and character development. It reads as if it's done effortlessly, and that's no small trick." —W.K. Stratton, *Dallas Morning News*

"Hap and Leonard, the East Texas duo of two-fisted do-gooders, return in the ninth novel about their adventures. The pair has always functioned as an odd mixture of shamuses, handymen, guardian angels, and no-nonsense fixers. . . . The series has a temperamental connection to the comic thriller as practiced by the likes of Carl Hiaasen and the late masters Ross Thomas and Donald E. Westlake. . . . But the camaraderie and down-home scatology carry the day. Let's hope there's more of that good feeling to come in this terrific series." —*Kirkus Reviews*

"Another jaw-dropper from the seemingly indefatigable favorite son of Nacogdoches, Texas. . . . Hilarious, crude, and violent, peppered through and through with unforgettable characters that leap off the page, dance around the room, and run off down the road. It doesn't get any better than this." —Joe Hartlaub, BookReporter.com

HONKY TONK
SAMURAI

HONKY TONK
SAMURAI

E R. LANSDALE

MULHOLLAND BOOKS

Little, Brown and Company
New York Boston London

Copyright © 2016 by Joe R. Lansdale
Excerpt from *Rusty Puppy* copyright © 2017 by Joe R. Lansdale

Hachette Book Group supports the right to free expression and the value of copyright. The purpose of copyright is to encourage writers and artists to produce the creative works that enrich our culture.

The scanning, uploading, and distribution of this book without permission is a theft of the author's intellectual property. If you would like permission to use material from the book (other than for review purposes), please contact permissions@hbgusa.com. Thank you for your support of the author's rights.

Mulholland Books / Little, Brown and Company
Hachette Book Group
1290 Avenue of the Americas, New York, NY 10104
littlebrown.com

Originally published in hardcover by Mulholland Books, February 2016
First Mulholland Books paperback edition, February 2017

Mulholland Books is an imprint of Little, Brown and Company, a division of Hachette Book Group, Inc. The Mulholland Books name and logo are trademarks of Hachette Book Group, Inc.

The publisher is not responsible for websites (or their content) that are not owned by the publisher.

The Hachette Speakers Bureau provides a wide range of authors for speaking events. To find out more, go to hachettespeakersbureau.com or call (866) 376-6591.

Library of Congress Cataloging-in-Publication Data

Lansdale, Joe R., 1951-
Honky tonk samurai/Joe R. Lansdale. —First edition.
  pages; cm
ISBN 978-0-316-32940-8 (hc) / 978-0-316-32941-5 (pb)
I. Title
PS3562.A557H66 2016
813'.54—dc23
                                                2015021762

10 9 8 7 6 5 4 3 2 1

LSC-C

Printed in the United States of America

For the Kelley Boys—Danny and Dennis,
our extended family

Just when you think you got things learned good, and life's flowing right, a damn Mack truck comes along and runs your highly attractive ass over.

—Jim Bob Luke

HONKY TONK
SAMURAI

1

I don't think we ask for trouble, me and Leonard. It just finds us. It often starts casually, and then something comes loose and starts to rattle, like an unscrewed bolt on a carnival ride. No big thing at first, just a loose, rattling bolt, then the bolt slips completely free and flies out of place, the carnival ride groans and screeches, and it sags and tumbles into a messy mass of jagged parts and twisted metal and wads of bleeding human flesh.

I'm starting this at the point in the carnival ride when the bolt has started to come loose.

• • •

The truck windows were rolled down and the heat wasn't quite unbearable yet, but the air had the smell toast gets as it begins to brown and you know the butter will spread clean. In less than a half an hour, about noon, my butt crack would be completely filled with sweat and breathing the air would be like swallowing fishhooks. I was already looking forward to loose clothes, a big glass of ice tea, and lots of air-conditioning.

We were sitting in Leonard's new-to-him pickup truck. He traded a lot. So did I. I'm not sure why, but we were always getting a different car or truck, usually used. This one was a Dodge and it was silver, and it was only a few years old. We were two blocks down from the house we were watching.

The guy who lived in that house, the fellow we were waiting on, had a wife who thought he was cheating and had hired the Marvin Hanson Agency to find out if he was and who with. She was brokenhearted and wanted everything to be all right, and if it wasn't she wanted to divorce him in a serious and financially lucrative way that would cause him to have to sell his balls for a place to sleep.

We weren't full-time employees, but we worked for Marvin quite a bit, a lot more lately. Divorce work, or potential divorce work, however, was not my idea of a good time, but the lady had hired the agency for two weeks of surveillance. We were on the last day of the job, and what we had pretty well determined was her sixty-year-old husband wasn't cheating on her at all, but he was going at odd hours to the gym, and we had a pretty good guess he didn't want to tell her.

Leonard thought it was because the idea embarrassed him, having to work out, or wanting to. That seemed peculiar to me, but Leonard understands that kind of thinking more than I do. For a gay guy he's much more tuned in to machismo than I am, so I guess he could be right. I figured the fellow was just going to surprise her with his new body, hoping one day she'd look up and say how good he looked. Maybe he kept going so much because she hadn't said anything.

Irony was, we had noticed that even in the last two weeks he'd dropped some pounds and muscled up a bit, and she had noticed over the last few months the same thing, but hadn't mentioned it to him because she thought he was dieting and buying new clothes because he had a chippie piece on the side. That's how she said it. "I think he's got a little chippie piece on the side."

I hadn't heard the word *chippie* used in many a moon, but the sad thing was I was old enough to remember when it was more common. I was starting to feel as if I were getting along in years and the recent ones were angry at me. By the time you're fifty you start to realize just how much of your time on earth you've wasted.

Anyway, we were sitting there watching him come out of the house, ready to follow, knowing full well by this time he didn't have a chippie piece on the side and that this was our last day so we would coast it on out for the dollar and give her our report. She had paid in advance and wanted two weeks, so I didn't feel we were sucking money she didn't want to spend.

I had been on a diet myself. I always exercised, and hard, and was usually in better shape than I looked, but lately I wanted to look it again, because Brett, my red-headed woman looked so good. I wanted to make my body more like the way I felt. But truth was, I had had to change my workout methods. I had dropped lifting heavy weights and gone to doing more reps with light weights. Jogging a little, but doing more walking than before. It seemed to be working. I was never going to be pretty, but I preferred not being able to rest a glass on my stomach when I was sitting down, as if it were an end table.

Even Leonard, who normally looked firm and ready for action all the time, had changed his eating and workout habits a little, because for the first time in a long time fat had crept in around his middle. He claimed it was protecting his gooey chocolate center. But since he was black as rich chocolate all over, I told him that seemed kind of redundant. And on top of that I didn't want to know about his gooey chocolate center.

There we sat, me reflecting on these things and holding in a wheat-bread fart out of courtesy, when Leonard said, "What the hell?"

He was looking at a yard across the street from our car. A man had a dog on a leash and the dog was cowered on its belly and the man was kicking it, and I could hear him screaming at it. The dog yelped a couple of times after the kicks.

Leonard was already out of the car by this time and crossing the street.

I got out and went around and followed, heard Leonard yell, "Hey, motherfucker, how about you try kicking me?"

The man stopped his dog abuse and looked up.

I let the fart ease out. I did it quietly, not wanting to frighten the dog. I left the fart where I had laid it like a rotten egg and moved away from the smell.

"Who the hell are you?" the man said to Leonard.

"I'm the man fixing to put that leash on your neck and kick you all over this goddamn yard like a soccer ball."

"You're trespassing," the man said.

"That's just where I start," Leonard said. "How about I put one of your goddamn eyes out?"

Appeared like a start to a fairly ordinary day for us.

I stayed at the curb while Leonard stood in the yard talking. I was waiting patiently, ready to stop Leonard from the death blow, which I was fairly certain might be coming.

"Take two of you to do it?" said the man, checking us both out. He was a pretty big guy, about Leonard's height, wider than both of us, bigger belly than us put together. He had the air of someone who had once run with a football and thought that gave him an edge for life. Maybe he should get with his neighbor who went to the gym, get some diet and exercise tips. Still, he was big enough to cause problems, even if it was just falling on you.

"No," Leonard said. "Just one of us."

I said, "And you can choose which one. Just for the record, I can hit harder. But I was thinking I'd rather not get all worked up. The heat, you know."

"He can't hit harder," Leonard said. "Faster, but I actually hit a little harder."

"He's a braggart," I said. "We both know I can hit harder, and I'm faster, too."

"You don't neither one of you look so tough to me," he said.

"Why don't you show us how tough you are?" Leonard said. "You do pretty good with a defenseless dog wants to please you, but we don't want to please you. Right, Hap?"

"Right," I said.

"Tell him again."

"Right. Not in the pleasing mood."

"Tell you what, ass wipe," Leonard said. "Give me the dog, let me take it with me, and we'll call it a day, and you get to keep your face like it is. With a nose on it and everything. Without me punching a fucking hole in it."

The guy laughed. "You are nuts. Both of you."

"That's what I'm trying to warn you about," Leonard said. "But I don't think you're listening."

By this point I could tell the man was starting to worry a little. That was a good idea. Leonard might truly be nuts. Some people didn't even think it was open to discussion.

"You want him, or should I go on and beat the shit out of him?" Leonard said to me.

"I'll just be here to stop you should you go too far."

"Hey, now," the man said. "You're in my yard. I'll call the cops."

"I don't think you'll make it to the door," Leonard said. "Got a cell phone in your pocket, you won't have time to punch in the numbers. I promise you that. And if you call afterward, it ain't going to help you none. The deed will be done. And they might have a hard time understanding you, as you might be missing some teeth, trying to talk with your nose gone. They might have to read your fucking lips you still got any. Now apologize to the dog and give the poor thing to me."

"Apologize to the dog?"

"Yeah, apologize."

"I'm not apologizing to any goddamn dog."

"I would if I were you," I said. "He means it."

"Fuck you. She's my dog."

"Not anymore," I said.

Leonard crossed the yard then. He moved swiftly. It was like those old Dracula movies when the vampire glides over the earth with the ease of a windblown mist. The man let go of the dog's leash. The dog, a young German shepherd mix, maybe a year old at the most, remained cowed.

I hated to see that. I loved dogs. I loved animals. People I'm a little more mixed on, so I didn't hate what was about to happen to the asshole in the yard, though I had to consider the cops might take a different view if the guy lived long enough and was strong enough to call them. Or maybe some neighbor looking out the window had already given them a call. Probably filming the whole thing on a cell phone.

The man put his hands up, clenched his fists in what he thought was a boxing position.

Shit, I could tell from the way he stood this wasn't even going to be a good fight.

Leonard didn't even put his hands up, just walked right up to the guy. The man threw a haymaker so slow and cumbersome we could have damn near driven home, had a cup of coffee, and come back before it landed.

It didn't.

Leonard looped his arm over the strike as he stepped in, most of the guy's force going around Leonard's back, the arm itself trapped to Leonard's side. Leonard lunged forward and shot out a palm that caught the guy in the nose and knocked him to the ground, or as close to that as he could get with Leonard still clutching his arm, partially lifting the guy's side off the ground.

The dog started to slink off on its belly like a soldier crawling in high grass. I went over and took the dog's leash. When I did the dog winced.

"It's okay, doggie," I said. "Uncle Leonard is kicking the bad man's ass."

By this time Leonard had let go of the man's arm and was kicking him sharply in the ribs, way that bastard had done the dog.

"How you like it?" Leonard said. "Enjoying that, asshole? Bark for me, cocksucker."

The guy didn't seem to be enjoying it. He started yelling, not barking. Hell, the dog had only yelped a little, this guy, you'd have thought was taking a real beating. And for him, I guess he was. Leonard actually seemed a little altruistic, I thought, considering it was all about animal mistreatment. Maybe he was getting old. Though actually he hadn't had much breakfast, so it might have just been his blood sugar was down.

After a bit, I guess Leonard got tired, because he quit kicking the guy, bent down, and retied his shoe, the string having come loose. When that was done I thought he'd go back to it, but he didn't.

The man, not learning his lesson, his face covered in blood from his nose to his chin, said, "That's assault, nigger."

"Couldn't leave well enough alone, could you?" I said.

Leonard had already grabbed him by the ears and was picking him up just enough to knee him in the face. Blood went everywhere, and the guy lay on the grass without moving. I hoped he had fallen in dog turds. I thought I saw one of his teeth gleaming wetly in the grass, like a cheap Cracker Jack prize.

Leonard came over to pet the dog. The dog let him. The dog seemed to know we were on her side. Leonard said to the dog, "When he wakes up I'll get him to apologize and maybe lick your ass."

"You didn't kill him, did you?" I asked.

"No, but I wanted to."

"Well, yeah," I said. "Me, too. But maybe it's best not to."

"Reckon so," Leonard said. "Still, not nearly as satisfying. Goddamn, what's that smell?"

"I'm having a little intestinal disturbance going on. My body does not deal well with wheat."

"Quit eating it. God, man. That's just foul and wrong. Let's move to some other spot."

2

I continued petting the dog, soothing it, and as dogs do, it stood up, wobbled, and licked my face. I think it would even have licked its crummy master's face. It's why I prefer dogs to cats. Cats aren't independent, they're just entitled assholes who want to be fed and do nothing. They're your owners. A dog just loves you. It's not about ownership or anything like that. They are sincere as death and taxes. They're the best creatures on the earth. Still, had it been a cat being mistreated, the bastard would still have gotten his ass kicked. But I would have taken a moment to tell the cat how I felt about his species. Not that it would have been listening or interested in thanking me. It would already be making its plans for the day. Lie around and shit in a box, puke hairballs on the floor, scratch up the furniture, and expect a treat for the effort. All dogs go to heaven. All cats go to hell.

The cops pulled up. One car. We were a little surprised to see Marvin Hanson, our boss, get out of the passenger side and stroll across the yard, look down on the guy, and say, "He doesn't look so bad."

The officer got out of the car. I didn't know his name, but I'd seen him around. Young guy. Leonard and I were no strangers to the police station. I tried not to worry too much about the cops' names, since they came and went faster than a john on holiday in Amsterdam. The young cop came over. He said, "Lady across the street called, said a guy was kicking his dog and we ought to come get him for animal cruelty."

"That's a good thing," I said. "But we thought it might take a little while, so we made a citizen's arrest."

"And trespassed and committed assault," Marvin said. His worn black face creased in a half smile. At least I think it was a smile. He might have been baring his teeth. I couldn't quite tell the difference. Marvin is not what you would call a pretty man.

"If you want to be that technical," Leonard said. "Sheesh."

"What are you doing with the cops?" I said to Marvin.

"He doesn't care what company he keeps," said the officer. He was a little guy, fat-faced, with stubby arms and legs, dark-skinned. He looked like a gingerbread man made with the last of the dough.

"Yeah, if my wife asks who I was with," Marvin said, turning to look at the cop, "for God's sake tell her I was buying drugs and was with a male prostitute. Don't mention the boys in blue."

"Done," the cop said.

"But between me and you," I said, "I still got to ask. What are you doing with the pigs, as we old rebels used to call them?"

"That's just mean," said the cop.

I liked this guy. I looked at his name tag. He might be worth remembering. Carroll was his last name.

"I been meaning to tell you," Marvin said. " I got my old job back. Police chief."

You could have knocked me over with a green pea. Before I could ask about the particulars, Marvin, who had recently abandoned his cane, though he had a slight limp if you knew to watch for it, strolled over and looked down at the guy, who was awake now and trying to sit up.

Marvin said, "Can you stand up?"

"I think so," said the man.

"Why don't you do that if you can?" Marvin said. "I'm with the cops."

"He called me a nigger," Leonard said.

"That's a tiebreaker in this modern world unless you use it in a rap song," Marvin said.

"I was just angry," said the man.

The guy gradually got himself collected enough to get to his feet. Marvin put his left hand on the guy's right shoulder, said, "Were you kicking this dog?"

"She kept pulling the leash," the man said. "I was trying to teach her."

"What were you teaching her?"

"To behave. To quit yanking me."

"So you kicked her?" Marvin said. "That was your instruction?"

"Had it coming. Hell, it's a dog. My dog."

Marvin's right hand moved then. It was quick, a slap to the guy's bloody face, a back hand, another slap, a swift knee in the nuts, and the guy was on the ground again. Marvin looked at the officer. "Damn if I wasn't just angry."

"You were just trying to teach him," Leonard said.

"I can't believe that," said the officer. "That son of a bitch tried to resist arrest. And to the brand-new police chief."

"Yeah, ain't that something?" Marvin said. "No respect for the goddamn law."

"Sign of the times," said the officer.

"Next the sun will go cold," said Leonard.

"I hear you," said the officer. "Just this morning, my coffee wasn't quite right."

"There you are," Leonard said. "It's already started. The end of the world as we know it. The goddamn fucking apocalypse."

3

She's got a busted rib—cracked, really. Nothing major. Used to wrap them up tight. Not the way it's done anymore." The vet, a stocky young lady who had thick shoulder-length blond hair slicked back with mousse, was telling us this as if we were potential interns.

"So she'll be all right?" I asked.

"Long as she takes it easy," she said.

"She will," I said.

"I'd like to have the bastard did this right here on my table," she said. "I'd cut his balls off with a dull scalpel."

"And we'd hold him down," Leonard said.

"When he came around, because he had a kind of accident and was out for a while, he apologized to the dog," I said.

"Apologized?" she said.

"Leonard there actually put the words in his mouth and made him chew on them and like it," I said. "But he had him say: I am sorry, little doggie, I am a shit-eating asshole and am not worthy to wear your dog collar. I have fleas."

The vet smiled a little, nodded at Leonard.

Leonard was sitting in a chair by the wall. He nodded back. Marvin was leaning against the open door frame. Officer Carroll had taken the dog abuser in. The dog was on a table, lying on her side. She was very patient and even cooperative. I liked that dog.

Marvin had let us take the dog to the vet. I guess he would have some paperwork to lie about, about how that bastard had jumped Leonard, who was merely trying to stop animal abuse, and then had turned on Marvin when he came to investigate. It wasn't legal, but it was justice. I could still visualize those slaps from Marvin. Marvin had fast hands.

The vet shaved some of the dog's hair and wrapped her up, but not tight. Just a little something to keep the rib firmly in place. She said it probably didn't need to stay but two or three days, and told us again about how it used to be done and how it wasn't done like that anymore. I guess she was practicing a lecture she was going to give. I paid the bill out of some of the money we had gotten for watching the guy go to the gym, and we drove Marvin to his car at the cop shop. He said he wanted to talk to us, said he'd follow us back to my place, that he'd come in a little while, had a bit of cop work to do. We went ahead.

Leonard had recently found his own living arrangements, a shabby place downtown in an old building that had once been a candy factory but was later cut up into apartments. Before the apartment, Leonard owned a house, but he had left that to John, then John left it, and Leonard sold it. Leonard actually made a small profit. This was rare for either one of us. A profit. Though for the first time in both our lives we had a bit of money tucked away and were what you might call almost comfortable. Redneck jobs are frequently short on career potential. You do one till you tire or get fired, and then you move on. We had moved on a lot.

Leonard's apartment was a kind of loft with a partition for the bedroom and the bathroom. The landlord was letting him build some new walls for some of the rent. Work he had to have done by a certain time. Leonard decided to hire someone to do it. It was not cheaper than the rent reduction, but it gave him a nicer place to live, and in time it would even out. There was talk of the landlord applying the rent toward a sale. The owner was old and tired of property and renters, and Leonard wanted to buy.

Leonard had been living there for only a short time, staying at our place a lot until some of the work on the place was done. Before that, he lived at our house full-time. We even had a room built onto it. I loved him—dearly—and so did Brett, but I must be honest: I was glad he wasn't there all the time anymore. Brett and I were happy empty nesters. We could have more time to ourselves, and we didn't have to be quiet when we were playing doctor, and my vanilla-cookie-and-Dr-Pepper budget would go down dramatically. This would also help Leonard's waistline. He loved those vanilla cookies and Dr Peppers severely, but he loved them even more when he didn't have to buy them. I think he saw eating my cookies and soft drinks as an accomplishment of great importance and took it as a matter of pride.

It had turned hot by the time we got out of the vet's, and it was only ten thirty or so. The sun lay down on us like a coat of heated chain mail.

When we got to mine and Brett's house and came in with the dog, Brett was home from her nursing job. She had quit nursing several times but was so good at what she did that she always got hired back. She looked tired but pretty, her red hair tied back in a ponytail. She said, nodding at the dog, "So we're having company for dinner? And I don't mean Leonard."

"Hey. I make good company," Leonard said. "What are we having?"

"Whatever you're buying," Brett said.

"Oh," Leonard said. "That limits things."

I looked down at the dog. "This is our true guest. This is . . . well, I don't know who this is."

"Follow you home?" she asked.

"Not exactly."

"Your new dog, Leonard?" she asked.

Leonard roved an eye my way. "Could be," he said. "Could be yours."

"Can I have her?" I said. I tried to sound winsome and wistful at the same time. Actually, I'm not sure which part of how I sounded was wistful and which part was winsome. Maybe you can't do both at the same time. Maybe one sounds a lot like the other.

"Will you throw a hissy if the answer is no?" Brett said.

"Probably."

"Oh, he can throw a grown-up big-ass cracker-style hissy," Leonard said. "I've seen him do it, and I got to tell you, I was embarrassed. It wasn't very manly."

"I can try throwing the hissy in a deep voice," I said.

"Nope," Leonard said. "That's not how a hissy works."

"First how about telling me how we've come by a dog?" Brett asked.

We all ended up around the table, the dog lying at my feet, and I told her while we all had glasses of ice tea.

"I can't believe people like that," Brett said. "This dog looks like a lover, not a biter."

"I don't think she's old enough to know what she is," I said.

"Well, I like dogs," Brett said.

The doorbell rang. I answered it. It was Marvin Hanson.

"So," I said as he came in. "Hello to the police chief who didn't tell us he was the police chief."

He sat at the table, and I sat down again. He leaned over to give the dog a pat on the head. "Nice dog."

"Police chief?" Brett said.

"Yep," Marvin said. "You know, that man might want this dog back, and I'm not sure how that will work out in court. He's going to get a fine for animal abuse and resisting arrest, but he could still throw some stink around."

"Give Hap some wheat bread," Leonard said. "He'll match him out, I bet you."

"I'm serious," Marvin said. "Could be some court stuff coming up."

"I don't know about court," Leonard said, "but I know how it worked out on his lawn. Not too well."

"We were bullies," I said.

"No," Marvin said. "We were the Fresh Fists of Vengeance."

"To be precise," Leonard said, "you were the Slap and Backhand of Vengeance."

"Don't forget the knee," I said.

"Yeah, and the knee," Leonard said. "But that lacks a certain ring."

"What's the legal damage?" I asked Marvin.

"For me or for you guys?" Marvin asked.

"Give us the whole package," Leonard said.

"Well, the police officer saw him attack me," Marvin said.

"Yeah, well, all right," I said. "Should we say we saw him attack you, too?"

"That would be handy," Marvin said. "But the lady next door saw it all happen, and she filmed it on her cell-phone camera. Got word of that on the way over. She called it in."

"Of course she did," I said, having expected just that sort of thing.

"But she said she didn't film the part where Leonard knocked cheese dick around, and she didn't film me slapping the poo out of him. She's just got the part where he kicked the dog. Said she thought he looked as if he was going to attack you two, and then me, so she put the blame on him."

"She's such a sweet liar," I said.

"Yeah," Marvin said. "And she's an old lady and looks very trustworthy, I hear. A little crusty, but all right, I think. I just got my description from Officer Curt Carroll, who had to drive back over there. He said the man who owned the dog was out on the lawn on his hands and knees looking for his missing teeth, thought maybe if he put them in ice they could be put back in. He's one of those guys thinks he knows all manner of shit but couldn't tell the difference between shit and wild honey."

"Very convenient the old lady looks trustworthy," Leonard said. "As for ass wipe, I hope he doesn't find his teeth."

"How many was he missing?" I said. "I only saw one."

"Two, I think," Marvin said. "Anyway, Gummy, as I like to think of him, isn't pressing charges. He at first had a different point of view, but I pointed out you guys were just good Samaritans who saw an animal mistreated and went to help. I think he bought that. There's some truth in it, but then there's that whole lying part about how we were attacked."

"He did swing at me," Leonard said.

"We'll let that count for something," Marvin said. "Thing is, he's done, you're safe, so am I, and besides, I'm the police chief."

"You were just trying to frighten us with that stuff about how he might want his dog back, weren't you?"

"Just a little," Marvin said. "I have to get my licks in on you guys somehow. You've certainly given me enough grief."

"There's a little something we're all curious about," I said. "How did that whole police chief thing happen? We work for you, you know— seems that would have come up."

"Does, doesn't it?" he said. "But it didn't. And I'll tell you why. I thought maybe I was being foolish, trying to get back on the cops. But now my leg's healed up and I'm able to work and I had a good record there, and better yet, the city council came to me. Seems they can't keep police chiefs or officers. They change all the time. They got a lot of quitters, one in jail for this or that. By the way, you know they painted the jail pink and make the convicts wear pink jumpsuits now?"

I held up my hand. "Been there, wore a jumpsuit."

"Pink," Hanson said.

"Yep, and a little loose-fitting, I thought, though more attractive than you might think. Comfortable because it was loose, I guess. The pink is supposed to be a deterrent to crime, embarrassing and all that."

"Do you think it works?" Hanson said.

"Not so much."

"Me, either. First thing I do next week is have all the jail cells repainted. They can keep the pink jumpsuits until they wear out. No. You know what? I'm ordering the standard orange ones right away. They can afford that. Can you believe that shit? People raping and murdering, and their conclusion is to paint the jail pink and have the shits wear pink jumpsuits. The goddamn death penalty doesn't stop them, but they think butt-hole pink will."

"It's a mystery," I said. "But I'm still more mystified that you're police chief."

"Yep, me too," Leonard said.

"I like pink," Brett said.

"The conversation has moved on, Brett," I said. "So why you, Hanson?"

"Oh, there's been some good chiefs, but so far the good ones have left because they can't stand how things get done in this town or because they got better jobs doing the same thing in places they like better. There's some good cops here, though. Kid that was with me you met. Some of the detectives like Drake and Kelso, few others. They've lasted awhile. But they want someone they think can hold things together better. They heard how I had an agency, was doing good physically now. How I had all that experience in Houston and here, so they came to me, hoping they could lure me away. They could."

"Don't they have elections for that sort of thing?" Leonard asked.

"That's sheriff," Marvin said. "Here police chief isn't an elected office, it's a pick-and-choose on the part of the city council. I got picked. I officially started today, but mostly I just rode from the office out to where you guys were. When I came in first thing, first day at work, first crack out of the box, I hear that a guy who's been kicking a dog was getting an ass-whipping in a yard near where I sent you guys to scout. I knew who it was, of course."

"We're so predictable," Leonard said.

"In some ways, yes," Marvin said. "Thing is, well, I can't keep the agency."

"There goes about a third of our employment," Leonard said.

"More like three-quarters," I said. "We've been prosperous these last few months, and now we won't be prosperous. It's back to day labor and field work."

"There's always bouncing, janitorial work, and sexing chickens," Leonard said.

"Yeah. I forgot we had so many options."

"It's a conflict of interest to have that kind of business and be in the law business, too," Marvin said. "Besides, I got to go more by the law now. I've turned back to being respectable."

"Clean underwear and all that," Leonard said.

"That's right," Marvin said. "I even change socks daily."

"You sure gave your first day a swell start," Brett said.

"Yeah, I know. I could have been back at the agency after one day, but it worked out."

"This what you want?" I said. "Police chief?"

"I loved my work there as a lieutenant, and I was practically police chief then, so I'm taking the job. I'm back in law enforcement. But thing is, I got to close the agency or sell it. I was thinking you two might want to take it over."

"What's the price?" Leonard said.

"What I was thinking," he said, "is you buy all the office equipment, take up the payments on the place, cause I'm buying the building, and you can start right away. Owner financed."

"Us?" I said. "You're really talking to us about owning a business? I don't know our names and 'business owners' ought to be said in the same breath."

"I know," Marvin said. "It's a scary thought."

"I don't know I want to run a business," I said. "I like the work all right, but that's just getting paid, not running the business—paying property taxes, insurance, and the like. Keeping up with this and that. What if a pipe breaks?"

"Fix it or get it fixed," Marvin said.

"One I don't like to do, the other one costs money," I said.

"Yeah," Leonard said. "That's not for me, either. Fixing pipes or running a business. I tried a lemonade stand once and had to fight two little white boys who called me a black cocksucker. I whipped the shit out of them. Hell, it was ten years after that before I sucked my first cock."

"It's good to be precise on cock sucking," I said.

"Have it your way," Marvin said. "But I'm selling out, and I'm offering you the best deal I'll offer anyone." He looked at Leonard. "Call it my cocksucker discount."

"That's nice of you," Leonard said.

"I don't know," I said.

"I'll do it," Brett said.

We all looked at her.

"I'm nursed out," she said. "I'm tired of the hours, and I'm tired of wiping asses and changing bandages. I'll buy out the equipment and take over the business, pay the bills. Hap and Leonard can work for me."

"You'll be our boss?" I said.

"We can make it work," she said.

"I don't know," I said.

"You know," Marvin said, "that's a good idea. Gets me out from under it, and you can make it work, Brett. You don't even need these two dopes. I can get you a private investigator license easy peasy. I know folks that know folks."

"I was thinking that," she said. "That I didn't need these two guys."

"Wait a minute," Leonard said. "Did I say I was out? I don't think so. I don't even like Hap."

"I'll provide a certain amount of vanilla cookies as part of your payment," she said.

"Dr Peppers?" Leonard asked.

"That, too," she said.

"Hell, then, I'm surely in," Leonard said.

"Hap?" Marvin said.

"Yeah," I said. "I guess so. We go on like we are? No license for us two, just slave labor?"

"Of course," Brett said.

"Yeah," Marvin said. "You work under Brett's license like you did mine."

"When does this start?" Leonard asked.

"Right now the business is going to close. I turned in the report to the lady with the gym-conscious husband, and that was the last of it. She owes one more payment. But the business can restart when Brett wants it to start, long as it's before the next building payment, and of course there's paperwork to do. Thing is, it's not going to cost that much to get started. It doesn't pay like nursing, though, Brett."

"Trust me," she said. "Nursing isn't exactly big money. Good, steady money, but not big money. Besides, like I said, I'm worn out with it. I'll give my two-week notice when I go in tomorrow. And I think they'll let me leave right away. They owe me vacation time."

And that's how I went to work for my girlfriend at what became the Brett Sawyer Agency.

4

At least Marvin had liked the paint. It wasn't pretty paint, and to be honest, I wasn't sure what color you would call it. Faded rust, perhaps. But it was the paint that had come with the inside walls, and there was nothing about it that bothered me, but Brett, she had other ideas. Leonard and I ended up painting the office a light mint green. It did look better, but I thought of it as a waste of time. It wasn't like we were trying to run a boutique. Next thing you knew there'd be flowers in vases, a bird in a cage, and a painting that looked like a bag of crayons had exploded.

Then again, we did work for Brett, and the boss was the boss. Course, what sucked was that she wasn't paying us for the paint job. Not that I expected her to or wanted her to. I'm just grumpy.

We got it painted, and Brett bought a new desk without coffee-cup circles on it, put out some coasters, and purchased comfortable office chairs and a new, streamlined computer. At least there were no flower arrangements or any of that other stuff I feared. She let me buy a movie-poster reproduction of the Robert Mitchum version of *Farewell My Lovely*, and I had that nicely framed and put on the wall. It was the only time in my life I actually did something more than buy a picture at a place like Walmart and frame it myself. I had someone who knew what he was doing frame it. It made me feel a little more like a real private eye, having that poster there. Of course, you got right down to it, I'm about as much like a real private eye as a weasel is like a kangaroo, but I like to dream a little.

The bathroom was kept simple. Clean place to do number one and two with plenty of toilet paper. There was a painting on the wall of water lilies. I thought that was silly. Really, did we need a painting in the shitter? And of water lilies?

Brett also got a better coffeepot for our kitchenette, as she called it, bought some gourmet coffee, and put a bag of vanilla wafers in the desk drawer. The vanilla cookies were the same cheap-ass brand we always bought, primarily for Leonard. He had three kinds of vanilla cookies he liked. The plain wafers, the ones with the cream in the middle, and any other kind that were vanilla. The drawer had a key. Two. I had one, Brett had the other. Leonard couldn't help himself. Came to those cookies, he was like a crack addict. We were there to protect him from himself. And the other thing I liked about it was it was kind of funny. He enjoyed tormenting me by wearing goofy hats and such, so I liked to return the favor now and again. It's what brothers do.

There was a little fridge with soft drinks and water in it, including Dr Peppers for Leonard, and there was a couch that could be pulled out into a bed. Brett and I tried it out one night when we were working late. Leonard had gone home to his new digs, and it was just us. We decided to break it in, so to speak. It was only a little more uncomfortable than the rack at the Inquisition. Next morning our backs were out of whack. Brett bought a thin foam mattress that she rolled up and put in the closet. You pulled the couch out, all you had to do was put that mattress on it and it turned the rack into something a little more serviceable and almost comfortable. We thought we might as well be ready. You never knew when you might need sex to bolster your serotonin, or whatever that stuff is that makes you feel happy. I always just thought it was fucking that makes you happy, so there you have it.

Our new dog stayed at the office with us during this time, wrapped in her not-too-tight but tight-enough bandage. While we were making love that time in the office, she watched us with curiosity from her doggie bed. I felt she was a little young for all that information. But I guess since I was taking her back to the vet for an operation that would end that whole having-puppies thing, it was all moot.

Night we were up there trying out the foldout couch, Leonard and John were having a get-back-together dinner. Leonard was making spaghetti with his famous sauce that he bought at the store ready to go. I hoped it worked out for him. He had been trying to put things back together for a while. He had just about thrown in the towel, and then John, who decided he was supposed to like women because he got religion, found out that women didn't really do it for him after all and maybe God would give him a pass on the whole male-on-male thing. Least that's where his head was at. I was beginning to think John, nice guy that he was, was just too confused and messed up to know what he wanted. Frankly, these days I avoided him. There was part of me that wanted to punch him in the mouth.

So the day after the night on the foldout, right after Brett bought the mattress and put it in the closet, it was just me and her, doing this and that to spruce up the new office. Mostly little things that I didn't think needed to be bothered with but that she thought were desperately important. We paused in our work and were both looking at the dog lying on her doggie bed in the corner of the office. Brett said, "You know, we got to quit calling her Her."

"You think?" I said. "It could be like that H. Rider Haggard novel *She.* That woman knew who she was. She was all the name she needed. Our dog could be Her."

"I don't think our She, or Her, is that confident," Brett said. "And besides, She actually had a name. Ayesha, I think."

"You got a point there."

"But she is starting to feel better, and she's getting fat, like you," Brett said.

"I lost five pounds."

"You need to lose twenty-five, dear boy."

"Yeah, at least."

"What have you been feeding her?"

"Nothing."

"Liar," Brett said.

"All right, now and then we go through the drive-through at Dairy Queen and I buy her an ice cream cone, plain, no chocolate. Chocolate is bad for dogs."

"I used to share chocolate candy bars with my dogs when I was a kid," Brett said. "None of them died."

"So they're all still alive?"

"Of course not," she said.

"See? Chocolate got them. It just took a lifetime."

"Ha," she said. "I think we should call her Spot."

"She doesn't have any spots," I said.

"That's the joke."

"We will not joke about our dog. I say we name her Ace."

"That's a boy dog's name."

"I always wanted to name a dog that because Batman's dog was named Ace."

"No. Not Ace. How about Buffy?"

"Like the vampire-slayer girl?" I asked.

"Yep. I like that name. More for dogs than for girls."

"That fits," I said.

"Let's call her Buffy the Biscuit Slayer. She does like dog biscuits."

I studied on that a moment, said, "Buffy the Biscuit Slayer is for formal occasions, when she has to wear an evening gown or be at a queen's coronation, but for at home and rides to the Dairy Queen, it's Buffy."

Our new dog was christened.

As this christening was going on, I was looking at Brett's legs. She was leaning up against the desk. She was wearing shorts and her legs were shiny and I was wondering if maybe we might try the couch bed again with the new mattress. That thought was destroyed when I heard someone on the stairs. It was a heavy sound, like a elephant loaded down with a raja and his escorts, and there was a clicking with it, like maybe the elephant had a large cricket for a friend or perhaps was wearing a tap shoe on one foot.

That's when the door opened and a lady came in who was older than dirt but cleaner. She had a cane, which explained the cricket, but the elephant walk was a little more confusing, as she wasn't much bigger than a minute. She had more dyed red hair than she had the head for. That hair seemed to be an entity unto itself, mounded and teased and red as blood. You could have shaved her like a sheep and knitted a sweater with all that hair, maybe have enough left over for at least one sock or, if not that, a change purse.

Her face was dry-looking. She had a lot of makeup on it, as if she were trying to fill a ditch, or several. Her clothes were a little too young for her age, which was somewhere near to that of a mastodon that had survived major climate change but was wounded by it. She had on bright red tight jeans and a sleeveless blue shirt that showed hanging flesh like water wings under her arms. Her breasts were too big, or maybe they were too exposed; the tops of them stuck out of her push-up bra. They looked like aging melons with rot spots, which I supposed were moles or early cancer.

She eyed Brett and me, said, "You two weren't about to do the dog, were you?"

"I don't think so," said Brett. "Our dog is a lady."

The lady eyed the recently christened Buffy on her bed in the corner. Buffy had lifted her head to check things out, but she quickly lowered her head again and lay still. I think all that hair bothered her. She probably thought it was a vicious animal ready to pounce.

"I mean screwing," said the woman.

Like Brett, I knew what she had been referring to, but still, she wasn't what I expected, though I suppose when I got that old, if I did, I'd still talk the same way I do now. Actually, the more I looked at the old lady, the more I thought the language suited her. She looked like a retired hooker.

"Why, yes, I was just fixing to drop my shorts and bend over the desk and ask Hap here to drive me home."

"You aren't shocking me, honey," the old woman said.

"Or you us," Brett said.

I was actually thinking I might be a little shocked.

"That was your game, wasn't it?" Brett said. "To shock us."

"Naw," said the old woman, finding a client chair and settling into it as if she were a bag with a bowling ball in it. "I'm just a vulgar old shit." She laid a heavy eye on me, said, "You're Hap Collins, aren't you?"

"I am," I said. "Do we know each other?"

"No, but when I was forty I'd like to have. You and me could have burned a hole in a mattress then. Course, you may not have been born. But you might want to lose a few pounds, honey. You're starting to chub up."

"He's taken," Brett said. "Pounds and all."

The old woman studied Brett. "Aren't you the Southern belle? I bet you could earn a pretty penny on a Louisiana shrimp boat and never have to toss a net."

"Listen, you old bag," Brett said. "Either say what you want or I'm going to stick that cane up your ass and throw you down the stairs so hard the dye will come out of your hair."

The old lady let out with a howl. "You are a pistol, aren't you?"

"And all six chambers are loaded," Brett said.

"Don't get your panties twisted up your ass," said the old lady. "I'm just fucking with you. I want to hire Hap here."

"I charge a little more for the position of male escort," I said. "And just so you know, I don't do anal."

"I might could arrange that—the male escort part," she said. "And I do do anal and use toys. Or used to. These days I'm so dry I have to grease up to pee." She said that and laughed. It was a good laugh and sounded young, right up to the end, where she got choked and suddenly sounded like a boiler about to blow.

When she got her pipes cleaned out, I said, "I don't know you, so how come you know me?"

"I saw you and your colored friend out in the yard the other day. And there's that sweet dog that got kicked. She looks much happier now."

I thought: colored friend? Really? Then again, she was old. Hell, she might have been near ninety. A spry ninety, but at least that age. I guessed she was entitled to the old proper style of identification for black people. Then again, the term *black* was fairly past its shelf life, too. The new word was *African American*, a variant of *Afro-American*, a term used in the sixties and seventies. Leonard always said it was obvious he was American and that the closest he'd been to Africa was a geography map. He thought of himself as black. Then again, me and him are about the same age. We like a lot of the same terminology. I just about always say *pussy* instead of *vagina*.

The old lady stirred a hand around in her purse and came up with what I still call an electronic device and everyone else calls a tablet. To me a tablet is writing paper between cardboard covers. I especially liked the old-style Big Chief tablets. I don't even know if they still make them.

She ran a bent finger around on the tablet, then turned it toward me. It was a very nice video of Leonard beating the shit out of the dog abuser. The sound was down. That was okay. I remembered everything that was said, and the machine probably hadn't picked that up anyway.

And then I understood. Of course I did. She wasn't just an old lady who had seen what had happened. She was the one who recorded the dog abuse, said she didn't have Leonard and Marvin recorded—but she did. She had filmed everything from the minute we showed up to the moment everyone left. It was pretty cool to watch, both Leonard and Marvin. I almost asked for a replay.

What kept me from asking for that, however, was I had a sinking feeling that I knew why she had come in.

5

Here's what I expected. She had blackmail material, and though I wasn't involved in the actual ass-whipping, I was there and was part of the deal by proxy, and the way it would come down was all of us on that video, and that included Officer Carroll, were about to get rubbed raw as hamburger meat.

"You think I'm here to blackmail you, don't you?" she said.

"Never crossed my mind. Why would a nice lady like you blackmail anyone?"

"Shit, boy, you're a bad liar. If you were a woman you couldn't fake an orgasm."

"All right," I said. "It crossed my mind. And just for the record, I think I could fake an orgasm."

"Totally," Brett said.

"I want you to take my case," said the lady, "if that's what it's called. Think that's what they say on the TV shows, or maybe it's movies. Are there private eye TV shows anymore?"

"I don't know," I said.

"Those were always kind of fun," she said. She seemed to be thinking about a favorite episode of something before she shifted to: "Here's the way I see it." She patted the tablet. "I want you to find my granddaughter. The cops gave up. For them it's a cold case, and from what I can tell it's not getting any warmer. I'll be honest. I don't have any illusions. I'm too old to have any. She's most likely bones by now, but I want her body found, and I want to know what happened to her."

"You don't need threats," Brett said. "We just need payment. Actually, I own this agency now, so it's me you deal with."

"Well, that's the rest of the problem," she said. "I got some money, but not what it takes to do the deed, cause I presume it'll take awhile, and usually this stuff is by the hour, right? That's why I brought the tablet. What's on it is my down payment. And if you're thinking of pushing me down the stairs, I got a copy of this elsewhere, somewhere where you can't get it. I'm pretty tech-savvy for an old geezer."

"I think you're a lying bitch," Brett said. "How much money you got?"

"How much you need?" the old lady said.

They went back and forth with that for a while until it was determined the old lady had about half of what Brett charged for a couple of weeks, having raised her prices from those Marvin used. I guess she was thinking about paying for the paint and the new furniture and a lot of vanilla cookies and the toilet paper for the snazzy bathroom.

When the money talk was done, and an inferior sum was agreed to, the old lady pulled a manila envelope out of her purse. Inside were some papers and photos of her granddaughter. She was a good-looking girl in a short white dress and those Greek lace-up sandals. She had thick red hair like Brett's and like maybe the old lady's original hair used to be. The girl was striking a model pose, which was appropriate, because her grandmother said, "She wanted to be a model when she was a kid, then she wanted to be a journalist. Her name is Sandy Buckner."

"What's your name?" Brett asked.

"Lilly Buckner."

"We have a painting of lilies on the bathroom wall," I said.

"What?" Lilly said.

"Never mind," I said.

Brett asked her a few questions, and I listened. Five years ago Sandy had gone missing. She had graduated college with a journalism degree and found that the newspapers and magazines that did hard news had gone the way of the dodo bird and drive-in theaters, so she tried being a weather girl, but she was no good at it. She looked wonderful on camera, but she had zip charisma, as her grandmother put it. It's odd how that works. There are people who in life are beautiful, but on film, beautiful or not, they have all the personality of a ham sandwich without the pickles, and then there are those who look all right, nothing special, a little too thin, but the camera loves them, spruces them up, makes them glow. Sandy didn't glow. She was just pretty. She ended up taking a job at a used-car lot that only sold high-end used cars—Mercedes, Lincolns, Cadillacs, muscle cars, that kind of thing—mostly old cars that had become rare and classic.

Sandy worked there six months and was making some money, then one day the boss called Lilly Buckner looking for Sandy. Hers was one of the numbers Sandy had left as a contact. She hadn't come to work, and she never showed up again. She hadn't been seen for five years. Her car, which wasn't up to the level of those she sold but was pretty nice, had been found in the parking lot of the apartment complex where she rented. It was a nice complex, and it and the pretty nice car led Lilly to think Sandy was making money that was a little too good.

The whole missing-person business had gone through cop channels without any solution. Lilly hired a private agency that had taken her money and told her what she already knew, then went out of business. The owner of the agency decided being a private eye lacked some of the excitement he had hoped for and had gone into real estate. Ms. Buckner said it made her happy the bottom fell out of the market right after he made that decision.

Then she saw us and the dog. She talked to the cops and got Marvin's name, and then she researched him, and that led to all of us. She did it, she said, because all she had to do was shit and eat. She discovered Marvin had an agency, and now Brett had it.

She researched us to brag on us saving the dog. She did in fact do that while she was with us, said good things about us, but thought Brett might could use a little less eyeliner, told her she had to watch tight shorts when they got sweaty. "You get a camel toe you're not careful," she said. It sounded like a sincere suggestion. Brett gave me a look that said: What the hell?

Ms. Buckner rambled on. She thought Leonard was good-looking for a colored man. Said she always voted against any politician if he smiled too much. She told us a lot about herself, pretty much everything there was to know except her personal laundry tips.

"This granddaughter," I said. "I take it you two had special feelings about one another."

That reeled her in a little.

"I understood her," she said. "I had been the black sheep of the family years before, and now she was. Modeling and journalism, any plan but marriage and being Suzy Homemaker, wasn't something my daughter Kate understood. Maybe that was my fault. I didn't set a good example for her. I had this stupid idea when I was younger that art trumped all things, including family. I thought I had great talent and great pride, but what I had was hubris. I still have a substantial dose of it."

"Oh, you don't say?" Brett said.

"You are a shit, aren't you?" Ms. Buckner said.

"Takes one to know one," Brett said.

"I was a bad mother, no doubt. I was always worried more about me than her. My daughter wouldn't have anything to do with me. She treated me like gas from a calf's ass after she left home. Not that I blamed her. She wanted things more conventional. Damn if I didn't outlive her. Cancer got her. Self-righteous and proper and all that, praying all the time, and she ended up wired up like a spaceman and easing away in inches and shitting in a bag. I saw her right near the time she died. I thought we might at least close our ledger. Kate didn't even know who I was. Poor thing, she looked then like I look now, and she was middle-aged. That cancer sucked the juice right out of her.

"My granddaughter had done the right things, gone to school, got a degree. Stuff her mother ought to have been proud of. Better than what I'd done by a long shot. But Kate thought Sandy should be going to college not for a BA but instead a MRS. Didn't matter. The degree didn't work out, but Sandy took a job. She was like this one." She nodded at Brett. "A pistol."

"How was her eyeliner?" Brett asked.

"A little heavy, you want to know the truth. I say go big, but don't go giant. Look like you'd like some action, but not like you're ready to pull the train on the local football team."

"So she was a pistol," I said. It was an attempt to get things back on track. I knew Brett. Once she decided she didn't like someone, it was hard to steer her out of a path of hit and run. Or, rather, hit and back over the bleeding corpse.

"Yep. She was indeed a pistol. Had all the chambers loaded, too, just like this one said. I liked her for that. I tried to help her here and there. I think she appreciated it. It was hard to tell. I think somewhere in there she had her own plans and thoughts, and I think she had a hard time expressing love and appreciation. I'm like that. You start showing me affection, I start waiting for the other shoe to drop, the trap to close. I don't know how to deal with it. Enough maudlin shit. I've told you everything but my shoe size."

"Would be about a man's ten, wouldn't it?" Brett said.

"That's just mean, girl," Lilly said to Brett. "Weight and shoe size on women is hitting below the belt."

"I know," Brett said. "I thought you had it coming."

"I may have. It was something I would have said for sure. Look. Enough shit. I want you to find out what happened to her, and bring either her or her bones back if you can. I need to know."

Experience gave me a thought. I said, "Let me ask you something personal. Did you ever loan her any money, give her any money?" I asked.

"Not exactly," she said.

"Let me put it another way. Did she ever take any of your money without asking?"

"I suppose you could say that. She took some things from my safe. Some of it was money, some of it was securities, things like that."

"How much money?"

"About fifty thousand dollars."

"Damn," Brett said.

"Yeah," Ms. Buckner said. "Damn."

"And the securities?" I asked. "She cash them in?"

"Forged my signature, worked her charms, I guess."

"You didn't look at that a little askew?" I asked. "That seems to me to not be doing everything right. A common name for someone like that is goddamn thief."

"She needed the money. Like I said, she had pride. She didn't know how to ask for it, so she took it. I think she would have paid it back. I think she meant to, anyway. Hoped she could. But then something happened. I'm guessing she got in some kind of trouble and had to have it and was afraid if I didn't give it to her things could be really bad. Whatever those things were, she didn't want to tell me."

"Sounds like to me it's what Hap was saying," Brett said. "She's a thief who stole your money."

"Maybe," Ms. Buckner said. "Maybe she did. I don't care. I loved her, and I don't love much, other than animals. I've had cats and dogs, and I loved them. Now I don't have any. Outlived everything I ever loved, it appears, and who the hell wants to get up early to take a dog out to shit? At my age I'm not adding anyone or anything new to the mix. The rest of the world can go to hell. Except for Sandy. Maybe she didn't always show good sense, even if I think she had it. I still want to find her."

Then she gave Brett a financial retainer and went down the stairs, doing that elephant walk with the one-tap-shoe sound. She had to struggle down the stairs in the way she struggled up. I think Brett would like to have helped her down by kicking her in the ass. I sort of wanted to give her a piggyback ride myself.

She was salty as a bar nut, but I got to tell you, I appreciated that. I like people with a little spice, even if it gives me a bit of heartburn. I looked out the window and saw her work herself into a vanilla Mercedes and glide it out of the lot, not bothering with the exit. She drove right over the curb with a thump, and then she was on the road. The middle of it. She struggled the car along without running over anyone, though she narrowly missed a parked car and a wandering squirrel.

She got to the end of our street, turned in front of brake-grinding and horn-screeching traffic, and maneuvered away slowly, like a blind turtle, until she was out of sight.

6

For someone who talks tough, I think she was all flatulence and no guts," Brett said. "Letting her granddaughter off the hook like that."

"Flatulence?"

"I was trying to class up our conversations."

"All right," I said. "But you should have said 'all flatulence and no intestines.'"

"It's so rare you're right," Brett said. "But when you are, you are."

We were lying in bed at home and had just finished what Ms. Buckner had called the dirty dog.

"I think she's tough, all right," I said. "I just think her granddaughter, Sandy, is her soft spot."

"Like Leonard is yours?"

"You and Leonard," I said. "Though maybe I'm Leonard's soft spot. If he was any tougher he'd be made out of leather and stuffed with nails. He should have been dead several times over, but he's too tough to die. He's waiting to get old so he can whip death's ass."

"You've survived your share of bad moments," Brett said.

"With Leonard it was toughness, with me it was luck."

"He's not always so tough."

"You mean lately?" I said.

"Yeah, the stuff with John," Brett said. "How does a gay guy stay a conservative, by the way? John's brother is a big-ass Republican, and he's always thumping the Bible and telling John he's going to go to hell for being gay."

"Well, Leonard has been hit in the head a few times," I said. "That could account for something. Frankly, he's been changing his political affiliation as of late. Thinks Republicans have become assholes, so he moved to the Log Cabin Republicans."

"That the gay Republicans?"

"Yep. But then he thought that was too much of 'an elite' club, so he's become a Libertarian."

"Aren't they just mean-spirited I-got-mine-and-fuck-everyone-else Republicans?"

"A lot of them are. But they're more like the old Republicans—least that's the way Leonard aligns himself. Eisenhower without a heart. He fits there."

"Except when he doesn't," she said. "He can have a pretty big heart."

"Yeah," I said. "He can. You vote Republican, don't you?"

"You've never asked before."

"No. But I've wondered."

"I don't really have a party I like," she said.

"Who does?"

"I vote mostly Democrat, though I voted for Reagan, to my regret."

"I don't fit neatly with either side," I said. "We're all like goats if we're honest. We find our pastures but we love to put our heads through the fence and nibble a bit of the grass on the other side. No one fits anywhere perfectly."

"I don't know," Brett said. "I can think of one place you always fit perfectly."

"Oh, you flatterer," I said.

"Yeah, well, I figured I needed to throw in a compliment so you wouldn't worry too much about me faking an orgasm now and again."

"Nice," I said. "The old lady got that on your mind?"

"I guess. Talk about soft spots: now you have a new one. Buffy."

I turned my head, looked at Buffy resting on one of the doggie beds we had bought her. We had one downstairs, one at the office, and one here, upstairs in our bedroom. She had to be coaxed to come upstairs, and then when she did she stayed there until we invited her outside to go to the bathroom. She seemed frightened to ask for the outdoors, the way a dog will do, poking you with its nose, wagging its tail, and barking. We had to take her out at regular planned intervals so she wouldn't hold it in. I felt like she'd do that until she burst.

"Stop overfeeding her," Brett said. "You're acting like a southern mother."

"She seemed a little skinny to me," I said.

"Well, you got her back on track now," Brett said.

I pulled Brett close to me. "Off topic, but have you been wishing you hadn't bought Marvin's business? Nursing was at least regular."

"I did wake up this morning wishing I could pour shit out of a bedpan, but other than that, and the long hours and the yelling doctors and men trying to put their hands on my ass and up my skirt, I'm not missing it as much as you might think. Besides, I got a nest egg for us. I can afford time off."

"I don't want your nest egg," I said.

"I know that. But it's there anyway. It's our nest egg. What's mine is yours."

"I found that out just a short while ago."

"You did, didn't you?"

"You know what I miss?" I said.

"What?"

"Leonard, damn it."

"Yeah. Me, too. He's so cute when he wants his cookies."

"Family couldn't afford a lot of extras. He'd go to his uncle's house, and Uncle Chester always had vanilla cookies and Dr Pepper on hand. I think it's a comfort food."

"That explains things."

"Yeah. You know the hats he likes to wear?"

"Childhood something or other?" she asked.

"No. He's just an asshole. I thought I should remind you of that before we became too nostalgic for him not being here."

"He is at that, but you can sure see the kid in him when he wants those cookies."

"He has eyes like Buffy's," I said.

"You're right. He really does. He was messy, ate all the cookies, drank up all the Dr Peppers, interrupted us during sex by knocking on the door, knowing full well what we were doing in here, and he stayed up and played the TV loud downstairs, left his dirty drawers on the floor between his room and the living room. Left them so I could get them washed."

"You made me do the wash," I said.

"I know, but I had to point the drawers out to you," she said. "Shit, aren't gays supposed to be neat and listen to show tunes?"

"Just the ones who do," I said.

"Still, I miss him."

"Me, too," I said. "Should I see if he wants to come back?"

"Not on your life," she said.

7

The car lot was called Frank's Unique Used Cars. It was off the major highway that ran through the center of town, Highway 59. In the town itself the highway had a street name until it came out on the far side in a wide band of concrete heading north. The car lot was tucked in near a bank and a money-managing firm, a stone's throw from a Burger King. It was a big lot, and the cars were in fact unique.

I had driven by there many times and seen those fine old cars, but it just then registered with me how rare and fine they actually were and how often I had looked at them. It seemed odd for our town to have that kind of business. Most guys I knew drove pickup trucks with dogs riding in the back, tobacco spit sprayed along the side of the truck, splattered like some kind of poorly executed racing stripe. Those trucks were frequently festooned with stickers about how proud the owners were to be rednecks and how they were going to cling to their guns until they were pried from their cold dead fingers. They often had stickers with beer and whiskey labels on the trucks as well. I guess they kept a dog in back in case they needed a designated driver.

The fancy cars were all parked out front on the lot, but you could bet they went into the huge building behind the office at night. It was a three-story building, and it looked like anything but a car lot. It had once been a fancy hotel. The bottom-floor wall had been knocked out and fixed with big aluminum doors, but the top floors were still the same, with broad windows and white shades over them. Not enough people came, so it closed down. Few years back it got a sweep-out and paint job, and its parking space became the car lot. A modern single-story office building had been built out front of the hotel, behind the display of cars, the glass reflecting the lot and anyone on it.

Leonard and I cruised by a couple times in a beige BMW we had rented from a place in Tyler so as to look prosperous. We were checking things out. Finally Leonard pulled us into the lot. Before we went inside, Leonard said, "I've driven by this place often in the last few years. The cars are still the same cars."

"Guess it's possible they are different cars that look like the same old cars," I said, "but I was thinking exactly the same thing."

We went inside, out of the intense summer heat. The office was large, a kind of showroom, mostly glass, but with no cars on display inside. It had the kind of glass that was hard to see through from the outside, appeared dark, but inside the glass had a different effect—you could see the outside clearly. A large part of the ceiling was made of glass. You could see clouds rolling by. It was bright inside and very air-conditioned, cool as a penguin's ass on an ice block. The sweat began to cool-dry against my skin.

"You'd think they were selling igloos instead of cars," Leonard said.

In the center of the room was a big clear plastic desk. At the desk sat a golden-haired beauty of a woman with two large, round tits from the tit store, firm as rocks. She had a nose by someone other than genetics and a lot of experience looking at her own reflection in the mirror, knew how to tilt her head just right, when to let go of her smile, like she was holding back a bomb until it was right on target. She let that bomb drop when she saw me looking at her. She was a lady who knew her chickens. Leonard, of course, was not going to be impressed. He was already scouting his eyes around for a male salesman that would be the lovely lady's equivalent, but none was visible. In fact, no one else was around but us and the blonde.

Just for the record, when it comes to tits and noses, I'm not one of those who worry about if they're real or not. If it doesn't appear to have been glued on, nothing falls off during sudden moves, and the smile doesn't look like a Great White gliding down on a tuna, it's okay by me. I'm true to my baby, Brett, but I have never lied about the fact that I got this whole biology thing going on, and I like to look, and this lady was well worth looking at. I imagined Brett looked at men, too. She could appreciate a nice shape, which is what makes me wonder why she stays with me. I like to think it's my massive pecker.

When the blonde stood up she looked even better. The surgery work had been mostly subtle. She wore a blue western-style shirt and a dark brown cowgirl skirt that was cut short, a little longer in back than in the front. I couldn't see her rear, but I had a feeling that dress was pressed against a butt firm as a fresh-picked apple. She had long, spray-tan legs that were lightly oiled and inviting. She wore red-and-blue cowboy boots with shiny white moons on the toes. The heels were high, even for boots, and when she walked, she knew how to do it. Had that runway-model approach. As she got closer I saw she was older than she looked from a distance. Not all her face had been sculpted. She had some corner-of-the-mouth creases, a few lines around her eyes, and a crimp on her forehead like she was about to make a decision. The lips were nice, and the cheekbones were high. I like to believe those were natural.

Me and Leonard were dressed in our most expensive casual duds, which were so seldom worn both of us had to send a posse into our closets to find them. Our outfits smelled a little dry, like old wallpaper in a damp room. The boots she was wearing were worth more than what both of us had on, right down to socks and shoes and all that was in our wallets, including the change in my piggy bank back home. I actually have one. A pink pig. I think it's precious.

It was a goodly walk to where we were. As she strolled, Leonard said, "She looks like your type, and I'm going to tell Brett if you smile too much."

Within a few seconds she was in front of us, standing in a way she knew was killer, one leg slightly in front of the other to accentuate her legs and hips. Of course, why anyone would stand like that normally is impossible to figure, but like I said, it had the desired effect.

"Can I help you gentlemen?" she said. She had the sort of southern voice that's a little bourbon-soaked and so smooth you'd think butter wouldn't melt in her mouth but a lie could happily live there. She let loose that bomb of a smile again.

I turned on what charm I had left, showed her my smile. At least I had all my own teeth. Except for the wisdom teeth. They were long gone, top and bottom. I have suggested many times that what was wrong with my life might be just that. No wisdom teeth.

"We'd love to talk to you for a moment," I said. I was so friendly and cheerful I wanted to pull up a chair and listen to me.

"Would you like to go out on the lot?" She posed that like it was a question up there with a possible discussion of string theory, and that the two of us might really have something profound to add.

"Actually, we're not here to buy one of those cars," I said.

"Oh," she said. "We do sell cars, you know."

"Yes, but I'm assuming you have others, ones not on the lot," I said.

"Of course. Come sit at the desk and we'll chat."

We followed her over. I watched her buttocks wrestle in the tight skirt. Both sides of her ass seemed to be holding their own. She indeed had a firm-apple butt, and the skirt fit tight, as if it and the ass were one and the same.

She took her chair, and Leonard and I took the two chairs in front of the desk. Those chairs were like settling down on a cloud. I felt sleepy the minute I got situated. I could feel the sweat freeze-drying at the small of my back.

"I'm Frank," she said.

"Hap," I said. And Leonard gave his real first name, too. We didn't offer last names. If it came to that we had already worked up some lies—Wilson and Smatter. He was Wilson, I was Smatter.

"Hap. That's an odd name," she said.

"It's rare," I said. "You don't look like a Frank."

"Actually it's Frankie," she said and shifted her legs so that I could be certain she was all woman, let her foot hang so she could dangle one of those fine boots. "But everyone calls me Frank. I thought it sounded better for the business."

I doubted that. She didn't seem old-fashioned to me, like she was trying to convince anyone a man ran the business. Maybe she was just trying to appeal to who she thought we were, a couple of male chauvinist pigs she could sell a car to.

I noticed her turning her head to the lot, checking what we drove up in.

"Would your car be a trade, if we were able to put you in a new ride? I must be honest. We don't give substantial trade credit. It's not our way."

"He drove his car," I said, indicating Leonard, "but I'm the one who's come to buy a car. I wanted him to check them out with me."

"He values my opinion," Leonard said. "Him being my sidekick and all."

She nodded. "That is so nice, to have a friend that dear."

"Isn't it?" Leonard said. "I get loose bowels thinking about it."

Frank gave him a look that showed she was trying to appreciate his humor.

Easy, Leonard. Pull it back. There were some days when you just didn't know which Leonard you would get. The sarcastically playful one, the deadly avenger with a heart of ice, or the snot-nosed little brother who wants his cookies and Dr Pepper and was easily bored. All the personalities that make up his overall personality were quirky at best.

"The cars on the lot, interestingly, are not for sale. They are showpieces, but we have others like them, and some even rarer. I mean, people can look at the ones on the lot if they want, but only to buy a car like it, not those cars."

"It's like when you get shown the dessert tray at a restaurant," Leonard said. "They look good, but they're shellacked over and not for sale."

"Sort of like that, yes," she said. "But you said you were looking for something different from what was on the lot."

"I did indeed," I said.

"Well, we have them."

"Good deals?" I said.

"I suppose that depends on how one looks at it," Frank said.

"How would one look at it?" I asked.

"Well," she said, "that depends on your bank account, to be honest."

"Or to be frank," I said.

"Yes, that's a good one, Hap," she said. "A good one." She made it sound like I was the smartest man who ever squatted to shit over a pair of shoes. She was already starting to irritate me.

"Our cars are reconditioned with all original parts, which we have to go well out of our way to find, and that's expensive. We don't use substitute parts or any modern part that might fit, and that is a rarer situation every year. Therefore, each year there is a rise in expense. Hard to find those parts. But for what we have to offer with the cars, and how unique our services are, it's worth it. You can look at one of our catalogs if you like. Not only pictures, but lots of explanation there."

She gave me and Leonard the catalogs. I studied them. Lots of nice classic cars with some very nice classic women leaning against them while wearing only enough to keep from being arrested. In fact, the girls were more prominent than the cars. Redheads and blondes and brunettes, white-skinned, dark-skinned, short, and tall, but each of them so good-looking they nearly brought tears to my eyes.

"There are a lot of side benefits to buying a car from us," Frank said. "If you want them. Were you recommended by anyone? Someone who might have told you about us, recommended our special services?"

I think it was the way she looked, the way she sat, the way she laid out the questions, that made me think what she was asking wasn't exactly what she was saying. I began to get some idea of what we had actually walked into.

I avoided her questions, and asked her one.

"Say we want to buy something to go along with a car."

She didn't even blink. "You don't mind expense?"

"I'm in a good financial position," I said. "Inheritance. Some patents. I'm well-off, to put it bluntly."

Leonard coughed a little.

"Are you all right?" Frank asked Leonard.

"Yeah," he said. "I think I swallowed a moth or something coming in."

"Really?" she said.

"I'm all right," Leonard said. "It was a little moth."

"Goodness," she said.

Her concern for Leonard dying of moth inhalation was brief.

She leaned forward, showing me her cleavage, which I should note was deep enough you might need mining equipment, a good light on your helmet, and some serious camping supplies to go down there and look around.

"What if I wanted something from your catalog?" I said.

"What kind of model are you looking for?" she said, leaned back and arched her back slightly. It was enough to give me a new and exciting view of the Grand Tetons.

"Something in your caliber," I said, and I was surprised to find there was a catch in my voice. I, too, must have swallowed a moth. "The sort of car you would drive, I mean."

"Of course," she said. "A nice, clean, serviceable model." She smiled to show me there was a joke in there somewhere.

Leonard cut his eyes at me. Buffy did that the same way. They really did have the same eyes. I put my attention on Frank. "Exactly," I said. "A nice, clean, serviceable model."

Now Frank laid it on thicker. She lowered her eyes slightly, gave me a sleepy kind of look, the sort she thought I might like to wake up to. Her voice dropped slightly, and you could almost hear panties drop and bedsheets being pulled back in that voice.

"Something sleek and fine-tuned. Something that could make you feel fine-tuned yourself."

"That sounds good," I said. "I mean, who doesn't want to be fine-tuned?"

She looked at Leonard, lowered her eyelashes, and gave him that sleepy kind of look.

"How about you?" she said. "You think you might decide you want a fine-tuned car, too?"

"Absolutely. Something that would just tune the shit out of me would be nice," he said.

She acted mildly shocked at such language, but in a pleasant way, as if she were a preacher's wife who now and then liked to have a beer and have her ass pinched.

"So we're talking a car for both of you?" she said.

"Oh, yeah," Leonard said. "I just came as his backup, but now that you mention it, hell, I might as well get one. Whatever he gets, I want one better. Fact is, make it bigger and longer than his."

"We've known each other a long time," I said. "We're a tad competitive."

"I suppose it's friendly competition," she said.

"Friendly as shit," Leonard said.

She smiled that killer smile again, settled back in her chair, and let her gaze hang somewhere in between us.

"Tell me how you heard of us," she said.

I had dodged that question earlier.

"I drive by here all the time," I said.

She gave me a stony look. That wasn't the right answer, but I was still trying to see how much of what I thought was going on was real and how much was my imagination.

I laughed. "Of course, as I pointed out, the merchandise I want isn't on the lot. I think I'm making myself clear, am I not?"

"I've explained about the catalog," she said. She was beginning to lose some of her giddy sweetness. She was definitely wanting an answer to her question. And the right answer.

"I've been told there are some things that come with the cars that aren't in the catalog," I said. "Or at least it can be that way."

She didn't bite. Just smiled. Not a very good one this time, just enough to show her teeth and wet her lipstick.

"I had a friend tell me about the place," I said. "He knew a lady named Sandy, and Sandy put him into a good ride at a fair but certainly upscale price."

The woman narrowed her eyes. "Oh," she said. "When was this?"

"Maybe five years ago," I said.

"Who was this man?" she asked.

"Fellow I met in passing," I said. "At a party. A party Ms. Lilly Buckner arranged. I met him there. Sandy was her granddaughter, and this fellow, the one at the party, he knew her a little. Actually he said 'a little but well,' if you catch my drift. Said she worked here. He told me a bit about what you offer."

"A little but well?" she said. "Kind of a contradictory statement, isn't it?"

"Not the way he meant it," I said.

"Of course," she said, but she had grown as cold as the air-conditioning unit since I mentioned Sandy. "We did have a Sandy, but she quit. Stopped coming in, actually. And this wasn't her work station. She was assigned to another office, another division of the business."

"Another division?" Leonard said.

"Another city, but she was here for a while, then she was gone. The other division, in Fort Worth, she just quit showing up there. Can't say I remember her that well. Well, right now inventory is small, Hap, but I'll keep you in mind."

"What about the catalog?" I asked.

"I think I misspoke," she said. "I realize I might not have what you want at all. The other services. Road check. Free tire rotation. That may not be available right now."

"It wasn't my tires I was hoping to get rotated," I said.

"I have no idea what you mean, but I made a mistake. We won't have any cars for a while."

"Not a good way to sell product," I said. "Not having it available after you say you do."

"We don't need to sell many of what we sell to make good money. We're expensive."

"I can afford the expense," I said.

"He can," Leonard said. "He's got patents on sex toys. Nice stuff—he ought to show you the line sometime. What's in *his* catalog is for sale. There's this one—a big purple rubber dick with metal studs on it—that will make you scream like there's a man with a chain saw after you. And me, I got some serious-ass money. A white couple left me their estate. I was their gardener for about ten years. They didn't know that secretly I hated them for their whiteness and called them ugly names behind their backs. Cracker, honky, and such. That old, wrinkly lady, and her having me stud her. Jesus. That was some tough work, I got to tell you. I'd rather have had a job wiping asses in hell. Dropped her drawers, lay down on the bed, that thing of hers looked like a taco rolled in hair rotting on a blanket. Paid all right, though. Still, you had to get past the smell and imagine it was a goddamn donkey to get a hard-on."

I thought: Gardener? White couple? Stud to a wrinkly old lady? Get past the smell? What the fuck?

"Is that so?" Frank said to Leonard. Under her green-eyed gaze I felt like we had gone from two wealthy buyers to a couple of yokels in mud-splashed overalls with cow shit on our shoes and the intellectual level of a bag of busted bricks.

"He's a joker," I said. "He's just not too funny."

"Oh, I'm not kidding. The old man knew how to keep an erection. Viagra. That's the drug for the aged; that's what I'm trying to tell you. I think for everyone over sixty they ought to pass it out for free. Put it in their fucking oatmeal and mashed peas. By the way, do you have a hat to go with that outfit? I think it needs one."

Frank stared at Leonard. I think she wasn't certain what she had just heard. When she was certain, she said, "I do have a hat. It matches the skirt." Then to me: "You have a card? Maybe I can let you know when we have new inventory. I can make my mistake up to you if something comes in."

"That sounds good," I said. "But I'm out of cards. I'll just write down a phone number you can call."

"Very well," she said.

I wrote my number down on a pad with a pen she handed me. I didn't put my last name, just Hap. Leonard didn't bother writing his number or name, just told her to call and make it two, but to make his more expensive and better. The competition thing. But by then Frank was like someone waiting for a train to pass.

I finished the writing, did it carefully, remembering where she had touched the pen. I didn't touch that spot. I looked at the pen when I finished. It was one of a handful in a small, decorative jar on her desk.

"Are these to spare?" I said, holding up my signing pen.

"Handouts," she said.

"Good," I said. "You'll call right away if something comes up?"

"Of course," she said.

Maybe saying there was a party at Ms. Buckner's was my mistake. Maybe she knew the old bat, realized she wasn't exactly a party animal. Then or five years ago. And, of course, Leonard had fucked up any chance I had of rescuing the deal.

We stood up.

Frank said to Leonard, "You must have been some gardener to inherit their money."

"Well, I was plowing a couple of fields in the house, not to mention the garden. I was good, though. I could make an old man scream and an old woman shit herself. I could grow a rose that would kiss your ass every morning and sing you to sleep at night. And petunias—oh, hell, they were so goddamn fine we had a paying tour come by once a year every winter."

"Petunias grow in the winter?" Frank said. She wanted us gone, but she just couldn't help herself. Maybe she was wondering if there was really something to it. A gardener gigolo.

"Mine grew in the winter, and that's why there was a tour," Leonard said. "Nuns. Boy Scouts. Mostly civic people. They were happy as hell to be there and see those petunias. Hybrids. Very special."

"I'm sure they were," Frank said.

We left. I made sure my grip stayed exactly the same on the pen. When we were back in the car, Leonard said, "Talk about going from hot to cold."

"Oh, really? I have patents on sex toys? A white couple left you money for being a gardener? And you secretly hated them and were plowing their fields, making them scream and shit themselves, and to fuck the old woman you had to imagine a donkey? Roses that could kiss your ass and petunia tours in the winter for nuns and Boy Scouts? What the hell, Leonard?"

"We were already burned," Leonard said, starting up the car, easing it off the lot. "I thought I might as well mess with her. I didn't like her."

"I guess you have a point, brother. It was over before we came in the door. I mean, she nibbled at the bait a little but didn't like the taste."

"Yep. She's not going to call," Leonard said. "Our pony stumbled into the ditch when you mentioned Sandy. And I think mentioning Ms. Buckner broke its leg."

"And you shot the pony in the head with that gigolo-gardener crap," I said.

"Someone had to put our bullshit pony out of its misery," he said. "It was kind of funny, though, wasn't it?"

"No."

"Hap?"

"It wasn't."

"Hap, come on, man."

"It was amusing to some degree. The old woman shitting herself was a nice touch."

"Told you. And I don't believe she had a hat to go with that outfit. I would have a hat with something like that. I like a good hat. She had a hat, she'd have had it on."

"You see her keep looking out at our car?" I said.

"I think she was memorizing the license number."

"If she's got the contacts, and I bet she does, she'll find someone who can trace it to a car rental."

"Yep. We're fucked on the secret-agent front," he said. "We were better at sexing chickens back at the chicken plant."

"Oh, I don't know," I said. "I couldn't tell a chicken wee-wee from a dee-dee. I could make a good aluminum chair, though."

"And I was a good bouncer."

"Until you got fired for kicking that guy's ass and peeing on his head."

"Yeah," Leonard said. "They thought that was excessive. Bunch of weenies. You know what we did do well? Rose-field work."

"We did. But it was hot in the summer and cold in the winter."

"Seasons work like that, Hap. It's not uncommon. Sometimes it rains, too."

"We're not actually too good at anything, are we?"

"Sadly, I was just thinking that," he said.

Leonard drove us to the office. I never let go of that pen. We pulled up in the lot. The sign for our office had changed, of course. It said BRETT SAWYER INVESTIGATIONS. That was done right away, and Marvin did it. He had to make sure no one thought he was working both sides of the street.

Just for luck, I checked for the bicycle lady and the shorts she likes to wear. She has a very successful store downstairs. You wouldn't think you could sell and repair that many bicycles, but then again, you got to see her in those shorts so much of the time. They make men and some women want to buy a bicycle or a hippopotamus, and catching sight of her in those sweet little things is as fine and satisfying as a tour of petunias in the dead of winter.

Neither she nor her shorts were on display. There were no petunias, either. Not that I'd recognize one if I saw it.

8

When we came into the office the air-conditioning hit us in a pleasing way. It wasn't as savage as the air in the car-lot office, but it was showing summer some anger. The couch was pulled out, and Brett and Buffy were asleep on it. Brett woke up when we closed the door but only moved a bit and didn't open her eyes.

Buffy raised her head in a tentative manner, like she was expecting a beating. When she looked like that I wanted to drive over to that fellow's house and pull him out of it and kick him around the way Leonard and Marvin had. I wanted to see him on a daily basis and do just what he had done to a helpless, loving dog. I wanted to see him flinch every time he saw me. I guess that made me the same as him. Naw. He's a grown-ass man. A dog expects to be loved. And deserves to. Any man that would kick a dog like that ought to have a knot jerked in his dick, the kind that could only be untied with a butcher knife.

"Been a tough day, huh?" Leonard said to Brett.

Brett cocked one eye open and left it open. The other eye finally followed.

"I didn't have a pillow, and the mattress is a tad lumpy," she said, "but I'm tough. I can handle it." Brett rolled over and put her feet on the floor, smacked her lips, and yawned. She had on jeans and a loose T-shirt. Her red hair had been pinned back, but part of it had come loose and hung across one shoulder. "Girl has to keep up her strength. Besides, I wanted Buffy to learn how to snuggle."

"How'd that work out?" I asked.

"It's a little like hugging a mahogany end table. Her legs stick straight out and go stiff. But she was sort of getting into it when you two interrupted us. How'd your morning go?"

"Not sure," I said.

"It does seem as if there's more than the car business going on there, though," Leonard said. "Fact is, I don't think the car business is going on in as big a way as monkey business."

"I'm not a fan of monkeys," Brett said. "Apes I like. Monkeys not so much. I think it's the screeching."

"Both monkeys and apes throw shit," I said. "I think we had some thrown at us today."

"Why are you holding that pen like that?" she asked.

I went to the desk drawer, where I knew there was a box of plastic bags we had bought for a variety of reasons, evidence being one. I unlocked the drawer with my key, which Leonard did not have a copy of, and put the pen in a plastic bag and left it in the drawer. I said, "I'm going to take advantage of our friendship with Marvin and see if I can get him to run the prints of a certain well-turned-out lady ape who I think may be selling more than cars and is the one who flung a lot of shit on us."

"Oh," Brett said. "How well turned out?"

"Nothing you have to worry about," Leonard said.

"No offense," Brett said, "but you aren't exactly the best judge of female flesh."

"You got a point there," he said.

"She was all right, but not my type," I said.

"I'll accept that," she said.

"On the other hand, maybe she thought me and Leonard were boyfriends," I said.

"If she did," Leonard said, "and I find out, I will personally set fire to that place, then shoot you."

I got comfortable in one of our nifty new chairs, said to Brett, "I think it's a place that gets a lot of people walking through the lot, but very few people ask about buying. I think they sell some cars but reckon they are mostly taking recommended clients, and it has to do with something besides automobiles. I got the vibe they were selling prostitution, but for all I know they got a big cookie-baking deal on the side, and that's what they're selling. I tried to make Frank—that was her name—believe I was a potential prostitute user or cookie buyer. Being with Leonard messed that up. He's like bringing a wolf to a butcher shop. He just can't help himself. He was all up in the pork chops."

"Oh, now you're blaming me," he said.

"I tried to sell us both, but I wasn't having any luck. Leonard was a bump on a log. He had nothing worthwhile to offer except claiming to have gotten an inheritance from rich white folks for his gardening expertise and bedroom prowess. Said he gave tours of his petunias. In the winter. He said I had patents for sex toys."

"I wish you did," Brett said.

"He's just pissed his charm didn't do it," Leonard said. "That he didn't have any."

"A little of that, yeah," I said.

Brett said, "No one should really let you guys out without a leash. And really, Leonard? Petunias?"

"I thought it made me sound sweet," he said.

"That'll be the day," I said. "And his story was a lot worse than that, but I'll spare you the details."

I got up and plucked us bottled waters from the little fridge. We all sat down and sipped water while me and Leonard told Brett more about what we may have found out. It all seemed less likely by that point. Frank hadn't really said anything incriminating, not actually. I began to think I had imagined a connection between cars and prostitution and Sandy's disappearance. I might as well have thrown in a Bigfoot sighting.

"It sounds way too precious," Brett said. "A car lot that sells poontang to rich people. Why bother? Why not just set up a simple escort service?"

"The cars are the lure, and the word gets around through satisfied customers. Expensive cars and expensive women. It could be a gold mine for them."

Brett shook her head. "I don't know. It may be monkey business, but it may be a totally different monkey than the one you're suggesting."

"Could be," I said. "But high-end clientele do things in different ways. No dimly lit massage parlors with stained towels or street-corner hookers with more germs than the Centers for Disease Control. That's too raw for them. This is elevated business for people who are willing to spend serious money. It may be hard to believe, but not only can they attract people from other places for the service, there are lots of people right here in town with money. Some of it is even legal. Lilly Buckner said Sandy came into some good money working for the car company, and then all of a sudden she wasn't in good money at all, or didn't seem to be, since she lifted her grandmother's goods. The good money could have been for the services that came with the car—sex, drugs, a party. I don't know. Maybe something happened, and she found out something else about the business she didn't like. Could be she was actually researching what was going on there to do an exposé—going undercover, trying to use that journalism degree."

"But she got caught?" Brett said.

"And she needed money to run," Leonard said.

"What I'm thinking," I said.

"I'm still skeptical," Brett said. "I mean, a car you can use every day, but this call-girl thing, paying that much money for a car and a one-time hump. No ass is worth that much."

"Except for yours, of course," I said.

"Oh, you are in for so much loving, Hap Collins," she said.

"What I'm saying is it could be like an exclusive membership. Now that you're in the club, the ass is there when you want it. You still pay, but not as much as the first time, because you were buying a car with it."

"Yeah, all right," Brett said. "I hear you. Still skeptical."

"I just want a cookie," Leonard said. "I know they're in that drawer and you have the key."

"What do you think about all this, Leonard?" Brett asked.

"I want the key to that drawer," he said.

"About the car lot and the prostitution business," she said.

"Oh. I think it's what Hap says, and I'd still like a cookie."

"Maybe tomorrow." I said.

"Don't be mean, Hap," Brett said.

"He needs to learn delayed gratification," I said.

Brett opened the drawer with her key and gave Leonard a cookie. He ate it slowly and happily. But he watched carefully as she relocked the drawer and put the key away.

"Dang it," I said. "You broke down, baby."

"Okay, laying the Sandy Buckner problem aside," Brett said, "there has been some good news. The lady who had you snooping on her husband came by and paid her last check and said she was happy with the results, though curiously she's divorcing her husband anyway."

"What?" I said.

"Said she didn't like him keeping secrets from her. But you know what I think? I think the marriage just played out, and she was looking for a way to end it."

"You figured all that because she gave you a check?" Leonard asked.

"No, actually she told me that," Brett said. "Said she was happy for twenty years, or thought she was, and then one morning she got up thinking he was cheating, and he wasn't, but she hoped he was. Said he's devastated and she feels a little bad about it, but she's moving on anyway."

"People are strange," I said.

"I called Marvin to offer him his part of the payment," Brett said, "but he doesn't want it. He says all of it is ours to have. He's keeping himself clear of the old business so there won't be any misunderstandings."

"Does this mean dinner out for me and you and John and Leonard?" I asked.

"Buffy would be alone," she said. "I don't think she's ready for that."

"Good point," I said.

"We could order something and have it here or at the house," Brett said.

Leonard shook his head. "John and I are going to pass. We're working on things. I think I need to sort of hang close. He's like your new dog right now. Vulnerable and confused. And me, I'm not too good at dealing with vulnerable. I kind of see it as a weakness. John comes and he goes. He's on about things. He's off about things. All that shit just makes my ass tired. I'm sick of talking about it, but I want a decision."

"He's vulnerable, like Buffy," I said, "but he acts like a cat."

"Tell me about it," Leonard said. "Just get over it or get on with something else and let me know where you stand. I hate all this back-and-forth bullshit about our feelings and such. My feelings are I care about him and I want to go to bed with him and I want to watch television with him, and now and again I want him to just leave me the fuck alone."

"That's part of the problem," Brett said. "You wanting him to just leave you the fuck alone now and again. Maybe you ought to at least pretend to be understanding."

"I suppose," Leonard said, shifting his butt onto the edge of the desk, crossing his well-muscled arms. "But you know what? Just pull your pants up and get on with it. I get so tired of all the whining. Do what it takes or shut up."

"Oh, that has got to be good pillow talk," I said.

"Pretty understanding and romantic," Brett said.

"Yeah, John don't care for it much," Leonard said.

"Sometimes a little white lie never hurts anybody," Brett said. "Tell him you feel his pain and understand his feelings, and that it's something the two of you will get through together. It might even come true."

"But it isn't like that," Leonard said. "I can't listen to that 'I'm a homo sinner' shit and not want to start tearing up the place."

"I bet that homo thing really goes down tight with the gay community," I said.

"I wouldn't know," he said. "I don't much like any community. I don't want to be part of anyone's goddamn club other than my own. I don't have problems with who I am. I don't want to tell a little white lie about how I understand where he's coming from, because I don't."

"Sometimes you have to lie a little," I said.

"So you lie to Brett?" Leonard said.

Brett was looking right at me.

"I didn't say that," I said.

"You just told me it was a good idea," Leonard said.

"Actually, she did."

"You just said the same thing," Leonard said.

"I was just saying who said what."

"And I'm just saying you were one of those who said what," Leonard said.

Brett was watching this like a Ping-Pong match.

Another five minutes and I had extricated myself from the mess with a few white lies, and Leonard and I left to return the BMW.

Leonard chuckled as we rode along. "Got you, didn't I, brother?"

"That stuff about lying was because of the cookies, wasn't it?"

"Most definitely was. John's not the only one on the fade right now. I am feeling quite vulnerable myself. For cookies."

"At least you're simple," I said.

9

That night I invited Marvin and his wife over after Leonard and I returned the car to the Tyler rental and I got mine back. Marvin said he would come, but not Rachel. I expected that. She hates me and Leonard. We saved her daughter once, and she's appreciative of that, but spending an evening with me would for her be like having her asshole worked over with a plumbing snake.

We ordered from a barbecue joint by phone. I drove over and picked it up about twenty minutes before Marvin showed up. I got Buffy a sandwich as well. Later, I'd take her to the drive-through at Dairy Queen and get her a vanilla cone, a double.

It was a good meal. The sandwiches. Ice tea. We also had some potato chips and a bit of pecan pie that had been frozen since last Thanksgiving. It tasted all right, though. Nobody died. All in all I was off my diet for one night, and I loved it. I felt good enough to give Leonard his cookies had he been there. Back at the office it had been a joke, but now I was thinking about his face and how he had looked. You had to know him well to know the difference, but there was despair there, as much as he knew how to show. Of course, John was the real problem, but a cookie wouldn't have hurt him. Or I could take him to the drive-through and get him a vanilla ice cream cone, too. He'd like that. Maybe tomorrow. I could even roll the window down and let him hang his head out the way Buffy likes to do. Of course, if he knew I was thinking like that, comparing him to a dog, he'd have my ass on a stick.

When we were done eating I went out of the room and came back with the bag with the pen in it. I told Marvin how I had come by it, told him what I suspected, told him about our visit with Frank. What we had said, what she had said.

"Seems pretty elaborate for a call-girl setup," Marvin said.

"What I thought," Brett said. "Ridiculous, really."

"Leonard agrees with me," I said.

"There you have it," Marvin said. "If Leonard thinks so, then we should consider no more. Where is that jackass?"

"Home with John."

"They're back together?"

"I think it's on the fence. One of those with twists of barbed wire along the top. John is feeling gay again and some of his religion and his brother's influence have faded and in the meantime his pecker has gotten hard, but Leonard doesn't like it."

"The pecker?"

"The situation," I said. "Doesn't like having to coax John along. Thinks he should just get over it."

"That time me and my wife had the troubles, I paid for that for years. Sometimes I still pay for it. Not that I didn't deserve it. Rachel took care of me through my accident, but we were split in a way, even then, because of me messing around. We were together, but we weren't. I was there. She was there, but we weren't there together."

"As a woman," Brett said, "I can see her position."

"As a man I can see it," I said.

"It was stupid on my part," Marvin said. "One of many stupid things I did. I'm glad we're back together, but there's times when Rachel's giving me the hairy eyeball, and I sort of get the wish we weren't together, that I'd moved on. And then I think of being without Rachel and I get sick. I'm sure Leonard is going through all that kind of thinking. And I got to admit, he may be on to something. You got to think there's a point where you either say high five or drown the son of a bitch."

"So how are things at home?" I asked.

Marvin laughed.

"Don't ask that," Brett said, slapping me on the shoulder.

"It's all right," Marvin said. "I'm not sleeping on the living room couch anymore. Being back in bed with Rachel feels funny. Like I'm sleeping in a bear's den and she's the bear and she's going to wake up and claw me to death and eat me and shit me out behind the house."

"Must make for some restless nights," Brett said.

"It does," Marvin said. He picked up the bag with the pen in it, turned it around in the light as if he might actually see her prints with his naked eye. "So you want me to run the prints? You believe there's something to it?"

"I do," I said. "See if there's anything on Frank, or Frankie." I placed her card on the table. "Note there's no last name on the card, either. Just Frank. The name of the business and a phone number. I left my name and cell number, but like Frank I didn't leave a last name. I don't think it matters, I said. I think she made me pretty quick, knew I wasn't legitimately rich. And then Leonard clinched it all with the sex-toy patents and the petunias."

"It's hard to know how to act rich when you've never been," Marvin said.

"Yep," I said. "Anyway, she made me and Leonard and that was it: we were given our traveling papers, and we were out the door."

"All right," Marvin said. "I'll look into it. Might be enough to reopen the cold case on Sandy."

"Do you know anything about that case?" I asked.

Marvin shook his head. "Been gone too long. But I'll look into it this week. My guess is she's growing grass somewhere."

"That's what her grandmother thinks, but she still wants her back," I said. "Even if it's just her bones or a hank of hair."

"I understand."

We had another cup of coffee, and then after an hour or so, Marvin said he had to go. Brett popped some popcorn while I drove Buffy to the drive-through for that ice cream cone. When we got back the dog consented to lying on the couch between us, but she was nervous every time we reached out to pet her. That, of course, made me mad at her previous owner all over again.

Other than that, it was a nice night. The popcorn was a little greasy, and it gave me a feeling of having a knotted rope in my stomach. But hey—compared to stuff that was going to happen, it wasn't so bad.

10

It seemed like forever before I fell asleep, and it seemed a shorter time before I awoke to Brett saying, "We got to go to the office."

"Didn't we just lay down?" I said.

"Nope."

"I feel like I just laid down."

"Was it night when you laid down?"

"Yes."

"It's day now, so you didn't just lay down."

"It's early," I said. "You own the place. I'm just part-time hired help. I been thinking about calling in a sick day."

"You're full-time. And when I go, you go. And you don't get sick days. Come on, lazybones."

"But why would I go to the office? I'm not a receptionist."

"Because I want you there. Either that or you and Leonard can get on the job and find out something about Sandy."

"We'll do that," I said and tried to cover back up.

"And you'll still get up," she said.

"What if I offered savage sex?"

"Would it have to be with you?"

"Yes," I said. "I think it would."

"Then get up."

While Brett made coffee, I put the leash on Buffy and took her out, and damn near jumped a foot. Leonard was sitting on our porch swing. He was pushing gently with his foot, back and forth. His skin, normally black as night, looked ashen. He had lines around his eyes and mouth and appeared to have shrunk into himself.

"What the hell, man?" I said.

"John went home last night. I didn't want to stay in the apartment."

"So you sat out here and sniffed under our door?"

"Yeah. Did you have barbecue?"

"We did," I said. "What happened, man? Did John leave angry?"

"I think so. I told him to go fuck himself, because I wasn't going to."

"I'm going to vote he was angry."

"Sounds right. He kicked one of my shoes on the way out and slammed the door."

"More evidence," I said. "What happened to get you in the 'go fuck yourself' department?"

"One whine too many. And then just before we got down to the business, he got on his knees by the bed and prayed to God to forgive him. That set a tone I didn't like. If he had been praying for strength, I could have got behind that, so to speak. But forgiveness? Hell, we hadn't even done anything yet. That wilted my pecker something furious, let me tell you."

"How long have you been here?"

"Since sometime last night. I dozed a little. I woke up, and a raccoon was in the yard. He looked at me like this was his swing."

"It is. He comes here at night. Likes to make it move by swaying from side to side. You're here tomorrow night, he might not be as accommodating. And he has friends. Come in. Have some coffee."

We went inside, me leading Buffy and Leonard. Brett glanced at Leonard.

"Look what turned up," I said. "And I still need to walk the dog."

Me and Buffy went back outside. The heat moved across the morning like an invisible truck, heavy and crushing, and with a hotter engine than the day before. It was the kind of heat that made me feel short and fat and close to the ground. It made me thirsty and made my stomach heavy as lead. I wished for rain, but knew if it came, even if it cooled things, when it passed it would be hot again and, worse yet, humid. Nothing helped but the arrival of winter.

Buffy sniffed where the raccoon had been, then did her business near the edge of the road under one of our trees on a patch of grass. I walked her down the sidewalk for about twenty minutes, then put her in the house, got the shovel from the garage, and cleaned up the dog crap, bagged it and trashed it. Time I got through doing that I felt even shorter and heavier and was sweated up and almost sick from the heat.

Inside we all had coffee, and I had a lot of cool water to boot, hydrating myself and thinking maybe I might move to Maine. I said that once to Leonard, and he said, "If it isn't the heat, it's the Yankees, and I prefer the heat."

You'd have thought he fought for the Confederacy.

Leonard and Buffy rode with us to the office. I suggested we get Buffy an ice cream, but Brett was against it. "She's been indulged enough. And besides, it's not good for her, and she shouldn't have something like that so early."

"Its not like drinking," I said. "It's okay to have a cone before ten. And she's not driving."

"It's important to set a good example," Brett said.

At the office we gave Leonard some cookies, primarily because he had a shitty night. I gave Buffy one when Brett was in the bathroom. I said to Leonard, "Don't tell."

"Only if the key to the drawer is mine when I want it," he said.

"You are an evil bastard," I said.

That's when the phone rang.

It was Marvin. He had some news on the fingerprints.

He drove over and we made more coffee, decaf this time, and got comfortable. Buffy climbed on the couch. She was starting to be bolder. I liked that.

"How's the new job?" I said.

"Fits me like a G-string," he said. "Nice and snug."

"You had to go there," I said. "Now I've got that in my head all day."

"If you can't stop thinking about it, call me later," Marvin said.

Brett came out of the bathroom then. When she saw Marvin, she said, "I was only in there to powder my nose."

"Of course," he said.

"I thought I heard the toilet flush," Leonard said.

"Hey," she said. "Who gave you cookies?"

"I may have heard the flush below, in the bicycle shop," he said.

"That fingerprint you gave me," Marvin said. "You'll like this. It belongs to a man."

"Interesting, to put it mildly," I said. "Frank didn't look like a man, in spite of the name. Maybe you ought to run them again."

"Frank, or Frankie, is really one Frank Chesterville from the old days, but she had the tree cut and the stump split."

"A surprise, but not a crime," I said.

"It depends on how big the dick was," Leonard said. "Some things, from my viewpoint, are a criminal waste."

"You're going there again," Brett said. "Lady present, goddamn it."

"The measurements were not in the report," Marvin said. "She does have a record, though. I guess that's right. She? Hormones and operations now put her in the female department. That's right, isn't it?"

"Why you looking at me?" Leonard said. "I'm queer, not an expert on every kind of sexual orientation in the world. I look at it simple. You got your good folks and your bad folks. They can be nudists, gays, trans doo-dads and no doodads, albinos, midgets and giants, black, white, brown, all the colors in between. I keep it simple. I think Frank might be a bad folk."

"I think you meant little people," I said.

"What?"

"You said 'midgets.' I think they like to be called little people."

"Fuck you," Leonard said. "And fuck the little people, too, right down to the ground. And piss on their little hats."

"Little hats?" Brett said.

"Oh, he is fussy today," I said.

"I just thought you might know what was what," Marvin said, shrugging his shoulders, looking at Leonard.

"So what's the past crime Frank committed?" Brett said. "You didn't wind up with her fingerprints in the system for nothing."

"You'll love this," Marvin said. "When she was a he, she was a pimp in Fort Worth. High-class, but a pimp nonetheless. Ran a tip-top joint, had people who took care of bad company, throwing them out, giving them an attitude adjustment now and then. No leg breaking, stuff like that, just kind of rearranging them for a moment. Keeping it all clean and calm and profitable. But Frank got nailed for pimping, did a little time and paid a fine, got out, had the sex change, and maybe changed her life. She may have gone on to better things and is a fine example of humankind and only works at the car place to finance her research into the elimination of cancer. Or maybe not."

Marvin paused.

"You want someone to ask, 'What do you mean "maybe not"?' don't you?" Leonard said.

"Thank you," Marvin said. "Frank did have a minor problem later with a man who said she was trying to blackmail him. That got swept under the rug, though. I think the guy got over being mad and started worrying about what his wife would think about some film that may or may not have been taken of him doing the sweaty-sheet wallow. He decided not to press the issue."

I thought on that a moment. "I don't know for sure she's still pimping, but it sounded like it to me. She was talking in a way where I could keep asking until I got the answer I needed. But I spooked her. I wasn't a guy with money, and she smelled a rat."

"Well, this isn't my problem just yet," Marvin said. "No crime is known. I'm just giving you a little information on the sly. If it comes to something, let me know. Frankly, I don't really give a shit if she's selling ass, as long as no one is underage or forced and they're keeping clean and not spreading disease. But you know, the law is the law, so if I should know it for a fact, I got to act. Blackmail is involved, that's a different matter. That one bothers me, and I damn sure need to know about it should you find out."

"Our business is finding Sandy," I said. "That's it. Wherever it leads."

"From what you've told me," Marvin said, "if Sandy went to work for them peddling tail, it's possible she moved on. Maybe she just didn't want anything to do with Grandma, and Grandma thinks she's dead, but she's moved on to be a hairdresser in Fort Lauderdale."

"That's possible," Brett said. "But I bet Grandma, who is, at least by her own admission, tech-savvy, has searched for her. It's harder to hide these days than it used to be."

"But not impossible," Marvin said. "People do it every day."

"We'll find her," Brett said.

"I love my girl because she's an optimist," I said.

"One week on the job and she's Sam Spade," Marvin said.

"Sammy Spade now," she said. Then looked at me, said, "You and me, baby, we need to talk."

"Honey, even if you were a horse in a past life, I'm satisfied," I said.

"I'm not sure what to think about that," Brett said. Then she whinnied.

11

We have this friend named Cason Statler. He works for a dying newspaper in Camp Rapture, which isn't far from LaBorde. He's one of those dark-haired guys that looks like an underwear model but is tough as sandpaper. Been in the military. Been to war. I don't know all the details, but he's done some things that have given him hard bark, even if it doesn't show right away. I like him.

Brett, on the other hand, thinks Cason's a little too free with the ladies, plays the field too much, but my take is if he's not making any promises to anyone, then so be it. Make it clear, and everyone knows the lay of the land, then it's all good if everyone is in agreement. Doesn't matter in whose garage he's parking the car.

We drove over to Camp Rapture and caught him at the newspaper. He didn't even ask for time off, just came with us. We wheeled over to a coffee shop downtown, where a very nice-looking, bouncy blond waitress wearing a short dress with barber-pole-striped stockings up to her knees put the hustle on Cason. Me and Leonard might as well have been extra chairs. Cason was polite with his smile, gave it to her freely, then ordered all of us coffee, and when she went for it, he said, "So you want me to be an operative of sorts?"

We had explained a bit of it to him as we drove him from the paper to the coffee shop.

"That's about the size of it," Leonard said. "Thing is, man, we don't know what's going on. It might be a legitimate car lot that sells expensive cars and we just looked like old biscuits, not new bread, so she was willing to let us pass. Then again, maybe Frankie was hiding something."

"Here's the thing," I said. "Frankie used to be Frank, but now she looks like a retired movie star planning a comeback. I don't know which way she swings. Men, women, zebras, or moose. But we think if you put on some nice duds, you got the look that says money, and you got the look she'd like if she likes men. I can't tell you which end of the farm she works. I don't know if she's hoeing potatoes or corn."

"What am I getting out of this?" he asked.

"The satisfaction of finding out if the place is actually a front for a call-girl service or something else nefarious. It's got a stink all over it. You could write a damn good article or two or three on that. We think that's what Sandy was trying to do—write an article."

Cason thought that over. He sipped his coffee, thought it over some more. "I could use a good article. I could make a series out of it if it's any good. Last piece I wrote was about the blueberry festival. Bad year. Lots of rot."

"There's always the cabbage festival next year," Leonard said.

Cason nodded. "Might be something there, except we don't have a cabbage festival."

"You could write like there's one," Leonard said. "Like it was a huge event, and everyone reading will think, shit, I missed the goddamn cabbage festival."

"No," Cason said. "I don't think so."

The waitress came with the coffee. She made some small talk, and we tried to make some with her, Leonard and I being witty and all, but she didn't think so. On the other hand, there wasn't anything Cason said that wasn't interesting to her. He asked for some Sweet'N Low. She went away and got it and was back faster than I could pour cream in my coffee.

Cason managed to end their conversation politely. When she left we noticed one of the artificial-sweetener packs had her name and phone number on it. This did not seem to take Cason by surprise. He stuck the packet in his shirt pocket without so much as blinking.

Okay. Maybe Brett was right, and he was a little bit too much of a player. Or maybe I was jealous he was so attractive to women. Leonard, of course, just thought it was funny. Hell, I think he had a mild crush on the guy.

"What we'll do is set you up with a rental," Leonard said. "Nice car, a bit of spending money. But please don't spend it."

"I may have to," he said.

"Only if you have to." I said. "Brett's money."

I took a moment to tell him that we weren't working for Marvin, how things had changed.

"How much money?" he said.

"A thousand," I said. "Plus the rental. You may have to get that in Tyler. That's what we did. But she might check the license plate."

He nodded. "I won't need a rental. I know a brunette lady who has a very nice old Jag. She'll loan it to me."

"All you have to do is wash it when you finish," I said.

"Maybe a little more than that," he said. "Still something that will get me wet, but nothing that hurts my feelings."

12

Cason told us he would start the next day, as he had a loose rein at the newspaper, could pretty much come and go as he pleased. He was the only one who worked there who at one point had been short-listed for the Pulitzer, so he was kind of their pet.

Since there was nothing for us to do but wait, we drove over to see Ms. Buckner. I had a few questions for her. It was a simple house with the grass grown up and a mailbox at the curb on a post that leaned a little. The garage was closed up tight where the Mercedes would be resting, ready to threaten cars and dogs and people on bicycles.

Once upon a time there had been a flower bed next to the house. Now it was weeds, and even they looked as if they were hoping for death. There was a stone Negro lawn jockey between the flower bed and the door. I thought he looked very hot and a lot insulted.

"Nice," Leonard said, studying the jockey.

I laughed at him and rang the bell.

It was hot outside, and it took her about the time it took for a roast to cook in a slow oven before she answered the door. She was wearing a loose white shirt with food stains on it and some yellow stretch pants that fit her a little too well, causing the bones in her hips to stand out. She had on fluffy brown house shoes. She studied us for a long moment.

"Found her?" she asked.

"No," I said.

"Then what the hell are you here for?"

"She is so endearing," Leonard said.

"Go fuck yourself," Ms. Buckner said, glaring at Leonard with two watery eyeballs.

"And her verbal skills are delightful," he said.

"Kiss my ass," she said.

"We just need to ask a few questions," I said.

"I hired you to find my granddaughter, not ask me a bunch of questions," she said to me. "What's he doing here, anyway?"

"She liked you better when you kicked the dog abuser," I said.

"I still like that part," she said. "But why is he here?"

"Just to be clear, Leonard works with me and the lady you met at the office."

"She's kind of a bitch," the old lady said.

"Wow, that is something," Leonard said. "If you weren't old and a woman, I'd punch you in the mouth. Brett's like my sister."

"Don't let the age stop you," she said. "I can still bounce a little."

Leonard actually laughed.

"Tell you something," she said. "I can use a cell phone, take photos with it, work a computer, and I can research on it. I don't need to call someone to change my TV channels, neither."

"No one asked you about your technical ability," Leonard said.

"Just thought I'd throw it out there," she said. "I wouldn't want you to think I'm past it."

"You know, I actually have trouble with the TV-channel part," I said.

"Of course you do," she said. "The trick is to actually read and study the goddamn instructions."

"That's true. I should do that. The questions I want to ask have to do with your granddaughter. I might get some tips on the remote later, but for now, it's her I want to talk about."

"I told you what I know."

"Okay," I said. "But would it be okay to ask just a few questions? There's some things you said that have got me to thinking."

"Don't hurt yourself, child."

"It does strain me a bit now and then, but if I lie down I get all perky again."

"All right, bring your happy asses inside."

We escorted our happy asses inside. The place smelled like old people. Or, in this case, an old person. I guess it comes with the territory. The room was way too warm for this time of year, at least for anyone with any skin on them. It was dark except for a crack of light from a split in the curtains, and in that light dust motes were spinning.

She poked a skeletal finger at the couch, and we sat down there. It was a couch so seldom used it was hard. Maybe we were the first ones to ever sit on it. I wouldn't think Ms. Buckner was the sort that attracted a lot of social visits. Any kind of visits, for that matter. So if Frank did know her, it was no surprise she knew she wasn't the party kind and that's why my cover was blown. And then Leonard had that whole servicing-the-old-folks bit going. Sometimes I really did want to throttle him. A lot of people wanted to do that. Only thing was, you had to bring reinforcements if you wanted to make that happen.

"You boys want something to drink?" she said.

"No, thanks," I said. "We're fine."

"Look, I'm trying to be a hostess. I'm going to have something."

"Sure," Leonard said. "Anything."

"You people like orange pop, don't you?" She said this to Leonard.

"We people sho' do likes us an orange, and you got some peanuts to po' in them, that makes it right special."

"Oh, go to hell. I drink them. Good enough for me, good enough for you. What about you, dipshit?"

"Dipshit will have an orange," I said.

She shuffled out of the room, the friction from her house shoes building up enough static electricity on the carpet she might be able to light her stove with nothing more than a touch of her finger.

"Goddamn," Leonard said. "She is just one big ole double-sweet sugar tit."

"Ain't she?"

We waited there in the smelly room with the slit of light and the spinning dust motes for a long time. This would be the crack of light at the window where she looked out and saw what was going on across the street, where she used her cell phone and transferred the video to her tablet with her high level of technical skill. She was probably drinking an orange soda while she did it, like Leonard's "people."

Finally she came back. She had three orange sodas in bottles on a tray she was holding with wobbly hands. When she came over, Leonard and I rescued our drinks, and she took hold of hers with one hand and just let the tray drop to the floor with a clang and a clatter.

"They make those damn bottles too heavy," she said.

She collapsed in a chair. She was breathing hard, and gradually she started breathing slower. Damn if I didn't think she was going to quit on us right there. But she finally came to herself, took a swig of the orange, said, "What's the questions?"

"You said Sandy had done good, gone to school, all that, but then you said something that kind of stuck with me. About her maybe living too high on the hog and having too much money. Did you let something out you didn't mean to?"

"I don't know I meant to or not," she said. "I say most anything comes to my mind these days. I thought I was pretty clear I suspected shenanigans. Damn. This orange is tangy, isn't it?"

"Quite tangy," Leonard said.

"So was there something?" I asked again.

"I know she was doing a bit of leg spreading for someone, making some money from it. You know, had a sugar daddy." She paused. "Maybe more than one. I'm not judging her. When I was younger I could do more tricks with a good long dick than a cowboy could with a waxed lasso."

I was feeling a little ill.

She saw it on my face. "Oh, hell, don't be such a prude. Look here." She got up and took her sweet time picking up a thick photo album on one of the end tables by a stuffed chair. She brought it over as if she were carrying the Ten Commandments down from the mountain, put it in my lap, went back to her seat, and did the whole breathing thing again. While she regrouped, I opened it.

After I had been looking a few minutes, Leonard leaned over to look, too. She said, "That's me. Nearly all those photos. I did some modeling. All we were showing back then in public was some leg and shoulders. In private men got to see a little more if I was in the mood. I was in the mood a lot. I liked pecker the way a chicken likes corn. When you get my age, look back, you got to wonder what that was all about. When the juices dry up the brain works better, at least in some ways. You know, I was actually in Hollywood. Believe that shit? In the old days. It was too vulgar for me, and I gave it up."

"That must have been some seriously nasty shit out there, then," Leonard said.

"What I'm trying to tell you."

I flipped through the photos. My God, even with the fashions then, the hairdos, she was one hot number. Considering the level of the photography at that time, she probably looked even better. She actually did look like a movie star, though a little short for a model. Still, she was the kind back then who would stop a man in his tracks the way a brick schoolhouse will stop a semi.

"I was in some movies," she said, as if she were reading my mind. "Some of those photos I'm a teenager. Some of the other shots, my twenties, then my thirties. I tried to settle down later, when the bit parts in the pictures played out for me. I was mostly the girl second to the left in a film with a couch audition on Sunday afternoons. I couldn't act my way out of a paper bag, but I was hell on that couch. That kept me working, if not in any big way."

"And settling down didn't work?" I asked.

"Couldn't keep my legs crossed. I was with every Tom, Dick, and

Harry that had pants, and I would have been fine with a man in a kilt. Couldn't help myself. I liked the men. Now not so much. Nobody too much. Except Sandy."

"So you're saying Sandy couldn't keep her legs crossed, either?" Leonard asked.

"I couldn't because I greatly loved sex, and I think Sandy did, too. But unlike her, I didn't do it for money. Oh, I got a coat and some diamonds now and then, a dinner, a play or a movie. A job. But hell. I was going to screw them anyway, so no big deal. By the time I did settle down and get married and had a child, I was almost too tired to fuck."

"I think that's a very modern way to look at things," I said, because I didn't know what else to say.

"Dontcha know it," she said, pushing her false teeth forward with her tongue. When she relaxed they jumped back into her mouth like a free throw. "Sandy, though, she might have been doing a little of the other, fucking for the buck. I got that impression. Then suddenly she didn't have money, and then my money went missing. I know she got it."

"You think this had to do with the car lot?" I asked.

"Expensive cars like those don't bring the cheapies around. So I figure that's how she started selling the old hairy triangle for the big bucks, and then somewhere along the way she either got greedy or got broke, because she played it stupid, took money from me. I like to think she didn't mean to take it forever, that she would have paid me back."

I could see the old woman thinking about that. I believe she decided it was too sentimental. She added, "I don't really give a damn. I can't spend money in hell."

"Did you ever meet someone named Frank?" I asked. "A woman?"

"Named Frank?"

"She goes by Frank or Frankie."

"No," she said. "I never met her, but I think Sandy mentioned her once or twice. The name Frank rings a bell. But then at my age everything seems slightly familiar and at the same time unfamiliar."

I looked back at the book of photos, closed it up, looked up to say something but didn't. Leonard looked at me. I looked at him. I placed the book on the couch beside me.

I drank the orange pop. I was hot, and it was good. Leonard swigged his. We wouldn't want to walk out and leave the bottles full—didn't want her to think we didn't appreciate it, the old witch. The clock on the wall beat out the minutes. We got up to leave and went out quietly, because she had gone to sleep in her chair.

13

Do you think while she was asleep we should have just gone on and smothered her and set her house on fire?" Leonard said.

"You are not a nice man, Leonard."

"How about I steal the jockey while she's sleeping?"

"It would look very nice in your new apartment," I said.

"Better at the dump."

I drove Leonard to our house so he could get his car. He surprised me by just going home. I guess that business with John had worn him down a bit. Not to mention the unpleasant old lady. He said he was going to see if he could stand to watch *Road House* again, as that usually cheered him up.

Of course he could. It was his favorite movie. I think he had a crush on Patrick Swayze.

I drove to the office. The lady who owned the bicycle shop was outside working on a bicycle chain. She had on those great blue-jean shorts, bless her little heart. Her legs were long and brown, and her hair was long and blond. I studied her as I walked to the stairway. She gave me a smile. It was one of those that said, "You're such a nice old guy."

It was chilly inside. Brett liked to keep it almost as cold as the office at the car lot. First few days she had it turned down to save money, but

East Texas summer heat can make you less thrifty. Sometimes someone from up north will come down to East Texas and say, "It's so hot, but living here all your life, I guess you get used to it."

No. You don't. You live in an air-conditioned house, dart from it to an air-conditioned car, then drive to an air-conditioned place. You spend time outside only when necessary. Some summers it's so hot dog crap fries on the ground. I used to work a lot of field work, but not anymore, and I hope never again. It was hard to believe that I had grown up with only a window fan.

Brett was at the desk chair, and Buffy was on the couch. Buffy raised her head to make sure I wasn't that other guy, the asshole who had kicked her.

Brett said, "Hey, we got a couple other jobs. Seem easy to me. Checking on a few things people want to hire us to do they could do themselves but are too lazy to do."

"That's good. I guess."

"Honey, it's good. We can always use the money."

"Sure. I was just thinking this current job might be a bit more demanding than expected."

"You thought it would be easy?"

"I thought the old lady would want to give up when we didn't find her granddaughter right away. I don't think so now."

"You talk to Cason?"

"I did. We're set."

"And your talk with Lilly Buckner—I bet that was a soul-enriching experience."

"Not exactly," I said. "But I like her. I can't help myself. I like her because she's got spirit and spunk and hasn't lived a life she feels a need to apologize for. I think she lived a tough life and was tough enough to live it and not care what anyone thought about it. Besides, she drinks orange soda. I like orange soda."

"I didn't know that."

"Me, either. I forgot. I had one today at her house."

"How did she and Leonard do together?"

"Like mother and son."

"That's a lie."

"Yes, it is."

I opened the refrigerator, took out a bottled water. We emptied a bottle, we filled it up in the sink, and cooled it in the fridge. It was the cool we liked. The water is the same, far as I'm concerned. Water that comes bottled—hell, fish shit in it. Ducks shit in it. Birds flying over shit in it. This way I can buy one bottle of water and use the bottle for a while without the payment.

I had marked the bottles with a marker. One mark for my bottle, two for Brett's, three for Leonard's, and sometimes I drew a smiley face on his. The dog drank straight tap water we ran into her bowl.

"There's something else," Brett said as I sat down in a client chair to nurse my water.

"Oh?"

Brett's face had a look on it like maybe she had been sitting on a tack and had just decided to pull it out.

"A girl came by," she said.

"Okay," I said.

"She wanted to see you."

"One of the cases?"

"No. But she knows a lot about you and us and that you were working for Marvin before I took over. She said I was pretty."

"You are."

"I told her you would be back, but I wasn't sure when, and it was best to either call or come by. Call would be best. I gave her the office number."

"Not the home or cell?"

"No. I didn't like that idea."

"Why not?"

"I don't know."

"You think this has to do with the car-lot business?"

Brett shook her head.

"Do I know her?"

"I doubt it."

"You're being very mysterious."

"Am I?" Brett said.

"You are."

"I guess I just don't know what to think about it. She wouldn't tell me anything other than she had to see you."

"What did she look like?"

Brett hesitated on that one. "She was young. I'm not sure how young. Twenty-five at the oldest, maybe a year or two on either side of that. She's well taken care of, but a little too thin, I thought. Like maybe she's missing some meals."

"On purpose?"

"I don't think so. She was maybe five nine, though she had on these wedge shoes with big heels, so I'm not sure. She was dressed nice, but nothing fancy. Older clothes well taken care of. Has jet-black hair and is dark-skinned, kind of Hispanic or Indian-looking, American Indian. I think maybe she dyed her hair, though my guess is it's pretty dark to begin with. She had that brunette look about her."

"If you say so. Whatever that is."

"She also had very nice teeth."

"That's good," I said. "If we need her to bite off a bottle cap, she's ready."

Brett said, "She had pretty gray eyes."

"Okay. I still don't know who she is. Did she leave a name?"

"She said she was called Chance, but she'd rather talk to you. So I didn't get a last name. She left, and I watched out the window. She talked to the lady at the bicycle shop a moment, then went out to a bicycle and rode away."

"She bought a bicycle while she was here?"

"I didn't say that," Brett said. "I said she rode away on one. I assume she rode up on it as well. Do you know anyone called Chance?"

I shook my head. "Can't say that I do. Mysterious, no doubt."

"I thought so, too," Brett said. "Buffy liked her. Actually got off the couch, came over, and licked her hand."

"Did she seem to know the dog?"

"I didn't get that impression. I don't think it was anyone working for the dog kicker, if that's what you mean. A daughter. A wife."

"I thought it might have been," I said.

"Didn't seem that way at all. I think she just liked dogs, and the dog liked her. Some people are like that."

I nodded.

"Besides," Brett said, "had she tried to take our Buffy, I'd have kicked her scrawny little ass."

Brett tried to smile after that, but the smile dissolved, like ice melting. I could see she was bothered by something. I went over and put my arm around her. "Here, now. You act like she's death come to visit."

"I know. I can't explain it. But somehow I think in some way she might be in trouble. That she might need us."

"She should have said something."

"I think for whatever reason she's waiting for you."

I didn't know what to do with that remark, and I let it lie.

We hung around for a while, me sort of hoping the dark-haired, gray-eyed girl on the bicycle would come around and solve the puzzle.

She didn't.

Leonard came over a couple hours later. He said *Road House* was as wonderfully bad as he remembered it. That was his way of saying he actually liked it a whole lot. I also knew that sometimes watching that movie was how he got his center back. It may be a hokey movie about a bouncer who has raised bouncing to a high art and reads Jim Harrison, but to tell the truth, in a way, Leonard was just that kind of guy. Only more dangerous. He made the characters in the movie look like the masters of the slap fight.

I had my jogging clothes and shoes at the office, and Leonard had his in the truck, so we changed and took a run along the street, on out to the edge of town and across to the park. It was a pretty place. Filled with pecan trees and a creek. We ran along the path that was by the creek. The late afternoon was still hot, but the shadows from the trees gave us shade. Our shadows piston-pumped along beside us.

There were women in shorts with dogs and Frisbees. Three college jocks were running along ahead of us. We passed them, and one of them said something about how he'd hate to see us die of exhaustion, old guys like we were, or some such thing. Leonard made a kind of circle while he was running, went straight to the guy, and only quit running long enough to punch him in the face, almost right between the eyes. It was a quick punch, a kind of half jab, and coming from Leonard that was still a lick, but it was a lick with a governor on it. Nothing full-bore. But it's all it took for the jock to hit the ground like a lawn dart.

The other jocks stopped running. They checked their man on the ground. He was way down in the deep siesta.

Leonard said, "All right, mice. You can squeak to the police or act like men. He can take it and live with it, and you can let him take it and live with it, or I punch you in the head, too. Which is it?"

No squeaking occurred. Leonard had appealed to their basic manhood. Don't be a squealer. Always a good weapon to attack the male ego; that's where great weakness lies. They were helping their dazed friend up as we jogged away. I think the guy they were picking up was trying to remember if his mom was picking him up from school, or if he had gym class and had remembered to bring his jockstrap.

"Kind of rowdy, aren't you?" I said as we continued to run.

"I just watched *Road House*."

"It's got you pumped?"

"I didn't tear his throat out like Patrick did to the bad guy in the movie."

"Yeah, after that guy Gazzara just looked like some goof stumbling around. See him rip the throat out of a truly bad guy, and then he fights an old man, a geriatric, and that's supposed to be tense?"

"Wasn't he about our age?"

"Maybe."

"That's what those boys back there thought we were. A couple of geriatrics."

"We're not that old, buddy," I said.

"To them we are. To them, anyone over thirty is ready for the boneyard. Irritates me. How about you?"

"Not today."

"But some days?"

"Some days. But I wouldn't have punched him in the face for that."

"No—I get to do the fun stuff. You have that thing about turning the other cheek."

"What did punching that asshole prove?"

"That I could knock him down," Leonard said.

I took a deep breath and blew it out my nose, picked up my pace. "Could John actually have something to do with your ill temper?"

"He could. He has made me an unpleasant man."

"More unpleasant than usual, you mean."

"True," Leonard said.

We ran for about an hour, then lightly jogged and walked back to the office. When we got there we were sweaty and we stank, but we were breathing fine. Our extra and revised workouts were starting to do us good. It was our plan to do some boxing later, some kickboxing, some shen chuan, then light weights. It's what we called the Master Fucking Plan.

Brett was wearing black workout shorts and a oversize orange T-shirt. She was on a roll-out rubber mat on the floor. She was doing some kind of stretchy thing. Yoga. Zumba. A version of the Elongated Man. I don't know. I kind of liked watching her do it, though. That girl was flexible. I knew that already, but it was nice to be reminded.

That went on for a while, and I enjoyed the view while Leonard fucked up his workout with some vanilla wafers and a Dr Pepper, which, according to our previous discussion, I had to let him have. I didn't even wait for him to ask for the key. I just unlocked the drawer.

Brett saw us. She narrowed her eyes, but I gave them to him anyway. I knew when it got right down to it, Brett was more of a softie than I was when it came to Leonard. She would never actually deny him a cookie. She was the one that always caved first.

I gave Buffy one of the cookies, too.

"Damn it," Brett said.

"She likes cookies," I said.

I reached down and gave Brett one of the cookies in the same way, as she was still on the floor stretching. She laughed and took it in her mouth like the dog. I decided to have one, and she fed it to me.

Leonard, wanting more, held up his hands like paws, but I put the bag of cookies in the drawer and locked it.

"Aw, come on," Leonard said.

"Nope," I said. "If you sit up only when you get a cookie, that's not good. You have to do it because it's the right thing to do now and then."

I insisted we call Jalapeno Tree for food. I made a phone order. We took turns in the bathroom changing back into our day-to-day clothes, washing our faces and hands. Leonard drove to Kroger to get some large diet sodas for us and some Dr Peppers for himself while we drove to the restaurant and picked up the food.

After that we drove to the Dairy Queen drive-through and bought a vanilla ice cream for Buffy, two scoops. By the time we arrived home, I had forgotten all about the girl Brett told me about. The one who said her name was Chance.

14

Leonard wasn't much for talk that night. After dinner he hung around for a short while, but I could tell he wanted to go home. He couldn't be comfortable away from home, because he wanted to be there if John showed up, but if he did show up, he wasn't comfortable with him there. That's love for you. When it's good, it's magic. When it isn't, it just pees all in your soup.

Leonard had pretty much decided John wasn't worth it, and then John came back and gave Leonard hope again, and then he was gone again. Leonard felt miserable. I didn't like John for that, but then again, you hurt Leonard and I'm not always reasonable.

Leonard went home, and while Brett showered for bed, I opened up the envelope Ms. Buckner had given us that day in the office. I had sort of forgotten we had it, which says something for my budding detective skills. I thought about the photos she had shown me at her house, and then I looked at the photos of Sandy in the envelope. I could see how much she favored her grandmother. They were both small and pretty, or at least Ms. Buckner had been pretty many moons ago. I moved the photos around and looked at the police reports that Ms. Buckner had gotten hold of. I wasn't sure how she came by them, but it might have been money that had helped that happen. Some of the last of her real money, back in the days when she had it and thought she'd have it forever.

There were some newspaper clippings about Sandy's disappearance there as well, but none of it meant a thing to me. I moved the photos around again, hoping something would jump out at me. There was a graduation photo. A couple shots that might have been taken in the mall with Sandy in front of one of the stores, one that was surely taken out front of Ms. Buckner's house before it went sad and dark, dusty and old, a tired, paint-chipped Negro jockey looking grim and lonesome by the flower bed. There was even one photo of Sandy with Ms. Buckner. Lilly Buckner still looked older than death in that picture, but she had a smile on her face.

My cell phone hummed. It was Cason.

"You up for some information?"

"Yep. Been waiting. Is it worth anything?"

"I think so."

"Let's have it," I said.

"Okay if I give it in person?"

"Should I put coffee on?"

"Probably won't take that long, but if you have decaf, that would be nice. I don't want to be up all night wrestling with caffeine."

"Milk and sugar?"

"I prefer Sweet'N Low."

"Would you like cookies and for me to wax your ass? Maybe a little hand job?"

"That would be nice, but you have to wear a blond wig and use baby oil."

"Well, you're shit out of luck on that."

"The hand job or the wig?" he said.

I rang off, warned Brett he was coming. She was in her pajamas by then. They were blue and loose and fell down on the tops of her feet. She went up to bed, and Buffy padded upstairs behind her. The dog was looking bigger, bolder, happier.

Like I said, there was something about Cason that Brett doesn't like. I knew I should pay attention to that, but right then, I needed him and his information.

I called Leonard and asked if he'd come over.

"Didn't I just leave?"

"You've had time to watch *Road House* again."

"Not quite," he said.

"John show up?"

"Fuck him."

"Sure. Fuck him. Cason's got some news for us."

"I'm coming over," he said.

It took Cason about twenty minutes. I had the coffeemaker churning in the kitchen. I was outside on the porch in the sweet dark, sitting on the swing listening to the crickets make their racket in the recently mowed grass of the front yard. I used to mow it. Now I hire it done. I guess for someone like me you could call that prosperous. Money got shy, I'd be pushing the mower again.

As I waited for Cason to cross the yard from the curb where he was parked, I could smell that unique smell that pines have when they've been heated all day by Texas summer, then slightly cooled by night, a kind of biting turpentine taste in the air and then in the nostrils and on the tongue. That smell was being carried a long way. I had an oak in the front yard and some sweet gums out to the side. No pines.

"Brett's gone to bed," I said as he came out from under the streetlights and up on the porch. "I'll bring our coffee out here so our talking won't disturb her."

This was a bit of a lie. She wouldn't hear us downstairs as long as we talked in an even voice, but I liked it out there. I liked that pine smell. It reminded me of when I was a kid growing up in the East Texas woods. Smells like that, along with honeysuckle, took me back to when I was young, sitting under a tree reading a book. The world seemed shiny and bright then. I wasn't thinking about trying to keep my life together, about living with failure. I was too young to consider anything but success. The world was my oyster. Since then I felt the shell had closed around me for the most part.

"Suits me," Cason said. "It's a pretty nice night."

Inside I got us two cups prepared, fixed his how he asked, went back out on the porch. He was sitting on the top step, and he turned in my direction. I gave him his coffee and sat on the swing, put my cup on the little metal table in front of me. Brett had bought it at a yard sale.

"This news I have, it's interesting," Cason said. "I don't know what to make of it, exactly, but there's some things in it that float, some others that might float to the surface if we stir them a bit."

"Then we'll stir," I said.

About that time Leonard pulled up in his truck. Unlike Cason, he pulled in the driveway next to our cars. He got out and strolled onto the porch and sat down on the swing with me. The pine smell was going away, and so was the wind that carried it.

"I like coffee," he said.

"Do you?" I said.

"I do. I'm smarter with coffee."

"Not that I've noticed."

"Well, I feel smarter."

I was too tired to jack with him as usual, so I cut it short, went inside, and fixed him a cup the way I knew he liked it, though I decided not to tell him it was decaf. I doubted he'd know the difference, nor would he be any smarter with caffeine. I brought out a bag of vanilla cookies with the coffee. I put the cookies on my side of the swing. There was enough glow from the streetlights for Leonard to see what I had.

"Manna from heaven, encased in a bag," Leonard said. "To me you are like a god."

"Thanks."

"Oh, no," Leonard said, smiling toward the cookies. "Thank *you*."

I turned to Cason. "You think you fooled Frank?"

Cason hesitated a moment. "At first. We got into a little more business than you did. I think she thought I really was a guy looking for a good car and a good escort and a trip overseas."

"Overseas?" Leonard said.

"Yep," Cason said. "That's connected to it. You can stay in the US, but they like this whole overseas thing. I think it makes what they have in mind easier to pull off."

"All right," I said. "How about you tell us what they have in mind?"

"Still a bit of guesswork," he said.

"That's all right," Leonard said. "So far we haven't got much but guess-work."

"I warn you, though, I didn't find out anything about Sandy," Cason said.

"Like you said. Let's stir it and see what floats."

"Cookies first," Leonard said.

I picked up the cookie bag, pulled it open, and shook it at him. Leonard took a handful. I poked the bag at Cason. He held up his hand like a traffic cop. "Don't care for vanilla cookies."

Leonard turned and looked at him but said nothing. I knew Cason had gone down a notch in Leonard's estimation. I was hoping the con-versation wouldn't turn to Dr Peppers. If Cason didn't like those, no telling where things might lead, especially since Leonard had watched *Road House* earlier and had already punched a smart-mouth college jock in the face.

"I went in for a little visit," Cason said, "like I wanted a car. Some of this is going to be familiar, but I'll try to hit the spots you know lightly and move on. I don't think you played it quite right when you were there, you and Leonard. They smelled shit in the air, and with me they were sniffing pretty hard. I started out with I had been recommended, saying I heard they sold very nice cars and there were a number of ser-vices that went with it. I even gave them a name. Before I went, I looked through the newspaper files stored in the computer until I found some reference to a car bought there, a black Rolls-Royce. Guy bought the Rolls was named Terrence Milden, had oil money out of Beaumont.

He bought a car there, and in this article—some fluff piece about the guy's car collection—his newest purchase was referred to in passing and where he got it. This guy was not so old, but he was retired. He came from Beaumont to here to live. I looked up more about him, asked around, did the reporter snoop, found out he was proud of that money and wanted people to know he had it.

"There were rumors about sketchy deals and such. Liked the ladies, drugs, and so on. Again, rumors, but he struck me as someone might have made a special deal at the car lot. So I talked to Frank like I knew this guy, like he recommended me. You see, he died of some disease or another—cancer, I think. Heart attack, maybe; not sure. I just know he's dead, so it's not like he can be questioned. It was a shot in the dark, but I hit the target. Frank got out the book of cars, all of them way over-priced, and sitting in each or leaning against each of those cars was a woman. Each of them looks so hot it's like the car will burst into flames. She starts talking around it, you know. So I say, 'Too bad the girls don't come with the cars,' and I looked at her and winked.

"She said they might. They could. Making it kind of a joke at first. We eased forward from there, and pretty soon I'm told how there are some nice women who work for their company that love to show buyers how the cars work. I asked what if the buyer was a woman. And Frank, she says there are some nice men who work for the company, too. Said they, too, like to show how things work, make sure everyone understands the product, inside and out. Like maybe I need help finding the clutch. It's like you guys thought. They sell a car, they sell you a girl. If you want to go that far. If they think that's your urge. Otherwise you can just pay too much for a fancy used automobile. They think you got serious money, and you take the car and the girl, you can get that foreign trip as well. I think it's a setup for filming."

"I was in the ballpark," I said.

Cason nodded, sipped his coffee.

"I don't think they're happy with selling just motors and snatcheroo. They want you to keep paying for it for a long time. They're not looking for repeat customers. They're looking for customers they can repeatedly blackmail."

"But what if someone doesn't care?" Leonard said.

"They still get money for the car and the girl, the trip overseas. They can let the blackmail go, they have to. Or they can wreck someone's life for the hell of it."

"What if someone turns them in?"

"Still has to be proved," Cason said. "Or maybe they know exactly how to set someone up they think is trouble, even if that person isn't really doing anything wrong. I don't know all the working parts yet."

"You're overseas, in some foreign country," Leonard said. "Makes you more vulnerable, more at their mercy."

"I got hints from Frank you could go places in the States, too. I think it's wide open. But the main thing is the blackmail. They asked me about my job. How I liked it. I played it up, about how important it was to me."

"To set yourself up for blackmail," I said.

"Exactly. Showed them I had something I liked and didn't want to lose it."

"That fits Frank's past MO," I said. "At least according to Marvin. Once a scammer, pretty much always a scammer."

Cason nodded. "But this scam is delicious, if that's the deal. I mean, I'm filling a lot in here based on a sideways conversation—all the things Frank said as well as the things she didn't say. Once they nail you good the first time, get you on camera, all they need is the blackmail. Though now that I think about it, they figure you're someone doesn't care if you get filmed, then they can keep selling you the girl if you want her. They think you repeat enough, there may be adequate money in that. Those gals in those photos, they don't get backstreet money. We're talking about high-dollar escorts."

"You got a lot from a mild conversation," Leonard said.

"As I was saying, I got some things, and the rest is reporter intuition."

"So you could be wrong," Leonard said.

"About some of it, but I think I read between the lines pretty well.

The blackmail idea, that's all speculation, of course. I mean, shit, she's not going to tell me they're going to sell me a ride and some ass, and then add, 'Oh, by the way, we're going to blackmail you so hard you'll be constipated.'"

"But you're in?" I said.

"I thought so. She pulled me up on a laptop right there, saw the job I had. I had to give her my name, you see. Got cornered. Could have given her a false name, but I wouldn't have had the cover. I tried to make out the Pulitzer nomination had led to a big publishing contract on a book I was writing on my time in Afghanistan. But she started pedaling backwards then. That was all stuff in the bush, not in the hand. She knew better. I think she believed I really had been given a recommendation for the place and that I had a job I loved, blackmail material, but she also figured if I worked at the Camp Rapture paper I wasn't making much. Not enough to be driving the car I was in and own it. Not enough to buy their kind of car and whatever else they were selling. She wasn't going to wait for me to finish a book. Frank's smart. She gets you right up to the door, cracks it a little, shows you some light, lets you hear a little music on the other side, but she doesn't let you in if you don't fit all the categories. I could tell she was clicking in that license number on the car I parked outside. I hadn't parked so she could see it, but some guy came out of nowhere, out there on the lot, looked at the car, and walked away. You can bet the license number came up on her computer."

"So you were fucked like us?"

"No. Lady owns it shifted it into my name, and we messed with the dates of purchase. You're not the only one who knows people. It'll only be that way for a few hours, then it goes back to the way it really is, so we don't get caught, but I was hoping that was enough."

"Does this lady of yours work at Motor Vehicles?" I asked.

"Yep," he said. "But she's got some inherited money. We take vacations now and again, on her dime."

Figures, I thought.

"But it doesn't matter," Cason said. "Frank has contacts, too, I figure.

Some blackmail victims, perhaps, or someone on their payroll. Might be dropping a few dollars at places where she can get things done, including the DMV. She figured it out pretty quick. She didn't say anything, but I could see it in her eyes. I had been squealed out, or something or other had gone wrong, because she knew from whatever she saw on the computer—whatever that guy in the lot saw and posted when he went back inside. She's getting information in real time while you sit there. Next thing I knew the catalog was closed, I had her card and a promise to call, and I was out the door. It was done so smooth I hardly realized it until I was standing on the lot."

"How it worked for us, too," I said.

"Actually," Leonard said, "our exit was less smooth."

"Thanks to you and the goddamn petunias," I said.

"I fucked it up," Cason said. "I should have spent a few days building a backstory, setting some things up with friends, contacts. I could have made it work better, but I was thinking it might all just be bullshit. It wasn't. Now I've got my radar up, and I want to find out more about the place. It's quite the scam, and it wouldn't surprise me if there's a lot more to it than what we think. I've got the nose for this kind of stuff, and I smell a big story here." He tapped his nose to assure us he did indeed have the equipment with which to smell a story. "I don't know what's making it smell, but I want to find out. None of that helps you with Sandy, but maybe she's in the mix somewhere."

"She was a journalist," I said. "Graduate in that profession without a job. What if she got wind of what was going on there and, being a looker herself, she thought she'd slip in, get a job as a car accessory, and find out the true story? She got past all the hurdles for what she wanted to do, slipped in and planned to write about it, and got caught."

"Maybe she just liked the idea of money from high-class hooking," Leonard said.

"Also a possibility," I said. "And some journalists go the whole hog, invest right down to the skin."

"That would be me," Cason said. "At least it has been me."

"All that is interesting," Leonard said, "but what we got to think about is Sandy, even if her grandmother ought to be run over by a truck."

"And after she gave you an orange soda," I said.

"I'm ungrateful sometimes," Leonard said.

I looked at Cason. "We owe you one."

"Oh, no, you don't," he said. "I'm still on this. You promised me the story if there was a story. I said I smelled one. I plan on keeping the nostrils wide open. I got contacts all over East Texas and elsewhere. There's this guy here in town called Weasel. He might be able to find me something. He's into everything, here and within two or three hundred miles of here. For all he's done he's only spent five years in the slammer. So he's pretty connected and pretty sneaky. Weasel may be our guy."

"Weasel?" Leonard said. "Now, that sounds trustworthy."

"I don't know his mother actually named him that," Cason said. "He's about five feet tall and slippery without being wet. He doesn't act dangerous, but I suspect he is, at least to some degree. He'll do most anything for a buck, and probably has."

"Can you trust him?" I asked.

"Not entirely, but enough to get what I want if I pay him a little. Out of the money you gave me, of course."

"So you're hanging on to that?"

"I'll give you half back now, but the rest I'm keeping for expenses and Weasel money."

"All right," I said. "For now, keep it all."

We talked a bit more about things, but it was just the same thing we had discussed recycled, and so we quickly called it a night. Cason walked across the yard and drove away.

Leonard said, "Is it a problem I sleep in my old room?"

"Of course not," I said.

Inside, Leonard headed to his room, the one we had built onto the house for him, and I went upstairs. Brett was lying in bed with the lamp on, reading a book. Buffy was lying beside her with her head in Brett's lap. I told her Leonard was staying the night in his old room.

"Okay," she said. "How'd it go with Mr. Slick?"

"A little of something and a lot of nothing," I said and told her some of what he told us, because as the owner of the business she needed to know.

"So Weasel's our next step."

"Unless we can find more steps," I said.

"This is turning out to be harder than I thought," Brett said. "This private-eye crap."

"Sorry you quit the nursing job now?" I said.

"Still not missing wiping asses," she said, "though now and again I long to change a colostomy bag. As for the detective business, what I'm feeling is I've bitten off more than I can chew with two sets of teeth. Now I'm worrying about paying the building payment, the lights, water, Internet."

"I always feel like I've bitten off more than I can chew," I said. "And usually I have."

"But it works out?"

"Mostly. I have to chew some of it for a long time, though. Sometimes a little of it slops out of my mouth."

I took off my clothes and put on my pajamas and crawled under the covers. Brett turned out the light. "No alarm tomorrow," she said.

"Suits me," I said, and we held one another. Buffy started pushing in between us, trying to find her spot.

It was very nice, very homey, and very comfortable. Why can't things stay comfy like that?

15

Me and Brett got to the office about ten. It beat going into the chicken-processing plant at 6:00 a.m. or working in the fields from daylight to dark, but the idea of being an office man hadn't quite taken hold of me. I had also given Cason our advance from Ms. Buckner, and that made me a poor office man and might require a bit of explanation to Brett later.

When Leonard came we went to the house to exercise. Out in the carport we lifted light free weights, then worked on a score of self-defense techniques, sparred lightly with boxing for a while, then switched to kickboxing. There was no way to do ground work comfortably, which is one reason it can be overrated. You fall down on cement or the hard ground, it's different than if you're working a mat or fighting someone whose basic approach you know, someone who doesn't have a knife or pistol in their pocket or a buddy around the corner, or doesn't have ring rules about gouging out your eyes. Going to the ground is not a choice I'd make on purpose. Still, it was a weakness in our game, because you don't always get to choose if you stand or go down.

Leonard and I went at it for a while, making light contact, not anything brutal, just keeping ourselves loose, but it was hot already and nearly lunchtime, and we weren't kids anymore, so we gave it up, went in the house. Leonard took a shower downstairs, and I took one upstairs.

Leonard still had some clothes in a drawer in his room, and he had those on when I came down. I had changed into something loose and comfortable. I decided to make sandwiches for all of us to have at the office. While I was opening a can of tuna and putting it into a bowl to mix, Leonard said, "Seems we're on to something, way Cason talked."

"Yeah," I said, spooning the right amount of mayonnaise into the bowl. "They're careful. Once they get their hooks in someone, they've got them in deep, and the cash cow just keeps supplying the milk until it can't anymore. Or they sense their victim is worn out enough to say, 'Get me some popcorn and I'll show the film myself.' Maybe then they back off. It could become a standoff. You don't care anymore, but now neither do they. So you don't speak up about it, and they don't show it to anyone. Everything stays even. I think it's a careful con. They've done it enough to know when they can't do it anymore, and I figure there's some law involvement."

"Some palms greased?"

"Yep. That way, say it's a guy, he keeps his mouth shut because he can't get any relief from either side, the law or the blackmailers. By just taking it in the ass, he keeps the wife, job, or both, or his civic pride, and they've made a healthy amount of money before whoever being blackmailed gets to the point where he, or she, doesn't give a flying fuck anymore."

"Thing is, our job isn't to worry about the whores or the blackmail, it's to find Sandy."

"But can we actually leave the blackmail part alone?"

"Probably not," Leonard said. "And they are most likely entwined."

We wrapped the sandwiches in plastic, put them in a paper bag, got some cans of diet soda out of the refrigerator, including a Diet Dr Pepper, which Leonard cursed but would still drink in spite of the lack of sugar, and headed out to Leonard's truck.

As he drove us over there, I said, "I'll just mention this once, and then you can do with it what you want. How is it with you and John? Done?"

"I hope so, but then when it gets late, I hope not. I miss him then.

I keep thinking if I had said this or that, or done this or that, it might be different. But I know deep down I wouldn't do those things. I'm not going to ask a god I don't believe in for forgiveness before I suck John's dick or he sucks mine. But sometimes, when it's late, I think I can do it for him. But a minute passes, and I know I can't do it for anyone. I guess I'm selfish."

"Just honest with yourself. After midnight everything is important, until about three or four in the morning, and then it's still important, but less so. And then when you wake up in the morning most of it isn't important at all."

"I appreciate your letting me stay with you and Brett again."

"You're my brother. You're always welcome, even when I don't want you around."

"It makes me feel better to know someone else is in the house, even if it's not my house. That I'm not all alone."

"And if John was at your apartment? How would that feel?"

"That wouldn't feel so good, either. I think I'd try again, long as I didn't have to play the games. I'd try until I pissed him off or threw him out. I'm actually thinking of buying a blow-up fuck doll. They have some very nice male ones."

"Please promise me you will keep it clean," I said.

"You have my word," Leonard said.

"And that you will keep it at your place. For all that is holy, I do not want to wake up in the middle of the night and hear you making plastic squeak in our house."

16

Weasel came by the office the next day with Cason. He was well named. He was small with a large nose and no chin and quick eyes and a wiry muscularity. He looked like he could squeeze through a hole smaller than he was. He was dark-skinned and maybe Hispanic, maybe black, maybe a whole gumbo of all kinds of folks. He wore a black shirt way too big for him. You could have housed two of him in it.

Even coming out of the heat and wearing black, he didn't seem to sweat much. He was as cool a customer as a corpse. He came in ahead of Cason, gave the room a sweep. He moved like a guy who was used to checking his surroundings, watching for predators or prey.

Cason looked his usual dapper self, though he had a sweaty glow about him, and the front of his blue shirt and the underarms of it were wet with sweat. No deodorant in existence could defeat the onslaught of East Texas heat and humidity. Unless you were Weasel.

Cason nodded at Brett. Brett nodded back. Neither seemed comfortable with the other.

Weasel's eyes continued to drift over all of us, then held on Buffy, who was holding down the couch. His eyes moved again, finally settled on Brett, who was sitting on the edge of the desk wearing white shorts and a loose green top.

Weasel said in a kind of Yankee voice with vowels so hard you could have used them to crack ice, "Oh, hell, lady, you are one sleek model."

"Yes, I am," Brett said. "Thanks for noticing."

Introductions were made. Weasel had a last name. Rolf.

Cason said, "Weasel's got some information. It's sweeter than we thought; not as sweet as we'd like. And I'm going to say it right up front. Maybe questionable."

"That hurts," Weasel said. "After all we've meant to each other you got to go on and say something like that."

"I can live with it," Cason said.

Weasel grinned, took a client chair, and crossed his legs carefully, as if he were a girl in a short skirt and had to be careful about giving a free show. "You let people smoke in here?"

"Only if they're on fire," Brett said.

"Fair enough. I got some chew. You got a bottle I can spit in?"

"I can give you a bottle, and you can take it home with you to spit in," Brett said. "There'll be no spitting in anything in here."

"You're a ballbreaker, lady," Weasel said.

"Just sanitary," Brett said.

"Tell them, Weasel," Cason said.

"I know a little about all this, cause there's lots of us off the grid, so to speak, who do know some stuff. Know what I'm saying?"

We didn't respond. He wasn't waiting for us to. It was just his way of talking.

"I ask around, and I say, what's the deal here, you know? Not that blunt, but that's what it finally got to, cause I know some people know Frank, and they think she's hot, but they don't know what I know, that she's an ex-con, a man that got his goober trimmed."

"So far," Leonard said, "you haven't told us anything we don't already know."

"All right, then," he said. "I'm coming to the good part, part worth the money Statler here is paying me. Some of this stuff I asked about, to my contacts, see, some I already knew. Intimately, you might say."

"By the way," Cason said to me. "When he says 'money' he means your money."

Brett looked at me.

"Takes money to make money," I said.

"Or it just takes money to lose money," she said.

"Hey, you going to let me say my say here or what?" Weasel said. "You paid for it, so let me give it to you. Otherwise I got things I can do."

"Go on," I said.

"There's a fellow I know, said he knows a fellow named Ron Bantor, and Bantor bought a car from Frank's place. This was, I guess, five years ago. In fact, this information is five years old, and the fella told me about it, he can't tell me anything now. But I remember the story."

"And how did this fellow know about Bantor?" I asked. "And why can't he tell you anything? Though I have an idea."

"Coming to that. So this Ron Bantor, he finds out with the car comes some A-one hole. Sorry, lady."

"Tell it however you will," she said. "There's nothing you can say that will cause me to like you less than I already do."

"So the snatch comes with the car, and the car costs more than it ought to, even with the snatch that comes with it, cause, hell, ain't none of that snatch made of platinum. And at some point, way I see it, a car is just a car. But more to the point, rumor was the snatch was named Sandy."

"You know that for a fact?" Brett said. "That her name was Sandy?"

"Heard this whole story from a guy what knew, and I've checked with some outside sources, got pretty much the same story."

"Pretty much?" Brett said.

"Not like this stuff gets written down, lady. It's a kind of story might grow some hair as it rolls downhill. I can only tell you what I know, hair and all. So Ron, he's got the car and the girl, this Sandy, but then he finds out it's got a trip goes with it to Italy, and he wants to take it. Nice trip. Nice tail. Figures then he can come home and ride around in a nice car."

"So far, so good," Cason said.

Weasel sucked on his teeth, continued. "He does the trio. Car, girl, and trip to Italy. Hear what I'm saying? Then he finds there's a fourth thing. They set him up in some nice Italian hotel, and they got a hidden camera and they got a movie, minus previews, of him putting the sausage in the grinder, you know. He finds this out when he gets home with the wife and the kids. Gets the bad news there's a film of his shiny, dimpled ass filmed by his automobile-and-poontang dealers. You following me?"

"Quite easily," Brett said.

"This Ron cat, he works for a big law firm here in town. Got a trophy wife and a lot of good connections. Plays golf with the right people. He's pulled the right dicks and pinched the right tits, if you know what I'm saying."

"Yeah," Leonard said. "We're with you."

"They start stretching those car payments, this car company," Weasel said. "He paid in cash, he was that flush, but now it's not enough. There's some side money they want for not showing the nice little film of him to the wife, film of him lowering the helicopter into the canyon with this Sandy bimbo in Italy. He was supposed to be on a business trip, and there he is on film, bare-ass, in living color. They send it to him on an e-mail, take a chance, see. Something to really scare him. He checks that e-mail, opens that video, sees himself swinging his pecker, shits enough bricks to build a cathedral, e-mails back with a what-the-fuck's-up comment. That's when the serious contact starts. Frank—she, he, it, whatever the fuck she is—starts having him come by and drop off little packages with sizable money in it. He don't even go home with coupons. Ron goes to this fellow I know, cause being a lawyer in a big law firm he knows some guys not quite on the straight and narrow."

"Like yourself?" Leonard said.

"Like me, and my guess is like you two," Weasel said, nodding at me and Leonard. "I hear some things here and there. You seem like a couple guys been around the block, and not walking around all of it on a direct path. Taking a few alleys here and there, climbing through a few windows."

"Go on," Leonard said.

"Ron goes to this guy he knows, one he got off a prison sentence for murder. He knows the guy was as guilty as O. J. Simpson, asks if he can help him out cause he don't want to keep paying. He don't want his naked skin on his wife's or boss's e-mail, spread around town, then on the Facebook thing, twittered or twatted or some such shit. I don't know how all that crap works."

I had a feeling he knew exactly how that stuff worked.

"Bring it back on topic," Cason said. "You're starting to break gravitational pull, getting way out there."

"So Ron asks this old client of his who is not a straight citizen, asks does he know a guy can whack someone, and he'll pay some serious jack to get it done so that he won't have to keep paying serious jack for the rest of his life, and, too, he's just mad, you know. This guy I know tells him no, cause he thinks the money, good as it is, is light in the pants for killing folks, but says he might know someone, and he puts me on it, asks me to see if I can find someone, cause I know the kind of crowd he needs. And Ron, because he has a big mouth, lays out to me exactly why he wants Frank dead. Here he is dealing with blackmail, worried about people knowing his business, and him a lying piece-of-shit lawyer, but he don't know enough to keep his trap shut. What he's doing is telling people he shouldn't all his business he's worried about keeping secret. I guess he figures he tells the slum crowd, he's all right, but when you get right down to it, that's not the crowd to tell. But hey, saying something and having a film of it is not the same thing. I mean, he knows that film gets shown, that's more than talk. That's the shine on the baby's ass. You with me still?"

"In the neighborhood," Leonard said.

"Got to be honest. Thought I could whack Frank for the dough Bantor was paying. I don't know why he decided on Frank, cause I figure Frank is just the figurehead, not the top of the heap, but hell, who knows? And money is money, and who is who in all this is not important when that stuff is being waved under your nose. Pussy and money can get a man to do most anything but clean a sink after shaving.

"Sandy was on his list, too, cause she set him up, least that's how he figures it. Don't matter. It was some serious jack he was slinging around. Even thought I might could find this Sandy and do her, too, you know, if all expenses are paid and there's a good fee for the final job. Thought I did good on Frank, I'd be willing to do Sandy, you see. Pop. She's gone. That's how I was thinking when the offer was laid out there. Gave it some serious goddamn consideration. Stayed up a night or two thinking on it, decided maybe it's not my line of work. So I tell this other guy I know might like the job, and finally Ron has his man. Thing is, the man, this hired killer, ends up whacked himself."

"Frank got on to the game?" I asked. "Beat him to the killing?"

Weasel shrugged. "Can't say. Could have been like that. I doubt it, though. Frank's not that tough, with a dick or without. Not a pushover or nothing, but killing like that, I don't think so. Like I said, I don't think Frank is the top of the heap. Bottom line is someone finds the would-be assassin Ron hired, this fellow I know and put him on to, finds him some miles from here in the Sabine River, or maybe it was the Trinity—shit, I don't remember. Finds him with no shoes and an engine block tied around his ankles. He's got a cut throat and no balls, and word around is the cuts on his throat and balls are from a sharp wire, not a knife. Imagine that. Snapping off a man's goodies with a wire. That's the rumor, anyhow."

"Lots of rumors around," Brett said.

"I'm going to believe it, myself," Weasel said. "You should, too. Guy did this knew what he was doing. You might call him a throat-cutting goddamn deballing expert. Cut the balls off cause maybe that was just part of the fun. Maybe he took them back to lay on the doorstep of who-ever wanted it done, like a cat will bring you a mouse. I don't know. But the balls weren't found. I guess they could be in the river, eat up by a catfish someone caught later and deep-fried, but I don't think so. The shoes. I think they just come off in the water, the current, you know?"

"This guy that was murdered," Leonard said. "He got a name?"

"Slide is what I knew him as. Black guy. Tough guy with muscles like you, had a shaved head, had that kind of look you got, except he was missing a light in his eyes. Kind of motherfucker makes a man nervous. Looked like he could spank a cougar and send it to bed without its supper. What he caught was meaner than a cougar. He put up a fight. I got word from a guy I know at the hospital that he had broken fingers, scratches, and one eye near torn out. So he fought back. They scraped under his nails, all that shit, but they didn't find anything but more of him. And he had been in the water and all, maybe a week. Fucks with the DNA, that water does."

"You sure know a lot of guys," Leonard said. "On the street, in the hospital. Lawyers."

"That's what ole slick-ass Cason likes about me. I'm connected with the shit on the shoes. That's why he came to me and how I've ended up here brightening your otherwise dreary day."

"Slide have a last name?" I asked.

"Don't know it," Weasel said. "Me and him knew each other pretty good, but last names didn't come up. We didn't discuss pork-belly futures none, either."

"You know all this and you don't know the guy's last name?" Leonard said.

"You just got to have it, I can find out, but who cares? This guy's deader than dirt. Now what happens is the guy Ron asked first, guy told me about it . . . and you need a name I got it. Thurgood Small. White dude. He'd have made about four of me, some of it fat. Everyone called him Red Mop on account of this toupee he wore and didn't think anyone knew it wasn't real hair. Looked like someone froze a fucking flame on his head is what it looked like. Whatever it was made out of, it wasn't hair. He done a little time, and it was rumored he'd done some murders for hire and got away with it. But Ron, he asks Red Mop again, and this time he puts some blocks under the money, adds in some more stuff with zeros, and Red Mop decides this time he'll do it. He'll go in and kill Frank, and then he'll put the pop on Sandy for another slice of the pie, and anyone else Ron needs killing long as the money keeps climbing. Shit, them two killings was probably more than the first two or three blackmail checks ole Ron paid, but Ron, he's mad now, feels like he got his asshole reamed, and he don't like it. Matter of pride, I figure, not so much the money.

"So Ron's guy, Red Mop, goes after Frank, and then next thing I hear, he's not doing so hot, either. Died same kind of way. Second smile under his chin, propped him up down by a railroad track somewhere in our small world, pants down around his knees, dick hanging out of his shirt pocket, balls whacked off and gone, along with his toupee. Now two of the guys I knew was in on the deal were whacked. That got the hair on my balls to stand up, so me, I went quiet as a mute mouse in house shoes. Looked over my shoulder for a while. Two, three years go by, and no one comes to kill me. So I'm thinking I'm sliding. They, being whoever hired this deballing fellow, don't know it was me that was the middle guy, or so it seems. I fell through the cracks. Two more years or so slip on, and I'm still here because I kept my big mouth shut."

"Until now," I said. "Five hundred dollars and you're singing."

"Cason told me a thousand," Weasel said.

I looked at Cason. He grimaced. "I did."

"All right," I said. "A thousand. But still, why now?"

"Haunts me some, you know. It's on my head. Never even seen the bodies, but I can imagine them cause I know people who know people who know the cops, and they got the news, the specifics from them, the cut throat and balls and all."

"You told us that part," I said.

"Did, didn't I? Man, I just thought I could do something like kill Frank and maybe Sandy. Just thought it. I see this dead dog got hit the other day, you know, on the highway, and I pull over and throw up. I know now I couldn't have done no such thing. Think I'm even more puny now than I was then. I can step on roaches and I can rat out people, but killing for money, I can't go there. That's some kind of house I don't want to live in."

"Aren't you scared to tell us all this after keeping quiet for so long?" Brett asked. "Even for the money?"

"A little," Weasel said. "You got big mouths, I'm scared a lot."

"They don't have," Cason said.

"That's some partial comfort, brother. It's bothering me, this thing I considered doing, and had I done it, I'd have that shit heavy on my head. I didn't, but I led to the hit men getting hit, and they could just have easily have done the job they were hired to do. That would have been on my head, too. That's why I'm laying it all out to you. And there's the money Statler here is offering, too, so I'm not claiming just to be a good fucking Samaritan. But my conscience, and the money . . . well, I think, why not? Next day or two I'll be out of town for good. Going back up north. I've been down here, let me see . . . seven, eight . . . no, nine years, and I don't get it here. I'm going back where plain old bad people are just that. They don't come with a side of 'honey chile' and grits, then a blackjack or a pipe upside the head and a soda bottle jammed up the ass, or throats and balls cut off with sharp wire. Now I get my money?"

Cason looked at me.

"What about Sandy?" I said. "She doesn't show up in this story a lot."

"Not a major player is my guess," Weasel said. "Think she did her part, and it was over. Could be Red Mop got to her before he got his balls lifted, and that's why she isn't around to spend Christmas. I'm going to guess she quit stinking about five years ago. But hell, I don't know. I know he didn't get Frank, so that means he may not have got this Sandy, either.

"Frank's company could have done this Sandy in for some reason or another. I don't really know Sandy, just of her. Couldn't pick her out of a fuck movie if her name was tattooed on her naked ass in neon. Never met her. All I know is the name Sandy, and I got that from the guy Ron talked to, Red Mop, one they found down by the railroad tracks."

"And Ron?" Leonard asked.

"He turned quiet, like me. Decided he wasn't such a manipulator. Quit trying to hire killers. He's still alive. I figure they figure he gives up on trying to be a gangster they'll let him keep living. Guy like that, he goes dead, it might be bad for Frank, or whoever he . . . she . . . is connected with, so they might think it's better to let Ron live. And maybe Ron's still paying the blackmail. I don't know. I know this. Me and him are alive, and my balls are still swinging, and whatever happens to him is on his head, and the same goes for me, and he ain't my goddamn worry. I'm taking the thousand, and couple days from now, I'm gone. I won't even leave any body odor."

"Oh, I don't know," Cason said.

"All right, look down on me you want, but you won't be looking long, cause I'm going to be out of here like a goddamn winter goose. I had to talk to people, ask about this shit Cason wanted, and one of them, well, they might see a dollar in it for them, and there's guys out there that would eat a pile of shit and call it a chocolate soufflé if they were getting paid. I figure they would spring it all loose on me first chance they got. Way I figure, on down the road, this Ron, he might turn up dead after all. You know, enough time goes by. Some kind of accident, you see. I don't want the same for me. Neither me nor Ron are talking, not about that, and not to each other, but could be at some point Frank, his bunch, his boss, they could be thinking they want to make sure that never happens, the us-talking part. So when we think we're safe and they got enough distance between what went on, they hit us. That's my thinking. About that money? Going to need that for traveling."

"You said Frank's bunch," I said. "Who does Frank work for?"

"You see, it's just that kind of thing made Ron quit. He realized he hits Frank, maybe this Sandy, that's just the tip of the spear. Ain't you been listening? I done said that more than once, that I don't think Frank is the brains behind all this. I know her a little, enough to know she's smart, but she ain't that damn smart. Ron figured out he would have had to hire someone to kill every goddamn body, and he wasn't even sure who was holding the cards."

"So who can you name?" I said. "Come on—toss us something for our thousand smackers."

"Well, a guy that's got a finger in the pie is Doug Creese. His father,

James, was just a bare-ass redneck that got lucky because he could make good barbecue. Said James used to find dead animals on the highway, fix them up good with sweet barbecue sauce and a long time in the smoker. Not unusual for old backwoods barbecue stands, using highway meat. People like that could barbecue a turd and make you think it was a sausage link. But his son, Doug, one you got to worry about, took it over, got prime meat and no more roadkill. He opened a string of barbecue houses. Played like they was upscale, charged more for a chopped beef than a filet mignon, and there was folks willing to pay the dough for it cause they thought they was, like, getting more for their money, it being on a fancy bun with seeds in it and shit. It was an all-right sandwich, but price like that, you could raise and kill a cow yourself and butcher it out cheaper. Well, all right, that's an exaggeration."

"Oh, really?" Brett said.

"Oh, hell, lady, you are so hot-looking I can take insults off you all day."

"Why, thank you, Weasel," Brett said.

"Creese's Barbecue," Leonard said. "Shit, I heard of that. Hell, I've eaten it. Good barbecue. But like you say, the prices are stiff. They're damn proud of it."

"Yep," Weasel said. "Creese's Barbecue. Doug wasn't really interested in barbecuing meat, though. He wasn't interested in having pocket money and a car didn't smoke oil. He wanted more. Wanted to fart half-dollars and shit thousands. He's that kind of guy. Hell, I'm that kind of guy, but I'm starting to know that isn't going to be how it is for me. It's always going to be pecking shit with the chickens, as you boys say. I come to that conclusion one long night after I looked in the refrigerator and realized I had a head of black lettuce and a bottle of water about half drank up."

"Actually," Cason said, "it's not your good or ill fortune we're interested in."

"Not that I was thinking it was," Weasel said. "Doug uses the barbecue success to finance some other businesses, ones not so on the up-and-up. Finally, the barbecue gets famous, and he sells the joints, and for big money. That sets him up high and tight, but it's still not enough. He was already running some low-level hookers in New Orleans. Had some meth labs cooking and all manner of shit going on. But now he has big money, and though he sold the barbecue places, he still gets a cut, so he's got that dough pouring in, so he starts running higher-class whores, ones who can walk on stiletto heels without wobbling and can cross their legs with a happy promise. He starts setting up more businesses for fronts, finds ways to make big money in a lot of ways, some of them legal, some of them not so legal."

"Like car lots and blackmail," I said.

"That would be it," Weasel said. "People don't really know the businesses he owns because of the way he hides them. Some he's up front with, but others he dresses down so it isn't so out front. He's the tail that wags the fucking dog."

"So it's really the former barbecue guy owns the car lot?" I said.

"That's how I hear it, and all that comes the fuck with it, but I tell you, that's just what I heard. All I got is what I heard. I heard most of it lately, when I was asking around, stuff I hadn't heard before, or stuff that didn't quite have a shape to it. Barbecue Doug may just be another cog in the wheel, which could be a really, really big wheel. One thing for sure, he lays low. Don't see him around much. He's tight to the house. Goddamn, I need a smoke or a chew. You know, I didn't chew until I got around all these goddamn cracker motherfuckers here in East Texas."

"Casting your nicotine habits aside," I said, "anything else?"

"Rest of what I got is old news. But the new news, it could get me whacked, so like I said, I'm traveling. When I get the money."

"You really just told us a lot of what we already knew," I said.

"Don't play me. There was some you didn't know, right?"

Leonard reached out and thumped a finger on Weasel's chest, causing him to wince.

"Better be telling the truth, Mr. Weasel, or you may never get to go up north, won't have to worry about Frank or Barbecue Doug catching up with you. Being lied to makes me itchy, and I don't like to itch, cause that makes me mad."

"Cason, he's used me before," Weasel said. "My information is good. I mean, I'm not saying some of it might not be rumor, but rumor is what I got. There's some stuff in there I think is real. Tell them I'm reliable, Cason."

"So far you have been," Cason said. "But there's been a time or two where your information has lived on the border."

"This is smack-dab in the middle of the territories with rumor on the edges," Weasel said. "I keep bringing up the money, but nobody moves."

Cason took out his wallet and pulled out the money for Weasel. Our money.

"Nice doing business with you, kind of," Weasel said. "And keep me out of it. I don't want to end up with that wire-cut smile and my balls buried in some nut's backyard."

"You're out of it," I said.

"Good," Weasel said. "I was you people, I'd be out of it, too. Messing with Doug or Frank could be bad for you. One of them, someone connected to them, knows the guy with the wire, and money gets waved at him, the right money, he'll pick up that wire again."

"We'll keep that in mind," I said.

"So you're not hanging it up?" Weasel said. "Even after what I've told you?"

"Nope," Brett said.

"Have it your way, honey," Weasel said. "Remember I warned you people."

"We got that sweet thought right up against our hearts," Leonard said.

Weasel shrugged. "Listen here. I got one more thing for you. I wasn't going to expand on this, go the whole hog, but I got to get right with myself—know I told you not only what I know is fact, but I got to tell you what might be rumor. Wasn't going to say, cause it sounds maybe too odd, but that don't mean it's not coming from a solid place. Word is this deballer guy, he's a company man carries their freight. Let me say it different. They got a man sometimes works for the company, whoever it is that owns the company, and he's a free agent kind of guy."

"The car company?" Brett said.

"The company. Doug's businesses. It's like a fucking octopus. There's more than cars and women and blackmail in all this. Shit, I done told you that."

"It's nice to know your story doesn't change up," Cason said. "So we can stand some repetition."

"Only a little," Leonard said.

"Keeping in mind I'm still saying it's rumor, and yeah, I know, I say it a lot, but it's said by some that this wire-using motherfucker has connections with all the Dixie-flag-waving jackasses and southern assholes you can imagine."

"Dixie Mafia?" I asked.

"Call it what you like," Weasel said. "Doug and his bunch may be the saltiest crackers you can imagine, a bunch of good old boys. They're shit-cracker tough guys with sweaty pits and bent noses and swastikas on their necks. They got women in that group, too, just as bad and mean as the men. Some got three teeth and two are in their pocket, but they also got sweet women with butter skin and a smile that looks like something you'd see under a magnolia tree with a picnic basket, but when you get close, those are shark teeth, and the basket is a fucking coffin."

"How poetic," Brett said.

"Make fun if you want," Weasel said. "But they got those folks all over, some in businesses that you wouldn't suspect. Some in back alleys, and some in stylish apartments in downtown Houston. They got gangs to do their work, and more than that, they got them a hitter more dangerous than all of them. Some think he's just a story. The Canceler, they call him, on account of he cancels your fucking ticket, erases your plans. He's the guy with the wire is what I hear. He's got other methods, but when they hire him it's because they want it done fast and smooth, otherwise they let the tattoo-necks do it. Those guys, offer them some cocaine, a twelve-pack, and a rubber pocket pussy, they're ready to rock.

But this guy, he's not someone I want looking for me, and neither do you. He gets the big bucks, and he don't get them by fucking up. What he gets paid is serious finance. The redneck Dixie-flag-waving cretins come and go, but this guy, he stays around. He hasn't got any agenda about the South, about family, or any such shit. He's got the ability if you got the money, and that's the name of that game."

"Have you seen him?" Leonard asked.

"I told you I don't even know if he's real. But someone is sure killing folks with a wire."

"Description?" Cason asked.

"If I had a description of him, way I hear it, I'd be dead before I could describe him. Ain't no one describing him, cause the ones might know him know better than to give that description. Just me giving out what I know, even if it turns out to be rumor, not fact, could be bad for me. Thus my exit plans, and I advise you folks to do the same."

"Thanks for the tip," I said.

"You think you're tough," Weasel said. "Word about you guys is you are. That you've seen some shit and thrown some shit around yourself. That you're like the brothers Death and Doom. Maybe you can handle the rednecks. You might do that all right. But this guy, let me tell you, whoever he is, he whacked two badasses I knew, maybe bad as you two, so whoever this guy is, this Canceler, he's a special-ass hired killer. Hell. He's the very devil."

"If he exists?" Leonard said.

"Somebody killed them bad boys I know. That's no rumor. The question is, how bad is the bad guy who done it? Rumors about him are true, then he's the baddest of the bad, and you don't want that hellhound set on your trail."

"We might have another couple of questions before you leave town," I said.

"I might can find out the name of the guy whose last name I can't remember, you just got to have it, but let me tell you, I'm not going out of my way to do it. I told you my plans, and right before I make with the runaway, I'm going to score me some cheap trim and some expensive whiskey, then I am gone. You might not think so, but you got your thousand worth and some change."

"Have a nice trip," I said.

"You know that's right," Weasel said.

"I'll run him home," Cason said.

"Drive fast," I said.

17

After Cason and Weasel left, Brett said, "This has gone from a missing-person case to blackmail and murder. Now we're talking an invisible hit man who cuts off balls. Anyone believe any of what Weasel said?"

"Some of it," Leonard said. "He kind of gets wrapped up in his own story, and it grows. He mentions the hit man and what he did, then at the end he tells us stuff about him he didn't seem to know at first, that he's part of a syndicate or some such, and he's just waiting for a phone call, carrier pigeon, whatever, to get his orders for another hit. I don't know what to think."

"A while back I didn't believe there was a guy and a woman who took in orphans and turned them into killers, but I was wrong," I said. "I should have believed it. Vanilla Ride is pretty badass, and this could be someone just as badass."

"Or it could be Vanilla herself," Brett said. "She might fit the time line, and she'd be a pro they might hire."

Brett did not have a soft spot for Vanilla, because Vanilla had one for me.

I said, "I don't think this is her style—the wire and the balls cut off—though a woman might think that way, cutting off the balls. It could be a comment on how she was treated when younger, and Vanilla wasn't treated too well. Still, I don't think it's her. She goes for efficiency, not statement."

"You have a blind spot for her," Brett said.

"He has a blind spot for just about everyone, you give him time to consider," Leonard said. "But I'm with him. I don't think it's her. Can't say why, but I don't. If this killer always does it this way, using the wire, maybe that's an MO he can't change, least not comfortably. It could be like a serial killer thing, a signature, except he gets hired to do it. He gets the pleasure and the money both."

"Other side is," I said, "maybe he does change up. Could be the employer is the one collecting nut sacks, way Weasel suggested. Hell, I don't know. Maybe he makes change purses out of them. But if he does a lot of hits, he may not do them all the same way, only does them that way because that goes with the payment."

"Good point," Brett said. "So see? It could have been Vanilla who did it, just fulfilling her boss's request."

"If it was, it wouldn't matter now," I said. "That's in the past. She's in Italy somewhere. Not here as a threat."

"So she told you," Brett said.

"I believe her," I said.

"Because she's beautiful?" Brett said. "That's why you believe her?"

"Her looks have nothing to do with me believing her."

"But she is beautiful, right?" Brett said.

"Some say so."

"Oh, Hap. Really."

"All right," I said. "There's nothing about her that makes you want to look away. Well, on second thought, she does carry a gun and will point it at you. She will shoot to kill, and we know she's blown a man up."

"Okay," Brett said. "That might make you look away. But you'd look as long as you could."

"You are putting words in my mouth. She's not my type."

"Damn, Hap," Leonard said. "That's one of them little white lies we were talking about."

"Whose side are you on, anyway?"

"Brett's."

"Thanks," I said. "Brett. She is not my type, because you are my type."

"And if I wasn't around?" Brett asked. "Honest answer."

"She might be my type. Except for that murderous assassin part. That would put me off."

Brett said, "Maybe it would be best if it was Vanilla did it—killed those two men, I mean. I don't think she'd bother you, and by extension, us. But if it wasn't her, and there is a Canceler, isn't that a bit scary?"

"I admit, it's a bit scary," I said.

She looked at Leonard.

"If he's out there I'd like a run at him," he said. "I think I can fuck him up."

Brett thought for a while. "Do we continue?"

"You're the boss," Leonard said. "I wouldn't trust Weasel to give me a cold. Hell, Cason brought him here, and he doesn't trust him. Not completely. Guy like that, he works like psychics. They listen around, figure out what it is we're interested in, then feed it back to us. He may have picked up clues from Cason when they first talked. I mean, Cason, he can be clever, but a guy like Weasel, fucking people around is what he does for a living. He takes a cold reading, swirls it around in his head a little, and by the time he comes to us he may have gotten enough from Cason to weave a story that fits the way we wanted it to fit. It's like making someone believe in flying saucers. You do the whole thing on a person's head, about how conceited it is to think we are the only thinking creatures in the universe, as if we think all that much. The flying saucers are a jump in logic. We are conceited, therefore extraterrestrial life is likely, therefore aliens have arrived on earth in flying saucers. But if that's logical, why do they always land somewhere weird with some two-toothed ignoramus standing on a stump with his dick up a cow's ass? The aliens cut the cow's udder out, haul Two Tooth off to some place high in space, spread his ass with salad spoons, play with his pecker, and send him home. Why is that? That makes no sense. They're so damn space handy why the fuck don't they just let everyone know they're here, hold a conference at the White House? Might be some folks out there that'll come in for a landing some day, but so far, not so much, and I'm not holding my breath. But you talk shit right, and people believe it."

Brett and I stared at him for a moment.

"What the fuck are you talking about?" I said.

"I'm using a comparison, you two. Surely you get it. Bullshit can be given a solid platform so anyone that's willing to believe it can. It makes sense if you think about it," Leonard said.

"You think?" I said.

"It doesn't matter," Brett said.

"Don't wave me off. The flying saucer story really has to do with what we're talking about."

"No, it doesn't," I said.

"Does too."

"You had that hobbyhorse in your mental garage and pulled it out. You been looking for some spot to put that in a conversation."

"Have not."

"Have too."

"Boys," Brett said. "That will be quite enough."

We gave each other a wicked look, and then we looked at the floor.

"Thing is, unless she was abducted by aliens, as far as Sandy goes, we still don't know dick," I said.

"He hasn't quit," Leonard said. "He's picking at me."

"Boys. I mean it. That's enough. Look, we got a missing girl. We got dead folks connected to the missing girl. There are no cow udders and no aliens."

"What I'm saying," Leonard said. "I'm not saying there are. I'm saying it's easy to believe in incredible assassins and all manner of bullshit if it's presented to you right. That's all I'm saying."

"And now you're done," Brett said. "Right?"

"Right," Leonard said.

"Here's some hard, cold truths," Brett said. "There's no more money coming to us on this, and I don't like the old bitch that hired us. Stay on this we go in the hole as far as money is concerned. It's all gratis. And by the way, it's a deep hole. Everyone got that?"

"Got you," I said.

"Just so you know," she said.

"We know," I said.

"Story of our life," Leonard said.

Brett was quiet for some time, but I could sense she was arranging thoughts in her head like a bricklayer laying bricks. She said, "I say we stick. See how this comes out. It's about a missing woman, and I have a daughter, such as she is, and I know how I'd feel, cause I been there."

I nodded. Leonard and I knew, of course. We had sort of rescued her daughter, Tillie, twice.

"Seeing it through, that's all right by me, but sometimes it's not a pretty picture," Leonard said.

"I been around you two long enough to know that," Brett said. "It's not like I haven't had my tit in the wringer a few times."

"You've shown you've got what it takes more than once," Leonard said.

"I think so," Brett said.

"No doubt about it," I said. "You got tough tits."

"You can say that again," Brett said.

"All right, then," I said. "We're in to the end. As for the Canceler, finding out about him, there's another person I can think of has an ear to the ground. Better than Cason, I think. Maybe better than Weasel. We need someone wades through shit on a regular basis and can turn it into tapioca."

"Ain't that us?" Leonard said.

"I think this is deeper than our usual crap."

"Oh, hell," Leonard said. "You don't mean that cornpone mother-fucker—"

"Jim Bob Luke," I said.

18

Of course I can figure it out," Jim Bob Luke said. He smiled like an alligator and moved a well-chewed toothpick from one corner of his mouth to the other with his tongue. "You do know who you're talking to, don't you?"

"We know, all right," Leonard said. "But ego alone won't solve what we're up against."

"Oh, I don't know," Jim Bob Luke said. "That's only true if I'm a blowhard. And I'm not. I can do what I say. It has never occurred to me but once—and I was feeling kind of sick that day—that there might be something I couldn't figure, couldn't solve. And by the way, that day I had my doubts, I solved it anyway. That cured me from doubting me. I always say: I want someone smart to talk to, I go out back of the house and talk to myself. I am fucking sterling company."

We were at our office, and Jim Bob, who lived in Pasadena, just on the other side of Houston, had driven down that morning after a phone call the night before, and he'd even brought doughnuts. They weren't on my diet, but damn it, I had two of the chocolate-coated kind. Brett had three, and Leonard asked for his cookies and we gave them to him. I have no idea how many he ate. Now, if I could only remember how many doughnuts Jim Bob ate, I'd be one happy man. I think he also brought apple fritters.

Jim Bob wasn't a young man, but he wasn't exactly old, either. He looked younger than he was. He was long and lean with a quick smile and eyes that sometimes looked green and sometimes blue and I suppose were actually a shape-shifting gray; they changed with the light or the clothes he was wearing. Today they looked blue in his tanned face. He wore a black shirt with snap pockets, what we used to call a cowboy shirt. He had on crisp blue jeans and black boots with red explosions on the toes, like he had kicked something dead and bloody. He had a white straw cowboy hat with a wide paisley band and a big green feather in it. He had taken it off and had rested it on his knee. He always looked wrong without the hat on. Looked like the kind of guy that had been born with it on his head. His hair was a little sweaty and hat-shaped.

As always, Jim Bob appeared happy and in a good mood, though I knew behind that friendliness was a granite-hard reserve and a dark streak. He seemed like the biggest redneck that ever walked the earth until you spent time with him. Then you realized that behind that rawness, that laid-back coolness, was a sharp mind and quick reflexes and street-fighting skills. I had seen them in action. Woe to the man that thought Jim Bob was a simple Texas goober. He could not only fight, he could also think, and he was as brave as they come without being foolish. He had depth that he kept hidden, but you could sense it was there, the way the smell of ozone alerts you to the approach of lightning.

Brett told him everything we knew, even her thoughts about Vanilla Ride, whom he knew. He knew damn near everyone who had ever done an illicit deed, and he had done a few himself here and there, but in his mind, and my own, it was for the greater good. Still, knowing that, and sometimes being a part of such myself, didn't help me sleep all that well at night. I think Jim Bob, like Leonard and Brett, snoozed just fine.

Jim Bob listened quietly, looking like he always does, like he's already got the answers before you get through explaining.

"Weasel tells a good story," Jim Bob said. "Some of it might have the whiff of bullshit about it, but I'm thinking it isn't all fairy tale. I've heard word of this Canceler. He supposedly wiped out an entire Mexican drug gang that was bringing dope into Houston, not because he was trying to do a humanitarian thing but because he got hired to whack them. And he kept on whacking them until what was left of them decided to stay down below the Rio Grande and sell tacos. They were bumping into the drug business in Houston, hurting some of the local boys' revenue. This Mexican gang, the Canceler took them out one by one, and though he didn't use a wire on all of them, it was mostly that. He isolated the ones he could, wired them, cut off their balls, and in the end I think there were four left, and like I said, they ran back to Mexico. Canceler followed them somehow, broke into their stronghold in Mexico, and killed all four. Took their nut sacks and left."

"That part sounds like some of Weasel's rumors," Leonard said.

"Wouldn't sound like that if you knew better," Jim Bob said. "Some of that gang was seriously bad and mean as a snake in a latrine. I knew folks dealt with them. Bought drugs. Not saying they're friends of mine, saying through my underworld contacts I came up against them, and one of them was an American beaner who did enough business with them he thought he might be next on the list."

"Beaner," I said. "Nice."

"Oh, hell, Hap. I got friends that are beaners, real friends."

This was the kind of stuff that made Jim Bob confusing, but I didn't say anything else. I had long ago given up on trying to sort out who was who by what they said. It was as Leonard said, "It's not what you say, it's what you do."

Jim Bob continued.

"So, as I was saying, this beaner named Miguel, who is not a friend but comes to me for protection, wants to hire me for it. Tells me this Canceler is real, and Miguel knows he's on the list, cause he's been doing drug business in a heavy way with the boys from Mexico, and now those boys are missing their balls, not to mention their lives, and he wants to hire me. I don't have nothing for that shithead, so I tell him no, and a week later they find him in a storage container out by the docks with his pants off and his balls gone, his throat cut. Maybe with a wire. No one knows what's true and what's myth about the guy, but this Canceler fella is real. My bet is he doesn't take the balls to prove he's done his job but takes them as a souvenir."

"I guess they don't give out awards for best serial killer," I said. "So he has to provide his own trophies."

"Unless you count the prize the press gives him. And this guy, he doesn't get treated like a serial killer. He's a hit man. He gets paid. For him, those men's nuts, it's like a little boy stealing girls' panties. He likes to take them out, look at them from time to time, maybe sniff them and bat them around with a tennis racket or some such, no telling what all, but he gets more respect than the dime-store serial killer, least among those who pay for his services."

"Does the Canceler kill women?" Brett asked. "I'm thinking I might get a pass if he comes after us."

"I think he'd kill anyone," Jim Bob said. "Maybe he's got some vaginas in his collection, too. I don't know. Stretches them over his head like a horse collar. How this all fits in with the car business and the blackmail I don't know. That's a lot of working parts, and some of those parts grind together a little. Think what we ought to do, since you two took a run at this Frank, and then your friend Cason did the same, is I take a run at her. I am one charming motherfucker when I want to be."

"Really?" Brett said.

"Really," he said. "Girl with a dick or no dick, I can make them smile."

"Or feel ill," Brett said.

"You good-looking little darling, you are so right. I can do that, too. But sometimes you got to play a different card in a different situation. I can smooth out when I want to."

"Cason is as charming as they come," Leonard said. "He kind of charms me. But you, charming? I don't know, man."

"All right, let's talk straight," Jim Bob said. "Am I good-looking?"

"Oh, hell, man," I said.

"Really," Jim Bob said. "Brett? What do you think?"

"You are a handsome man," she said. "And to tell you true, if I didn't

already have my man, you'd butter my biscuit, no doubt. I mean I'd probably kill you in a week, but as much as you're arrogant, you are somehow
appealing, like whipped cream, which also makes me sick. I think calling
people beaners and such would wear on me, and that toothpick annoys
me, and I don't like the hat, unless it's to shit in, but as long as we didn't
talk all that much, I can see you being appealing enough. I'd think of you
as someone who could hit the high spots."

"I think I'm wounded to the bone," I said. And I was a little.

"All is well," Brett said. "I'm just giving my honest opinion as a beautiful and highly appealing woman."

"There you have it," Jim Bob said and winked at Brett. "Thank you,
you fine-looking honeypot, cause your opinion really matters to me.
Hell, Leonard there, even he's thinking—and tell me if I'm wrong,
Lenny—you're thinking: that is one fine-looking man, and I'd like to do
him. Aren't you, Leonard?"

"Hardly," Leonard said, but I thought there was a bit of a catch in his
voice.

"Well, we need not worry about that. I don't throw the saddle on ho-
mos, just women."

"You are going to get hurt," Leonard said.

Jim Bob laughed. Unlike most people, Leonard didn't faze Jim Bob
in the least. He liked messing with people, pulling their strings. Life
was his oyster, and you were living outside the shell as far as he was
concerned.

"Here's the thing," Jim Bob said. "I got me a date with a barrel racer
tonight, a twenty-nine-year-old big-tittied blond home wrecker if you
ever saw one. Fortunately for me I don't have a wife, so there's nothing
to wreck. I don't even have a hog farm anymore. Sold it. But I do have
that date."

"This might be a little more important than dating a barrel racer," I
said.

"You haven't seen the barrel racer, Hap. She's got legs so long you
want to climb her like a tree. Least up to where it forks. I mean, yeah,

she's younger than me by some years, but shit, way I see it, if she dies she dies. But here's the other thing. I don't want to go into this car place looking to buy a car close to when all you numb nuts went in. I say we give it a week or so, let this Frank get your visit off her mind. She's bound to have her flag up and ready to tussle. So I don't want to make her think I'm part of the problem. I want her to see me as a mark."

"Makes sense," Leonard said.

"Also, I got to tell you, since you went in there and pulled on Frank's string pretty hard, I figure she went to her boss and pulled on his string. People like that, they don't like their strings pulled. If they're connected like this Weasel says, they may not like it so much you might even get a visit from them, and they won't be bringing flowers and a bottle of wine. On the other hand, they may just figure you guys aren't really on to shit and are no threat."

"Good," Leonard said. "Then we get to meet the Canceler sooner than later."

"I don't think so. Guy like the Canceler, they don't pull him out for just any old hit on a peckerwood and bop-a-nigger job."

"Hey," Leonard said.

"I'm telling you how they think, Leonard. First rule of becoming a good detective—not something I think is in your immediate future—is you got to think like they do, and sometimes you got to be them, at least in spirit."

"Call me a nigger again and you'll have my spirit up your ass."

"Trying to say watch your backs, cause they might send problem solvers, one of those that's on the low end of the totem pole. Not some hot-dog professional but a crowd of dick draggers that come cheap. Eyes and ears open, and keep your left up. And by the way, since you didn't mention pay, I suppose this is one of them jobs where I'm doing this for you to have the pleasure of my company."

"Looks that way," I said. "Maybe something comes along later that we can't do, don't want to do, we can throw it your way, something has money in it, I mean."

"Thoughtful. I figure it's most things you three can't do when it comes to real detective work, so I might have a long line of referrals coming my way. No offense, Brett, you can learn, these two, I'm not so sure. They are blunderers. How they have lived as long as they have and managed to have all their legs and arms is beyond me. Deal is, I'm going back to Houston."

Jim Bob looked at his watch.

"I got time to get there and shower up, put on some smell-good, buy a couple packs of rubbers, and meet my barrel racer."

"Couple packs of rubbers," Brett said. "Very romantic."

"Ah, honey, I'm taking her to dinner first, and I always let the woman put the rubber on, and I think two packs is enough. And don't worry. I need an extra pack, I can send her to the drugstore. I got a bicycle in the garage."

"You can leave now," Brett said. "Wouldn't want you to miss your barrel racer."

"And she wouldn't want me to miss, either, in more ways than one. But as you know, I'm a straight shooter."

He stood up, put on his hat, and went out.

As we listened to him going down the stairs, I said, "He can rub a dildo wrong when he wants to."

19

I won't lie to you, next few days I was jumpy. I had a snub-nosed .38 revolver that I gave to Brett to keep in her purse, and I kept the same kind of gun in my glove box, and in the house I had a twelve-gauge Remington handy. I had another stashed in the attic. There were shotguns tucked into the closet at the office. Leonard was armed as well. I always felt like a hypocrite with all those guns, and I was. I hated them, but once you felt their power, they owned you to some extent. I disliked being owned by machinery.

Frank, if she had checked the car I rented as a decoy, and had a few contacts, it wouldn't have taken her long to figure out who rented it and connect me to it, which connected Brett to it, if just peripherally. And Frank probably figured out who Leonard was, too, being as how there was no winter petunia tour, and the Internet probably revealed everything but our shoe sizes. If the car lot people were as sneaky at business as they seemed to be, as wealthy as they appeared, they could get things done, not only in finding us, but hurting us, if they were willing to go that far. When it came to bad criminal business, a few dollars and a hard piece of wood upside the head or a loaded gun works a lot better than a smile and a kind word most any day.

Few early mornings later, a weekend, I was in the kitchen reading the newspaper and drinking a cup of coffee. Our local paper was now about the size of a grocery pamphlet. It had an online presence as well, but I missed holding a heft of news sheets in my hand. I loved newspapers, and they seemed to be a near-lost business. News had become primarily a bunch of folks quarreling on TV and giving opinions about the news even before it happened. The actual news itself was hard to seek out.

I was thinking on all this because I was reading the newspaper for my entertainment, but the last few mornings Cason let me come over to his newspaper office and see the papers in the morgue—those that had been copied to their computer. Camp Rapture, where he worked, had as much news about LaBorde as LaBorde did, and I thought it might be wise to get their take on our news.

Leonard had taken the mission to look through the records at our local newspaper, telling them he was doing some research for something or other, which in a way he was. But we thought saying we were looking for clues of a prostitution-and-blackmail ring and a serial killer who cuts off balls might not be something to spread around. He did this while I was at Camp Rapture. What we were specifically looking for were articles, bits and pieces here and there about certain murders, that would substantiate what Weasel told us. Other murders of a similar nature, that sort of thing.

So far Leonard hadn't found anything in our local papers that I hadn't seen, and none of what I had seen seemed to matter. I had burned out looking through the Camp Rapture records and was, as I said, home that day, having my coffee and contemplating if driving over to Camp Rapture again was even worth it. Seemed to me I would have heard of those murders Weasel told us about, and if I hadn't, there would at least be some reference to them in the newspapers five years back.

Nada.

Could something like that be kept secret?

I called Marvin and left him a message, was waiting for him to call back. I was trying to keep him and the police out of it as much as possible, at least at this point, but I figured desperate as we were, it might be time to drag him in, if only for information he might have available to him that we didn't.

I called Cason next. He told me where Weasel lived, and after I had finished the paper and was sipping another cup of coffee, I decided not to go to Camp Rapture. I called Leonard, and he came over.

Me and him drove over to Weasel's joint for a closer talk. He was most likely long gone, but if he wasn't, Leonard suggested we start breaking his fingers off in his ass until we got some real answers. Leonard had the frame of mind now that Weasel wasn't giving us rumors but was in fact shining our ass a little. Giving us some real information but holding back things we needed, things he knew but wasn't saying. I didn't have an opinion on the matter. Truth was, going to see where Weasel lived, hoping he might not have gone north yet, was something to do other than look futilely through old newspapers. I liked my fresh morning paper, but those made my nose itch.

Weasel's place was a duplex. There were some standard box houses on both sides of the street. His apartment was upstairs. The bottom apartment seemed uninhabited. Windows were knocked out of that one, and there were no curtains and no sign of occupation. The duplex was the only one on the short block divided from the box houses by tall untrimmed hedges on either side, and there was a car parked out front. It was an old Ford that looked to have been bullied by other cars on the highway. There were dents, and the windshield was cracked in a spider-web pattern, and it was plastered green and yellow with bugs that had chosen the wrong flight pattern. The tires were a little low. The trunk had been closed poorly, and a black rag dangled out of it.

We climbed to the top floor of the duplex and knocked on the door. No one answered. We gave it a good banging with our fists and worked the doorbell, which didn't work at all. That brought us back to more door banging with the same lack of results.

As we came down the stairs a black cat came out of one of the lower duplex's missing windows, jumped to the ground, then eyed us like we might be trespassing on his property.

Leonard said to the cat, "Get your goddamn windows fixed."

It was late morning by then, but no one seemed around in the yards or looking out windows. The area struck me as the sort where people minded their own business in case your business might be bad business they didn't want to know about.

Driving away, I called Cason and described the car we saw. He was the one who introduced us to Weasel, so I hoped he knew a little about him and the wreck he drove. When I described the car, he said it indeed was Weasel's wreck, but he thought it might have been something he'd leave behind. It was about twenty years old, and besides needing an oil change, probably had a lot of miles on it.

We went back to my place. Leonard dropped me off and headed for the LaBorde newspaper. He figured he had to take advantage while they were still friendly enough to let him sit in a chair in their morgue room and read the papers on computer and microfiche.

I went straight back to the kitchen table and resumed drinking coffee, decaf now, because I had swigged so much pure black coffee over the last few days I was almost dancing everywhere I went.

Sitting there at the table, thinking on these matters again, I came up with nothing. Brett, who had been sleeping in while Leonard and I had been out, came into the kitchen. She was wearing one of my long shirts, an old paint-stained one that she sometimes slept in. It wasn't pretty, but she made it look good, way her legs showed.

Pouring herself a cup of coffee, she said, "What you thinking?"

"Weasel's full of shit."

"Jim Bob verified some of what Weasel said."

"I know. But still, though there may have been some truth in there, nothing he told us shakes out. Not in the papers; no word of it anywhere."

"You may not be thinking this through," Brett said.

"How's that?"

"He said one body was down at the Sabine, or the Trinity, and one near a railroad track. He wasn't specific, didn't seem sure about any of it, not even sure which river was involved. I got the idea he knew the stories, but none of it first-or even secondhand. That could be the rumor part he was referring to."

I let that sink in.

"Could be," I said. "But I'd have thought something as bold as a killer taking someone's balls and cutting their throat and leaving them out to be found would have shown up in the papers, even if it didn't happen right around here."

"Maybe, and maybe not," she said. "Still, doesn't mean it didn't happen. Weasel is oily, but I don't think even he is that good a bullshitter. He seemed legitimately scared of this guy."

"Lying is his stock-in-trade, dear," I said.

Brett nodded. "Yeah. I guess at this point we're just circling the airport. So maybe we ought to get on with it, see if we can land this baby."

Someone knocked on the door. Since what Jim Bob had told us was more than a little fresh on our minds, I was cautious about answering it. I went to the kitchen cabinet and opened the drawer and took out a little flat automatic I had put there since Jim Bob and Weasel had warned us. It was small-caliber and didn't have that much stopping power, but it was something. I still had the revolver, but I liked to keep it in my glove box.

I eased to the window by the side of the door, edged back the curtain, and looked out. A young woman I judged to be in her twenties was standing there. She was very pretty, with black hair and dark skin, long-legged in blue-jean shorts, wearing red tennis shoes. She had on a loose shirt, black with red and blue parrots on it. She didn't look like a Jehovah's Witness.

I put the automatic at the base of my spine and pulled my shirt over it and walked over to the door. Buffy, who had been on the couch, got off of it and strolled over. Even she was curious.

I opened the door.

The girl stared at me. She reminded me of someone. A battered old brown Cadillac was parked at the curb.

She said, "Are you Hap Collins?"

"Yes."

"Funny. I thought you'd be taller."

"Okay. Do I know you?"

"Not exactly. What a pretty dog."

"She is, yes."

Buffy had eased out the door and was sitting now, looking up at her. The girl patted the dog, and Buffy liked it.

She looked up and studied my face. The way she looked at me, I don't know if I can describe it. Wistful. Hopeful. Scared. Nervous. All of the above.

"Do you remember May Lynn Gomez?"

I did. We had dated awhile after the divorce from my first wife. She had been divorced, too. We pleasured each other, mostly, and it wasn't exactly much of a relationship. She had been a fine-looking woman with a lot of problems. Other than her beauty and those problems, I didn't really remember all that much about her.

"Yes," I said.

"She has died," the girl said.

"I'm sorry to hear it. Are you Chance?"

Brett came to the door, said, "Hello, dear."

"Miss Sawyer."

"Call me Brett. Dealing with getting older is not working out as well as I thought it would."

We stood there in the doorway looking at Chance. Nobody spoke. Nobody barked. Buffy slowly wagged her tail.

"Mom thought I should look you up."

"And why is that?" I asked.

"Mr. Collins . . . Hap. You're my dad."

20

You could have pushed me down with a hummingbird fart.

Almost. I actually remained on my feet, though a bit stunned and confused.

Brett said, "Come in, Chance."

Chance came in. She looked so much like her mother, though taller, and with a different sort of movement.

When Chance was inside and Buffy had followed, I found enough of my brain to remember the door needed closing. I did that, then wandered along with her and Brett into the kitchen, where Brett asked her to sit down at the table. Buffy trotted into the kitchen with them, lay down near her food bowl by the stove.

Chance sat and folded her hands together on top of the table.

I sat down across from her.

Brett said, "Have you had breakfast, hon?"

"No, ma'am. But I'm okay."

"No problem to fix you something," Brett said.

"It's all right," Chance said.

"No, really. No problem. Right, Hap?"

"No problem."

"Okay, then. I guess I am a little hungry."

"Hap, fix her something," Brett said.

I looked up at Brett and smiled at her. Then I looked at Chance.

"What would you like?" I said and gave her some offerings.

She decided on toast and coffee and scrambled eggs. While I fixed those, Brett talked to her in a general way, things like where are you staying, simple stuff. I listened as I cooked. Chance said she had been living out of her car. I liked the way she talked. She sounded East Texas, but there was a kind of smoothness to her manner and movements, and I could sense a wounded confidence, like a tiger that had survived a gunshot wound.

I put breakfast in front of her, said, "Eat first, then we'll talk some more."

I poured Brett and myself coffee, then sat down at the table. I glanced at Brett. She glanced at me. I felt shell-shocked. Could it be true?

I studied Chance. She was about the right age, midtwenties. And she sure looked like May Lynn. Had beautiful coffee-colored skin. I remembered May Lynn saying something about being Hispanic, and what was it? Choctaw? I didn't remember exactly. Frankly, we hadn't been that close, except in bed. But the question wasn't if May Lynn was her mother. The question was, was I her dad?

Chance finished eating and sipped at her coffee. She had been polite and careful as she ate, but it was clear she was hungry.

"Me and your mom, we only dated a little while."

"I understand when it comes to sex," Chance said. "It only takes the one time."

"True enough," I said. "But it's been years. Why now? Why didn't she come to me earlier? What did she die of?"

"Lot of questions pretty fast," Brett said.

"Sorry," I said.

"She didn't blame you for anything," Chance said. "She had sex, she got pregnant, the two of you moved on, and she never told you. She said the two of you hadn't been that close."

"Except for at least one time," Brett said.

"Yes, ma'am," Chance said. "There was that one time."

"It wasn't quite that simple," I said.

"The drinking. She said that's what did it. You liked her, but she drank, bad."

"She had problems with the liquor," I said. "Nice lady. Except when she drank. We never truly became an item."

"She always loved me and treated me well."

"I'm glad for that," I said.

"She quit drinking for a while. I had a passel of unofficial stepdads. Not legally, but she lived with different men. She wasn't strong. She drank a lot, and so did the men, but they came and went. It was really just me and her, and then she drank so much it ate her up inside and she died. She left me what she had. Five hundred dollars in the bank, her lifetime of savings, and then there was the car and a bicycle. Thank goodness the Cadillac is big enough to sleep in, though it hardly runs. A 1975 model. She bought it used, and it got really used after that. I also got a box of belongings in the trunk of the car. I pawned the bicycle."

"So May thought you were my daughter?"

"She didn't think, she knew."

I nodded, not really knowing what else to do. I looked at Chance even more carefully. She looked like May Lynn, but I was starting to see myself in her face—little things, like the mouth and nose. Or maybe I was just reading that into place because I thought she might in fact be my daughter.

I sipped some coffee I didn't want, searched for words, and didn't find any.

Brett said, "Honey, here's the thing. If you are Hap's daughter—and I'm not saying I doubt you; you look a little like him, but you know, to be sure—we need to take a paternity test. It's the right thing to do, just to prove what you and your mother believe to be true. Because if it isn't, then you need to know that, too."

"Mother was certain," Chance said. "She said there was only Hap, and then she was pregnant, so it was him unless it was immaculate conception."

"Of course, but she may not have judged everything correctly," I said. "I mean, at some point there were others, your stepdads. There could have been someone else. And besides, she said she was on the Pill."

"She was. It was that rare, rare chance when something that shouldn't happen does, in spite of the Pill. It's nearly one hundred percent, but not quite. Mr. Collins, I'm not asking you to be a dad, not asking you for money. I just wanted to see you. Have some idea what you look like, how you are. I researched on you for the last year. Asking around, finding out this and that. Mom only told me about you a year ago. By the way, a lot of people don't like you."

"And maybe with good reason," I said. "Understand I didn't mean what I said to sound like, well, that—"

"That you were saying my mom was a tramp?"

"Yeah. I didn't mean that."

"What did you mean?"

"What he meant is this is new for all of us," Brett said. "It'll take a bit of time, but a paternity check would figure it out for us. I think that's only fair, to be sure. Your mom told it the way she remembered it, but say she was off by a little, forgot a few details?"

"That's a big detail," Chance said, and she turned her head slightly, and when she did I could see her mother quite clearly. She had a habit of doing just that, kind of turning her head to one side, as if it gave her greater perspective on an idea. Her mouth trembled ever so slightly. "She had a number of boyfriends later, but she wasn't a slut. She wasn't."

"No one is saying that," Brett said. "Not even close. I'm not Hap's first, nor is he mine. It's the way life works. It's just if your mother was mistaken. If. Then you wouldn't want to miss out and not find your real dad, if you haven't already found him."

"If you're my daughter, Chance, then I'm more than fine with that. Completely fine. It's like Brett says, though. We need to be sure. For all our sakes. Before we invest hearts, we need to invest DNA and be sure. That's fair, isn't it?"

Chance looked into her coffee cup. She stared at it so intently you would have thought a small shark might be circling in there.

She lifted her head, settled her eyes on me. "Sure. That makes sense. But I haven't got money for that kind of test."

"We do," Brett said.

•   •   •

That night Brett and I lay in bed together in the dark while Chance was sleeping downstairs in what had been Leonard's room. Buffy was in her basket near the bathroom door, asleep. She made little growling noises as she slept. I think she was thinking vengeful thoughts about her former master. Or maybe she was just being beaten up by a rabbit.

I had made a move on Brett to make love, but Brett said, "Not with Chance downstairs."

"As you say, she's downstairs, not under the bed."

"It just doesn't feel right. Your daughter . . . possible daughter . . . right under us, and us, you know . . ."

"You know?"

"Making love."

"You're the one invited her to stay. I also want her to, but . . . hell, I don't know what I think. I like her, I know that, and I wouldn't mind her being my daughter."

"What if she's not your daughter?"

"She still doesn't need to sleep in a car."

"Why I asked her to stay. I want us to help her."

"But on the other hand, I sensed hesitation from you, a fear she could be down there putting the silverware in a pillowcase."

"I didn't say anything like that."

"Didn't you?" I said.

"No. I said I didn't want to make love because it makes me uncomfortable that she's down there."

"How about taking a pee? Will that make you uncomfortable knowing she's down there?"

"Don't be cute," she said.

"It wasn't that cute."

"No, it wasn't. It's just that if she is your daughter, what do we do? If she isn't your daughter, what do we do?"

"I really just wanted to make love and go to sleep," I said.

"We have to do something for her."

"We fed her. We gave her a bed. And if she's not my daughter, we'll see what we can do to help her get started. Until then, we let her stay, have her take a paternity test, and take it from there."

"My daughter doesn't come visit," Brett said.

"She hasn't asked to come visit."

"You don't like her."

"I think her nearly getting me and Leonard killed twice and her going back to being a drunk and a druggie on a regular basis is part of that."

"She has problems, too, Hap. Is it one daughter over another?"

"I don't even know Chance is my daughter."

"But if she is?"

"I said already. We help her out."

"My point. Your daughter we help, my daughter we don't."

"Would you consider me and Leonard, and even you, nearly getting killed one time, and then me and Leonard nearly getting killed a second time, helping her out?"

"You said that already."

"I think it has a certain significance."

"If my daughter had a home to come to, then it might be different. She might do better."

"Tillie has her own house. What she does there and who she brings there is her problem. And sometimes ours. And she's in her thirties now. This girl is young."

"I handled myself then."

"So did I, but that's not the point."

"I'm not trying to be a bitch, Hap."

"You're doing a pretty good imitation."

She turned the light on.

"Are we going to go there?" Brett said.

"You're the one that said you're a bitch."

"I said no such thing. I said I'm not trying to be one, and you said I was one."

"An imitation of one."

"Don't start splitting hairs with me, buster. You not only aren't getting any pussy tonight, you might prepare yourself for what certainly could be a long drought."

"Baby, come on."

"So now I'm your baby, not your bitch."

I could see this was going downhill fast. I said, "Sorry, Brett. I'm as confused, surprised, and startled as anyone. I go from one end of the spectrum to the other on this. I'm happy about it in an odd way, confused in another. I hope she is my daughter, and I hope she isn't. But she's a person."

Brett turned off the light.

In the dark, she said, "I know. I'm sorry. But I don't think you've given Tillie a chance."

"Well, speaking of Chance, let's see if this girl deserves a chance. Even if she doesn't I still want to help her. And it's not like I haven't tried to help your daughter, but Tillie—"

"I know. It's different."

"I was going to say difficult."

"You wanted a family. And now you just may have one. But I won't lie to you: I'm uncomfortable about it. Maybe I'm jealous of one daughter over another, or at least that's how I'm seeing it."

"If she is my daughter," I said. "Seems to me we have to let this lay and see how it plays out for now."

I could hear Brett breathing gently in the dark.

After a long while she spoke.

"I guess. And Hap?"

"What?"

"We don't actually have any real silverware."

By the time we quit talking things had smoothed over pretty well, but I still didn't get any.

•   •   •

I finally got up and slipped out of the bed silently and went downstairs. In the living room I picked up a book on the coffee table, an old Bill Crider western, and started reading it. I had read it some years before, but now and again I have to read or reread a western.

I had just started when I heard the door to Leonard's old room open. Turning, I saw Chance, dressed in a pair of Brett's footy pajamas that were too long for her, come into the room.

She came to the edge of the couch where I sat, smiled at me. "Brett is tall," she said. She lifted one foot, and I could see the footy was dangling.

"She is at that."

"She's so different from my mom."

"Yes," I said. "She is. What you doing up? You look tired."

"I am. I thought I might have some warm milk. What are you doing up? You look tired, too."

"Wanted to read."

"At three in the morning?"

"I thought two was too early and four was too late."

She chuckled slightly.

"Come on," I said. "I'll warm us both some milk."

We went into the kitchen, and I poured milk in cups and placed them one at a time in the microwave. When we both had our warm milk we sat at the table. We looked at each other. I think we both had a lot to say but had no idea how to say it.

"I have something special," I said. "Well, I find it special. I hide it so Leonard doesn't get it."

"I know he's your friend, but nothing else."

I got up and opened a cabinet, and from behind a box of rice and a can of whole jalapenos I pulled out a box of animal crackers. It was one of those small boxes that has a zoo on the front and animals behind bars. Never liked zoos or circuses, really. Felt sorry for the animals. But I liked animal crackers.

"Oh, I love those," Chance said.

"So does Leonard," I said. "Vanilla cookies of any kind, animal crackers, Dr Peppers. Why I hide these."

"That's mean."

"He's a cookie-eating machine and kind of a bastard about it."

She showed a lot of pretty teeth. "You two sound like kids."

"In some ways we are. You end up staying around us, you'll find we're very juvenile and pretty crass."

"Mom said she thought you were a fine man."

I didn't know how to respond to that, so I merely opened the box of animal crackers, divided them up between us. When that was done we both had a small pile of them in front of us, along with our warm milk.

"I guess I should have got a plate," I said.

"No, this is fine."

"Sure?"

"Yeah."

"I could get a plate—a saucer, or something."

"No, really. This is fine."

"Not a great host," I said.

"We don't need the good china for animal crackers," she said and popped one in her mouth. "Oh, wow, these are good. When I was little Mom would get me animal crackers and a carton of milk, put me in front of the TV, and let me watch cartoons. She used that time to drink. Still, it's one of my fondest memories—eating animal crackers, drinking milk, and watching Ren and Stimpy, whatever she recorded for me. I had stacks of those VHS tapes, and out in the car I have a box of DVDs I've used to replace them. I still like cartoons."

"I like the Road Runner in those old Warner Brothers cartoons."

"Oh, yeah, he's great. And Wile E. Coyote always going off a cliff, and there's that slow drop and the big pow and the cloud of dust that floats up."

"You bet. What kind of music do you like?" I asked.

"I'm eclectic. I like some rap, but not much. Sounds alike pretty quick. Liked more of it when I was younger."

"You're pretty young now."

"I don't feel all that young," she said.

There was a slight darkening of tone, so I said, "What else do you like?"

"Country, some. Kasey Lansdale."

"Oh, hell," I said. "Leonard adores her stuff. I like it, too, but he's a fanatic. He likes to sit around and be moody to country music, usually the older stuff. Hank Williams, Johnny Cash. I like all that, too. Patsy Cline. Loretta Lynn. And have you heard Johnny Cash's son's music? John Carter Cash. Man, he is different. I have a CD of his that I've about worn a groove in."

"I don't know Hank Williams's music much," she said. "I kind of like Hank the Third, some of it. I know who his dad is, and know songs of his sung by other people, but not him."

"Real deal, Williams."

That line of talk ran out, and we sat for a while drinking milk and eating cookies. I was glad I had the milk and cookies so I wouldn't just sit there and stare at her, still trying to see myself in her.

"I have a degree in journalism," she said.

"That's good," I said.

"Did I already say that?"

"I don't think so."

"I worked at a paper for a while. I had a short story published in a literary magazine."

"Really?'

"Yeah. *REAL,* out of Stephen F. Austin University. I didn't get paid."

"Still, it was accepted."

"Yeah."

We minced around for more conversation, but by this time the animal crackers had run out.

"I feel better now," she said. "Sleepy."

"Me, too," I said.

"Thanks for the milk and the animal crackers."

"No sweat."

She stood up from the table.

"I guess I'll go to bed."

"Me, too."

"Should I put the glasses in the dishwasher?"

"I'll do that. You go on and get some sleep. Wake up when you want."

I think we were both trying to decide if hugging was appropriate. We decided without a word that it wasn't. She lingered, standing by the table for a moment, then said, "Good night," and went away.

I got up and rinsed out the milk glasses and put them in the dishwasher. I threw the box that had contained the animal crackers away. I dampened a sponge and wiped the table clean, pushing crumbs into my palm and dropping them in the trash.

I climbed the stairs, and by the time I got to the bedroom and slipped under the covers my eyes were wet with tears that I couldn't entirely explain.

21

We still hadn't heard from Jim Bob and Marvin.

On Sunday me and Leonard went fishing. I'm not really much of a fisherman, but now and again I enjoyed casting a line in the water. If I caught fish I sometimes ate them, but more often than not threw them back.

The main reason I went was to get my mind off things, both the case we were working on and my possible fatherhood.

It was a private lake we had access to, thanks to a friend of Marvin's. More of a big pond, actually. We had borrowed a small boat with a motor, and the lake was infested with fish and alligators, not to mention ducks and all manner of swampy growth poking up through the water. The sunlight hit the water with a vengeance, and where the greenery was tall in the water, it made a lot of little shadows. Out in the center it was clear and deep-looking, and there was a sheen that made it look more like oil than water. On the banks birches grew, alongside a scattering of willows and elms, their roots spreading into the water where the shore had broken away.

Leonard was sitting at the bow, and I was at the stern. We both had on wide-brimmed straw hats to keep from cooking, and the brims made shadows on our bent knees. The air was stiff and hot. We were drifting near the middle of the pond, casting our rods. I always loved the moment when the cast happened and the line whizzed out and sometimes you would get a flick of silver from the sunlight falling on the business end of the line.

We had brought along a lunch in a big cooler, and besides thinking about Chance, I was thinking about food. I liked lunch. I checked my watch. Damn. Still two hours away.

"Where is the girl today?" Leonard asked.

"She and Brett went to Tyler for lunch and clothes shopping. They'll spend the day. Why I thought it was okay for us to go fishing. Course, Chance doesn't know about the business we're into. I mean, she knows what we do, private investigations, but she doesn't know exactly what it is we're working on, and I don't see any reason to tell her there might be danger in our lives."

"If someone were going to hit us, wouldn't they have already done it?"

"We have some reputation, Leonard. They might be waiting for when we least expect it."

"Good point. About the daughter thing, though. How's Brett dealing with this?"

"Truth is she was a little shitty about having Chance there, even if she invited her, but she isn't shitty to Chance. I think she kind of likes her."

"She's being shitty because of her own daughter. That's it, isn't it?"

"Damn, Leonard. You are alert and tuned in."

"I read a book once. It had lots of pictures, but it led to me thinking a little."

"Oh, did I tell you? Chance has your room now."

"I have things in that room."

"No," I said. "Your shit is in a cardboard box under the stairs now."

"That's my room."

"You sound like a teenager come home from college to find his room is now a home library."

"Well, it is my room."

"Was."

Leonard pouted for a few minutes, then said, "So you don't know for sure she's your daughter?"

"And if she isn't, you want your room back?"

"That would be nice. If she is your daughter, I guess she can keep it."

"Big of you."

"If she is your daughter, it will change some of my thoughts about you."

"How's that?" I asked.

"I thought you were lying to me about having sex. I though you were just masturbating and pretending to have sex. You have a daughter, that means you really did have sex. Yuck."

"What do you think Brett and I do?"

"I don't like to think about it. I don't think Brett would do something like that."

"Yes, Leonard. I may have a daughter. Fruit of my loins."

"I was sort of hoping you were the end of your bloodline."

That stopped the talk for a while, and we drifted in the boat and fished. We ate our lunch. When we finished eating, Leonard pulled the previous conversation out of the bag again.

"Do you want it to be your daughter?"

"Been thinking about family a lot in the last few years, like maybe I want one that's bigger than the one I got, which is pretty much you and Brett. I even in a moment of odd weakness tried to talk Brett into us having a child."

"Well, she looks fine, and I want to put that on record, and though it's coming from a queer, I think I can safely say Brett has held age off better than just about anyone I know, but a little old for child rearing, don't you think?"

"Like I said, it was a kind of irrational thought, not much weight behind it."

"She's got a cool name," Leonard said. "Chance. I like that."

"Chance told me this morning her mother had quit drinking when she was pregnant. That it meant that much to her. And that May Lynn talked about me all the time, like we had been together forever. Told Chance she thought I was the one and she had missed the boat, and that she didn't want to disrupt my life, because except for when she was pregnant, she knew she couldn't stop drinking."

"You're one of those that thinks alcohol is a disease, aren't you?"

"Don't you?" I asked.

"I don't think all alcoholics are that way because their body reacts to liquor in a different way than someone who can take a drink. I think it's true of some, but I think a lot of people just find something for a crutch, take hold of it, and support themselves with it. They can quit but won't. I don't think it's always about disease. It's like me being gay. I had no choice, it was in the DNA, but I think it can be a choice, too. I think you can just decide you want to suck dick, out of adventure or the fact that you think, hey, I'm bringing up my average of having sex with a warm body."

"I believe they call that bisexuality," I said.

"I don't know if that exists or not. I don't care. I say you want to suck dick or mess with the other, no matter what your DNA, that's up to you. Me, I don't get any urge to do the other. I like men, and it's that simple. But I think for some it's choice. Hell, prisoners fuck each other all the time, get out of prison, and never fuck someone of their own sex again. Provided they don't end up back in prison. Everyone is looking for a warm hole, Hap."

"Don't go changing, Leonard. Stay the fine and romantic person you are."

"I'm just saying how I see it. Some things are more habit than disease. And I'm not saying being gay is a disease. I'm just saying a lot of things can be by choice. Might be a bad analogy, since I don't have any problems with sexual choice, but I've known some drunks who I think just liked to wallow in self-pity."

"I don't know," I said. "Bottom line, May Lynn was a drunk, by choice or disease or DNA or whatever."

"When do I meet Chance?"

"Whenever you like. I guess I didn't want to put her in with all the family until I was sure she was family. It's a dumb thought, but there you have it. We've already had swabs done to check for DNA. It takes some time, though. We have a wait of a month or longer. Private business that does those tests, they're pretty backed up. Rest of the time, well, me and Chance, we've been talking. I'm getting to know her, and she's very sharp and likable. It's like finding a puppy that has a collar and is well cared for and you put an ad in the paper, flyers, and any day you expect someone to call or knock on your door looking for that puppy. And there you are, having invested all your heart into them, and someone shows up with a leash and a dog treat."

"Speaking of pups, how is Buffy?"

"Tip-top. Brett actually boarded her for today. Picks her up tomorrow. Vet is giving her the once-over, checking that rib."

"I hate to veer from all your boring personal matters, Hap, but this stuff with Frank, the car lot. Jim Bob might ought to have his tree shook."

"We do that, a barrel racer might fall out."

"Maybe the horse, too. But we will shake his tree. Right?"

"Right."

"Wait a moment. Think I have a bite."

He started reeling it in. It was a bicycle tire and wheel.

"Ah," he said, releasing the wheel from his hook, tossing it in the boat for us to dispose of. "The rare bicycle fish."

22

We fished, and the day slipped away comfortably. For a pond full of fish, we weren't having a lot of luck. We threw back three fish and kept the bicycle tire. Mosquitoes were becoming a real problem.

Running the boat back to shore, we packed up and loaded the boat on the trailer. As we were driving out of there my cell rang. It was Jim Bob.

"We got to talk, Hoss."

"You saw Frank?"

"Yep. We need to talk."

"We're talking now."

"In person. Your house?"

I hung up and looked at Leonard. "Guess who?"

• • •

By the time we dropped the boat and trailer off and got rid of the bicycle tire, it was close to dark. Leonard drove us down back roads of red clay and sometimes gravel and blacktop.

Once East Texas had been the land of bears and honey and even parakeets. These days the bears and parakeets were all shot out, and the bees weren't doing all that well, either. There were cows, though. We spotted them when we came to gaps in the trees and saw pastures. The cows looked happy and content. They didn't know they were waiting to be hamburgers.

The dwindling sunlight wrapped through the trees and darkened into black ribbons of shadow, and by the time we broke out onto the main highway it was full dark. With the night having arrived, the air was cooler than before. We turned off the air conditioner and rolled down the windows and let the night air in. We passed houses with lights on inside them. A few cars zipped by, headlights shining bright and then gone.

Twenty minutes later we were in town and came to my street, arrived at the house. I noted there were no lights on, not even a porch light. I glimpsed flashlight flares in the yard. We cruised by, down to the church parking lot below the house. Leonard parked on the far side of the lot behind the church. You couldn't see the car from my house.

Leonard said, "You saw them, too?"

"Yep."

"Jim Bob?"

"Did you see his Caddy at the curb? Anywhere?"

"Nope."

"Lot of flashlights," I said.

"Yep. Maybe Jim Bob brought friends. The barrel racer?"

"Not unless she brought her horse and he has a flashlight, too."

"I judge there were three lights, so at least three guys, wouldn't you say?"

"Shall we surprise them?"

"Ain't nothing like a surprise," Leonard said.

"One thing first." I dialed Brett on my cell.

She answered with, "Hap. Sorry, hon. We been shopping, got caught up. We're going to have dinner then be home. You ought to get with Leonard and eat something."

"I will. So you're still in Tyler, then?"

"Like I said, we're going to have a late dinner."

"Okay. Well, take your time. Love you."

"You sound a little funny."

"Tired. Long day fishing. Talk later."

I turned off the phone and put it away.

"So?" Leonard asked.

"She and Chance are still in Tyler."

"That's good," Leonard said.

"Didn't see any reason to alarm her."

"Shall we see if we can give the people in your yard reason to be alarmed?"

"They could be folks looking for a lost dog."

"They could."

"Or kids prowling the neighborhood."

"Also possible."

"Termite exterminators at the wrong house."

"Less likely," Leonard said. "They could also be assholes out to do you and your bunch harm, too. And that would include me."

Leonard cranked the truck, drove out of the lot by the back way. This led to a road that ran behind our house. There was a two-acre pasture of overgrown grass directly behind our house to the road. There were houses elsewhere, but whoever owned this property had never developed it. I hoped they never would.

We parked at the curb by the pasture. Leonard leaned across me and got my revolver out of the glove box.

"That's my gun," I said.

"You pick up a stick or something."

"You have my gun."

"Very observant."

"How'd you end up with my gun?"

"Do you really want to talk about that right now?"

"What if we're not being that sneaky and they're in my backyard?"

"Then the surprise will be on us," Leonard said.

Crossing the pasture, I half expected to be shot. I've been shot at a few times. It makes a memorable impression. There were streetlights behind us and some from houses back there, and that framed us nicely for a shot if anyone was looking in our direction.

No one shot at us. I did have some grass burrs sticking through my pants, but other than that, so far so good.

There's a chain-link fence at the back of our property, but on the right side there's a tall redwood fence. Someone started building it years before we bought the place but never finished. Maybe they ran out of money.

There's no gate directly at the back. It's on the far side, where the redwood fence dies. The gate opens between the fence and the back wall of the house. To get to the gate from the direction we were coming from, we had to cross our next door neighbor's property. A few dogs barked, but none of them were going crazy. Maybe our intruders would think nothing of it.

We eased through my neighbor's yard along the redwood fence. I saw lights in one of the windows of the neighbor's house, and I could faintly hear the television. I was sweating more than the temperature demanded. My hair was dripping with it. When we got to the gate I used a key to unlock it, and we eased it open and slipped into the backyard. For once I was glad the automatic light we had above the back door was out. I had been meaning to replace it.

There was a shed out there, and it was locked. I got out my key and unlocked it and got a crowbar off the workbench. So far the only work I had done on that bench was lay the crowbar there. I had arranged some tools on the wall, none of which, except for the hammer, I knew how to use. If I couldn't fix it with a hammer, it would remain unfixed.

I felt the heft of the crowbar in my hand. It slipped against my sweaty palm.

Gently as possible, I unlocked the back door and cracked it open. I could hear someone jacking with the front door, picking the lock, most likely.

"I'll surprise the folks at the door," Leonard said. "You want to check out the garage?"

"Try not to shoot anyone if you don't have to."

"You're no fun," Leonard said. He slipped inside and gently closed the door. I went back through the gate and along the grassy path between our house and the neighbors, came up alongside the garage. I guess it's more of a carport than a garage. It's open in the front, and there's no garage door.

I crept and sweated along past the neighbor's window with the glow and the television sounds coming out of it. I got out of the path of that light as quick as I could manage. I slipped forward until I got to the front edge of the garage.

I took a deep breath. There was a time when I kind of looked forward to this sort of thing. These days I just wanted dinner, a comfy bed, and Brett. I could hear someone in the garage, trying to walk softly but not managing too well. I heard someone say, "Shall we jimmy the door?"

That would be the door from the carport into the house. It led directly into a hallway that led to Leonard's room. Chance's room now.

I took another deep breath and let it out slow and easy and quiet. I thought about hitting someone with the crowbar and didn't like that idea, unless they had a gun. If they had a gun a crowbar might not be enough.

Soon the one who was picking the front door lock would be in, and when he came in, there would be Leonard. It would be like expecting the lady and getting the tiger.

I heard a loud noise, like someone slapping water with their palm. It came from the front of the house, and I knew that would be Leonard. He hadn't shot anyone, but he certainly had hit someone. Maybe they hit him, but I didn't think so. I knew in that instant, the same instant I thought all these thoughts, that my time wouldn't get any better than right then.

I rounded the corner and stepped into the garage as two men ran out of it and headed toward the sound. They didn't see me, as their backs were to me. They had heavy flashlights, and they were big men. That's all I could tell from the glow of their lights. The streetlight out front of the house was out and there was no moon and they were mostly just shapes with a light going before them.

I heard another sound, scuffling, then that smacking sound again. I saw someone fall backwards off the porch. His flashlight went flying, and I saw a beam from one of the flashlights gleam against a shaved head of one of the men in the yard. I could make out Leonard standing on the porch.

I was right behind the two men with flashlights. One of them raised the light onto Leonard, who was leaping off the porch. The man had a gun in his hand, and he was lifting it when I came up beside him and struck his gun hand with the crowbar as hard as I could swing it.

I knew from the way the crowbar felt in my hand I had broken bones. The gun dropped, the man went to his knees, sick with pain, and now the other man was turning toward me. I stepped right into the middle of him and twisted my body and hit him alongside the knee with the crowbar. He let out a scream, staggered back on an uncertain leg. I dropped the crowbar and stepped in so close we were almost in the same pair of pants. I hit him with a straight right that I knew was a good shot because I hardly felt it. He went down and tried to get up. I kicked him in the head, and he rolled over like a doodlebug, the flashlight flying from his hand and rolling across the grass where it came to rest on the concrete driveway.

I picked up the crowbar and gave it to Leonard, searched for guns, found a very large automatic on the unconscious man by the porch. The guy I had hit on the knee was unarmed except for a blackjack. I gave it to Leonard. He stepped forward and hit the man holding his knee with the blackjack, a short, sharp blow to the back of the head.

"Goddamn," said the man, shifting his hands to his head. "My leg is done broke; wasn't no need for that."

"I felt there was," Leonard said.

"You broke my arm," said the man I had hit on the arm with the crowbar.

"I would be disappointed if I hadn't," I said. "And you, asshole. How's your leg?"

"Broke, I done told you," said the man.

"Good," I said.

I went over and collected his gun from the driveway while the man with the broken arm bent over and threw up in the grass.

That's when a car glided up at the curb.

23

Jim Bob parked near a big tree and got out. I could see someone else was in the Caddy, but couldn't make them out. Just a shadowy shape. Jim Bob came strolling up with a big revolver dangling from one hand and a flashlight in the other.

"Y'all having a yard party?" he said.

"You could call it that," Leonard said. "Though I think me and Hap had the party and they mostly just rolled around on the yard."

"You got you quite a few little souvenirs there, don't you?" Jim Bob said, looking at the guns in my hands.

"They weren't offering T-shirts," I said.

Jim Bob walked around, looked at all three on the ground, one completely out, two others moaning. He put his flashlight on them. One of them, the unconscious one, wore leather pants and a jean vest, was bare-chested under it. He had a belly like a hairy boulder. The other two wore jeans and dark T-shirts. White guys, all three. All with shaved heads and scraggly beards, faces that looked to have been boiled before they were arranged over the skull.

"Man, they are indeed the warehouse for ugly," Jim Bob said. "Might want to drag these fuckers inside or somewhere before the neighbors wonder what you're doing."

We didn't ask who was in Jim Bob's car. We knew he would tell us in good time, and we didn't want to share any knowledge with whoever it was lying on our lawn.

Leonard turned off the flashlights in the yard except the one that I took to use. He tossed the crowbar and the blackjack in the grass by the driveway and dragged the unconscious man into the carport, the man's boot heels scraped along the concrete.

I put two pistols away in my waistband and one in my front pocket. Me and Jim Bob took hold of the other two guys. I clutched the one with the injured leg under the shoulders and slid him along on his ass, managing to stick the flashlight under my arm and clutch it there while I did. Jim Bob pulled the other one to his feet, and we got them inside the carport.

They were too weak to fight. We got them in there easy. It was dark inside the carport, and we didn't turn on the light. What light there was came from Jim Bob's flashlight and the light I had. There were steps leading from inside the carport into the house. We sat our catch on the top steps, except for the unconscious guy. Leonard left him lying in front of the steps.

I said, "Who the hell sent you and why?"

"Fuck you," said the one with the broken arm.

Jim Bob strolled over and slapped the man twice, grabbed his injured arm, and cranked it. The man squealed, and I winced.

Jim Bob slapped him again. "That's for yelling."

"This is brutality," said the man.

"I know," said Jim Bob.

"Easy, man," I said.

Jim Bob looked at me. "You talking to me?"

"Yeah."

Jim Bob waved the revolver at the thugs, said, "All my life, doing what I do, I have dealt with the scum of the earth, the shit on the bottom of my boots, boots into which I stick my highly attractive feet, and tonight I'm fed up with it. Got no pity left for creeps. I don't know why they're here, who they are, if God or genetics made them ugly, but I know you guys are not the problem without even knowing how this got started. They are the problem. I know a place when we're done here we can bury them. Only way they'll be found is if the earth cracks open on the Day of Judgment."

"There's a shovel in the storage shed," Leonard said. "I don't believe in God, so I'm not expecting that big Day of Judgment other than what we dole out. So I reckon they'll stay hidden for good."

"Guys," I said. "Let's don't let this get out of hand."

I couldn't clearly see the expressions of the two that were sitting on the steps, but their body language told me they were scared. The man lying on the floor of the carport I was starting to wonder about. He hadn't so much as groaned. Leonard can hit pretty damn hard when he wants to.

"Who are you?" I said. "And understand that in this carport, I'm as close as you got to a friend, and I don't like you at all."

"That don't give me any confidence," said the man with the broken arm.

"Nor should it," Leonard said. "Come to my brother's house carrying guns and badly shaved heads, you got to understand how much I'd like to just blow a hole in your meat and dump you in a ditch and piss on you."

"I wasn't even here when it came down," Jim Bob said to the man, "and I don't like you."

"You've made that clear," said the man with the broken arm.

"I can make it clearer," Jim Bob said.

"It's now or never," I said to the men, hoping Leonard and Jim Bob were just playing roles, but with those two, you could never be sure. I knew Leonard better than anyone in the world, but there was a place he could go I couldn't. Jim Bob was even more unpredictable. We could be standing there one moment, next moment all three of those men could be dead and in the trunk of a car on their way to someplace dark and wet.

The man with the broken arm looked so much like the other two, the only way I could tell the difference was in tattoos. He had a tattoo at the center of his throat, like a wishbone. It was not attractive. It looked to be made with a ballpoint pen. Jailhouse tattoo was my guess. I thought of him as Wishbone. I moved the light off of him and pooled it at the base of the steps.

"We was sent by the boss," said Wishbone.

"Narrows it right down," Jim Bob said. "Shall I come over and yank on your arm some more?"

"The Big Dog."

"Who's the Big Dog?" Leonard said.

"Boss we don't never see. We just been told Big Dog has money to pay for certain things being done, and one of those things was you guys, and the ones was told to do it was us. Big Dog ain't really our boss all the time, but he hires us from time to time. You might call us freelance."

"I might call you stupid," Jim Bob said.

"I think you ought to consider a career in macramé if your arm heals," Leonard said. "You damn sure aren't any good at this business."

"So you guys are some kind of crew?" I said.

"Bike club," he said. "Apocalypse on Wheels."

"I heard of them," Jim Bob said. "I think they ride tricycles."

"You ought not talk too mean," said the man with the banged knee. "You might write a check with your mouth your ass can't cash."

"You boys are any example of the badass Apocalypse on Wheels," I said, "then you ain't so much. We can write as many checks as we want."

"We got taken by surprise," Wishbone said.

"Yes," I said. "You did."

Wishbone wanted to say something mean, but instead he was wise enough to sit and smolder. There was an air about him like the school bully who had been beaten up by the ninety-eight-pound math nerd.

Apocalypse on Wheels were known to be dangerous. Drug dealers, primarily meth. They were also known for dog-fighting rings, which in my view should have been punishable by a death sentence.

"Where's your bikes?" Leonard said. "You boys come by stick horse instead?"

"I said tricycles," Jim Bob said.

"Yes," Leonard said, "you did. But I just graded them down another notch. Next Hap can say roller skates."

"Oh, I got you," Jim Bob said. "But wouldn't skates be better than a stick horse?"

"You have a point there," Leonard said.

"Car," said Wishbone. "We parked on a backstreet and walked over."

"Car?" Leonard said. "What kind of self-respecting biker gang comes by car?"

"Easier," Wishbone said.

"Yeah, well, let's get back to what you were saying," I said. "Hired by Big Dog, who you claim you don't know, to come over here and do what? Sort my shit?"

Wishbone held his arm, winced a little, said, "Pretty much. Supposed to be a warning. Give you a good ass-whipping."

"You know where I live," I said, "so you know who lives here with me, don't you?"

"A woman."

"You come here in the middle of the night with guns and flashlights, and you were just going to sort me out? What about her?"

"I guess we would have put some smoke on her, too."

"All right," I said. "Officially, I'm no longer even a faint resemblance to a friend."

"Nothing happened," he said. "We got hurt. You didn't."

"And man, that saddens us," Leonard said.

"You were going to whip my ass for what?" I said.

"You know," he said.

"Why don't you define it for me?" I said.

"Well, we don't get no details much, just the job and some street cred. We was told you was meddling where you shouldn't be meddling, and that we was to whack you around a little, say stay out of business where you don't belong."

"But they didn't tell you the business?" Jim Bob asked.

"No. Didn't matter. It was a job."

"What were you getting paid?" I asked.

"It was to kind of go on our credit."

"Credit."

"We're acolytes," he said.

"Goddamn, that's a strange word to come out of your mouth," Jim Bob said. "I think you even pronounced it right. What you mean is you're trying to get into the gang as a full member and not just a wannabe. Right?"

"I suppose you could say that," Wishbone said. "I like acolyte better."

"So who came to you and said Big Dog wanted me worked over a bit?" I asked.

"They wanted the nigger popped around, too," Wishbone said, avoiding my question. "We thought we'd catch him at his place. He, like you, was easy to find. They gave us your names, and we went straight to the Internet. Wonderful thing that is."

"Ain't it?" Jim Bob said.

"Who is this cowboy fuck?" Wishbone said, nodding at Jim Bob.

"Hell in a cowboy hat," I said. "That's all you need to know."

"No," Jim Bob said. "I want you to know who I am, so you can maybe take a run at me if you survive, and I can fuck you up. I'm Jim Bob Luke. I live in Houston. I love a good enchilada and a medium-rare steak, a good-looking woman with a free spirit, and you couldn't hurt me if you was three people apiece and had three friends just like you. Fuck, you couldn't roll me over with a pry bar if I was dead."

"You just fucked up," said the one with the injured leg. "We'll damn sure remember you."

Jim Bob said, "Most people do." He stepped forward and popped the man with the bad leg in the nose with a sharp left jab. "That's for talking out of turn." Then Jim Bob hit him again. "That's for flinching." Jim Bob slapped him once across the cheek. "And that's for calling Midnight a nigger."

"Oh, thanks," Leonard said.

"My pleasure," Jim Bob said.

"Midnight?" Leonard said.

"I thought it made me seem less politically correct," Jim Bob said. "I got to keep up an image to work with the people I work with."

Bad Leg held his hand to his nose. In the beam of my flashlight I could see blood running between his fingers and down his face.

I said, "You haven't given us a lot of information."

"It's all we got," said Bad Leg.

I thought it might well be.

"You said you were hired by Big Dog and someone else," I said. "Who is this someone else?"

"Our club chairman. Samson House."

"Ah, hell," Jim Bob said. "I know that son of a bitch."

"You do?" I said.

"Nice guy, ain't he?" said Wishbone.

"A peach," Jim Bob said. "Same as his brother, Moses."

"Moses is dead," Wishbone said.

"I know," Jim Bob said. "Why don't you boys take us to Samson? I'd love to see him. I'm only pretending to ask, by the way."

"You know," said Bad Leg. "My leg ain't broke like I thought. I think it's going to be okay."

"You'll never know how that has made our day," Jim Bob said.

"Still hurts, though," Bad Leg said.

24

I soon found out who was in Jim Bob's car. To say I was baffled is to put it mildly.

It was Frank. She was wearing jeans, a T-shirt, and red running shoes. She had her hair tied back in a ponytail and wasn't wearing makeup. She looked good. That she had once been a man was hard to figure on my end. I guess it shouldn't matter, but the idea of her being male before she was female didn't exactly evaporate from my mind.

I walked out to the car with Jim Bob to see her while Leonard kept the three in the garage occupied by pointing one of the guns at them. Sleeping Beauty had finally stirred and was sitting on the steps with the other two.

Frank nodded at me as she got out of the car, but nothing was said. Jim Bob guided her into the house, and when he came back out, we got the bad guys out of the carport. None of them had seen Frank. Jim Bob made it clear we didn't want her seen and took Leonard aside to explain that she was in the house.

We tied up and gagged all but Wishbone, put the gagged ones in the trunk of Jim Bob's Caddy. Bad Leg was right. His leg wasn't broken. He managed to limp out to the car without assistance, moving the way you might if someone had taped your dick to one leg.

After they were tucked nicely inside the trunk, I noted there was plenty of room for them and the spare and maybe we could stuff Wishbone in there, too, if we needed to. But he was our pathfinder, so we placed him in the front passenger seat. Leonard sat behind him with a pistol. I stayed at the house.

Jim Bob drove away slowly. I drove Frank to our office, arriving well ahead of him. He was taking the long way around so Wishbone wouldn't get a chance to see her.

I put Frank inside the office, made the bed for her, showed her where the bottled water was, the coffee and such. We didn't discuss anything, nor did she offer any explanation for why she was with Jim Bob. I got three twelve-gauge pump shotguns out of the closet and a box of shells, told her to make herself comfortable, that I wasn't sure when we'd be back, and to stay inside and not answer the desk phone, then I left out of there.

In the parking lot Jim Bob was standing outside the Red Bitch, as his Cadillac was known, and Leonard was sitting in the backseat with the revolver. Wishbone was in the front seat, being very cooperative. Jim Bob walked over and helped me with the shotguns, taking two of them off my hands, leaving me holding one in one hand, the box of shells in the other.

Jim Bob said, "Got her set?"

"Yep. But I don't get it."

"You will."

"What if she runs away?"

"She won't."

"She might."

"She'll stay until we get back."

I looked at the biker dude in the Red Bitch.

"Considering where I think we're going, what happens if we don't make it back?" I asked.

"I always come back."

"But if we don't?"

Jim Bob shrugged. "Eventually she'll get bored and leave."

I could tell Jim Bob wasn't going to explain shit, least not right then.

"Was it like we thought?" I asked him.

"You mean the cars and the women and the blackmail?"

"No. I wanted to know if without her original elongated wee-wee can she piss up a rope. Of course I'm asking about the cars and such."

Jim Bob was unfazed.

"More to it than we thought. Not exactly like you figured. Think you and your buddy have opened up one big-ass can of worms, and these worms have some serious teeth. But we'll start with these assholes. We finish that, I'll explain about Frank. She can help explain. We don't get these honky tonk samurai sorted out, we might not need an explanation. What we're going to do is nip them in the bud."

"Frankly, I don't see how three of us can sort out a biker gang."

"No doubt it will be precarious," Jim Bob said and raised an eyebrow at me. "You scared?"

"Yeah."

"Not me."

"Liar."

"Okay," Jim Bob said. "I'm slightly nervous. I'll own up to that much. But I got a plan. I'm not sure it's a plan makes any sense until we get where we're going. It doesn't, well, we change plans. We shoot these three in the head and leave them in the woods."

"I don't like that plan," I said.

"Then you better hope plan A works," Jim Bob said. "Look. I know something about these bike-club sucks. They are part of the Dixie Mafia. You might even say they are actually a wing of it. They are connected to just about everything that smells bad in Texas except a little roadkill. Not just East Texas but the whole goddamn state. These biker fucks are mostly muscle for people with more brains and bigger plans then these guys got. Guys in your yard tonight, they are the lowest of the low. They were probably going to get their bones for putting you and Leonard and Brett out of the way. They were there to kill all three of you, not sort you out, but it didn't work out for them. Their boss figured you guys weren't much, so he sent some hitters who weren't much, but don't think there isn't some serious trouble with these boys, and you want to nip it in the bud, and quick, or they will keep on coming until one of them gets lucky. Bottom line is, instead of talking to these three lame-ass soldiers, I say we talk to their main man. That doesn't work out, then we shoot everybody."

"How many is everybody?"

"How would I know? More than ten, twelve? Enough to make a biblical epic? I don't know."

"Not comforting."

"True, but I think it's best to confront them. You want them to at least think they got to consider twice they throw down on you. You can't show weakness with them. Some of the Dixie Mafia head guys, you might even reason with them they see a profit in it. But these biker goobers, not so much."

"And I'm saying you don't crawl down a hole full of rattlers and expect to come out unbit."

Jim Bob nodded slightly. "I hear you. Like I said, I've dealt with them before. They kind of lump up together like dog turds out Etoile way. We were in Houston, thereabouts, I'd know exactly where they are. Here, I just know the general location."

"You know a lot of shit, Jim Bob."

"That's because I walk through it every day. Someday soon I'm thinking I'm going to throw in the rope and take up pig farming again full-time."

"I didn't even know there was a biker gang around here."

"Did you know there are some Amish here in East Texas, north of town? The men use power tools and have cell phones and drive cars, but the women live on the farm, wear bonnets pulled down around their faces, and, unlike the men, only use hand tools."

"I don't know from Amish," I said. "How did we get on the Amish?"

"It seemed like a natural segue. Bottom line is we need someone knows more than the bikers' general whereabouts."

"Meaning the young gentleman with the fucked-up tattoo in your front seat is going to be our guide?"

"Bingo."

"You know, one thing we ought to take into serious fucking consideration is we got shotguns and revolvers and everyone else has automatics and rifles that can spray bullets faster than we can."

"Yeah, I know," Jim Bob said. "But I do so hate change. I haven't got over that whole business about Pluto. I think Pluto got fucked, you know. One day it's a planet, and the next day it's not. I hate change, Hap. I'm the same with guns. Like to keep it old-school."

"Well, when we get back, if we get back, we'll draft a stiff note to Congress about that business with Pluto."

25

Inside the Caddy I laid a shotgun across my lap. Leonard placed one across his, the other I put on the floorboard at my feet. Leonard was still holding the pistol pointed at the back of Wishbone's head. I hoped we didn't hit a bump.

"Well," Leonard said. "You guys certainly took long enough. I hope you got some shit sorted out and it's nothing I need to know."

"We had some serious things to discuss," Jim Bob said. "We didn't need you for it. It would have been over your head."

"Nice," Leonard said.

"The guys, they do that to me all the time," Wishbone said. "I always feel like they're talking behind my back, like maybe the ass is ripped out of my pants and I don't know it."

"You shut up," Leonard said.

Outside of LaBorde, the trees grew thick and even thicker as we headed eastward.

I sent Brett a text that said I might be home late, maybe even tomorrow morning, and I'd explain later, and not to be surprised if she found a strange woman sleeping on the sleeper sofa at the office. I didn't tell her it was Frank. I thought about it some more and sent another text. RENT A MOTEL TONIGHT FOR YOU AND CHANCE. DO THIS. TRUST ME.

DON'T GO HOME TONIGHT. NO EXCEPTIONS. NO EXCUSES. IN FACT, NOW THAT I THINK ABOUT IT, DON'T GO TO THE OFFICE UNTIL I SAY IT'S OKAY. LOVE, HAP.

I wondered what Brett would think if I didn't come back. Where is he? What the hell is he doing? What the hell was that text about? Will there be coupons this Sunday in the newspaper for granola bars and panty liners?

And then there was Chance. If she was my daughter I damn sure hadn't gotten to know her very well. She didn't know me well enough to miss me when I was gone. I really should just try to get a regular day job that didn't involve getting hit or shot at and that maybe came with health benefits and a retirement plan.

I glanced at Leonard. He was just a dark shape in the car, but he turned his face toward me. He sensed what I was thinking. He often knew what I was thinking. He said softly, "It's cool, man."

He'd say that with the hot wind of hell blowing in his face.

We passed very few cars, and in fact the presence of their headlights out there in that lonesome country was almost alien, like spaceships cruising close to the ground, zipping by so fast even the big Cadillac vibrated.

Wishbone sat stiff, giving directions, mostly saying, "Keep going."

Finally we came to what had once, in the 1950s, been a prominent highway. Now it seemed narrow, and the old yellow stripe down the center of it was worn so dim you could hardly see it in the headlights.

It was two lanes, and we didn't pass a single car as we went along. We traveled down it for a goodly stretch. The trees closed in on both sides and limbs came together overhead and made a kind of canopy. We had to dodge some rotten limbs that had fallen in the road, and once we had to stop so I could get out and drag a big limb away so we could continue. Finally we came to an asphalt road, the sides of which bled off into deep bar ditches on either side. Wishbone had us turn down it. In the woods I saw fireflies glowing in spots, winking out, then winking back into view.

The headlights caught the glint of standing water in scattered spots. A mosquito paradise.

"All right, fuckhead," Jim Bob said to Wishbone. "You better not be leading me on a wild goose chase, or you will be a cooked goose."

"We're down here on purpose," he said. "It keeps prying eyes out, and the club owns the land."

"How close are we?" I asked.

"I don't know," Wishbone said. "A mile. Maybe two."

"Tell me well before we get there, and don't be cute about it," Jim Bob said. "We show up in the midst of your comrades before we know it, you get it first. *Comprende?*"

We came to what was nothing more than a deer trail. Wishbone told us to turn down it. Jim Bob pulled off the road and onto the trail and stopped, turned off the headlights. He turned in his seat and looked at Wishbone.

"What?" Wishbone said.

"How close now?"

"Real close. You go down here a piece, then it widens out. It's been logged down there. You'll see a patch of trees beyond the bare spots, though, and on the other side of them is another bare spot, and you can see some mobile homes we got there, a big shed. That's where they cook the meth. And there are a bunch of dog pens where they keep the fighting dogs, though there ain't none there now."

"Tell you what we're going to do," Jim Bob said to Wishbone. "I'm going to get out of the car, and then you are going to get out. You are going to walk around to the rear of the car. My boys here will follow out after you."

That was just like Jim Bob. My boys. He had taken over. Thing was, right then, that was fine with me.

"Are you going to shoot me when I get out?" Wishbone asked.

"That's up to you," Jim Bob said.

Wishbone and Jim Bob went to the back, and me and Leonard followed. The air outside of the air-conditioned car was as stiff as wire and uncomfortably warm. Jim Bob opened the trunk and shined his flashlight into it. The two thugs hadn't evaporated or died of a carbon monoxide leak. They had been trying to work the ropes loose, you could tell that much. They were both still gagged.

"All right," Jim Bob said, and without being asked, Leonard readjusted the wrist and ankle ties on the two in the trunk. There was more nylon cord back there, and Jim Bob got that out and tossed it to Leonard, nodded at Wishbone, said, "You don't mind, tie his ass up and gag him and put him on the back seat floorboard. I just wanted to see how these guys were riding back here."

He reached down and pulled the gag from Bad Leg. "How's the ride?"

"Bumpy. And my leg hurts."

"I can live with that," Jim Bob said and readjusted the gag.

When Wishbone was well tied up by Leonard and lying on the ground, Jim Bob stood with his hand on the trunk lid, looked down at Bad Leg and Sleeping Beauty, and said, "Good night, sweet assholes. Better hope we don't get killed. It's going to be real hot tomorrow, and then you're going to get thirsty, and then, well, it's not a nice way to go."

There was mumbling behind the gags and a lot of squirming. Jim Bob closed the trunk. I got hold of Wishbone's head, and Leonard got his feet. We lugged him around and put him on the floorboard in the back of the Caddy.

Jim Bob said, "Let's go."

Leonard got in the front passenger seat, and I sat in the back with all the shotguns in my lap and my feet on Wishbone's head. I found it was a little uncomfortable. I don't know how Wishbone felt.

Jim Bob backed us out of the narrow trail and drove the Cadillac slowly and without lights down to where there was an indention in the woods. He pulled in there. There was a small trail off that. He drove down it a few yards, stopped at a dead end, and me and him and Leonard got out. Wishbone was thrashing around on the floorboard like a beached whale, but I had seen how Leonard had tied those knots that held him; he wasn't coming out of that without assistance.

I sorted the shotguns out. We walked away from the car and then stopped underneath a black willow tree that was growing near a little runoff of water that trickled down through the brush and trees.

"Thing we don't want to do is get surprised," Jim Bob said. "We'll do the surprising."

"How surprising are we going to be?" Leonard asked.

"The surprise is they'll never know we were here. But we'll get a lay of the land this way. This Samson fellow, like I said, I kind of know him. We find Samson, he can give us a more direct note on who hired him to hire the numb-nut squad, and that can lead us more directly to the problem you boys got. That and Frank. She had plenty to say, and I think she's got more."

"And you know Samson on sight?" I asked.

"You might say I knew his brother, Moses, better, but yeah, I know Samson on sight. Probably can smell him."

"What about Moses?" I said.

"He met with an unfortunate accident."

"What kind of accident?"

"Well, I had some run-ins with the Apocalypse bunch in Houston," Jim Bob said. "It don't matter what for, as it was a complicated mixture of events that involved a variety of nasty happenings. It ended with me getting outsmarted, which is a goddamn rarity in this universe. But it happened. I think I'd been a little sick that week."

"You mess up, you always say that?" Leonard said.

"I wouldn't want you thinking it's my fault. Thing was, it was a temporary lapse, but at the moment I'm telling about, they had me by the nut sack. I was caught up in something that got me taken out to their compound outside of Houston. Kind of like what's out here. They moved here not long after that. I didn't know exactly where, but knew it was in this area. You can bet I've kept an ear to the ground. They made a few runs at me afterward, but it didn't turn out well for them, and in time they quit. At least for a while. So knowing this location, and if Samson's here, I can also make sure I don't get run at again. They aren't known to be smart, but they aren't known to give up.

"Thing is, I killed a few of them, and that was their main point of contention. They were mad at me over some things I had done for a client that didn't do them any good, so they started sending these guys to hit me. I had three runs at me and was successful each time. But this time I'm talking about, I turned left when I should have turned right. To put it in a nutshell, they nabbed me, kicked me around a little, but didn't kill me. They had other plans, had me dead to rights, and they hauled me out to their compound so I could meet their head asshole, and he's talking about chopping off my head and doing some nasty things to it. I says to the brother, Moses, I says, 'You're pretty tough with me handcuffed, but for all your tough-ass talk, you couldn't pull a cotton wad out of a dead man's ass. What you got is muscle all around you. Those men of yours I killed, they came for me, and I took them on face-to-face and killed them.'

"Anyway, they've got me. I'm handcuffed, and I got some knots they knocked on my head growing larger by the moment, and one of my eyes is starting to close a little. Moses is going on about how he's going to cut my head off, pull out my intestines, stick a hot poker up my ass, pull my dick off with pliers—none of this laid out in any particular order—and it all sounded quite convincing. You can bet my asshole was puckering wind about then.

"I says to him again: 'You talk big with all these swinging dicks around you. How about it's just me and you, and that decides it?'

"Let me tell you, conditions I was under, I was throwing some serious pecker around. They wanted me to grovel, but I wasn't going to give them that. I was playing with pure shit talk and ball sweat out there, let me tell you. Had it been some of the other criminals I know, they would have just laughed and shot me in the head. But I knew how those suckers thought. Moses says, 'All right. Let's do it. How about a duel, pistols with two loads at thirty feet?'

"Now, that is my meat, boys, and I thought, I could do that and have as good a chance as most anybody. No use lying. I knew I'd win that way. Course, I did win, I wasn't certain they'd actually let me go. But right then the choices were shoot it out or have my dick pulled off with pliers. Dick like mine ought to be bronzed, not mistreated. But then Samson, he says, 'Do it the old bowie fight way.' He says he's done that and come out on top, and he lifted up his shirt and showed us some scars that looked like he'd been caught up in a very large electric fan. Samson says his brother, Moses, ought to do that, show me and anyone that would find my corpse that you don't mess with the Apocalypse fuckers, and so on and so on. He went on for some time. Another few minutes and I would have died from boredom."

"I know what you mean," Leonard said.

"Fuck you," Jim Bob said. "You love this and you know it. Well, now, this knife-fight idea was far less appealing to me. A knife fight, even one you win, usually ends up with you cut, and maybe you only win because the other guy dies first. I don't like knives. But that's not to say I don't know a thing or two about them. I been in a knife ruckus or two, but not like they were suggesting. You see, turns out these guys are fans of Jim Bowie, and not just the knife. There's this old story that back in his time Bowie fought a knife duel in a dark room. Story being Jim had a bowie and the other guy had a common butcher knife. Bowie won, though a lot of people don't know the part about how he was laid up with knife wounds and such for a long while. Add to this, Samson and Moses aren't little folk, and it seems when they aren't killing people, doing meth, they're lifting weights. They got so many muscles, they move and it looks like gophers running under their skin.

"Still, it was a chance to walk out with my head on or go down fighting. So I'm watching Moses, looking confident and just a little bit contemptuous, using my Elvis smile on them. I have practiced that motherfucker a thousand times in front of a mirror. I know how powerful it is.

"Thing is, this hat I'm wearing, with its high crown, same kind I had then. I got a little automatic pistol clipped in there, then and now. It's just a little homemade thing with a little silencer on it and it shoots two twenty-two rounds, and for it to do any good you got to be close and accurate. It's what we used to call a Saturday Night Special. So this crack team of bikers that searched me and took my larger artillery didn't no more see the gun in my hat than they noticed I got a couple of dark spots on my nuts. I mean, they searched me and left my hat on. Their stupidity that day worked in my favor. And before you worry about those dots on my nuts, it's not cancer, just some natural markings, like a spotted pup."

"Now we can sleep with comfort," I said.

"So the brother, Moses, agrees, and they give us both big ole bowie knives. These were like swords, man. I think they was over twenty inches and wide as my hand, sharp enough to shave with. And into this shed we go. It was about twenty by thirty, which is small to begin with, but when you get in there and the other guy has a knife, it's smaller yet. He got one corner, and I got the other, and as soon as they turned out the light from outside and locked the door, I took off my hat and got the gun out of the little holster in the crown, tossed the hat in his direction. I hear him yell, thinking I touched him, and I could hear him grunting and the knife slashing the air. I got down on my hands and knees, stayed against the wall, and started crawling. His grunting and such had pinpointed him for me. I was close. I tried to see if my eyes would adjust, but it was so dark in there you couldn't find your ass with both hands.

"I bided my time, worried he'd walk up on me, bump into me, and stick that big knife in me. I had my bowie, of course, but I had stuck it in my belt at the back. What I had that gave me the edge was that tiny silenced pistol."

"Didn't know they could put silencers on little guns like that," Leonard said.

"Silencer is built in," Jim Bob said. "It don't come off, and it doesn't really work that well, but then again, it's not a gun makes a lot of noise to begin with. Anyway, I'm creeping around on the floor like a cockroach with a little pistol that feels small in my hand, something I hadn't never used on a human being and feared might not stop a mouse that had had a good breakfast. This guy is going nuts. Screaming at me, saying, 'Say something, cocksucker. Show me how tough you are.'

"I crawled along, and damn if I didn't run up against his legs. I might near blew a turd that was such a surprise. I had figured on where he was, but of course by the time I got that figured he had moved. I grabbed his legs, still clinging to my pistol, pushed my head forward into his knee, and took him down. He sat up, and that knife come around and I heard it whistle just over my head.

"I ran my gun up along his chest so I could put it right up close to his head, cause that little gun has to be right on you to do much good. When I had it under what I figured was his chin, I pulled the trigger. The gun coughed, and it was louder than I counted on, but it didn't sound like gunfire. It sounded like someone letting out his breath real hard. I felt Moses stiffen and fall backwards from where he was sitting, and his head cracked on the concrete floor. I dropped the pistol and got on him and pulled the bowie and went to work. I got hold of his head, pushed it back, and cut his throat, then stabbed the living dog shit out of him. When he was still and not breathing and I was wet with his blood, I felt around till I found where that twenty-two shot went in under his chin, up and into his brain, which I figure was a lucky shot there, that dude's brain having to be about pea size. I felt and cut around his chin with that bowie, so there wasn't no bullet hole visible. I wiped my hands on him, felt around until I found my gun, put it back in my hat, which I also had to hunt around for.

"It was then I realized I had been cut. I don't know how I got cut. I guess Moses still had some juice in him when I took him down and was trying to work that pistol under his chin. Anyway, I was cut in a few places, all of it superficial stuff, my manly beauty not being seriously marred. I figure the scars I got, they just give me a kind of rugged charm."

"You are one of the most delusional fuckers I've ever known," Leonard said.

Jim Bob laughed. "But there I was. Bloody and cut, and Moses lying there leaking in the dark, and I'm thinking, okay, I won."

"You cheated," I said.

"Wouldn't you have?"

"Yep," I said.

"Oh, yeah," Leonard said. "Big-time."

"Thing was, I had won, and they didn't know how I won. I'm thinking, all right, when I open that door they're going to be on me like bears on honey, and it won't matter I won. But there was one door in that shed, and one way out, so I didn't have no choice but to go out of it. I decide, all right, if I'm going to go out that door, I'm going to go out of it with the knife in one hand and have that dead fucking Moses by the collar with the other. And that's what I done. I knocked on the door with the butt of the bowie. They opened it, and I come out with the knife in one hand, dragging Moses with the other. There were a few steps leading up and into that shed, and I bumped Moses's big dead ass on every one of them, dropped him on the ground.

"I said, 'Next.'"

"Always a step too far," I said.

"Can't help myself. But you know what? They let me go. Samson insisted."

"Honor among thieves and murderers," I said. "How refreshing."

"Uh-huh," Jim Bob said. "But he regretted it. One of his boys took a run at me not so long ago, and, well, as you can note by my presence, standing here upright before you, I came out all right. Since then, no trouble. But I don't like him, and like I said, they got long memories, and that honor-among-thieves shit is only if they're in the mood to be honorable or feel they have to appear that way at the moment. But in the middle of the night, when they're considering on things, they frequently have a change of heart."

"What I figure," I said, "by the time we quit listening to you and get around to doing something, it'll be full morning."

"Believe me," Jim Bob said. "There will come a time, if we don't get killed, when you will in memory cherish moments with me like this."

26

We came out of the trees and started down the road then, being watchful, and finally we could hear noise. Men and women laughing and cutting up. We had been using a little penlight Jim Bob was carrying to make our way, but now he shut that off. We stopped and stood in the black night awhile, not talking. We were letting our eyes adjust to the dark as much as possible.

After a few minutes we started traveling again, but it was so dark we had to stay on the road and not go back into the trees. You could hardly see a thing down there in the woods, and the road was only slightly better. The air was full of the stench of something that had died and was decaying, and it was intense. The sound of voices swelled.

In short time we put most of the stink behind us, kept on keeping on. Then we began to hear music, faint at first, but growing louder as we moved forward, loud enough to damn near make your ears bleed. Acid rock from ages gone.

Finally the road emptied itself into a field, and in the field we could see a huge bonfire. It was so large and so bright it was as if the shadows were on fire.

There were about twelve men and twice that number of women

around the fire, which appeared to be fed by railroad ties, dead wood, old car and truck tires. The group was all white. Not exactly folks known for diversity was my guess. The music was coming from some device with real power inside a mobile home near the fire, and not far off were three other mobile homes. There was plywood over spots where windows had once been.

There was a horde of bikes parked out front of the mobile home where the music was coming from, and the door to the home was open. Now and again men and women staggered out or staggered in. As I said, I had counted twelve men in the yard, and twice that many women, but with people going in and out of the home, it was hard to say how many were actually there and how many, if any, were in the other homes. Out to the left was a long row of doghouses inside metal pens. There were ten pens. I didn't see any dogs.

Bright as it was, we decided we could enter back into the tree line that connected with the field and see quite well because of the bonfire. We slipped in among the trees—oaks, pines, and sweet gums. The air was rich with the stink of that fire, the mix of creosote and burning rubber, as well as the sweet smell of the gums and the turpentine-like bite of the pines swaying in the wind.

There was great light from the fire, but as the wind whipped it, it grew greater and flicked and flowed like levitating lava, rose up high against the sky. There were shadows and shapes of people dancing around the fire. I was reminded of the old Tarzan books—where they had dum-dums, which was a kind of wild party of apes with Tarzan himself, dancing and whirling, working themselves into a frenzy.

"Jim Bob," I said, "I don't know if you have enough fingers and toes to keep up with the number of folks out there, but you have enough to know there are only three of us."

"Yeah, that puts them at a disadvantage," Jim Bob said.

Leonard sighed. "Got to agree with Hap, Jim Bob. Those numbers bite the moose."

"Boys, I never had in mind we were going to ride in there with guns blazing. I thought we might catch them at low tide, so to speak. Maybe only a few around, and we could sneak in there like bandits and nab Samson, get his firsthand take on the dealership, folks he's working for. The Big Dog. That don't look like such a good plan now, way things are set up. We can go back, get Marvin in on this, have the three back at the car tell him what they told us, and he can send some cops out here to break this shit up. I bet they find drugs and all manner of illegal stuff. I think these are the kind of boys would steal, don't you?"

"Oh, no, I can't imagine a nice, clean-cut group of folks like that stealing," Leonard said.

Jim Bob said, "Yeah. You're right. Hard to imagine."

"We go to the law, how's it going to go down with us riding around with our friends in the trunk and floorboard?" I asked.

"We made a citizen's arrest. We get all these other biker turds arrested, we can get them off your backs, maybe permanently. If not, we may have to find a way to mess their shit up big-time."

"Weren't you the one that said we couldn't get them all and that we had to worry about them showing up later?" I said.

"I did say that," Jim Bob said. "But I'm feeling more optimistic now, and besides, I don't know what else to do. There's just no easy way to slide in there like I hoped."

About then we heard motorcycles humming, saw headlights from them. We got down low and stayed behind the trees, saw three bikes pass on the road. They were heading toward the compound; I guess you could call it that.

Guy on the lead bike was so big he looked like a bear riding a motorized tricycle with the seat stuffed up his ass. Bearded, broad-shouldered, hulking, knees bunched up high because of his size, wearing what looked to be a leather cap. Under the cap his long, dark hair snapped in the wind. He probably weighed three hundred pounds and was at least six feet seven without the cap. I noted he had a very large scabbard on his hip in which was placed a very large knife—a bowie, most likely. Behind the bikes came an El Camino, one of those car-truck combinations, this one being one of the last in the model run, made in the eighties. A man was driving. A woman sat in the middle. Another man was on the passenger side. I was already feeling nervous, but now I felt really uncomfortable, like something with a beak and tentacles had parked itself inside my head.

When the truck passed, a couple other bikes behind that, Jim Bob said what I expected: "Big dude on the lead bike, that's Samson."

"You say his brother was the same size?" Leonard said.

"Moses was the baby brother. Not quite as big as Samson. But it would have been a difference mostly of who had the most change in his pocket."

"Good thing you had that pistol," Leonard said.

"Why I always carry it now. Experience. But a guy size of Samson and Moses, you got to place the shot just right, otherwise the bullet might bounce off."

27

Having found out where the base camp was, all we had to do was go back to the car, take the boys in the car back to Marvin, and have the law descend on the place. That was the plan. But, as is the usual situation with anything that has to do with me and Leonard, things went wrong.

Creeping back on the road, staying close to the trees, ears cocked for bikes or cars, we were hustling along pretty good, and then those cocked ears of ours got filled with sounds.

More bikes.

We edged off the road again and hunkered down behind some trees. That dead smell was strong now, strong enough to gag a vulture. The bikes, two this time, went by on the road. When they were past, Jim Bob said, "I think we can use the penlight if we flash close to the ground. Think the Red Bitch is over there."

Jim Bob pointed.

That was about where I thought it was, too. Me and Leonard were both pretty damn good in the woods. We had grown up living in the country and knew our way among the trees and bees, as they used to say. It was towns and cities I had the most trouble navigating.

Going along, the stench growing stronger and stronger, my gag reflex causing me to heave a little, we came to a large ditch, cut there naturally by time and runoff water. There was a little scummy water in the ditch. We could see that when Jim Bob flashed his light down there. But there was plenty of something else.

The decaying bodies of dogs. Dozens of them. Flies, startled by the light, rose up in a nauseating buzz, and the dim moonlight between the trees filled with their collected darkness, and then the flies split and the dull light came through again.

Most of the dogs were of the pit bull persuasion, full-blood or mixed. Some of the bodies were fresh, but most were not. The less fresh ones were terribly ripe, bony, and decayed.

"The motherfuckers," Leonard said. "They fight them, then toss the dead ones in this ditch."

"They don't always die from the fight," Jim Bob said. "A dog loses, they figure it'll never be good in a fight again, so they shoot it in the head to get rid of it or just to show it who's boss."

"I'd like to show them who's boss," Leonard said. "Jesus. How can those pieces of shit think of themselves as human?"

"A monkey thinks more profoundly than those hunks of crap do," Jim Bob said.

While we stood there, looking down on that sorry sight, our noses plugged with that dead smell, I felt the uncomfortable thought I had felt earlier when I saw the El Camino go by with its passengers. The thought started to float to the surface like a corpse floating up from the depths of the sea. I thought again about the woman I had seen in the pickup. I had a sudden flash. At first it was just a passing flash, and then it came back and swelled into a thought that was more substantial. I said, "Goddamn it. Woman in the El Camino. It was Frank."

"You sure?" Leonard said.

"I think so. I mean, now that I think about it, it looked like her. I saw her right off, but it didn't register. She shouldn't have been in the truck. She should be tucked tight at our office."

"They found her somehow," Jim Bob said.

"I can't be sure," I said.

Leonard said, "I say we get in the Bitch, roll down the windows, and drive that motherfucker right into the midst of them, shooting the shit out of the place and packing Frank up and taking her out of there."

"Need I add it would turn out bad and not in our favor, and we might end up shooting her," Jim Bob said. "Remember it was you guys telling me about the finger count. They are many. We are three."

"Here's a little something I just thought of," I said. "What if she called them? What if she's in cahoots? What if she's the Big Dog?"

"There's a thought," Jim Bob said. "I don't like that thought, but it's something. She got on my side of the game pretty quick. I'll tell you about that later."

That's when a roar went up from back at the camp. We were a goodly distance away, but the sound of that roar was heard clearly.

None of us said a word, didn't discuss it, but we automatically started easing back toward the sound, which had been replaced by hooting and yelling and laughing.

When we got back where we were before, the trees near the clearing, the fire was blazing higher and it lit the place up almost as bright as day.

Like ants, the bikers were moving into a wad around something, and since the pickup was parked near where they were gathering, I had an idea what it was.

"That doesn't look like a welcome-home committee," Leonard said.

"Thinking on it," Jim Bob said, "I can't see Frank coming out here to party. She's a little too high-class."

I had my palm against a sweet gum. I looked up. The bottom limb was well above my head. I put my shotgun on the ground, said to Leonard, "Brother, give me a boost."

Leonard put his shotgun down, cupped his hands. I put my foot in them, and he lifted me up. I grabbed the lowest limb and pulled myself higher into the tree. I could damn sure feel those extra pounds on me.

Normally I'd have been up that tree like a young squirrel. That night I was a plump old squirrel, and less spry.

I climbed up higher, going slow. When I found a limb high enough and big enough for me to stand on, I did that and put my hand against the tree for support. It wasn't a great view, but I could see who was who.

It was Frank. She was in the middle of a circle made up of the biker gang, men and women. For her, things didn't look so good.

28

The circle closed around Frank. She was being shoved, felt, and snatched from all sides. Even the women were giving her hell. Pack mentality, wolves with a single lamb, and the wolves were hungry.

I started down. Leonard grabbed my legs when I dangled from the lowest limb, helped me onto the ground.

"It's her," I said. "And she's not here for a hootenanny. She's meat. Someone gave her to this bunch for whatever reason, and I think they are planning a series of festivities that she won't enjoy."

"How many of them did you see?" Jim Bob asked.

"I didn't count them," I said. "But it's more than before, and not just the ones who rode in a while ago. Trailers must have been full. I think every man in that group has plans to wet his wick in Frank's handmade doohickey, and the women might have something special in mind as well. There will be no get-well-soon cards."

"That clears up our plan," Leonard said. "We go in."

"It's already too late to help her," Jim Bob said.

"I think it's only going to get later," Leonard said.

We gathered our weapons and started hurrying back to the Cadillac. It took a full fifteen to twenty minutes, tearing through the brush. The roar of those beasts back at the compound filled the night.

. . .

In the car, Jim Bob driving, me riding shotgun, Leonard in the back, we took off.

"We have the element of surprise," Jim Bob said as he drove the Red Bitch onto the road and gunned it. He had yet to turn on the headlights.

"More like the elephant of surprise," I said. "I think they're going to hear us coming."

"Then we'll give them plenty of noise," Jim Bob said. He had laid his shotgun on the floorboard, at my feet. He had his revolver in his lap.

"Can you shoot left-handed?" I said.

"Hell, I had to, I could shoot left-footed and reload with my dick."

No wane in confidence there. I had to say that for him.

"You think the boys in the trunk are enjoying the ride?" I said.

"I hope not," Leonard said. "The boy here on the floorboard is a little wiggly."

"They should all go 'Whee,' " Jim Bob said.

"They're gagged," Leonard said.

"Oh, yeah," Jim Bob said.

"Hap," Leonard said.

"Yeah."

"Brother, in case things go wrong, it has been quite a ride."

"Oh, yeah," I said. I jacked a load into the twelve-gauge and prepared to hang my body out the window. My hands were shaking.

"Can you actually see the road?" I asked Jim Bob.

"Not really," Jim Bob said. "I'm guesstimating."

Jim Bob let out with a cackle and floored the Red Bitch.

Man, that motor did howl.

29

Situations like that, it's like you and time are frozen in amber.

And then the amber breaks, and you're not frozen, but everything moves for a time in slow motion. If it's your first time or two doing something like that, going into the midst of danger and uncertainty, you have tunnel vision. You see what's in front of you as if looking down the length of a tunnel. Everything to the right and left of you is a black wall. But if you've been there before, it's not that way. On some level, like the samurai of old, you have accepted your death. You are neither there to win or to lose. You are there to be in the moment. Things may be slow, but they are viewed wider with experience, not inside that fearful tunnel of the neophyte. That's how it was with me. I could see clearly. I could feel clearly.

I might add right here that I say fuck the samurai. I planned to win. I planned to go home. And I knew that plan had about as much chance as a slug in a salt block. I knew, too, I had survived worse situations. And as that thought galloped through my head, another less pleasant thought showed up.

Sometimes your luck runs out.

So on we went, the car seemingly hanging in time, moving slowly in my mind's eye, but in actuality barreling down on that crew at a rate of at least sixty miles an hour. We came off the road and hit the pasture with a bumping motion that jarred my teeth. The Red Bitch went hopping over that rough ground like a metallic rabbit, and then everyone in the camp turned to look at us just as Jim Bob hit the headlights and put the pedal to the floor. The pasture in front of us was flooded with gold light. I glanced at the speedometer. I could see it because Jim Bob had turned on the lights and the dash light had lit up. The Bitch jumped to seventy and was growling as the needle on the speedometer swung wide to the right.

Jim Bob hit the horn and didn't let it go, guided the car by using his other hand to precariously hang on to the suicide knob. If that thing snapped we'd end up in a ball of hot metal and shredded tires rolling along the countryside.

I was partly out the window now, and Leonard was hanging out in the same way from the back driver's side window.

Now, let me tell you, a big red Cadillac bearing down on your ass will do one of two things. It will cause you to stick to your spot like a tree, or you will attempt to spring away like a deer. The ones who stick to the ground like a tree are not going to turn out well, and the ones who spring away like a deer, well, truth is, a deer is quick, but a big red Cadillac going over seventy miles an hour is far quicker.

When the Red Bitch hit into them we discovered that the old adage is wrong. Men can fly. So can women and motorcycles. Jim Bob hit the brakes as we came up on them, but not completely; just a firm tap and a turn of the wheel. We slid into that circle and hit three or four of those fuckers and knocked them into the air, slammed a bike so that it went skidding past Frank as close as a foot. Had our luck been off by a hair, had the bike hit her, we could have just backed out and yelled a polite "Sorry" and gone home.

Way we hit caused a stocky woman with short ragged hair to do a sort of cartwheel that whirled her past Frank and a big man in the middle who was clutching Frank's shoulder. Frank was wearing only a bra and fragments of blue jeans, which had been cut or ripped off of her.

Frank and the man, the mighty Samson himself, watched the biker bitch twirl by, performing a dynamic cartwheel. Samson seemed calm, like a paying customer observing a circus trick. I hung out the window, fired the shotgun, and blew a tire out on the El Camino. Leonard slithered out the window on his side and blew the leg out from under a big blue-jean-wearing guy with no shirt and a belly big enough to have contained a few cases of beer and a Thanksgiving turkey. The man's kneecap went flying out of his torn pants, and then he was on the ground. Those blue jeans were ruined.

"Oh, goddamn it," the man said. I could hear him clearly as I hung out the window, and then his forehead went to the ground and his shot-up leg extended behind him. He had passed out from pain and shock. The air smelled of burning rubber, and it made my eyes water. I wondered how they stood it, standing near that fire. Besides, the night was too warm for a fire. It was too warm for a cup of coffee. I guess devils like those don't mind a little heat.

All of a sudden I was out of the car and into the crowd, which was no longer a circle but instead a clashing mass of flesh. A big woman next to me, wearing a bandanna with bits of hair hanging out from under it, reached for a little gun that was hanging out of her baggy pants pocket. I hit her with the stock of the shotgun hard enough to see teeth fly. I was all out of chivalry. I would have gunned down Minnie Mouse had she pulled a pistol, a pocket knife, or a too-large comb.

I heard one of the shotguns go off behind me and didn't realize until later it had been a warning shot by Leonard, a blast over the crowd's head.

I had the shotgun to my shoulder, and I knew there were people closing in behind me. A shotgun barked again and I heard someone scream and then there was a rustling as people ran for it, knowing now we weren't fucking around. I walked right up and took Frank by the elbow, said, "Come with me."

Samson let her go. I turned with her then, knowing Jim Bob and Leonard had my back going in and had it as I walked out. I pushed through a few bikers who wanted to be tough but were a little weak in the knees from our arrival; I could smell shit where some of them had crapped themselves.

Directing Frank to the car, I noticed that the Bitch's front tires were pretty deep in grooves of dirt they had plowed. I was hoping in the back of my mind the Bitch would back out of there without a snag, because if she didn't, our moment of shock and awe was over with, and all that was left was us being thrown in that ditch with those poor dead dogs. Our elephant of surprise was near over.

Frank got in on the backseat passenger side of the Bitch faster than the snap of a whip. "There's a man here," she said.

"Put your feet on him." I said.

Jim Bob, who was holding a shotgun, tossed it through the window onto the front seat, got in behind the wheel. He had left the motor running. In the car lights the crowd had begun to clutter up like moths before a porch light. Leonard and I stood with our shotguns, pointing them, moving them from side to side, trying to take it all in, hoping no one moved. It was so quiet you could have heard houseflies fucking.

Leonard got in the backseat, closed the door, and dangled himself out the open window with the shotgun. I stayed where I was for the moment. If we lived through this, I would tell Leonard later that with him hanging out the back window he reminded me of a black Labrador with a shotgun.

Samson moved forward, close to the car. He yelled out, "Jim Bob, I'll get you, you son of a bitch. You are mine."

Jim Bob stuck his head and arm out the window, pistol in his left hand. He said, "Samson, it is so nice to see you."

He shot Samson in the throat. Samson dropped to his knees as if in need of sudden prayer, then rocked forward on his face.

Jim Bob said. "Hap. Get in the fucking car."

I swung the shotgun from side to side, but no one asked for a load of buckshot. I got in, and before I could close the door, the Red Bitch was in reverse and we were flying out of there backwards, spinning dirt so hard it flew up and over the front of the car. By then the biker assholes had their brains back and had found guns. Bullets popped around us. One, a rifle shot, I'm sure, hit the windshield and went through it like a hot knife through butter. It zipped between Frank and Leonard and took out the back windshield. The front windshield merely had a hole in it, but even as we bounced along that pasture in reverse, Jim Bob looking over the backseat, eyes squinted, trying to see what was behind us in the red taillights, the front windshield collapsed like a Baptist deacon's morals at a strip club.

We were really being fired at now. One of the headlights went out as we backed up, and I could hear little impacts as shots popped the Caddy, but it didn't slow us and we didn't lose a tire, and none of us gathered up a bullet.

Jim Bob, soon as those tires hit the road, jabbed the brake and whirled the wheel, still holding on to that stupid suicide knob, and all of a sudden we were turned completely around and roaring down the blacktop, shots snapping in the air and some of them still hitting the Red Bitch. But she kept running, and away we went, our visibility based on one headlight. There was a kind of rumbling from the back of the car. Something was rolling around in the trunk.

Oh, yeah. Now I remembered.

30

The Red Bitch was rocking along, that one remaining headlight punching the night like a Cyclops with a heat beam. Through the busted-out windshield the air was smashing into us like a fist. The little hula girl and the plastic Jesus stuck on the dashboard of the car did the shimmy-shimmy-shake in overdrive. I think even Jesus was worried how all this was going to come out. My hands were trembling.

Jim Bob saw a little cutoff into the woods, about bicycle wide, shot past it, braked hard, burned rubber, backed into it, and kept going in reverse. Limbs scratched the Caddy, bent the aerial. Jim Bob bounced the Bitch along quite a ways until the limbs grew closer and began to brush over the car as thick as shadows. He turned off the one remaining headlight.

"Let's get out of the car," Jim Bob said.

We all had shotguns with us when we got out, except Frank, of course, who paused long enough before getting out to wipe her feet on Wishbone. Got to stay tidy, even if you're barely wearing pants.

Outside the car we'd at least have a fighting chance. We moved to the back of the Caddy, pushing through the tight mesh of limbs and brush. There was tapping going on in the trunk. There was a bullet hole in the trunk.

Jim Bob snapped the stock of his shotgun down on the trunk, said, "Quiet in there."

The tapping ceased.

"At least one of them is alive," Jim Bob said.

"I'm sorry," Frank said. "This is all my fault."

She stood there shaking in fear, dressed only in the fragments of her jeans, bra, and shoes.

"I was thinking it might be," Leonard said. "I was thinking that a lot."

"Save it for now," Jim Bob said. "I'm pissed off enough right now without having to hear something stupid. We'll hear stupid over a cup of coffee or some such later."

I don't know exactly how long we stood there at the back of the Bitch, but finally we heard the roaring of motorcycle motors. I wondered if the burned-rubber smoke and smell was still in the air, that they'd notice there was probably half the Caddy's tires on the road out there.

"They come down this way," Jim Bob said, "is it every man for himself?"

"Nope. Musketeer way," Leonard said. "All for one and one for all."

"Suits me," I said.

"Done," Jim Bob said.

"I'm out," Frank said. "They show up, I'm into the woods like a goddamn rabbit."

The roar of the motorcycle engines grew louder, and then we saw headlights from the bikes striking the road. The bikes came flying by. One, two, three. After a bit I lost count. But a lot of bikes shot along that road and past us.

We stayed there for a while, not moving. Then Jim Bob took his keys, found the right one by lighting a match, and opened the trunk. He held the match in such a way we could see inside. No one had turned to smoke and slipped through the cracks. A bullet that had gone through the trunk had passed above them. Later, Jim Bob would tell us he found that it had passed through the trunk, split the backseat between Leonard and Frank, and had killed the radio on the dash. As for the two in the trunk and the one lying on the floorboard, they were all alive but un-comfortable.

We waited a bit. No one came back for us. We pulled Wishbone out, dragged him to the back of the car, and laid him out on the ground.

Jim Bob reached in the trunk and pulled a little bag out. Leonard and I picked up Wishbone and put him in the trunk with them. Tight fit. We bumped some heads pushing the trunk lid down.

"I figure they're all right for a few more hours," Jim Bob said.

"They'll get pee-pee in the trunk of your car," Leonard said. "May have already done it."

Jim Bob opened the bag from the trunk and got a dark western shirt out of it. He gave it to Frank. "Put that on."

She did. It fell down over her thighs, giving her a little more dignity than before.

Another twenty minutes passed, and it was a good thing we waited, for during that time a couple more bikes roared along, having gotten into the mix late. After a while, though, we decided we'd pull out. We did that and went along in the direction the bikes had taken, and then when we got off the back roads and onto the main highway, we tooled right on into town. No police pulled us over for having one headlight, a broken aerial, and three thugs in the trunk.

"They could be waiting at your place," Jim Bob said. "The three in the trunk know where you live; so may the rest of them."

"Good point," I said. "And since Frank is with us, I'm going to guess they know where the office is."

"They do," Frank said. "I fucked up."

Frank started to cry. I wondered if she cried like that when she was a man. I was her right then, I would have cried. Hell, I wanted to cry, and I wasn't her.

31

Well," I said, "at least one of the bikers out there is dead for sure, unless he has been resurrected. Maybe more. Depends on how hard the car hit them and if the guy without the kneecap died. The one I know is dead is named Samson. Jim Bob said his last name is House. Like in Son House, the blues guy. Jim Bob shot him in the throat."

"Ah, shit," Marvin said. "Is there anything you didn't do? I mean, you might as well add you got through shooting folks, you dug up a corpse, fucked it, and named it Dixie."

"I can honestly say we didn't do that. We named it Ethel."

I was sitting on the bed in a motel room talking to Marvin on my cell phone. We were all in that room, us and the biker shits.

We were lucky that night. Lucky to have pulled through and lucky the motel was mostly empty. The only gun we decided to take with us inside the motel was Jim Bob's pistol. Jim Bob had plunked down in a chair by a desk that was under a TV screen mounted on the wall and laid his gun hand across his knee. Leonard stretched out on the bed, his back against the headboard. There was a table with chairs, and Frank sat there. I found myself checking her out. I felt funny about that. An old East Texas boy studying her curves, trying to imagine what she had looked like as a man. We sat all three thugs on the floor with their backs

202 • JOE R. LANSDALE

against the wall. Wishbone and Bad Leg complained, the third man had still yet to say a word.

When I finished up with Marvin, he said, "I hate you guys. See you in thirty. Hey, you aren't going to shoot anyone else or burn anything down in the next thirty minutes, are you?"

"We have plans for a time of solitude," I said.

"Good. I need to shower and have some coffee and eat a bite. Make it forty-five minutes to an hour. Again, can you stay out of trouble that long?"

"I think so," I said.

When we were through talking, I told them Marvin was on his way.

"Oh, good," Jim Bob said. "I'm sure he'll be thrilled to see us and get more details."

"Who the fuck is Marvin?" Wishbone said. We had removed their gags but left their hands tied, though we had only fastened down Wishbone's unbroken arm by tying it to his belt. The broken one we put in a sling we made with a bath towel. They were all three at a point where they couldn't have outwrestled a dying frog in a best two out of three, but we kept their hands tied anyway.

"Someone you won't like," Leonard said.

I said, "I was pretty thorough with Marvin, don't you think? I didn't tell him about the dead dogs because I didn't want him to be really mad. He thinks we should just take these dudes off in the woods somewhere and shoot them in the head and let the buzzards sort them out. Oh, yeah, he said if we decide to do that, we got to get rid of the gun."

The thugs sitting against the wall gave me a look and shifted on their asses.

"Nah, he didn't say that," I said. "Just fucking with you."

"It's an idea, though," Leonard said.

"Oh, man," Frank said. "I really messed up."

"Hold that thought," Jim Bob said. "We'll come back to it in short order. Right now I'm still as mad as I want to be."

We allowed them to go to the toilet one at a time with the door open and Jim Bob standing there with the revolver. "Jesus," Jim Bob said to Wishbone. "Do you have to shit now? I don't want to see that."

"Think I like doing this? I'm modest."

"Just get it done," Jim Bob said. "Oh, man. I'm going to have to light some matches for sure. Maybe get a fucking blowtorch. Have you been eating something dead off the highway?"

"How am I going to wipe my ass with my hand tied and one arm broke?" Wishbone said. "You doing it for me?"

"Not likely," Jim Bob said.

He ended up untying Wishbone's hand. Wishbone took his time in there. He had really been saving up. The other two, thank goodness, were quite content with number ones.

When everyone had their bathroom trip finished, and all had washed their hands, using soap, as Jim Bob instructed, and when Wishbone was tied up again, we lined them up against the wall and had them sit as before. We let them keep the gags off. They promised to be good boys.

The one with the injured leg was starting to look bad. He had beads of sweat on his forehead, and his lips had grown pale. His leg was outstretched and had swollen bad enough Jim Bob had to cut the fellow's pants open to accommodate the swelling.

"Can we order a pizza?" Wishbone said. "I'm hungry enough to suck shit out a pig's ass."

"Eeew," Frank said.

"Would you like us to rent you a movie, too?" I said.

"That would be nice," Wishbone said. "But nothing violent."

"You're showing your spine, ain't you?" Jim Bob said.

Wishbone shrugged. You'd have thought we were all old buddies, way he acted.

"Can I bum a cigarette, then?" he said.

"Nobody here smokes," I said. "Jim Bob just carries matches."

"I wouldn't mind taking you outside and setting you on fire, though," Leonard said.

204 • JOE R. LANSDALE

We ended up ordering a couple of large pizzas anyway. Hold the pig shit.

Forty-five minutes passed, then an hour, and still no Marvin.

About an hour later there was a light knock at the door. It could have been Marvin, the pizza, or the bikers having figured out where we were.

I glanced through the peephole.

Marvin.

I let him in. He looked around the room, settled his eyes on Frank for a moment, trying to figure who she was and what the hell she was doing there. He looked at the three men sitting on the floor. He grinned at Wishbone, said, "Jared Fonteneau. My man. How's the old hammer dangling?"

"It's waiting in the toolbox until needed," Wishbone, a.k.a. Jared, said.

"And Thomas Peers. Or should I call you Hopalong Dumbass? Man, you don't look so good."

"Leg's fucked up," Thomas said. "I could walk a little an hour ago, now I can't."

"I can see that."

"I need a fucking doctor. A nurse. A goddamn big-ass dog with a barrel of brandy hung under its neck. Something, man. I'm in pain here. I'm starting to get way past not feeling so good."

"You do in fact look as if you might be moving past your expiration date," Marvin said.

Marvin moved his gaze to the man who was yet to speak. "And Mute Boy Gavin. Tongue hasn't grown back, has it?" Then to us: "Mute Boy there. He don't say much because he can't. He was five his mother decided he talked too much, and it was screwing up her crack high, so she used a pair of pliers and some pruning shears and took to his tongue."

Mute Boy gave Marvin the finger.

"He has, however," Marvin said, "acquired some ability with sign language."

32

The pizza came. The pizza boy looked like he just got his driver's license.

Leonard gave the pizza boy money, said, "You took long enough. You have to go to Italy to get it?"

"It's a busy night," the pizza boy said.

"I'm so busy you're not getting a tip," Leonard said, taking the pizza and closing the door with his foot.

I got up and went out and gave the pizza boy a tip. I said, "It's all right. He found out today that his penile implant isn't going to work."

"Oh," the pizza boy said and went away.

Wishbone said, "I told you no onions."

"Shut up," Leonard said.

Everyone ate, onions or no onions, though Bad Leg was good for only one piece. He really was starting to fade. Wishbone was actually starting to be jovial, even cracked a few jokes. I think he was a little delirious from the injured arm and all that had happened to him. He told us a limerick—not that we asked for it:

There was an old hermit named Dave
Who kept a dead whore in a cave.

He said, I'll admit
She does smell a bit,
But look at the money I save.

On that note, me and Marvin went out of the motel and took a ride in his car. I got picked because Leonard didn't want to do it, and that was that. As we cruised, I told Marvin what I had already told him. I explained about Frank. At least all the stuff I knew, which was pretty much that she had showed up with Jim Bob, been nabbed, been rescued, had enjoyed pizza with us in the room, and had said little to nothing since we pulled her away from the bikers and the party in her honor.

"Frank was a man?" he said. "That's hard to believe."

"I try to be cool about it," I said. "You know, moving with the times, but the whole thing jacks me around some. Odd thing is she looks damn good. I mean, now that he's a she she does. Am I saying that right? Shit. You know what I mean."

"She's got good legs, and I like the way that shirt hung on her, minidress-style. I saw her, I felt my dick wiggle. Don't tell anyone."

"Lips are sealed. By the way, you took long enough to show up."

"The missus felt friendly. She doesn't always feel friendly. I thought I ought to take what was offered."

"That explains a couple of minutes," I said. "What about the rest?"

"You are not nice," Marvin said.

"I will say this, you don't need any outside dick wiggling if there's wiggling at home."

"I agree," he said.

No use denying it. Men, even honorable ones, can think like dogs. There's an old joke about a guy that's been without loving so long, a friend takes him into the woods and suggests he fuck a knothole in a tree. The other guy says, "Does it have to be just that tree?"

I told Marvin how those motorcycle shits were most likely out there looking for us and that if they found us it wouldn't be good, us no longer having the elephant of surprise on them.

"Don't know how you two do it," Marvin said. "You could start trouble at a kid's birthday party. And Jim Bob, too. You two and him, that's a disaster in the making. It's the *Hindenburg* and the *Titanic* and the Great Hurricane of 1900 on Galveston Island all rolled into one big mess. Look here, Hap. Seems to me this is some bad poo-poo. Getting you out of it, I'm not sure it's worth anything to me."

"I can understand that. New job and all."

"Guys came and attacked you in your yard, that's easy to make self-defense. But you put them in the trunk of a car, took them for a ride while you went out there after the others, shot and killed one, at least. Blew a kneecap off another and knocked some folks around with the car. That shit there, that's hard to explain."

"Knowing their location was a self-defense move, way we saw it."

"Making that play so anyone believes it, that'll take some work, buddy."

"I know. But that's all we intended. The other, rescuing Frank—that just happened. We had to do it. No red-blooded American would have done any less. I think we could ride the hero horse with a jury, it came to it."

"We might have to dress it up a little, buy it some new shoes, but it might work."

We rode up North Street and on out of town, along the highway, where the trees were thicker. Marvin turned around in the driveway of a liquor store that was oddly placed out in the middle of nowhere, then we started back south, driving slow. We didn't talk for a while. Marvin was considering.

"Tell you what," Marvin said. "I can go in and talk around things a little, see how things hang, so to speak. But if it doesn't hang so well, I got to throw you boys to the dogs. Maybe I can do it so you only spend most of the rest of your life in prison, and I'll have them put you in with some nice man won't hurt you too much if you call him Mama."

"That's not much relief."

"What the fuck you expect? Jesus, Hap. Look here, what we'll do is we'll take those three in, get that one with the messed-up leg to the hospital, get a cast for the one with the broken arm. In the meantime, I'm going to call the sheriff, see if he can get his men out there in the county. I can probably have a few of our local cops go out there, too, without there being some big jurisdiction battle. Thing is, we'll check the place out. We'll check your house and Leonard's place. Where the hell is he staying now?"

I told him.

"Shit," Marvin said. "Brett. Where is she?"

"A motel somewhere," I said.

"Good."

I decided to tell him about Chance.

"Man, that would be something. A grown daughter. Think of all the money on formula and diapers you saved. And there's that prom-dress thing."

"Leonard said pretty much the same thing."

"That's because he's a thinker, Hap. He's the thinker of you two. That prom-dress thing, by the way. Wouldn't believe what something like that costs, and for one night. There's also weddings and such, and you have to deal with son-in-laws, and ex-son-in-laws if they divorce, and they got kids, it's a real fucking stinker. Worse, you get other in-laws, and some of them are no treat. I know. I been through it."

"If she is my daughter, maybe I can still catch the marriage part, the grandkids, the angry ex-son-in-laws, and the shitty in-laws."

"Being a father is very rewarding, except when it isn't. And then there's being a grandparent—same thing. That can be great, and it can suck. But then you remember Gadget and how that went?"

I did. She was Marvin's granddaughter. Real name Julia. Nickname Gadget. Me and Leonard had once rescued her from some drug dealers. As well as from herself. She seemed to be doing much better these days. Had married to what I understood was a pretty good guy with a handful of college degrees and some family money. They had moved off to Wyoming, where they both ended up working in real estate.

Marvin drove us back to the motel, having called some law on our way back. When we got there a city cop had already arrived, and right behind him came an ambulance. People were poking out of doors and standing on the landing watching Jared and Mute Boy being loaded in the cop car. Bad Leg was fading, so he got placed in an ambulance and driven away fast with lights and sirens.

When the cops and ambulance had gone away, Marvin stood out in the lot by his car talking to me and Leonard and Jim Bob. Frank was in the room.

"You could have had the cops come without lights and sirens," I said. "It makes us stand out like sore thumbs."

"Truth is, I wanted for it to be a big to-do. That way it looks like we mean business and that we've brought in some real desperadoes. That part could be good for you, being involved with bringing in these three. Truth is, these guys aren't so tough, and I think if I put the screws to them a little, they'll speak in tongues I ask them to."

"You sound a bit more optimistic about our chances than you did earlier," I said.

"I've been thinking on it," Marvin said. "And I got an idea or two. I'll put a couple of cops at your place for a few days, Hap, until I can sort things out. You might want to stay away from the office, and Leonard, you shouldn't go home. I hate to bring it up, don't know how things are between you and John, but he shouldn't show up there, either."

"Don't worry about John," Leonard said. "I changed the locks with extreme prejudice. May that motherfucker go with Jesus and Mary and the Holy Ghost and the young Casper."

"Just stick with Hap," Marvin said. "And Jim Bob, no use talking to you, as you'll do what you want. In the long run, so will these two. I could have made friends with quieter, more agreeable people, I guess."

"But you wouldn't have all the excitement we bring to your life," Jim Bob said.

"That's sort of what I meant," Marvin said.

"I can tell you this," Jim Bob said. "I leave here, I'm going to take my now wreck of a car back to Houston and have it fixed up so that it shines like a newborn fawn. You need me for something else, I'll come back. Give me a call. Hell, I got my sneak-around cars and my old wrecks at home, so I'll come back a little quieter and a little less shiny."

"All right, we got one last thing before we call it a night and I find out if you boys are going to jail. Explain to me about Frank. Got the general business already, but I got a feeling there has been a new portfolio added. Hap only knew so much."

"Tell you what," Jim Bob said. "Let's the four of us retire to the fine living arrangements of this cheap-ass motel, sit with Frank, and me and her will sort you out on that new portfolio. It's a doozy."

33

I don't have a comb, makeup, or anything," Frank said.

We were all in the motel room. I was starting to come down off my action buzz, beginning to feel tired. The pizza had not settled well with me. I needed an antacid. It felt like a dogfight was going on in my belly.

"You look fine," I said.

"Thank you," she said.

"Yeah, you're all right," Marvin said. "Way you look isn't what I'm concerned with here."

He looked at me, remembering full well his comment about the shirt she was wearing.

I smiled at him.

Marvin cleared his throat. "I got some of the story, what Hap and Leonard know, not what you and Jim Bob know. What I want to know is why Apocalypse on Wheels put the nab on you. How do you figure in this story, front to back? Tell it straight. It might mean the difference in you having to wear an orange jumpsuit and share a cell with Big Bertha, or spending lazy weekends at home with a beer and a vibrator."

"That's just vulgar," Frank said.

"I'm up when I should be sleeping, and I'm going to guess you are involved in what I like to refer to as nefarious fucking shit, so don't get holy on me."

Frank nodded. "Jim Bob came to see me, lying about wanting to buy a car. Almost fooled me. But I have a kind of radar, like with you two and Cason, who, though a dreamy piece of meat, I figured was in with you guys, me being able to radar things, which is why I have the job. Though I got to tell you, that stuff about the petunias and screwing the old folks sort of had me going for a moment, and I almost thought Hap here might have patents on sex toys. Bigger the lie, easier it is to believe. Well, truth is, that was too big a lie."

"Get to the backbone of it," Marvin said.

"Jim Bob came to the dealership, told me his name was something or other—"

"Tommy Jasons," Jim Bob said. "It's a name I use now and again, even have an identity established online, a past, whole shooting match, right down to my shoe size."

"Jim Bob was very convincing, but I had some small doubts, an itch at the back of my mind, and after he left, after I told him I could put him in a car and a vagina, I looked him up—or, rather, I looked up Tommy Jasons—on the Internet. Did that, I knew I was being scammed. Never scam a scammer. Guy Jim Bob hired to build his past has a certain method for building those sites, a certain look. He changed them up, of course, and he was good. But I saw plenty of things he did for our own business. Pasts he had built. I recognized his style. No matter how differently he approached those sites, constructed those pasts for certain people, he had signatures that I recognized, same as a fingerprint. I knew him personally, too. Called him up, got it confirmed, found out Tommy Jasons was Jim Bob Luke. That's when I looked up Jim Bob, read about him and his agency. He didn't have a photo there, but as I said, I knew it was him. Saw what he did, private investigator. I did a bit more research, decided he was exactly what I needed to get my ass out of a crack. I called him on the Tommy Jasons number, told him my situation."

"Which I'm still guessing at," Marvin said. "And this guy creates false identities. Going to need to know more about him. Sounds big-time illegal."

"Here's something cute," Jim Bob said. "He is better known as Weasel."

"Oh, shit," Leonard said.

"Yep," Jim Bob said, pulling a toothpick from the band of his hat, sticking it in his mouth. "He is in fact a weasel. I didn't know he was your man until Frank told me. That makes some things fit together, don't it?"

"Like fingers in a glove," I said.

"There's a lot of lawbreaking going on among friends here," Marvin said. "I can't like that too much, you know. And I'm a cop. Not a game-show participant. I'm not here to guess what the fuck is going on. Tell me straight out and avoid taking the long path to the rabbit hole."

"I'll get there," Frank said.

"Yes, but will you arrive by Shetland pony?" Marvin said.

"When I saw that site, I called Weasel and asked him about it, about Jim Bob's connection. He didn't know Jim Bob was connected, but he figured it all pretty quick, told me he had to lay some bad words down about me to you boys, but nothing that really got me in trouble, just some smoke-screen stuff."

"Was any of what he told us true?" Leonard asked. "Like that stuff about the Canceler?"

"The Canceler is true, though I haven't heard anything about the company using him in a while. I never had anything to do with that. I've never seen him, only heard of him. I was a figurehead at the dealership. I do the front-end work. When a deal is set, others take it from there. I know cars and peddling ass, but the blackmail stuff, that came from on high. I didn't have anything to do with it."

"But you knew what was going on."

"Got set up by someone else. Not me."

"Who?" Marvin asked.

"Never met them. Didn't want to. Car company is just one head of the hydra. It's hard to know which head is in charge. I went with the blackmail because I was getting paid extra, but to tell the truth, I didn't see any harm in it. Men they blackmailed were mostly entitled shits cheating on their wives, talking false about family values at community meetings and political rallies. They had money. Plenty of it. It wouldn't hurt them to let go of some of it, but then things started changing. They got tougher. A mark didn't go for the blackmail, or someone got too far out of line in some way or another, they brought in the Canceler. It wasn't like that when I started; that kind of too-tough business wasn't the way then. Things shifted. First a little, then a lot. It got grittier. Not just the blackmail but money laundering. They'd go to one of the rich guys, one of the girls would, or one of the men who was servicing some rich woman, and say, 'Hey, I got this money, couple hundred thousand, and I need it to sort of find its way into the system without going through normal banking channels.' Rich folks always knew someone who knew someone, and they'd get the deed done. Next thing you knew, FBI was on them."

"FBI?" Marvin said. "Damn, call me a fart and paint me green."

"Top of the game, someone giving information to the FBI as confidential informers. That made them paid informants, and it gave them a lot of liberty as well as a lot of money when it was a high-profile case. FBI wanted to close cases more than they wanted someone running a prostitution ring. They wanted it bad enough to turn their backs on the prostitution, blackmail, and even a lot of the thug work. That included the Canceler. They just greased the CI with olive oil and let him slip through the cracks. The feds were protecting the Canceler and the rest of the car-lot owners as government informants, and they were getting paid serious money, too. Way the feds saw it, the Canceler's killings weren't nearly as important as the info they were getting, and it was an easy way to solve cases. Saved legwork and having to deal with killers that might kill them."

"Law enforcement isn't quite like I thought it was when I was a kid watching *The FBI Story*," Leonard said.

"I been here before," Jim Bob said.

"What's that mean?" Marvin asked.

"Means I've been in on a bad deal once where the FBI were protecting someone they shouldn't have been protecting."

"How'd that turn out?" Marvin asked.

"Messy," Jim Bob said. "Thing is, FBI gets concentrated on one thing, they can't see the forest for the trees. They focus on what they're trying to accomplish, and if they are using people, so be it. Sometimes guys they got as informants are doing just as bad or worse than the ones the FBI is concentrating on. FBI gets focused, they're willing to give themselves a hand job and call it pussy if it meets their needs."

"Not much justice in that," I said.

"That's where we come in," Leonard said.

"I didn't hear that," Marvin said.

"Just because you're a cop doesn't mean you're out of it clear and free," Jim Bob said. "You show up too big and tall, they might want a big ole piece out of your ass."

"Puts me where it puts me," Marvin said. "But I don't need to be supporting you guys on vigilante missions."

"What about Sandy?" I asked Frank. "That's what we're really after, though it has sort of morphed into something else."

"I don't know any more about her than I've told you. I'm being honest with you. I just want out of this mess."

"Want a deal," Marvin said, "got to tell this to the DA, and it's got to pan out. Though I'm going to tell you, I think you might have had your finger in the pie a little more than you're letting on."

"If I can give you most of the pie and most of the fingers in it, that would help me, wouldn't it?"

Marvin creased his brows. "Might. Time you and me went to the station, Frank."

"Can I have a private cell?" Frank asked.

"We have one cell we call the suite. Just like all the other cells but only has one bed. We'll start there. In the morning the DA will take your statement. Got to tell you, though, I still don't think you grew a conscience, and I want you to know where I stand. I think you'd feed shit to children and tell them it's chocolate."

Frank looked hurt, but when Marvin's expression didn't change, she said, "I had a feeling they wanted to replace me. I had been borrowing a bit of money from the dealership, and I hadn't been paying it back. They take things like that seriously, and their severance package doesn't contain a golden parachute, just a hole in the ground, or maybe they grind you up for sausage. I don't know. But it wouldn't have been good."

"Why tease the tiger?" Marvin asked.

Frank gave that beautiful smile. "Once a con, pretty much always a con. Doing it the wrong way always seems right to me."

"And you ended up in the woods with a bunch of bikers how?" Leonard asked.

"Started having second thoughts," she said. "Thought maybe it wouldn't be so smart to go to the police after all. Decided since the FBI was in on this, they and my employers might find a way to seriously get me messed up or killed. I called a friend in the business with me. I thought she and I were close. Thought for sure she would be sympathetic. I decided I'd get out altogether and not tell the police anything. That I'd run for it. You know, got cold feet. It was stupid. She told someone at the top, and they sent someone at the bottom to collect me. By the way, I think you'll have to replace your door. It got kicked in and is still standing wide open, far as I know."

34

When we came out of the motel it was cool for a change, and there was the smell of rain in the air. A pink glow rose in the east and expanded and turned gold. Some dark clouds floated overhead.

As we stood there by Jim Bob's busted Chevy with Marvin's unmarked car parked next to it, Marvin said, "I'm going to make some calls, and then maybe you can go by your house just for a moment, because I'm going to have a few cops there, though it'll take me a bit to line them up. I can't afford to post a long-term guard. Go there and get some things you need, and then leave. I'll have a place for you to go. We have a couple of safe houses that the city owns, and we can put you up in one of those for a while."

"How safe is a safe house the city owns?" I said.

"Safer than being home," Marvin said. "In the meantime, I'm raising a posse and we're going to try and go out to where you said the bikers are. They are bound to have given up on you guys by now. And if not, we can toss their place because we have cause. The dead dogs you told us about. A suspicion of dogfighting is a good way in. Now draw me a map to the place."

"Shit," Leonard said. "We'll just go with you. We might as well."

Marvin thought on that awhile. We all stood there while he considered, watching the morning grow older. Frank was leaning against Marvin's car. In the light she looked older and more tired and considerably less full of beans than when we first met her.

"All right," Marvin said. "Here's the thing. I'm not going out there with just us. We got our own little SWAT team here, and since mostly they don't do much, and the equipment they use is going to waste, I'll rally them, and off we'll go. I got to get Frank squared away first. Meet me at the station in, say . . . oh, how about two hours? That will give the bikers time to drift back. And they will. We're not talking brain surgeons here. They won't figure you guys going to the cops, not after what you've done, Jim Bob. From what I'm understanding, you killed a man, and that is eventually going to at least bring you downtown for a cup of our bad coffee."

"I'll pick up some creamer," Jim Bob said.

"Tell me he was armed."

"He might have been, but he was threatening me, and there were a lot of folks around him that had guns, and he was their leader, so to speak."

"Not as good as I had hoped for," Marvin said. "And Hap, if there are others dead, and one of them is missing a kneecap, like you told me, you might have to have that cup of coffee, too. Right now, do what I've told you, and we maybe can get things to shake out how we want them. Even Frank might end up with the FBI giving her a nice little retirement fund. They're on the other side now, but this is going to put their reputation in a blender we let it out. They may be willing to make a lot of concessions for all you guys. Frank, too, though that irks me a bit."

"I haven't hurt anyone," Frank said.

"That's a matter of angle," Marvin said. "I want you to get in my car and sit and close the door and be quiet."

Frank got in Marvin's unmarked car and sat quietly.

Marvin said, "Hap, you asked me about the stuff Weasel told you. Why it's not in local papers."

"Yeah."

"That's because it didn't happen here. It happened on the outskirts of Houston."

"You're saying he had the murders right, not the location?" I said.

"Exactly. Why he didn't tell you the exact spot I don't know. Maybe he didn't really have as much contact with what went on as he wanted you to think, and maybe he didn't want to be too specific. Figured you didn't find mention of it locally, places he said, you'd give up, figure he was bullshitting. He'd have your money and be on his way up north. Want more, check the *Houston Chronicle*. I'll send you some special links you can check out. It fits with what he said happened."

"Thanks," I said.

"See you in a couple hours at the cop shop," Marvin said.

· · ·

Jim Bob drove us to Walmart in the Bitch. It was just then solid daylight, and when we parked and got out, he looked at his car and moaned. "Goddamn them," he said.

"Man, there are lot of holes," Leonard said.

"Good thing is, none of them is in us," I said.

As Walmart was open all hours, we went in, and I bought a hammer and nails, and Jim Bob drove us over to the office. Upstairs we found the door kicked in, as Frank said. We closed it and used the hammer and nails to sort of jury-rig it shut until we could call someone to fix it.

After that we went straight to my house. The cops hadn't been put on duty yet. No motorcycles were in the yard. No bikers had built a bonfire with our furniture. No machine-gun nest. No meanies had soaped our windows.

We drove past. Jim Bob wheeled us to Leonard's ride on the backstreet where we had left it, and Leonard drove me and him around to the house. Jim Bob followed.

Leonard parked in the driveway, Jim Bob at the curb. We got out with shotguns and stalked over to the front door. I hoped no neighbors were up early to see us carrying heat. I went through the carport, unlocked the door, went inside. Leonard came through the back door, Jim Bob through the front.

We looked through the house. Leonard went to check on the cookies. They were intact. No one appeared to have been there beyond the three we had nabbed, and they had never made it beyond the front porch, the yard, and the carport. So far so good.

I relaxed and gathered up a few clothes and toiletries, simple stuff, and put them in a suitcase. I went into the closet and stepped up on the stool there and opened up the little trap to the attic, reached around until I found the two revolvers I had there. I always had a scattering of guns around due to the fact that Leonard and I had made a few enemies over the years. The ones in the attic were clean guns, not traceable, and if we used them, they would be tossed. There was ammunition up there, too.

I pulled a pillowcase off a pillow and slipped the guns inside of it. They would leave an oil stain on the pillowcase, and Brett would give me hell, but right then I couldn't worry about that. I gathered a couple books off my nightstand, a Bill Crider Sheriff Rhodes mystery I was halfway through and a book by Lewis Shiner I had been meaning to read. I went to Brett's side of the bed, and out of the nightstand I got her Kindle and charger. I gathered up some DVDs and stuck those in the bag. I could just have gotten the porch swing in my suitcase I could have a home away from home.

Downstairs I found Leonard brewing coffee. I sat the suitcase and the pillowcase full of guns by the couch. Jim Bob was helping himself to eggs and bacon in the refrigerator. I showed him where the frying pan was, and he went about frying us up breakfast.

I tossed some bread in the toaster, then went upstairs again, sat on the bed, and called Brett on my cell.

When she answered she sounded like a sleepy bear. I realized then just how early it was. "Sorry to wake you," I said. I gave her a quick rundown on things, asked that she and Chance hang tight where they were, because we'd all be moving to a safer place late morning or early afternoon. I told her she might as well tell Chance what was going on but to keep details down to a minimum. She deserved to know what kind of mud she was in just by possibly being my daughter. That alone might send her packing. If she was my daughter I didn't want that to happen, though it might actually be a hell of a good choice, blood kin or not.

"I might wait awhile on that," she said.

"You be the judge, hon."

"Being in love with you certainly never gets boring," Brett said.

"I could actually use a little boring," I said. "Chance?"

"I think I love her and wish she was my daughter," Brett said. "Though she knows more than I ever wanted to know about James Joyce."

"I'll have a stern talk with her and give her some Steinbeck."

Finished with the call, I went downstairs and ate breakfast with the guys. Every now and then I got up and looked out the window. Still no bikers. It was beginning to rain lightly.

Jim Bob said, "If they come, my thought is they'll show up in the dead of night. They like to do that. Cover of darkness; unsuspecting, sleeping prey. I once heard there's an hour of night when even watchdogs aren't very alert. I think it's something like three or four in the morning. I doubt that's true, but I've heard that."

"Me and Leonard won't be here for them to sneak up on."

"Thing to do is let them sneak, but be prepared," Leonard said.

"Too many of them," Jim Bob said.

After eating, I wanted to sleep, but that wasn't in the cards right away. I had two cups of coffee, went upstairs, showered, and put on clean clothes while Leonard did the same in the downstairs bathroom. Jim Bob was sitting with his revolver on the table when I came back down.

"No ninjas showed up?" I asked.

"Nope."

I looked out the kitchen window. Still raining. It was a light and simple rain, but steady. I liked a rain like that. I liked to sleep to the sound of it.

No thunder and lightning, just rain. Right then I so badly wanted to go upstairs and go to bed.

"I'm heading home now," Jim Bob said. "Putting the Red Bitch in the shop. Then I'm going to nap and find that barrel racer and show her a few tricks that don't involve barrels. I'm a phone call away."

"You've already done a lot," I said.

"I have, haven't I?"

Leonard came around the corner then. He wasn't wearing a shirt or shoes. Just blue jeans. He may have gained a few pounds, but he still looked like he could turn over a truck, fuck it in the gas tank, and make it raise his gassy children.

Jim Bob shook hands with us and left.

35

We drove over to Leonard's place. I waited outside in the car in case any baddies appeared. After a while Leonard came downstairs carrying a small canvas bag with clothes and such in it.

At the cop shop we met up with Marvin, and then we led him out to the bikers' lair. I like to think of it that way. A lair. I've read far too many Doc Savage books.

Behind Marvin came a few unmarked vehicles and some guys in a couple of Humvees and a green pickup truck, probably army surplus. German Shepherds were in the truck bed. The dogs, with their tongues hanging out, looked like they were going to the dog park.

The lair was easier to find in the day. When we got near it, Marvin pulled over, and the Humvee pulled up on the passenger side. Leonard rolled down his window.

"Go in and check it out, Billy, and don't get shot," Marvin said to the Humvee driver, who had gotten out and was leaning on Leonard's door, looking in through the rolled-down window.

"Yes, sir," Billy said. He was a stout man, probably in his forties, who had kept himself in shape. He had a series of small moles along the side of his nose that resembled stair steps leading to his forehead. He had the air of someone who could take care of himself. My guess was he had actually been a soldier and had probably seen some action. Then again, maybe he was just constipated and wanted to go home.

Leonard explained where the place was and how to finish getting there. He told him where the dog bodies were as well. Billy got back in the Humvee, and away they went. We let the two Humvees move ahead, the pickup truck following. The dogs looked happy. They didn't know they could be shot.

We waited where we were until we got a radio message from Billy.

There wasn't much to it. Happily, it was anticlimactic. They found most of the bikers sleeping around the remains of the tire fire and in the trailers like a bunch of kindergarteners who had played too hard and had gone back home and were taking their naps. There wasn't any resistance. They had used their energy chasing us.

Cops had a warrant, so they searched the place good, found meth and meth-making supplies. They found a lot of weapons and ammunition. When they went out to the place in the woods where the dead dogs were, they found Samson on the pile. Regime change had taken about one evening and possibly part of an early morning. Sentimentality was not strong among that biker club. In that crowd you're the head badass until you aren't.

At some point, whoever took over decided they had chased us enough and it was time to start fresh. They hadn't even so much as thrown Samson in the ditch before they got high on their own product. As an old gray-haired addict called Two-Toe George told me and Leonard once, "When you start wanting meth more than you want pussy or a rib-eye steak, then you know you got, like, a serious fucking drug problem."

Two-Toe George was a philosopher. He was, as you might expect, short in the toe department, having cut off a chunk of his right foot with an ax while trying to smash a snail with it. He said he did that when he was high. Was certain right then that the snail was actually a spy machine made to look like a snail, that it had cameras and was watching him.

Turned out it was just a snail. But the loss of those toes put Two-Toe on the clean-and-sober chart for three days, and then he went back on the meth as soon as he could. Couple years later, in a scummy motel outside of Lufkin, Texas, he put a cheap automatic he had used the day before to rob a gas station of sixty-five dollars and a Peanut Pattie to his head, told the whore he was with he could bounce a bullet off his skull, and said he'd like to show her. He proved in a split second he could in fact not bounce a bullet off his head. It blew his brains all over the motel wall. The whore stole his meth and was caught four days later by the cops trying to sell her three-year-old child for a fix.

Fortunately, the addicts the whore tried to sell the child to weren't as far gone as she was, and they turned her in. The child went to Texas Child Protective Services, and she went into the system, was probably making license plates or such somewhere in a big concrete compound with guards all around.

More cops arrived. Two of their vehicles were large vans. They put their captives in that and drove them to the police station. The guy with the missing kneecap was still alive, and nobody else had died from the car collision, though the woman who had done the nice cartwheel had a broken arm and a broken ankle. She was so high she was feeling no pain. Billy said she tried to get up and dance a step or two to show she hadn't been using. Her ankle cracked, and down she went. She and a few others got a ride to the hospital.

When we were back at the cop shop we didn't go inside. Marvin thought it best we not see any of the bikers who might have seen us.

"Doing what I can to slide you two out of this," Marvin said. "Here's the address where you're going to be. Bring Brett and Chance there as well."

"What about Frank?" Leonard asked.

"We decided no cell for now. We got her tucked away in a nice little apartment with a twenty-four-hour guard. Next thing is to figure how much of her story is true and how much is bullshit."

"Quite a coincidence that Weasel, who helps people create new identities, is also the guy who helped Jim Bob create one."

Marvin nodded. "As I've said before, coincidences do happen. I can live with that if the rest of Frank's story checks out."

As we drove away, I called Brett, told her to stay where she was for a while and that I'd get back to her and tell her where to meet us before too long. I gave her a bit of the rundown. She took it in stride, switched the subject.

"You know what?" she said.

"What?"

"Me and Chance, we've had a lot of fun."

"That's good. What's she up to?"

"She's showering, and I'm making motel-room coffee. It smells a little like the dirty-clothes hamper. Chance and me, we just been talking, almost nonstop. It's like a mother talking to a daughter, for real. My daughter I mostly yell at and try to tell her how to screw her head on straight. Chance, she's got some emotional wounds, but overall, she's okay. Shit, Hap. If she isn't your daughter I'm going to be disappointed. I think there may be a real monkey wrench somewhere in her path."

"You explain to her about what me and Leonard were doing?"

"I decided not to even play with that idea. Not just yet, anyway. I'm working up to it. Thing is, it's hard to explain what you do."

"She doesn't need to know all the gory details," I said.

"Sandy? Anything?"

"Nothing, really. That girl disappeared off the face of the earth."

"More likely she is in the face of the earth," Brett said.

"Looking more and more that way."

"Shower has quit running. I'm going to let you go. Call me when you're ready for us to come home. I think I can keep us busy for a while. I like spending money."

I rang off.

"You're already starting to look like a concerned parent," Leonard said.

"Think so?"

"Oh, yeah. You want that girl to be your daughter, don't you, brother?"

"I think I do."

"Family isn't always about blood. We prove that."

"Yeah, we do. But it would be cool if she was. I think she may be someone special."

"You can help her, kin or not," Leonard said. "Shit, man, that's what you do, help people."

"So do you."

"Yeah, but except for a chosen few, I don't really like them."

"There is that," I said.

The phone rang. I looked. It was Brett again.

I answered it, but it was Chance, not Brett.

"Hey," she said.

"Hey yourself."

"Last night we bought some animal crackers out of the motel vending machine, a carton of milk. It made me think of you. I enjoyed our talk."

"Me, too. I don't remember what we talked about, except animal crackers, but I enjoyed it, too."

"We talked about music and warm milk," she said.

"We did at that."

"I just wanted to tell you about the animal crackers."

"Yeah, well, that's good. I'm glad you had some more. Watch Brett, though. She'll eat them up."

Chance laughed softly. "She is so cool."

"Tell me about it," I said.

"You go on and take care," she said. "I'll see you soon."

"Sure," I said, and she rang off.

Leonard looked at me. "I think I detect a mist over the eyeballs."

"Fuck you."

"A tremble of the lips."

"You heard me."

"She's your daughter, can she call me Uncle Leonard?"

"She can call you Uncle Asshole. That would be more accurate."

"I like it," Leonard said.

"Listen," I said, changing the subject. "Maybe we ought to go back and see if Weasel really left town. He might be still hanging around."

"Why would he?"

"Because he may never have been under threat like he wanted us to believe. He and Frank may both be in on this deeper than they admit. Weasel wanted that thousand, told us enough to make us happy to let him have it, but maybe he knows a lot more. Like who this Canceler actually is."

"All right, then. Let's saddle up."

36

Weasel's place hadn't been urban-renewed since last we saw it, and no volunteers had dropped by to brighten it up with fresh paint. The bottom part of the duplex still had the windows knocked out. Weasel's car was still parked where it had been before. It hadn't been detailed. It looked like the same piece of shit.

We put on cloth gloves we kept in the glove box, which was a swell place for them, went up the stairs again, and leaned on the door. It was still locked. There were windows on either side of the door. We tried them—Leonard one, me the other. They both slid up.

I looked around. There didn't seem to be anyone watching. In fact, there didn't seem to be anyone around at all. It was like it had been last time. The whole area looked abused and then forgotten. The morning light didn't freshen it any.

I climbed through the window I had opened, and Leonard went in through the other. We both had handguns.

The house smelled stale from having been closed up, and it was hot because there was no air-conditioning—no electricity, in fact. It had that odd feel you get from an empty house. Then again, that didn't mean it was really empty. We went through the house with our guns and looked around. There was one very nice room with a bed in it and a computer on a desk, and there was a laptop in a case by the closet. I opened the case up and looked at the laptop. The closet was full of clothes. The desk drawer had a number of flash drives in it.

I joined Leonard in the kitchen. We looked in the refrigerator. There was food in there, lots of it. Of course, he decided to leave, he could have abandoned the food. But his clothes and the laptop? The place wasn't much, but it was clean. I hadn't expected Weasel to be a good housekeeper.

We sat at the kitchen table, having helped ourselves to cold diet colas from the fridge, our guns on the table.

"Could be the computer is here because he's coming back," Leonard said.

"Maybe it's like I thought. He isn't really on the run. But then again, I get a feeling he hasn't been here in a while, so I'm starting to shoot down my own theory. But if he did run, would he leave the computers? They're the tools of his trade. Or at least part of it, creating identities. He'd make a false one for himself and not leave anything behind that might incriminate him if the cops came looking."

"And maybe he writes letters to the editor on one, watches porn on the other."

We drank the diet colas and took the cans with us, trying not to leave any DNA around that might come back and bite us on the butts in the future.

Outside on the landing, our pistols tucked under our shirts, we pushed the windows closed, went downstairs. We were about to get in the car when something struck me. I turned and looked at Weasel's junker and that black piece of cloth hanging out of the trunk. I was thinking I knew what that cloth belonged to.

I pointed it out to Leonard, said, "I got a shitty feeling."

In the back of my car is a tool case with tools I mostly don't know how to use, but there was one thing in it I could handle. A crowbar. I could break an arm and I could jimmy a lock with it. After the hammer, it was my tool of choice. I got the crowbar and Leonard looked up one side of the street and I looked up the other.

Nothing but a black cat crossing the road. I thought it might be the same cat that Leonard had told to clean up the bottom of the duplex the first time out.

At Weasel's car I stuck the crowbar under the edge of the trunk and tried to pry it. Leonard said, "You're being so goddamned delicate you're making me nervous. Give me that."

He took the crowbar and rammed it into the crack of the trunk near where the black cloth dangled and sort of squatted as he pulled down on the bar like a handle. There was a snapping sound and the trunk popped open and out of the trunk there came a smell that once you smell it you never forget it.

There was the rest of the black cloth. It was part of what Weasel had been wearing the day we saw him. A loose black shirt. Weasel didn't really look much like Weasel now. The heat and time had done some work. He was lying on his side away from us, but his head was turned as if he were trying to look over his shoulder, and his mouth was open. There were teeth missing. One of his ears had been cut off. I could see that his throat had been cut. His pants were pulled down to his ankles, and one knee was lifted slightly. I had an idea that if we were to roll him over and look he'd be missing a set of balls.

"Well," Leonard said. "He's had a bad day."

"Yep."

"Seems he wasn't making that stuff up about the guy who cuts throats with a wire and takes balls away with him. He really should have left town sooner."

We closed the trunk and put the crowbar back in my car and looked around. Still nobody. Even the cat was long gone.

We rode away.

37

The address Marvin had given us for the safe house was on the edge of town, and just five years back would have been in the country, but the town had spread out and almost met it. Few more years and it would be part of LaBorde. But for now the little yellow house was off the highway and down an asphalt road, set back off that by a long gravel drive that ran straight up to the house.

There was a faded gray garage separate and near the house, and the garage door slid up to let cars in and had to be opened by hand. Inside there was room for two cars. We opened it and parked the car inside but left the garage door up. Across the asphalt road was a large pasture with a big barn on it. It was worn and made of logs and the logs had began to rot; it was for the most part a full structure, though there were gaps in its side and you could see hay stored in there in bales.

The house was small and untidy. The living room had a saggy paisley-covered couch and one fat matching armchair and a coffee table with so many coffee rings stained into it it almost appeared to have been designed that way. There was a small TV on a stand. It was an old-style TV. The face of it was about the size of a microwave oven. There was a DVD player stacked on top of it. A wire ran from it through a gap in the wall. Apparently we had cable.

The kitchen smelled of old grease, and the floor was covered in cheap yellow linoleum with blue flowers and some long-ago stepped-on cockroaches. When we walked, something sticky on the floor grabbed at our shoes. The linoleum was curling where it met the kitchen cabinets. The cabinets were stocked with quite a few canned goods, and that was swell if you wanted to eat beets or green beans, because that's all there was, except for a can of cranberry sauce with the berries in it. There were blue plastic plates and jelly jars to drink out of, and the kitchen drawers were stuffed with utensils, including a few plastic forks and spoons. There was a kitchen table with a series of mismatched chairs drawn up around it.

I sat on the couch, and the cushion sagged. I called Marvin, told him what we had found at Weasel's place and that he ought to get over there while there was evidence to get.

Marvin sounded worn-out and anxious and was in no way pleasant.

"I told you to go to the safe house," he said.

"We're here."

"Now you are. You had suspicions, you should have called and told me. I could have checked out Weasel's digs myself. What the fuck, Hap?"

"No one knows we were there," I said. "Though we did pry the trunk with a crowbar."

"Damn it. Don't mention you were there or that you pried anything open. That part will be marked down to a worn-out trunk that popped open. You wipe prints?"

"Duh. We wore gloves."

"Actually, that was pretty good detective work. Don't tell Leonard I said that."

"Leonard, he said we did some good detective work."

Leonard saluted.

"Funny," Marvin said. "Go to bed. We'll discover Weasel on our own."

There were two bedrooms. Leonard was quick to choose the larger one and make camp. I slung my overnight bag into the other one, pulled the blinds to keep out the morning light. I climbed out of my clothes and into bed in my underwear. I lay there and listened to Leonard snoring across the hall. I had meant to close the door but had been too tired to do it. I thought I really ought to get up and do that. That was going to be my next move, but to do that I first had to open my eyes and will myself out of bed. I was seriously planning that when I fell asleep.

Late afternoon we were up and dressed. We split the can of cranberry sauce, said to hell with all this sneaking around, and drove to town. We do not follow directions well. I remember my kindergarten teacher telling my mother, "Hap would do very well if he could just learn to follow directions."

And I remember my mother sighing and saying, "Tell me about it."

We bought a large cardboard container of coffee at Starbucks as well as a quickie breakfast of eggs and bacon inside what might have been an English muffin and drove back to the safe house and ate and sipped our coffee. When we finished, I called Brett. She answered on the first ring.

"How are you?"

"Peachy," I said and gave her a rundown.

"You had quite a night. I can tell by your voice that you're not quite right."

"I saw a person shot, some people hit by a car, blew a man's kneecap off, was shot at, a lot, was chased by thugs, scolded by Marvin—unfairly, I think—and me and Leonard found Weasel dead in the trunk of his car stinking to high heaven. And the toilet here is small and rocks when you sit on it. So the usual."

"Sorry, Hap."

"My own fault, getting into shit like this."

"So nothing on Sandy?"

"Zip," I said. "I get to thinking she might be out there, alive, hiding somewhere, or maybe just a stack of bones and rotting clothes under a rock, and mostly what we do is ride around and shoot at people and take a regular shit."

"There's not much else you can do, Hap. It's been some years since she disappeared. And if she's dead, and I don't mean to sound cold, but what's the hurry?"

"*If* she's dead," I said.

"What do you think?"

"That she's been fertilizing the soil for some time, but I don't want to think that. What if I'm wrong, and she's in some hellhole being forced to whore out? Maybe they're doping her, hurting her. I think about it too long I feel sick to my stomach."

"I know how you take things to heart," she said, "even when it's not your fault and there's nothing you can do about it. You can only take it a day at a time, love."

"Look," I said, "I think you should stay where you are. There's not enough room here, really. And I think it's best we just stay separate for now. Can we afford for you to stay where you are or someplace similar?"

"For a while," she said. "Then we're going to have to make new plans. And Chance, she doesn't know about all this, not the real inside scoop, anyway. But she's no idiot. I can't find my way into 'Daddy is back home shooting the kneecaps off bad guys and breaking legs with crowbars, so we have to stay away right now.'"

"I assume she is not in the room with you."

"Downstairs having breakfast. She thinks we're just spending time at the hotel because you're having the house sprayed for termites."

"That was your story?"

"I thought about telling her you and Leonard had been quarantined for bubonic plague, but that seemed a little extreme."

"You told the right lie. You know this means we are no longer empty nesters. We have a dog and maybe a daughter."

"At least it isn't Leonard. I say that with love."

"Damn. I didn't even think to ask I've been so preoccupied. What about Buffy?"

"Right here beside me. We got her from the boarder, brought her back here this morning. We couldn't leave her, Hap. She is really doing well. I think hotel life agrees with her. They not only allow dogs here, they have dog treats and doggie beds and a place outside for them to poop, provided you clean up afterward. This is a life Buffy could become accustomed to. She seems to like watching cartoons."

"Sounds fun."

"It is, but what I'm thinking is maybe we should get out of East Texas for a while. I'm thinking up a big lie to justify that, and I may be getting one cornered. I'm going to lay it on Chance when I get it worked out. I have to tell her something. Say I was planning a vacation and she ought to go with me, all expenses paid as long as they aren't large expenses. I think I can talk her into that, justify it with some bullshit. But Hap, she isn't stupid. The girl is smart. She's going to know I'm telling her shit don't smell when it does. It might take a little time, but she'll come to it."

"If anyone can sell her on a line of shit, it's you."

"I'm not sure that was a compliment. You know, Hap? I really, really like her."

"I don't actually know anything about her. I want to like her."

"You can't help but," Brett said. "I'll be devastated if she isn't your daughter. She's a buddy. We have so much in common, and she's so young to be such an old soul."

"Or you're a young soul," I said.

"Aw, how sweet. I like that. Baby, I feel like I'm running out on you. Taking a sabbatical during a time when you need me there with a shotgun and some face paint. I just don't know what to do with Chance under the circumstances. I don't mind putting my ass on the line, but not hers."

"You're making the right choice. Let her have some time when she's not scuttling to survive. Daughter or not. You like her, that's enough. And there's really nothing you can do here. To be honest, I'm not sure there's much further we can go as far as Sandy is concerned. She dead-ends at the dealership."

"So you want to throw in the towel?"

"Just because I don't think there's much further we can go doesn't mean I'm smart enough to quit."

"You're a terrier, and Leonard is a pit bull."

"Technically, I think pit bulls are terriers, too. Leonard is waving hello."

"Wave back. And let him have his cookies, and don't get killed, okay?"

"Not in my plans," I said.

"Tell Leonard I said to watch after you."

"He always does."

38

I guess we had been at the safe house about a week when things changed. Brett was traveling with Chance and Buffy on some of our money stash, and I had been keeping in contact with her on a daily basis. She said Chance had never been out of East Texas, except for Louisiana, and was having the time of her life. She said this as if she and I were great world travelers.

They did a tour of Sun Records in Memphis, went to Nashville for a few days, and were uncertain where they were going from there. Thing was, they had to come home sometime because the money would run out. It might not be so bad now. The bikers were still in the can. Frank was stashed away somewhere, and if she were able to give a bit more insider information than she already had, she might do a lot less time, not that she deserved less. Jim Bob wasn't off the hook altogether, and neither were we, but so far we were still footloose and fancy-free.

I called and had our mail and newspapers held until we were ready to pick them up. I wondered if Chance's DNA test was in the mail. I was almost afraid to find out. The door at the office had been fixed, but except for the workmen who had been out to do the job and our dropping by quickly to check on the door, we had mostly laid low at the safe house. As for leads on Sandy, we were out of ideas.

We were sitting on the porch in lawn chairs, letting the hot air settle on us, trying to figure what we were going to do next, when Jim Bob showed up. He wasn't driving the Bitch. He came in a late-model black pickup truck. It looked like a lot of trucks. Nothing fancy. No dice hanging from the window. No plastic Jesus. No curb feelers. He parked in the drive in front of the garage.

He got out and came across the yard. "*Qué pasa,* motherfuckers?"

"How'd you find us?" Leonard asked.

"I'm a detective. Don't be silly."

"Marvin told you, didn't he?"

"I was smart enough to ask, wasn't I?"

"For a moment I thought the safe house wasn't so safe," Leonard said.

"I'm sure it isn't," Jim Bob said. He came up on the porch and sat on it with his feet on the steps. The gray boots he wore had blue stars sprinkled over the toes. His snap-pocket cowboy shirt was blue as well. He took off his hat and placed it on his knee.

"So far no trouble," I said. "And we're ready to go home."

"You might want to hold up on that one," he said. "Unlike you, I haven't been hanging out on the front porch of a supposed safe house eating cookies and drinking coffee and playing with my pecker."

"We have neither coffee nor cookies," Leonard said.

"Guess not," I said. "Leonard ate all the cookies and drank all the coffee."

"I drank coffee because we are out of Dr Peppers."

"Well, we do have peckers," I said.

"You got some news?" Leonard asked.

"Well, me and the barrel racer broke up. I had too much stamina."

"That's your news?" I said.

"No. I been researching our hired killer with the comic-book name— the Canceler—and I been looking deep into the car company where Frank worked. I have friends in the FBI, some others on the edges of organized crime, and a few snitches I wouldn't call friends but I would call reasonably reliable. I been putting together quite a résumé."

"Where is it?" Leonard asked.

Jim Bob tapped his head with a finger. "Right'cheer. That car company has its main hub in Fort Worth, but its tentacles stretch all over the place. Houston. Austin. Dallas. There's one in Tyler and one in El Paso. There's one in Denver, Chicago, Los Angeles, and a number of other places. LaBorde must have been a long shot for them, but then again, they've been here for a while, so they are doing well enough. Most people here don't have money, but the ones who have it really have it, and some of the ones who have it really want cool cars and women and long trips to Italy. Course, they didn't know being blackmailed came with the deal.

"As for the Canceler, well, he's supposed to have killed a lot of folks in a lot of places, people who seem to have something to do with the car company. Clients turn up dead, maybe because they wouldn't pay or got sideways with the companies. Maybe they threatened to go to the police or were going to testify. I don't know the reasons, but that's fair-enough guessing. Also others that may or may not have bought cars but were internal problems or external problems—snoops. Weasel would be a prime example. I heard about him, by the way. He sure could build a good website."

"Marvin told you?" I said.

"Yep."

"Sandy could have been one of those snoops," Leonard said. "And she might have paid for it."

"A cog in the wheel that didn't quite fit. Don't know yet. But the thing that doesn't add up, when I started looking at all the similar killings my FBI buddy let me in on, is the timing. Too many killings too close together, happening in too wide a range to be one person. There's a crew. Have guns, will travel. They operate to create this idea that it's one deadly bastard, but it's several mean-ass bastards. They get paid well to do what they do and to make it scary. That way, word gets around, especially to the underworld: you don't fuck with the dealership, because if you do, you get whacked and lose your balls. It's all been men they've whacked that I know of, but maybe they just aren't as theatrical with women. Sandy, for example. Which may be why she hasn't turned up. Thing is, they fucked up by being too generous with their killings. That way, cause of times and locations, we know it's not one killer, it's several. And from what my friend at the FBI says, sometimes it's several of them on one job. Inside sources think it's eight people, and they think they know who the eight people are, but they won't get nailed because the FBI has contacts in the organization that are helping them out."

"It's like Frank was saying," Leonard said. "They let some bad people go to nail other bad people."

"Yeah," Jim Bob said. "It's fucked-up, man. I always say when the law breaks the law, there isn't any goddamn law. I don't care who they're nailing: if there's stuff going on as bad as what they're focused on, it's still bad. For them it gets down to closing high-profile cases. At the moment, bunch of dead rich guys, or a bunch of dead thugs that were going to challenge the company, are no skin off their asses if they can nail some others more easily. That fake money-laundry business, for one. That's just folks being set up by the bad folks so they can turn them in and get paid, and paid a lot. I told my friend this, the fed, and he says, 'We know. But it's easier to nail the money-laundry folks, even if they're innocent, than a bunch of bad motherfuckers that will kill you.' "

"Damn," I said.

"Our friends in the government," Jim Bob said. "Tomorrow the worm may turn, but right now the feds are getting what they want out of the deal. In the long run, even if they turn on these guys, they'll end up letting most of them go, giving them new identities and hiding them in the witness protection program. That could mean the Cancelers, too. It's less embarrassing for the FBI that way. They don't have to admit they been ignoring crime to catch crime. Of course, these guys, they get new identities, and pretty soon most if not all are back at their original business, and it becomes even more embarrassing for the feds, so they got to continue keeping it under wraps. Deeper they get into this, the more desperate they are to hide it."

"That is fucking wrong," Leonard said.

Jim Bob nodded.

"Knowing that and changing it are two different things. Thing is, the car company is vengeful, and since their cheap biker help blew the job, well, they'll send someone from the crew, or all the crew. The Cancelers, if you will. Local law enforcement will suddenly find their hands are tied, at least where it would matter to us. The feds will put the pressure on them. The bikers will get tossed into the deal as patsies and serve time, but the real big wheels, they'll keep on turning, and so will their hit men, ones who grease the wheels for the real owner, who seems to be our Barbecue King."

"So it's just a matter of time before the Cancelers know where we are," I said.

Jim Bob made a clicking sound with his tongue.

"It's possible we might negotiate our way out, say we're going to hang up investigating Sandy. We could be put with the right people to have that meeting. Kind of a catch-and-release program, but then again, you have to know they might catch and not release."

"You know us better than that," I said.

"I do. You're not smart enough to quit."

"And besides," I said, "we slither out of the deal for now, who's to say they won't come back later and whack us just to make sure?"

"My thoughts exactly," Leonard said.

"And mine," Jim Bob said.

"So what do we do?" I said. "Wait until they decide to hit us?"

"That could be an idea," Jim Bob said. "Thing is, it could be any time. Now. Tomorrow. A month from now. What we got to do is prepare, and then we got to annoy the shit out of them until they come out of the dark. Or find a way to take the fight to them."

"The Barbecue King?" Leonard said. "We brace him."

"That's a good idea," Jim Bob said. "Go to the top."

"That will get the shit stirred, no doubt," I said. "But we do that, and there really are eight of those guys, then we got to consider all eight might come after us at once."

"Three into eight goes how many times?" Leonard said.

"It goes badly," I said.

"We need a crew," Jim Bob said. "I'm sure we would do just fine, the three of us, but I don't know about you guys, lately I get a little more tired than I used to."

"Me, too," I said.

"Not me," Leonard said. "I can fight all day and fuck all night."

"Sure you can," Jim Bob said. "But maybe we ought to put this crew together anyway."

"I have an idea or two," I said.

"Good," Jim Bob said, standing up, talking as he walked toward his truck. "Me, I'm going to venture out into the wilds, fearless and handsome. Strong and noble. One man alone against the elements."

"So what's that mean?" Leonard said.

"Figure we're in for a long haul, so I'm going to go buy some groceries and such. I'm not back in a couple, three hours, you fuckers start looking for my balls. If you find them, find me next. I'll need them back."

39

I gave Cason a call.

"Hey," he said. "I been researching the shit out of things. Or, rather, I got a friend here at the paper who has. He's like a computer wizard. You know what he figured out?"

"That there is more than one killer?"

"There goes my news."

"Weasel's dead," I said.

"No shit? Damn. I didn't like him and can't say I miss him, but I got some good information from him. I had already sort of cut him loose, though, knowing he was planning to move. Guess he didn't do it soon enough."

I told him what we knew about Weasel. "That's not for public consumption, but in time it can go into your article, leaving me and Leonard out of it."

"Who's going to believe an article about a league of assassins?"

"I don't think they're quite that impressive. Eight guys who kill people is all they are."

"That's pretty impressive."

"It's presumptuous, but me and Leonard want to set things right."

"No way that can ever be done," Cason said.

"Not completely," I said. "But in increments. I'm tired of not sleeping in my own bed. I'm tired of being nervous. I'm tired of Brett being gone on a permanent vacation until this is over. I want my life back. We need to put together a crew to help us get things straight."

"That won't be me. I did a thing not long back for an old army buddy, and it wasn't a thing I wanted to do, but I went against the grain and did it. I've had enough. But I know a guy who lives for this stuff. He throws in with you, long as you don't fuck him over, he'll stay until things are done. Someone else comes along next week, hires him to whack you, well, he might just sign up. You can never tell about Booger."

"Booger?"

"What he prefers to be called. And believe me, he is a booger."

"I can't promise money."

"Can you promise bloodshed?"

"Most likely, but if I find a way to do it without killing, that's the route I'll take."

"Just so you know, he's violent, efficient, but hard to manage. Kind of guy you don't know much about, because there's not much for him beyond the moment. He only likes a few people, and who knows? One day he might get out of bed, have a tough bowel movement, and decide to kill everyone in the house. With him it's like playing Russian roulette with a one-shot revolver."

"Don't sugarcoat him so much."

"Oh, actually I am sugarcoating him."

"Well, we're not looking to have someone to do the dishes and macramé sweaters."

"Good thing. You want me to call him?"

"Yeah. I'll chance it."

"Let me know where you're staying, and he'll come. I'll be with him, but I won't stay. Later, don't say I didn't warn you."

When we rang off, I turned to Leonard, said, "We got one more."

"I know of another," Leonard said.

40

Couple years back I started getting cards from places in Italy. I knew who was sending them. I only knew one person in Italy. The cards were random kinds of cards. Christmas, birthday, get well, Halloween, all manner of things. There was a stack of them. There were no notes in them. Only a single number. Except the last card, which read: IF EVER.

Me and Leonard drove to my house and parked boldly in the drive and went inside. Leonard stood near the front door while I went upstairs and climbed on a footstool in the bedroom closet and removed the little door there that led up into the crawl space. I still had a few cold guns and some ammunition up there. There was also a small metal box. It had those cards in it with the random numbers. I carried it to the bed. I removed the cards from it. I looked at the envelopes and laid them out by date. Then I took each card out of its envelope and lined up the numbers by dates. I had figured out months ago what they were. If you arranged them in order, then put Italy's country code in front of it, it was a phone number. Plus the card that said: IF EVER.

Brett knew about them and knew what they were. She didn't like it, and I said I would throw the cards away, but I didn't.

I used a pad and pen by the bed and wrote out the complete number and put it on the night table by the bed, sat on the bed, and used the home phone to call the number. It rang for a long time. A machine picked up. The words were first in Italian. I had no idea what was said. I kept listening. Then in English. "Dry cleaner's. Leave a message." It was one of those mechanical female voices, robotic and clear.

I said, "It's if ever," and hung up.

I tore up the number I had written out and tossed it in the trash can, put the cards back together, placed them back into the metal box, and put it back where it belonged. I went down, said to Leonard, "Now we'll see."

"All right, then," he said, and we left.

41

When we got back to the safe house Jim Bob was inside making lunch. He had cooked steaks and baked potatoes and had bought all the goods that go with them. He had bought a six-pack of Dr Peppers for Leonard, two jugs of unsweet ice tea, and a six-pack of Lone Star for himself. He had bought an apron and was wearing it. It had writing on it where it draped over his chest. The writing read: KISS THE COOK.

Over lunch—which, I might add, was well prepared—we told him we had one thug lined up for sure and a professional who might come on board.

"That makes four, maybe five," he said.

"I want to talk to the Barbecue King first," I said.

"To rile him?" Jim Bob said.

"Maybe."

"What I'd suggest heavily is that if we want to take the fight to them, let's not just march up to his house and start some shit. If he's behind this, and it looks like he is, he might have a little army at his command. There's the eight guys, but then there's the Barbecue King's own guys."

"Technically he doesn't run the barbecue business anymore," Leonard said.

"Beside the point," Jim Bob said. "He's rich. He's powerful. He owns the car company, and that means he runs the illegal side businesses, which will make him cautious in the extreme. Guys like that, they are always scared, because there's always someone looking to take over, and frequently they plan to do it by giving their rivals a nice vacation, so to speak. Give me a few days to do a bit of surveillance. I'd rather do it alone. Easier to hide one than two or three. So in the meantime, hang out and stay cautious."

* * *

After two days a small four-door white pickup pulled up out front, and a man got out on the driver's side. He was tall, dark of skin, but it was hard to get an ethnic take on him. His head was shaved and shiny. He could have been black, Samoan, American Indian, or maybe even Asian. Probably all those things. He was wearing a tight white T-shirt that showed he worked out. He wasn't bulging with a lot of theatric muscle but instead was lean, had a boxer's build. He was carrying a compact leather bag. He moved like a cat.

There was a man on the passenger side, and he got out. It was Cason.

It was just me and Leonard in the house. We were in the kitchen looking out the window at their arrival.

"Looks like Cason has brought us the cavalry," I said.

"Looks like one big asshole to me," Leonard said.

We went on the front porch as they walked up. The big man moved as if well oiled but not in any hurry. He had the languid but somehow threatening stride of a tiger. When they were standing at the bottom of the porch, Leonard and the big man took to eyeing one another immediately.

"This," Cason said, "is Booger."

"How you fuckers?" Booger said. He had a sweet baritone voice that might have encouraged his mother to have enrolled him in the high school choir.

"Us fuckers are fine," Leonard said.

Booger gave him a Cheshire Cat grin.

"Where's Jim Bob?" Cason said.

"Out," I said. He had, of course, been gone a couple of days, and we hadn't heard a peep yet.

"How about all us fuckers go in the house?" Leonard said.

Booger made with his Cheshire Cat grin again.

We went in the house, and Booger went straight to the refrigerator and looked inside. Leonard had been doling out his Dr Peppers since Jim Bob brought them. There was one left. Booger grabbed it and swigged about half of it down instantly.

Leonard looked at him as if he had just taken a shit in the middle of the floor.

I touched Leonard's arm casually. He turned and looked at me.

"Son of a bitch," Leonard said.

Booger swigged more of the soft drink, wiped his mouth with the back of his hand, said, "What was that you said, Leroy?"

"Leonard," Leonard said. "I said, son of a bitch. That's my Dr Pepper."

"Not anymore," Booger said. "Maybe I can save you a swallow."

"I'm the only bad nigger drinking Dr Peppers in this house," Leonard said.

"Now there are two bad niggers," Booger said. "Though, technically, I'm as much of this as that. I'm what you might call a mutt. More of a junkyard dog, really."

"That's not what I was thinking of calling you," Leonard said.

"Come on, guys," Cason said. "I'll buy more Dr Peppers."

"A case," Leonard said.

"A case, then," Cason said.

After a while Cason went away, left Booger with us, and let me tell you, there was one big draft in the room when he departed. Partly it was due to how Leonard and Booger felt about each other, but it was more than that. Booger was like a slice of cold shadow.

Late afternoon we fixed supper, sat and ate at the table. I said, "Booger, we're glad to have your help, but the pay sucks. Meals and this roof over your head and a chance to get killed."

"I won't get killed," Booger said.

"You know what we're up against, or may be up against?" I said.

"Cason told me."

"Maybe eight guys, and who knows, it could be more."

"That's all right."

"Course, we got to find them. It may take time."

"I got time."

"We'll have to fix you up with some guns."

"Got my own equipment." Booger looked at Leonard and smiled. "When's Cason bringing those Dr Peppers?"

"You know," Leonard said, "one day you're going to pull on the wrong rope, and it just might be tied to me."

"Wouldn't that be delightful?" Booger said.

"Maybe less so than you imagine," Leonard said.

"You look to me, both of you, like you might be getting a little past it."

"There have been various opinions on the matter," Leonard said. "The ones who held your opinion lived or died to regret it."

Booger grinned, leaned back in his chair, said, "You going to make coffee, Happy?"

"Hap," I said. "And you can make your own damn coffee."

"You old men watch football?"

"Not really," I said. "But there's a TV here if you want to watch it. Keep it turned down, though. I plan to read."

"I hope you plan on being alert," Booger said.

"How alert are you if you watch TV?"

"I can hear a dog taking a dump in the yard and watch TV at the same time."

"And leap small rivers and buildings at a single bound, and you're half horse and half alligator," Leonard said.

Booger gave Leonard a cold smile.

"You know," Booger said, "I killed my mother and fucked her dog, and her I liked."

I wasn't sure if he was kidding.

Leonard said, "Yeah, but what if it had been a Doberman, smarty-pants?"

Booger delivered his cold smile again.

After a while Booger padded lightly into the living room and turned on the TV. He found a sports channel and watched an old classic football game.

Me and Leonard went out on the front porch. We sat on the steps and watched the day grow gray. Leonard said, "I don't like him."

"If he's as bad a dude as Cason thinks, as Booger himself thinks he is, we are going to need him."

"What if he isn't?"

"Then he'll get himself killed. Does he make you nervous?"

"No," Leonard said. "He irritates me."

"Sure," I said.

"Okay," Leonard said. "A little."

"What makes him scary is that he doesn't seem to really have anything or anyone inside that shell. He's here so he can kill someone, and that's it. Maybe some odd loyalty to Cason. But in the end, it has nothing to do with setting things right. It's a whole different country where Booger dwells. My guess is he isn't all that different from those we have been calling the Canceler. They're serial killers who have made killing their profession. Slight bend in the road, and Booger could be one of them."

"I believe that," Leonard said.

"Believe he killed his mother?" I asked.

"No," Leonard said. "Well, I don't think so. He might have fucked a poodle, though."

"Do you believe he can hear a dog shit in the yard from inside the house while watching TV?"

Leonard gave me a serious look. "Can't everyone?"

42

The days were hot and the nights were warm, but in the house around Booger there was a coolness stronger than the air-conditioning. Sometimes Booger decided to talk, and he talked at random about all kinds of things, sports and such, and he loved to talk about dead things, and things he wanted to make dead, and it was a long list and seemed to be made in order of desire.

We had one CD that Leonard had brought with him, and we played it on the laptop I had brought with me. It was *Restless* by Kasey Lansdale. Booger took to playing it more than us. He played over and over one cut in particular. "Sorry Ain't Enough." I wondered if those words meant something to him. I doubted he was sorry, but I figured anyone who had done him wrong, at least in his eyes, could never be sorry enough to please him.

We hung out like that for three more days, growing nervous about the wait, and me and Leonard growing nervous because of our companion. I could hardly sleep at night for worry Booger might get bored and decide to kill us in our sleep. But on the last of those three days of waiting, midmorning, Jim Bob showed up.

When he saw Booger he did a kind of double take. "Who's this? The fucking golem?"

"You can ask me," Booger said. "I know all about me."

"Okay," Jim Bob said. "Who the fuck are you?"

"Booger."

"Ah, well, that clears it right up," Jim Bob said. "And I don't like the way you're looking at me, asshole."

"The hat and boots, you look like one of those little dolls you buy in Texas souvenir shops," Booger said.

Perfect. Jim Bob and Booger, like Leonard and Booger, were already in love. Soon bloody kisses would follow.

"I've known you a few seconds, and I wish you dead," Jim Bob said.

"You can't imagine how important being liked is to me," Booger said and showed that smile again.

"Son, you maybe ought not mistake a rattler for a king snake."

"Here's a little conversation starter," Leonard said. "Booger here killed his mother, who I think was a mountain lion, and fucked her poodle, who I actually think was a stuffed plush toy."

Booger and Leonard did a stare-off. I could see this was not going the way I wanted.

"We're all on the same team," I said. This was kind of like that lame invocation "Why can't we all just get along?"

Leonard spent what seemed like an eternity trying to stare down Booger. Booger didn't even seem to notice. He yawned.

"Again," I said. "Same team."

"Yeah, well, same team or not, right now, since I'm the one with the information, I'm the goddamn quarterback," Jim Bob said.

"Call the play," I said.

"You sure this fucker is okay?" Jim Bob said.

"You can depend on me," Booger said.

"Cason vouched for him," I said.

"Don't let us down, kid," Jim Bob said. "You turn out to be someone doesn't know the difference between diarrhea and hamburger gravy, you may not only get yourself killed, which I can live with, you might, most importantly, get me killed, and that would be a fucking loss to the world, I guarantee."

Booger's face was a blank.

"According to Cason, he's done stuff," I said.

"All right, then," Jim Bob said, and he finally quit glaring at Booger. "Here's the score. I got our Barbecue King's schedule down. He's got a couple of bodyguards, which tells me that any doubts to the contrary about him not being into some shit other than barbecue royalties can be tossed. If you're just making money off a barbecue deal you don't need thugs."

"There are just the two?" Leonard asked.

"From what I can figure. You wanted to talk to him, Hap, and I think that's a good idea. As far as a squad of hit men, I got nothing out of my surveillance. Not that I expected them to all be hanging out at his house eating free barbecue and swapping recipes for making their own ammunition. I only got his schedule down for a week, but it seems pretty rigid. He gets out and about some, but it's the same thing over and over, and then he stays home a lot. I watched his house for so long I began to know the birds that were sitting on the telephone wires and named each and every one. The house has a very tall fence around it, but if you drive up Livery Drive and park up there, you can look down over the fence. Nothing odd seems to be going on, but then again, not every week is going to be go-daddy time. Here's the thing, though. Every day he goes to a Japanese restaurant to eat sushi. I guess he's had enough barbecue to hold him. Doug looks to be in his fifties, good shape, gray hair. Looks like a retired businessman. Polo shirts and dress pants and comfortable but expensive shoes."

"How would you know a good shoe from a bad shoe?" Leonard asked.

"I know lots of things," Jim Bob said. "Thing is, I think the best time to brace him without everything going Sam Peckinpah is to catch up with him at the Jap joint."

Nice. Jap joint.

"The bodyguards don't even go inside. I don't think he's really worried about anyone wanting to snap his ass, and that makes me wonder about some other things."

"If he's actually connected to all this?" Leonard said.

"Maybe he just thinks he's invincible," Booger said.

Jim Bob gave Booger a stare. There was a lot of malice in that look. It didn't change Booger's demeanor at all. He could have been talking about gutting someone or going out for an ice cream.

"All right," I said and looked at my watch. "He eat at noon?"

"For whatever reason he's at the restaurant twelve-fifteen on the dot. I watched him go there every day. One day I went in and ate not too far away from him. He sits by himself. He has his phone with him, and he puts it on the table, and now and then texts or e-mails on it. He takes his time. He's there at least an hour, sometimes longer. I think it's kind of a temporary office. He finishes, pays his bill, goes out to the car, where the two guys are waiting. They drive him home. Actually, once in a while it's just one guy. Like I said, the bodyguards seem more out of habit than need. Like he's keeping up appearances. I haven't got that figured altogether."

"I think it's best I go see him alone," I said. "We don't want to overwhelm him with numbers."

"You know what you're going to say to him?" Jim Bob asked.

"It'll come to me."

"All right, but one of us, at least, ought to be nearby," Jim Bob said.

"That'll be me, of course," Leonard said.

"All right, then, you watch his back, and me and Booger will not be far from there, a phone call away if it comes to that. There's a Burger King just down the road."

"I don't like fast food," Booger said.

"Then order a fucking salad," Jim Bob said, "or just hang over a soda. I don't give a shit. Anyway, things go bad, you got Leonard, and all he has to do is have a text prepared and punch it. We'll be there in two or three minutes. I think the two of you can probably handle two or three minutes."

"I doubt it will turn ugly, not in public," I said. "I like bearding him in one of his neutral dens, so to speak, see if it causes him to get the hit crew stirred and moving in our direction. That will be our chance to clean out that nest, provided it comes to that."

"It better," Booger said. "It was a long drive from Oklahoma."

"We only go code red if we need to," I said.

Booger grunted.

"And somewhere in all this," Leonard said, "I hope to figure out what the hell happened to Sandy."

43

We arrived at the restaurant at straight-up noon in my car, but with Leonard driving. Actually, we parked down from the restaurant a ways, but we had eyes on it.

Leonard said, "I hate waiting around."

"Me, too."

"I'd rather have to fight and mate with a wild tiger in a ditch than just sit around waiting."

"No tigers in a ditch for me, but I do hate waiting."

"If you didn't have to fight the tiger, but just mate with it, how would that be?"

"Female tiger?"

"In your case, yes."

"Count me in."

"You know, Hap, I think we ought to smother Booger in his sleep. He doesn't seem trustworthy to me."

"I haven't seen that he sleeps much."

"Every time I get up to go pee, I see him sitting up in a chair with the light on. Reading books you brought. He always smiles at me. He has a creepy fucking smile."

"We may in fact be getting old. We're sleeping, he's watching."

"You got a point there," Leonard said. "I sleep light, but I sleep. He seems like a fucking machine."

"What he is is a sociopath. Cason said as much, and I guess he's as close as Booger's got to a friend. I think he seems odd because he doesn't quite understand human discourse. I think when he gets our goat, he believes he's being pleasant or friendly. He doesn't really know what that's supposed to look like."

"Jim Bob, like us, he's been around, and when he was talking to Booger the other day, talking tough, you know what I thought I saw?"

"A moment of hesitation." I said.

"Like maybe the tiger saw the elephant."

"Thought I saw it, too. Thought I saw the same thing in your eyes a couple times."

"That was a trick of the light, buddy boy, nothing more," Leonard said.

"All right, then. But I assure you, he makes me a little weak in the knees."

"Hey, that may be your man."

A black SUV pulled up in a parking spot near the front of the restaurant. A big man with black hair who looked like he lived in a gym got out on the driver's side, stepped to the back driver's-side door, and let a man out with stylishly cut gray hair. He was slim and wore blue dress pants and a lighter blue polo shirt. I didn't notice if his shoes were expensive or not, but they were black.

He went inside.

I said, "Okay, heads up, brother. I'm going in."

I got out and strolled along the sidewalk to the Japanese restaurant and went inside. The place had a few scattered customers. The waitress, an attractive Asian lady, asked me how many.

"I'm joining a friend," I said and nodded toward the booth where Doug Creese, the Barbecue King, sat.

"You're the first."

"How's that?"

"You're the first to ever sit with him."

I walked over and sat down in the booth across from Doug. He looked older close up. There were lots of lines in his face, and his mouth drooped at both corners. He studied me for a few seconds.

"Do I know you?"

"No, but I thought you might like to."

"You're not selling insurance, are you?"

"Depends on how you look at it."

"How should I look at it?"

"Like I'm here to save us both a lot of problems."

"Yeah?"

"My name is Hap Collins."

"I know of you."

"Really?"

"Yeah. I hear you're a cracker that runs around with some queer nigger named Leonard and you think you're a tough guy and he thinks he's tougher."

"That's us. And by the way, he just might be tougher."

"I haven't got any business with either of you."

"Then how come you know who we are?"

"I hear about you because I've known some people who know of you. The name stuck with me. Hap. Unusual. Hap and Leonard. I remember that."

I nodded.

"Word is you own a car lot downtown, the fancy one."

"That's the word, huh?"

"Yep. And word is you don't just sell cars. You sell pussy, too, maybe dick, and you like film, especially ones where someone with money is caught naked with his pecker hanging out and a prostitute dangling on the other end."

"You heard that, huh?"

"I hear, too, when people cross you, there's these guys known as the Canceler, except there are several—eight, I believe—and they get a ticket to kill, and then they get paid really well for it. That's what I hear."

"You're hearing from all the wrong people."

"Am I, now? Funny. No matter what we hear, it always comes back to you."

The waitress came over.

Doug gave his order. I told her I'd have the same. I said, "I'll even pick up the bill."

She went away.

"You're ruining my lunch," he said.

"What I'm doing is telling you that I'm not going to stop what I'm doing, and the people I have with me are not going to stop, either, and we are going to put holes in anyone who wants to cut off our balls or any variation thereof that leads to any of us being dead in any manner, shape, or fashion or, for that matter, just made unnecessarily tired."

"You should do that. It's got nothing to do with me."

"I'm also saying the only thing we really want is to find a lady named Sandy Buckner, and if we can do that, we can save a lot of trouble, because if we know what happened to her, where she is, or where what's left of her is, we'll take our toys and go home."

"How nice."

"We think so. We wouldn't want to mess up your lunch routine by you being dead."

"You threatening me?"

"I'm telling you how it might work out if you start the ball rolling. But on the other hand, you don't want to cooperate, I got one guy with us who will kill anyone for anything and skull-fuck them. Hell, he scares me."

The waitress brought us both unsweet ice teas. I reached over and got an artificial sweetener from the rack on the table, tore it open, and dumped it in my tea. I stirred it with the straw.

"Collins, I'm tired. Real tired. I just want to spend the rest of my life being comfortable. I don't want any shit. None."

"We're in the same ballpark."

"No, you have on the wrong uniform and have showed up for the wrong game."

"Have I?"

"Listen. Ten years ago I'd have been all over this. I'd have wanted war. I'd have had so many men and resources at my service you'd be dead by the time you left here to get in your car. Your car would be dead. I'd have it shot in the engine block. I'd have your house burned down and your plumbing dug up and have your shit shot, turd by turd."

"So what's wrong now?"

"I'm retired."

"That's lame."

"I didn't choose retirement. I was forced into it. The car lot—I don't really own it. Haven't for years."

"I'm not sure I believe that."

"Believe what the fuck you want. It's still in my name, but own it? Only on paper. It and damn near everything I ran at one time is no longer mine. I had a good business; some of it was legit. I made good barbecue. You know, I don't actually own that anymore, either. I get some payments, a percentage, but I sold that off. I sold it off so I could retire, and I got paid good to let the car lot stay in my name, but I don't make money off of it anymore. I'd like my name off, but part of the deal was it had to stay attached, at least as the owner. That keeps the real owner at a distance. I'm a fucking lame duck in an orthopedic shoe. I can still quack, but I got nothing left to quack about."

The waitress came over with our lunch. It was sushi and California rolls. It looked good. I asked for a fork due to the fact that I might put my eye out with chopsticks. She went away and came back with a fork. I thought she looked a little disappointed when she gave it to me.

I reached for the soy sauce.

"Put some wasabi down first, spread it around, mix the soy in that, gently, and then dip the food in it. It gives it real taste."

"I've had it before," I said.

"Yeah, but you don't know how to eat it. It's a one-bite thing, you know that? Though it should be done with chopsticks, because a fork gives it a funny aftertaste. Stir it around in the stuff, and then eat it."

"I appreciate that," I said, "but I kind of had another conversation I was interested in. One about you not owning anything anymore."

He ate a piece of sushi. He put his chopsticks down and sipped his tea. He said, "I got drummed out, and if you got a beef, it isn't with me. I can tell you some things, though, things that might even help you, and I don't mind doing that. I got my own ax to grind. That said, I ask you to keep me out of it."

This was an interesting turn of events.

"All right," I said. "Tell me some things that might help. I'll decide if they do."

"I'm a king without country, Hap. I still got a big house and nice cars and some money, good money, but I have about as much power as a toddler. I'm almost in prison, you want to know the truth."

"I been to prison once. I didn't care for it. Comparatively, what you got isn't nearly so bad."

"That's because you don't have what I have. And in fact, guy out there in the car, he's my bodyguard in name, but not really. He watches me. He sees you in here, well, he could make trouble for you."

"I got so much trouble now that adding to it doesn't matter much. Besides, there's someone out there watching after me who might as well be named Trouble."

"You are in deeper than you even imagine, and you still haven't got a clue what's going on. I think you think you have a clue, but you don't."

"Are you going to enlighten me?"

"I'm trying. Just listen. Don't talk, don't answer unless I ask you something. Just listen. Let's start with Sandy Buckner. Few years back she went to work for me. I had the car company, and I was peddling tail on the side, and she comes in wanting to work for me. Talks to Frank first."

"That right?"

"Yeah. You know Frank's a split stump?"

"Heard that."

"Frank tells me about Sandy, cause then I was boss. Called the shots, hired the help. Frank tells me there's this girl I might like to hire, a real looker, and I set up an interview. Sandy's well turned out. I don't trust her at first. Did a bit of research, like I always did. She had a journalism degree, and I'm thinking she might be playing *Brenda Starr, Girl Reporter*. So I take the position that I'm interested, but she's got to give me a sample of the goods. I'm thinking this might be the breaking point, that she won't let the beaver loose if she's just there to do an exposé. I mean, sure, she could not care, but it was one way to test. Not definitive, but something. She did me more ways than I thought could be done, and hell, I was running a high-class whorehouse. Still, I was cautious. Time passes, a year or so, and she does her job well, and I think she's all right. Next thing I know there's some guys come to talk to me, my own guys. They say, 'Hey, we're going to put you in more of a consulting position.' My own fucking business. I hit the roof, of course. Consulting? Who the fuck are you? Well, know who they were?"

"How many guesses do I get?"

"The new owners. They didn't buy shit, but they had someone who invested a little money in the right place to get the right guys interested, some real hardware slingers from Houston. They got businesses all over the United States and overseas."

"You got steamrolled."

"That's right. Sandy had some money of her own, quite a bit of it, I think, and she goes to these guys, says she's investing. Besides money, she offers something better, says she's got all the inside dope on the business. And she did. She had done her fucking homework. She tells them she can go wider, spread it overseas.

"Turns out, too, she's been doing this blackmail thing, and she tells these Houston guys, these bent-nose motherfuckers, they can do what she's doing on a wider scale, cause they got some real dough to expand. They dive in, and all of a sudden I'm sitting home with the cold fucking north wind whistling up my asshole. They pushed me out and told me to eat shit and call it caviar."

"Sandy did that?"

"Goddamn right. She is one smart hot-ass bitch, and she screwed me not only on the couch in my office that time, she screwed me over and took my business. Went to work for these Houston turds. Bottom line, I was out, she was in. That's when this Canceler crap got started."

He paused, ate a piece of sushi, put his chopsticks down, and drank some tea.

"Woman you're looking for, she's the fucking mastermind. She doesn't call herself Sandy anymore. She's wheeling and dealing. These guys, these hit men you got the fancy name for, I think they're all kin. Brothers, cousins. Maybe there's some friends thrown in. And Sandy expands the business with them. Used to be one guy, or maybe it was two. I'm not sure, but pretty soon it's a family business for a family of fucking psychos. I've done my share of things, Collins. Or had it done. Some bad shit. I knew it was bad shit when I did it, but I didn't lose sleep over it. It was business."

"Well, then, that makes it just fine," I said.

"Don't even know I disagree with you. Being away from it, I got to say, what the fuck was that all about? I started out selling my dad's barbecue and peddling used cars, next thing I know I'm in the sewer without any hip boots."

"I doubt that was an accident of nature."

"I'm not asking for pity. I come from a family that was so poor the soles of their shoes were the bottoms of their feet. I come from ignorant shits, and my old man was the one taught me how to be crooked. But I was better at it than he was. I got some education and I got some plans and I got rich. I liked being rich. I'm still well off, but I haven't any power, and these bodyguards, they don't give a flying wet sausage in a whorehouse about me. Long as I keep it simple and don't go much of anywhere without them, don't try to take the business back over, they're all jake with me. I had that business back, you know what I'd do? I'd get rid of all those high-end cars and go back to selling Chevrolets. On a bad day I'd sell a Ford. I'd quit running poontang, and there wouldn't be any blackmail. I know it's rare and hard to believe, but I've grown a conscience."

"I think what you've grown is desperate."

"Have it your way."

"So Sandy, she runs your business now?"

"What I said, and someone runs her business. The Houston people. But here's a bit of a rat turd in her soup. What she don't know is I got some records that I kept, old-school, on paper, and I got that and I could maybe cause her a real pain in the ass I was to give it up to the law. It's stuff happened under my watch, but now she'd get asked about it, long as someone knew to ask her. She could have me whacked at any time, though. I expect it every day. One day I go to eat sushi, and instead I'm in a lake somewhere and the fish are eating me. It could happen. Truth is, you sitting here could cause me serious problems. Bodyguards have got more lax in the last few years. They're not right on me like they used to be, but I don't want them to think I'm spilling out of school."

"But you are."

"Suppose I am. Thank God they don't like sushi, which is why I eat here. They're the greasy hamburger types. They think class is what they attended in school. If they went."

"Are you offering this information to me? Sounds like it."

"I'm looking to get out of this trap, but I'm not giving anything to anyone with those hit fucks out there."

"The Cancelers?"

"Who else? Yeah. Them. Listen to me. What I'm thinking is you want what I want."

"Not exactly," I said.

"Yeah, but you want it close enough it works for both of us. What you want is to take their bad asses down. The real ones. The ones that really own the business. Sandy, too, and the ones they hire for the big kill jobs.

Start with the teeth, the Cancelers, and you get rid of a whole lot of their bite."

"They'll just buy implants, new killers."

"Not if you go after the teeth, then get them while they're nothing but gums.

"Let me tell you something, Hap. I heard through the grapevine about the biker screws you messed with. I heard that from someone who's part of that club, one of the few spies I got left out there. He's damn near worthless to me, really, but now and again I get some news because he wants some money. He said three guys came down on the whole fucking club and shot the shit out of them and ran over some of them with a car. He said two of those guys were you and this Leonard Pine."

"That sounds about right," I said.

"Who's the third guy?"

"You don't need to know."

"They said Frank was there and you came and got her from them."

"Right again."

"You trust her?"

"No."

"Good."

"But she gave us a bit of information. Some of it would groove nicely with what you're telling me. Some of it. I think Frank might have a way of dressing up things so that it's all in her color. Know what I mean?"

"Frank is an opportunist. She didn't mind I got skunked and Sandy took over and that the Houston people took Sandy over. Long as she has a job and the money comes in, she's hunky-dory with it. Don't start thinking she's got a conscience."

"No need to worry," I said.

"And Sandy, that bitch, she doesn't get her clock cleaned, another five years and she'll be running the Houston group, you mind my words."

I thought: damn, if he's telling it true, I've found Sandy, but Lilly Buckner will not have the cockles of her old and somewhat creaky heart warmed by my discovery. The thought of that made me feel deeply disappointed, as if I had somehow expected something different from the human race.

"Thinking about what you did to those bikers, and you coming here to talk to me, bold as the pope in his underpants, it's got me thinking you might can find a way out for me."

"Does it?" I said.

"It does."

Doug leaned out of the booth and looked outside. I looked, too. His so-called bodyguard was in the front seat of the car with his head thrown back and his eyes closed.

"See?" he said. "Something happens to me, no one's crying. But if you were to get rid of those hitters, then I'm not scared of who else they might bring. But you see, the cops, they can't protect me from those Canceler motherfuckers, because cops and feds, they're all entwined. Some of those Cancelers might just walk into the police station and shoot hell out of everyone while the cops are busy trying to open a box of fucking doughnuts. But if the Cancelers are gone, I would start to believe I can be protected long enough to squeal like a dying rat. I got stuff the feds would want. More and better than what they're getting now. I got about twenty years' worth of material, a lot of it on the Houston guys, the ones who have their peckers in most of the serious moneymaking crime in Texas, might be something the feds would trade for. I used to deal with the Houston assholes all the time, but they didn't own me until Sandy came along, the crafty cunt."

"So what you're saying to me is I should see that the Cancelers are canceled, and then you'll come forward and pin the tail on the donkey?"

"That's the size of it."

"How do I know if I get rid of them you won't just go back to doing what you were doing before? Laying low and having sushi for lunch?"

"Because I want a nice witness relocation by the sea somewhere. Hell, I'd settle for the high desert, fucking mountains. I just want to start over and live the rest of my days reading books and pumping some good-looking widow with grown or dead children. Preferably the latter. Saves money at Christmas."

"If I were to think this was a good deal, where would I find these Cancelers? How spread out are they? Where would I locate Sandy?"

"Sandy works out of Houston. She goes by the name Florence Gale. There's some humor in that name somewhere. People she works for, the Houston crowd, they've done her up right. Got her named changed, given her a nice clean business front that hides the dirt under her finger-nails."

He reached out and touched my hand. I wasn't expecting that.

"Do this for me, get rid of these Cancelers, then I'll help you, and that will pull Sandy into the light. I'll take my chances with the feds."

I eased my hand away from his, leaned back in the booth, fastened my eyes on him.

"Let me explain something to you, Barbecue King. We do this, and then you welch, you won't be doing any better than before, cause we'll have to come see you. Understand?"

"You're able to take out the Cancelers, then I figure you can take out me. I haven't any reason to play you."

44

They are believed to be of one family, and their father was a man named George Greely," Doug said.

George Greely. It came back to me. He had been in the news some years back and is now part of criminal history as well as criminal legend, but not for being a mastermind—simply for personifying evil in human form.

George Greely had been in the military, and according to all the psychoanalysis by people who knew something, or people who knew nothing but thought they did, all the editorials and comments and news reports, Greely was the kind of guy that should clear your head from thinking everyone in uniform, or that's worn a uniform, is a hero. The military suited him because it gave him structure. Something he hadn't had early in life, as his father died when he was two and his mother left him to a couple who in turn gave him up to a orphanage. He became a bully, taking out all his anger for being abandoned on anyone smaller than him. He was a giant of a man, tall, with a barrel chest, dead-white skin, shark eyes, and a thick gray beard. I remembered seeing his photo in the newspapers.

When he left the military he lost his structure and tried to re-create it for himself with rigid rules about what he ate, when he ate, how he slept, and so on. He'd sleep on the floor with the window open in winter with nothing but a thin blanket over him. He read the Spartans did that, and it made them tough, and that's what he wanted to be, a kind of Spartan.

He married a woman he could control. Told her what to wear and how to talk and who to talk to, kept her from using makeup and perfume, even body deodorant. Showers were once a week and don't waste water and to hell with soap.

Greely finally decided she didn't need to talk to anyone but him, period. He isolated her on a farm outside of Crockett, Texas, away from everyone, and there over the next thirty years he built a junkyard and scrap metal business. He and that poor woman had a passel of kids. Greely had kids not only by his wife, but in time, by one of his own daughters. Pretty soon this compound he made of mobile homes linked together was surrounded by a concrete-block fence ten feet high with barbed wire at the top. His land was a hundred acres bought when land was cheap, and five acres of that was Greely compound central.

Later, when they came to take away the bodies, they determined from survivors, cause there were a lot of children there, that the daughter Greely had a child by had managed to move out of the compound by not coming home from school, and in time, a year or so later, word drifted down to him that on the outside she found a boyfriend. Greely felt like a jilted lover and coaxed her and her boyfriend to the compound with promises of money and a slice of the land.

They showed up, he murdered them, and killed two of his older children just for sport while the others scattered like quail. He put their bodies in a pit that was beneath an outdoor privy. He then drove into Crockett with a plan to kill anyone he saw. His first pick was a police officer. Greely's gun misfired, and after a ferocious fight, in which the police officer was assisted by citizens, Greely was arrested and taken away.

Greely told his story in a matter-of-fact way, and the papers were full of it for weeks. He mainly talked about guns and large knives and how he loved them, how he knew things that others didn't, had some direct insight with God. He said God told him to do what he did, and no matter what man's law was, he was right with God. God was testing his faith, same as Abraham and Job.

Bottom line was, some few years later the state of Texas gave him a hot shot. But the family, mostly boys, a few girls, survived. When the news lost interest in them, they slipped into obscurity. According to Doug, the Greely survivors had not learned a damn thing and had taken up their father's habits of incest and fanatic gun and sharp-weapon love. Children were born between daughters and brothers, and they were raised in Greely's unique way, out there among the junk in the compound; it was a family tradition.

In time most of the folks in the compound drifted away, a few died there. That left seven or eight boys. The number varied, depending on who was telling the story. No one knew much about them after that. The Barbecue King knew more than most, because he knew about the Cancelers, and he knew some of the people who hired them. They were all Greely men from early thirties on up. They had found their niche. In time they became the go-to boys for the Houston crew, the Dixie Mafia.

They were perfect. They killed as much for love as money, and they were isolated out there on their land, inside their compound. No one knew what they did or how they lived, because no one was allowed out there, and there was very little contact between the general population and the Greely clan.

"You know something about Greely," Doug said, "then you know the Cancelers. They aren't a bunch of fucking masterminds. It's not like you could get them in a room and they could explain to you why they do it, other than for money. I would do it for money, situation was right, and I could see it as business, but not pleasure. They enjoy it. They have a need to do it. They are stone-cold killers, plain and simple. I've heard a rumor they're all mute, but that could just be a story that gets told because there's so little known about them and nothing known that came directly from them. I also know that the ones out there are the last of it. I guess they ran out of sisters to fuck. You won't find a damn thing about them anywhere, because except when they're on a job, they're to themselves. You aren't going to find some profile, or a list of crimes, because they've never been caught. Not because they're so smart but simply because they know one thing. Isolate the prey and kill it, take the nut sack, leave. Here's the good news, though. I do know this because I do get a whiff of what's going on through my former company now and then—someone will drop something and I'll hear it, pick it up, and tuck it away. I'm not a hundred percent isolated. Ones out there, those boys, they're the last of it. When they're gone the Cancelers have bought their last pairs of underwear. If they wear them."

"You're sure these guys are it?"

"One of the few things about them I'm sure of. As much as you can be sure of anything. I can't be certain exactly how many of them there are, but I think what I've told you is more than reasonably accurate."

"All right, then. Can you tell me where they are?"

45

With directions from my new pal Doug, me and Leonard drove out beyond Crockett, named after frontiersman Davy Crockett, who stopped there on his way to the Alamo and his date with destiny. We drove through Crockett into the boonies, where the woods grew wild. The hundred acres the Greelys owned were thick with woods, and there was one narrow dirt road that led into it. It was dark down that road, even in dead-solid daylight. Tree limbs came together from either side and knotted up with branches and leaves and made a kind of canopy over us. There was brush growing on the sides of the road, and there were long stems sticking out of the brush, waving in the gentle wind like great insect antennae.

I said, "This looks like the road to the witch's house that Hansel and Gretel found."

"What if it's just a bunch of inbred motherfuckers he's sent us out here to see? Shit stains on the ass of humanity, but maybe not killers at all."

"Occurred to me," I said.

"We get the gang together, come out here and kill them all, and they got nothing to do with any of this business. That would suck."

"It would," I said, "though I think Booger would be happy either way."

We drove down a ways and found a gap where the local assholes tossed their trash instead of taking it to the dump. There was all kinds of rotting garbage there, including a dead white cat with its feet sticking out of a dilapidated plastic trash can crammed with all manner of stuff. Next to the trash can was a couch with springs poking through it, coiled and bobbing in the wind. There was a thin, well-worn path next to the road not too far from the trash heap, and that was the path we wanted.

I said, "Wait a minute, brother. Stop the car."

Leonard stopped near the garbage heap. I got a shovel out of the back of the car and dug a hole by the trash can. I levered the cat out of the can with the shovel, dumped it into the hole, and covered it up.

"All done, Saint Francis?" Leonard said. He was still in the car with the window rolled down.

"All done," I said and put the shovel away.

It was midafternoon, but as I said, it seemed later due to all the tree shadows and ink-dark clouds clustering together in the heavens and showing through the gaps in the trees, threatening rain. Leonard pulled the car up farther into the gap with the trash, pulled around behind a tree. It didn't totally hide the car, but it was only noticeable if you were looking in exactly the right place.

We got our handguns, and Leonard got a pair of binoculars that were on a strap from the trunk of the car. He slipped the strap over his head and put a penlight in his pocket.

We walked back to the long road that led to the witch's house and started down it. There were NO TRESPASSING signs as well as others that said TRAVEL AT YOUR OWN RISK and one that showed a gun pointed at us and the words: WE DON'T CALL 911.

We walked a long way. Finally the trees opened up and there was cleared land. Wild grass grew on it in spurts of green and yellow as well as twisted dead, gray grass. We walked along, and then Leonard said, "Hold it. Look there."

The wind had done us a favor. It had lifted a patch of the dead grass enough that Leonard had spotted the outline of an opening in the ground. We moved over there cautiously. The dead grass had been dug out in lumps and stacked on top of a piece of thin ply board. Leonard got out his penlight and shined it into the crack. There really wasn't anything to see. Leonard found another place to duck down and poke the light. Finally he laid down on the ground and lifted the ply board slightly and poked the light in.

"There's a pit under that ply board," he said. "It's wide, and it's very deep. They must have used a backhoe to make it. I could see a bit of water shining at the bottom. My guess is that ply board is just strong enough to hold the wads of grass, but had we walked across it, it would have folded. There's a smell in the pit, like old shit. There are stakes down there, and the shit looks to be smeared on them. It was one of the Cong's favorite tricks in Nam. You not only got the spikes, but if you survived, you got a tremendous infection that worked in the long term as well as a bullet. Old Man Greely spent time in the military, maybe Nam. He could have passed that on to his family, such as they were. It's a fucking booby trap, and I'm going to guess there are others."

"They may not use the road much," I said, "but they use it, so they have some way around this stretch of land."

"Exactly what I was thinking."

We went back up the path a ways, stood and looked. It emptied right into that field, and beyond the booby trap was a thick swath of trees. The path split through them and turned slightly left. There was nothing visible of it beyond that.

"Look there," Leonard said.

He was pointing to a spot to the right of the road. There were no trees there, just tall brush, and the brush was dead like the grass on top of the ply board, touched with dust from the road in a way that made it look as if it had been sprinkled with nutmeg. We walked over and peeled back the brush and took a look. On the other side of it was a narrow road, more of a trail, really. It wound down between the brush and trees.

"They have their own secret road," Leonard said.

We got hold of the brush and found it was all wired together and on a wooden swivel. We pulled at it, and it slid back like a door.

"Let's do a bit of recon," Leonard said. "But watch for booby traps."

We found one right away. There was a wire across the trail. I walked to one end of it, Leonard to the other. There was a little wooden box on both sides. Leonard said, "My guess is someone trips this wire, the box opens, and something shoots out, backed by an explosive. It could be glass, nails—hell, anything."

"I'm starting to get nervous," I said.

We stepped over the wire and went along. No more traps were discovered. In time the trail wound around a large patch of trees, and then there was another clearing, and in the center of that clearing, about an acre away, was a great wall of concrete blocks, just as the newspapers and the Barbecue King had described it. A huge Dixie flag snapped in the wind above it on a tall pole made from a skinned tree.

We squatted down at the edge of the trees and studied the place.

"See those cameras?" Leonard said.

I looked and saw. They were positioned in several places along the wall.

"Think they can see us?" I said.

Leonard lifted the binoculars and studied the wall.

"They look to be pointing down. I think we got within twenty feet of the wall they'd pick us up. I can see lights mounted near them, probably those automatic things that come on when they sense movement."

"This seems to be more complex than I expected."

"They may be white trash—inbred, fun-for-the-dollar killers," Leonard said, "but that doesn't mean they're stupid. Inbreeding doesn't always result in people with quarter-sized moles on their faces and a hole where their noses ought to be. It doesn't do much for emotional development, though, and it confuses folks at family reunions."

"What's our plan now, bwana?"

"We play Jungle Jim. You see how the woods narrows when you look to the right side of the compound fence? We ought to go that way, be in the tree line. Might be the best bet for taking a closer peek at the place."

46

The woods was full of heat-wilted greenery, crosshatched limbs, and briars, and it was dark and deep and painful to make our way through. I was stabbed and poked, ripped and torn, and I could feel ticks and chiggers crawling on me, racing over my flesh on a mission to create a warm nest of my pubic hair.

We came to a rise in the forest where the trees draped over a hill and thinned enough you could stand in a clearing and look at the compound. The narrow trail had some deeper grooves there from vehicles going down and climbing up the hill. The concrete-block wall did not go all the way around. There was a medieval-looking gate in the side that was wide enough to let a tank through.

The concrete wall, except for where the gate was, was in the front and on both sides, but at the back there were tangles of barb wire fence fastened to metal poles. In front of the metal poles was a wide ditch, and there was mucky water in the ditch and no telling what else. The ditch ran along the back side and draped in at the corners toward where the barb wire fence met the concrete blocks.

Inside the compound we could see cars and trucks and all manner of equipment, most of it rusted and weather-pocked. There was a Ferris wheel and sections of tracks and fragments of old rides strewn all about like dinosaur bones. The sunlight sticking through the trees coated those "bones" with a blood-red sheen.

In the center of the compound, drawn in a circle, like covered wagons defending themselves against Indian attack, were a series of mobile homes, and near them was a large wooden shed. There were ten homes, and they were all connected by slapdash ply board walls, and in some cases only by porches, from one to the other. There were outhouses out back and around the circle of homes. There was an old-fashioned satellite dish weathered to the color of dirt. There were no trees in the compound, no grass, and no sign of life.

I turned around and looked behind me. More trees, but at the top of the hill and slightly to the back of it was a weather-peeled deer stand. It was set back in some trees. From there you could look down on the compound.

"We have to decide: is it over the wall or through the wire?" Leonard said.

"Wire and that ditch are a lot of trouble."

"Over the wall?"

"Ten feet is ten feet, and then there are the cameras and the motion-sensor lights."

"Thing to do, I guess, is go back and tell our bunch what we've found and put some plan in action."

"I don't see a car or truck out there that looks like it could run," Leonard said. "That may mean no one is home."

"You wanting to investigate?"

"Best to come back at night," Leonard said.

"And if there are traps out there?"

"Someone will be really surprised."

"We should send Booger across."

"I was thinking that," Leonard said.

• • •

We worked our way back to the gate of dried brush and closed it and tried to make it look the way we had found it. After walking out, we got in my car and drove back to the safe house, but we stopped and ordered hamburgers and french fries first. By the time we got back the day had mostly run its course. The safe house was dark. Jim Bob's truck was out front, and Jim Bob and Booger were on the front porch, sitting on the stoop. I wondered if there had been a moment of bonding. I dismissed that when I got up close and saw that neither was talking. Jim Bob looked unpleasant, and Booger looked bored.

"So, nice fun day?" I asked.

"Well," Jim Bob said, "it's been a day."

"You two boys been playing pretty?"

"Shit, yeah," Jim Bob said. "Me and him, we're fucking."

That made even Booger smile.

"Then there have been no harsh words, slap fights, or water spitting?" Leonard asked.

"So far so good," Jim Bob said.

"We made some hot chocolate," Booger said. He seemed very happy and sincere about that event.

"We did," Jim Bob said. "I brought a few things in my rucksack. What you guys got there?"

"Hamburgers. A few extra if anyone feels really hungry."

"I could lick shit off the sidewalk if there was undigested food in it," Jim Bob said.

"This will be better," I said, and we all went inside.

At the table, in the dark, we ate our meal without turning on the lights. Leonard told them all that we had found and what we feared about more booby traps beyond the ones we knew about. He explained that it would take some work to get inside.

"We just have to prepare for the mission," Booger said. "Go prepared, go in quick, and then get out."

"We didn't see anyone," I said. "No movement. No signs of life. Not a working car there. Electricity is probably from a generator or generators. No wires were visible outside the compound. Us not seeing them could mean they're out on their various missions. Or on a singular mission together. Or they're just real quiet. What I fear is that Dougie may have given me a line of manure, and they may just be a bunch of crazy fucks who like to be alone so they can diddle each other in the ass."

"No," said a voice from the dark of the living room. "It's not like that at all."

We all nearly turned the table over when we leaped up, grabbing at our weapons. A light was turned on by the armchair near the living room window. In the chair sat a fine-looking woman with long blond hair and a silver dress that fit tight and rode high on her thighs, rode low at her chest, revealing the tops of two creamy white mounds, as they used to say in the sex books. Her long, pale legs were crossed, and one very uncomfortable-looking white shoe with a heel designed by Masochist Incorporated dangled off the end of the toes of her crossed leg.

"Oh, they might be diddling each other in the ass," she said. "But they aren't just a bunch of crazy fucks, though they are crazy."

She smiled. "Hi, Hap."

"Vanilla Ride," I said.

47

I have arrived," she said.

Her message in the greeting cards had worked, and she proved she could still move like a ghost. I wondered how long she had been inside the house, in the dark. I tried to remember if I had even looked in that direction.

Booger stepped forward, ahead of us, eased into the living room and closer to Vanilla.

"Who are you?"

"I'm the cavalry," she said.

"You?" Booger said.

"Me," she said.

Jim Bob laughed. "I know you."

"Yes, you do," Vanilla said. "Not well, I might add."

"We can remedy that," Jim Bob said.

"It's so sweet of you to think so," she said.

"You look like a wispy piece of ass, you ask me," Booger said.

"No one did," she said.

Booger was still holding the gun he had drawn, and now he pointed it at her and walked over closer. "Shit, I could jerk you up from there, pop you like a whip. Pop you so hard your snatch will snap off and smack the wall."

"So," Vanilla said. "How was charm school?"

Booger put the gun in its holster. Vanilla flicked her foot. The shoe popped off and snapped Booger between the eyes. He yelled, lunged forward, ready to grab Vanilla. She was on her feet then, one foot lower than the other due to the height of the one shoe she was wearing. She reached out and took hold of the hand he was reaching with by one finger, quickly, and made a slight movement, pulling her little finger in just below the joint that connected Booger's finger to his hand.

He hit the floor on his knees hard enough to jar John Wayne's hairpiece, and Wayne had been dead and in his grave for years.

Vanilla manipulated the finger until Booger, who was trying to reach for his gun with the other hand, was stretched out on his belly. He made a mewing sound that was music to my ears.

Vanilla said, "Up, up, up."

She turned his hand over, palm to the ceiling, and that made him come to his knees. She turned slightly, putting his hand against her chest next to her throat, and pressed his finger. He came to his feet with a grunt, tried to dance around her in a circle. She went under his arm, still holding his finger, and with a twist of her wrist sent him hurtling over the couch. He hit hard on the other side of it.

When he rose up from behind it he had his gun in his hand. Vanilla had one, too. I had no idea where it came from. It was very small and shiny, and the barrel was pressed up against Booger's forehead. She said, "I think I snapped you hard enough your dick came off, don't you?"

"You bitch," he said.

"Now you know my middle name. Drop your gun on the couch, or I'm going to give you a small, bullet-size ventilator shaft."

Booger dropped the gun, and Vanilla reached out and snatched it up with her other hand. Slowly she pulled the gun back from his forehead, slipped it into the gap of the dress at her bosom. She tossed his gun into the chair where she had been sitting.

Smiling at me, ignoring Booger, she said, "Hap, honey, you have any more hamburgers left in there?"

I nodded.

"I don't normally eat that stuff, but right now I'm hungry. It was a long flight and a long drive, and then I had to sit in the dark all by myself while you boys discussed things."

"How long have you been here?" Leonard asked.

"Long enough. If this is your idea of security, I can tell you now, you boys are screwed, considering who you're up against. They aren't smart in the normal way, but they are stealthy and determined."

"Never had anyone sneak up on me before," Booger said, massaging his finger.

"Now you have," Vanilla said. "And leave the gun in the chair for now, or I'll shoot you before you can pick it up."

Booger didn't move.

"You know who these killers are?" I asked.

"I do."

"How could you possibly know what we're up against?"

"I have quite the network, Hap."

"Baby," Jim Bob said, "you are my goddamn dream girl."

Vanilla gave Jim Bob one of her wide, wicked smiles.

"Girl? Girls play with dolls. I'm a woman. I play with men. I can even get them to dress up funny."

"Better yet," Jim Bob said.

48

Booger was out from behind the couch now, but he was moving slow. He was glaring at Vanilla. She didn't seem to care. I knew better, though. She was aware of his every move.

"You can have your gun now," she said to Booger.

He picked it up and eased it back into its place.

"When did you get in?" I said.

"A bit ago. Bad flight and bad food, and then a drive from the airport in Houston. I came by Harley-Davidson."

"We didn't hear you come up," I said.

"I know that. I hope you boys are going to perk up, otherwise the Canceler—and he is a group, which, from listening to you talk, I see you've figured out—is going to have your itty-bitty testicles for lunch."

"How long were you sitting there?" Leonard asked. "Answer straight."

"I was here before you guys came home. I was here while Jim Bob and Sore Finger were here farting about on the front porch."

"In that chair?" Jim Bob said.

"No. In the back, and later in the chair, when it started to get dark."

"Goddamn," Jim Bob said. "No one, but no one, sneaks up on me like that."

"That's what he said," Vanilla said, nodding toward Booger.

"You are one lovely, mysterious woman," Jim Bob said.

"Tell me something I don't know," Vanilla said.

"Come," I said. "Sit down at the table. You can have Booger's chair."

We all sat down at the table again, except for Booger. He came and sat on the kitchen counter with his legs hanging down. It was the first time I had ever seen him look less than confident, and maybe it was the first time he had ever felt less than confident.

"Me and the Cancelers are in the same business," Vanilla said. "Or were. I'm what you might call semiretired. We didn't run in the same circles, exactly, but our circles crossed now and then. Gets right down to it, they're nothing but backwoods rednecks who like to kill."

"You've done some pretty brutal things yourself," Leonard said.

"For money. But I'm what you might called reformed. I have a new way of looking at things. Now I only kill those who need killing, or I do a few favors for friends."

Vanilla reached out and patted my hand. God, I loved Brett, but when Vanilla did that an electricity went through me that made my pants strain at the crotch.

"How good a friends are you two?" Jim Bob said.

"Not as good as I'd like," she said.

"I don't get it," Jim Bob said. "Booger you just made piss himself—"

"She did not," Booger said.

"Leonard is queer, and Hap looks like he's been through the mill, and here I sit, a handsome piece of meat wearing manly footwear and a cowboy crown, and you're patting his hand."

Vanilla grinned at him.

"I don't understand it, either, but Hap here stirs me."

I felt myself blush.

"And I thought I'd seen every strange thing there was to see," Jim Bob said. "And I once saw a fellow eat a dog turd for a dollar."

"Goddamn heterosexuals," Leonard said. "What you guys see sexually in women confuses me."

"It should," I said. "But just for the record, me and Vanilla are only friends."

"Unfortunately," Vanilla said.

"I agree with the fag," Booger said. "You guys are making me sick."

"Enough bullshit," I said. "Vanilla, you know anything about this bunch that could be helpful?"

"Basically the best thing to do is kill them all."

"I'm liking you a little better now," Booger said.

"How nice," Vanilla said.

"I prefer we turn them in," I said.

"Please, brother, please," Leonard said. "That stuff where a guy goes into a psycho's den and shoots the gun out of his hand and asks him to give himself up—and the guy does—is for old *Lone Ranger* episodes."

"I like *The Lone Ranger,*" Jim Bob said.

"Yeah," I said. "Me, too."

"But," Jim Bob said, "I have to agree with Leonard."

"We saw their nest," Leonard said. "It's a bitch to navigate."

Me and Leonard went on to explain in more detail about it. I drew a map on a burger wrapper, drew a kind of design of the compound as we knew it. "As for what's inside, we have no idea."

"Seems to me," Jim Bob said, "the weak spot is that hill you guys said you stood on. You can see right down into the place."

"We were thinking the same," I said. "That would be the spot for a lookout."

"But you don't know that anyone's home," Booger said.

"We didn't see cars that looked like they would drive," I said. "So we figure they were out. Hell, for all we know they're killing folks in Maine right now, packing up testicles to mail home, and won't be back for a while. They might decide to take a holiday. It could all be futile, but it's the only plan we got."

"There was a big building in the middle of the compound," Leonard said. "Storage shed, maybe, or that could be where they keep their vehicle or vehicles. They may be home and are tucked up in one of those trailers playing cards or stringing their collected testicles on strings for Christmas ornaments for all we know."

"Hap ought to be posted on the hill," Leonard said. "He can shoot well. He'd be best with a simple twenty-two rifle. It would do fine from that range, way he shoots. He could kill them with that, and there wouldn't be a lot of noise. It might make it harder for them to figure where the shot is coming from."

"It might take a bit more firepower than that," I said.

"I can do it," Vanilla said. "I have my own gear, including a sniper rifle. Depending on how far away the hill is, Leonard's right. A twenty-two might be the thing. These days everyone thinks they need a rocket launcher, but it's loud and messy and may take out more than you want to take out."

"I bet that gear of yours was rough to bring in your carry-on," Jim Bob said.

"I don't carry it with me. I have suppliers in a lot of places, and I have the money to buy it. I'll pick it up later."

"You are so cute when you talk about guns and murder," Jim Bob said.

"I say we lay out the plan, get anything else we might need, and to-morrow night go out there and see if they're home," I said. "If they're not, we might have to regroup at a later date."

"This is the full run for me," Booger said. "I just want to have fun and go home. I don't know I could stand you people again."

"I don't know we'd invite you again," I said. "And if your ass feels chapped, you can leave at any time. Vanilla promises not to twist your finger and make you cry."

Booger frowned.

"All right, I'm in, now or later," he said. "Let's just do this thing."

49

We bought some supplies the next day and then rested as much as possible at the safe house, except for Vanilla, who brought out the Harley she had hidden in the barn across the way. She told us she needed to make some preparations, that she'd be back in plenty of time. She put on purple leathers and a helmet and rode into town.

When she was gone, Jim Bob looked down the road she had taken, said to Booger, "That little wisp of a girl sure made you eat shit, didn't she, big'n?"

"She surprised me," Booger said.

"That's what she does," I said. "Surprises folks. Sometimes she surprises them to death."

"I respect that," Booger said. "I made a mistake. I underestimated."

"Being underestimated physically is her greatest strength," I said. "That and the fact she's quick and smart and knows some tricks and carries a gun and can shoot the eye out of a gnat in the dark."

"And she's got that long blond hair, those sleek legs, and a face like a goddamn rodeo angel," Jim Bob said.

"You really are smitten," I said.

"One time with her would bring me closer to God," Jim Bob said. "I might even start believing."

Me and Leonard grabbed a couple Dr Peppers, went outside, leaving Jim Bob and Booger in the house. We walked across the street toward the old barn, slipped through the barb wire fence, and kept walking. We hadn't discussed doing this, we just all of a sudden did it, somehow knowing it was something we both wanted to do.

We opened the Dr Peppers and walked out to the barn, went behind it, and leaned against the old log wall and looked at the sky. It was late day, and the sun was beginning its slide to the west, like a fried egg on a tilted Teflon skillet.

"We'll be all right," Leonard said.

"Sure," I said. "We always are."

"I guess we'll be all right until we aren't."

"There you go."

"Think we can trust Booger?"

"I don't like him," I said. "But yeah. I think we can. Cason says he's reliable, and I think he wants to kill someone so bad he'll do the job. I only fear he'll want to do it too well."

"You still thinking you're going to bring some of the bad guys in and that the cops are going to go, 'Oh, sure, you went out there alone and brought them in without telling us, and we have to trust what you told us is true. We like that. Thanks, boys. You can go home now. Here's a lollipop.' "

"I just don't like the idea of shooting them down in cold blood."

"You knew it was leading to this."

"I know. But I don't have to like it."

"I don't like it, but it is what it is, and I do believe there are just some folks that need killing. You and I, this isn't our first county fair, now, is it?"

"I know."

"If I was making a list, brother, these motherfuckers would be right at the top, just under some that are already dead, like Hitler and Jack the Ripper and some that ought to be, like the Pillsbury Doughboy."

"You know I hate that doughy bastard, don't you?"

"You always say you want to take a rolling pin to him."

"I'd make cookies out of that cocksucker," I said.

"And then eat them."

"You got that."

"Vanilla, the extract, not the woman, would be added for me."

"You know it."

"We could dip the cookies in coffee."

"You know we would."

Puffy clouds were blowing across the sky like marshmallows floating in water. We watched them. I didn't say it, but I knew Leonard was probably thinking the same. What if this was the last time we ever paused long enough to study those clouds? It was an odd thought, really, because if we died we weren't going to miss them. I didn't believe in life after death, only in life, and I wasn't sure how good I had managed mine, but I liked it enough I wanted to hang on to it.

We sipped our drinks. It was really hot out there, but the heat felt good. I liked it on my face.

"In case anything happens," Leonard said, "I have a confession."

"All right."

"One time I used your toothbrush."

"What?"

"You heard me."

"Goddamn, Leonard. Recently?"

"Yep. Last time I stayed overnight at your house. I wanted to clean the toilet, and it was handy."

"Oh, go fuck yourself," I said, and we both laughed. Right then anything could be thought funny. We leaned there for a long time and drank our sodas and watched the white clouds rolling over the high blue sky and were pleased to have a breeze come up. The hot sun felt good, but the breeze drying the sweat on our faces felt even better.

50

Vanilla came back when the long blue shadows began to crawl and there was only a strain of daylight left. She was in a black Buick Grand National sedan, circa 1980s. It roared into the drive like a lion. We all went out and looked at it. I don't really know diddle about cars, but I knew it looked cool.

Vanilla was wearing black leather pants so tight you could see the outline of a quarter in her pocket, a black shirt, black leather jacket, and tall black boots. She got out and walked around and leaned on the Buick like she was about to have her picture taken at a car show.

"Where'd you get this?" Jim Bob asked.

"Don't ask," she said.

"Stolen cars will give us an unneeded headache."

"It's not stolen," she said. "But still, don't ask."

She opened the back door and took out two large black metal cases. I stepped over and took one from her. It was light. We took the cases in the house and placed them on the couch. Vanilla opened one of them. There was a series of black tubes and truncated rifle stocks inside, along with a scope and boxes of ammunition—.22 longs.

"I brought a very large van with me from Houston. Inside is the motorcycle and this stuff. I had the car arranged for here. Stored the van and bike in town at a storage unit. The car is a 1982 Buick Grand National. Last of the good muscle cars. I hope we won't need the speed, but if we do, we're ready. I'd prefer to just kill them, drive back slow, and have a small decaf later here at the house."

"It looks brand new," Booger said.

"Freshly repainted to match the original. It has a four-point-one liter turbocharged V-six, two hundred thirty-five horsepower. Go to sixty miles an hour in five seconds in spite of its size. Six seconds is common, but this one has had some serious modifications. It also has nice cup holders. Drinks gas like a fish drinks water. But the thing we really need is the stuff in this case."

"I don't recognize these weapons," Booger said.

"That's because they are special made. Not from any gun company. Light. Durable. Heaviest stuff on this trip will be the shotguns you carry. I saw them in the closet."

"You are quite the snoop," Leonard said.

"I like to know my surroundings. This one"—she pulled out two pieces of black gun barrel and screwed them together—"shoots a twenty-two round. Technically they have a bit more firepower due to the design of the rifle. Screw these barrels into this"—she reached in and pulled out the body of the gun, and then the stock, which was black and shortened at the back—"and you load it and go. It has a light clip, holds twelve shots. There are spare clips under the foam padding. There's a night-vision scope that fastens on it."

"I know what a night-vision scope is," Booger said.

"Good for you," Vanilla said.

"What's in the other case?" I asked.

"My underthings and changes of clothes."

"Can we look at those?" Jim Bob said and gave her his charm-them-out-of-their-pants grin.

Vanilla said, "No."

51

The Grand National roared through the night, Vanilla at the wheel, me in the front seat. Behind me was Leonard and Booger and Jim Bob. It was a wide car, and there was plenty of room in the backseat, even if Booger took up a lot of it.

It was just after midnight, and we were tearing through the dark and out into the hinterlands, as I liked to think of it, where the evil bastards lived in their dark little mobile houses with their sharp little wires and their grim little thoughts. Right then, my thoughts were pretty damn grim. I thought of Brett, and I thought of Chance. I even thought of our rescued dog, Buffy. But I didn't let myself think too long.

We hummed along, and I showed Vanilla how to go. When we turned off onto the back road, Vanilla went slow. Hot summer road dust swirled in the headlights and settled on the windshield. We came to where I buried the cat, and Vanilla parked behind the tree and brush where me and Leonard had stopped before.

"Walk in from here," I said.

"Turn off your phones," Vanilla said. "Anyone gets a phone call while we're sneaking, I'll take him out. I'm not getting killed for stupid reasons. But you will."

We checked our phones. Everyone was dressed in black. Vanilla had changed the black leather pants for black leotards. They fit even tighter than the leather but were far more flexible. I know, it's sexist, but I notice that kind of thing, and just about every heterosexual male who walks the earth and isn't neutered or too old to know ducks from chickens, and some that don't, notice those sort of things. It's biology, and it's a bitch. In polite society what you say to an attractive woman who is dressed in a way that makes you understand the power of biology is, "You look nice."

Vanilla had Booger hand her the case from the floorboard of the backseat. She put her rifle together. I knew, too, from watching, she had that little gun of hers in one leather jacket pocket, and strapped on her in clear sight was another pistol, also an automatic and also made of plastic, light as a child's dreams.

We got out of the car and walked to the back and got some rolled-up thick blankets out of the car. That part had been Jim Bob's idea. It was a good idea, but I'll come to that. There was a coiled rope with a grappling hook. Booger took that and draped the coil over his shoulder. Me, Jim Bob, and Leonard grabbed the shotguns. All the shotguns had shoulder straps on them, so we slung them. The shotguns were fully loaded.

We all had extra shells. I had a cold-piece Smith & Wesson revolver with me and it was loaded and the belt it was holstered on had shells in the bullet loops, just like an old cowboy gun belt. Booger had only his bag and whatever it was he had in it.

We walked together, watching for headlights, but there weren't any. Finally we came to the path through the woods with its tight limbs and brush and went along that. Once a raccoon darted across the road in front of us and was nearly shot by all of us who were carrying shotguns. Vanilla didn't so much as quiver.

We stopped at the brush gate and looked around carefully with our penlights in case new booby traps had been placed there, but found none. We opened the gate and went through, and when we came to the wire across the path, Booger studied it with the light, went to one end and used his knife to pry the top of one of the wooden boxes. We stood there with our assholes clenched while he did this, but he knew what he was doing. He said, "The wire pulls a trigger, and it causes an explosion that launches whatever is packed in this plastic bag with gunpowder. Looks like glass and nails."

That was as I had figured.

"We can just step over it," Jim Bob said.

"Yeah, but we come back this way quick we might not want to worry about it."

"Fair enough," Jim Bob said.

Booger used his knife to gently cut the string that pulled the explosive into action. "You got to cut it smooth and without much pressure. This stuff, it goes off, it sprays like skunk stink but hurts more."

He went over and cut the cord on the other side. He tied off the cord to limbs on either side so it appeared to be rigged.

"Now, we come back through here hauling ass, forget about where this is in the heat of the moment, we don't have to worry."

"Good job," I said.

"I know," Booger said.

We went on up the narrow trail, came to where it rode up on the hill then coiled down through a small patch of divided trees and on down to the compound. At night there were lights in the compound. They were on the wall and inside on large posts, and there was a small light coming from two of the trailers.

"Either someone's home," Leonard said, "or they just left a few lights on for giggles."

"There's the deer stand," I said and pointed. "I can position myself there."

"You're a good shot," Vanilla said, "but I have the rifle for it, and I'm used to how it works. I think that should be my job."

I nodded. "Take it."

"All right," Vanilla said. "Good. Stand has a clear look down on the compound. I'll use it as my crow's nest. I feel like I need to come down and join you boys, I will. Otherwise, I'll be shooting from there."

"Well, don't shoot us, baby girl," Booger said.

"Baby girl shoots you, then you know I did it on purpose. I don't miss a whole lot, not when the target is standing still and doesn't know I'm out here, and a lot of time even if they do."

"Holding you to it," Booger said.

"First I need to take care of the motion lights," she said.

Vanilla went to the deer stand and climbed up the little wooden ladder quiet and quick as a squirrel. A moment later I saw her rifle barrel poke out of a slot in the stand.

"Do you think me and her might hook up later?" Jim Bob said.

"I wouldn't know," I said. "Keep your mind on the business at hand."

"I can be easily of two minds and know what I'm doing. Don't you worry about that. Have I ever given you cause to worry?"

"No," I said.

"Still," Leonard said. "I worry a little."

"Shit, Leonard. You can fold those worries into a little square and set fire to it when I'm on the job," Jim Bob said. "You can rub my head for luck."

"Still a little worried," Leonard said.

Booger opened his bag, took out a sawed-off shotgun. There was a holster of sorts that he draped over his back and slipped the weapon into. He already had a Colt .45 automatic in his hip holster; it looked like a collector's item, had pearl handles. He had a knife on his other hip, and I knew in his boot he had another. He had a pair of small wire cutters stuck in a little bag on his belt. He had a light that fastened to the top of his sawed-off. We all had that, though Booger's rig was special made; mine and Jim Bob's and Leonard's were rigged with duct tape.

Booger stood up and said, "No one leaves anyone behind. That's the military way."

"I'm not, nor have I ever been in the military," I said. "But I'm with you on that one."

I looked down at the compound and the lights around it. It wasn't that well lit, really. In fact, the center of it was dark and shadow-crowded. I thought of the compound Vanilla Ride and I had broken into once, but she had known the place, and it was more organized and easier to navigate. Down below was a pile of mobile homes and carnival junk and old cars and a lot of unidentifiable metal. It made me a lot more nervous than the other compound had.

There was a hissing sound, like an arrow in flight, and one of the lights went out, and the sound was followed by others just like it in rapid succession. The lights on the wall, and the motion lights that would come on if we came within range, were out of commission. Vanilla took them out quickly and efficiently, and she didn't miss once. It was dark on that side now, and it would stay that way.

I glanced toward the deer stand, raised a hand in acknowledgment, and then we slipped down the slope of the hill, using the road. We were about a hundred feet outside the wall when Booger said, "Hold it."

We stopped and waited. "Look out there," he said.

We looked. I didn't see anything.

"You see how the moonlight hits along that line of grass there?"

I looked and saw that there were spots of yellowed grass about ten feet apart, and the spots went on for a long ways.

"Grass is green between, but in those spots it's yellow," Booger said.

"Traps," Jim Bob said.

"Mines is going to be my guess," Booger said, "cause if you look carefully, real carefully, between each spot is a strand of wire. Can you see it?"

I saw it.

"Hit one of those and it'll pull two of the pins off, and when they explode, my guess is they're the sort that will go up and out."

"Sure they're mines?" Leonard asked.

"No," Booger said. "But sure enough."

"The wire is designed so you hit it and it tugs, it'll go. I've seen mines like it before, or similar, in war. All you got to do is not step on the cord. You cut it gently, don't tug it or push it, it'll release tension on the mines. You step on one it'll still knock your nuts up under your chin, but I'm going to slip up there and cut the cord and then we'll go through. If they're real clever, they'll have another line not far from it. That way you see one, the other one will be behind some grass, and you think you're home free, trip the second one up, and—"

"Balls under your chin," I said.

"You get the teddy bear," Booger said.

"Here's an idea," Leonard said. "Let's just go down the road."

"We could do that," Booger said. "It even seems smart, but I got a feeling that road isn't all it looks to be, either. I think you'll note there are holes in the gate, and if you look carefully, there are gun barrels poking out of the holes, and I'll assure you, they are not manned, they are gimmicked. One of them comes in, they most likely got it rigged so they hit a switch, a button, whatever in their automobile, and those guns are disarmed. Way they're set now—and again, this is me guessing, and you're welcome to walk up the road and check out my theory—but way I see it, that's how they're set. Got to be disarmed by some device that we don't have. So we take our chances with the mines. I'll do that part."

He moved then, and I started to come up behind him, but Jim Bob caught my shoulder, said, "Let him run it through. That way, we lose him, it's only one man down."

"And it's Booger," Leonard said.

"Yeah, he'll be missed all of five seconds, though we might be wearing parts of him."

"He blows up, the noise will give them a small clue we're out here," Leonard said.

"Yes, but Booger will be gone, and we'll live to fight another day."

"Good point," Leonard said.

Booger eased forward, took out his knife, and clipped a cord between two spots in the grass, then he eased forward, found another cord, and cut it.

"Damn," Jim Bob said. "He made it."

Booger stood up and waved us forward, showing us where to go between the mines he had disarmed.

We ran along then, and when we got down to the wall, Booger uncoiled the rope and tossed the grappling hook over. It caught in the wire at the top easily enough. Booger pulled on it, and the wire sagged but held. Booger took one of the rolls of blankets we had brought, tossed it over his shoulder, and started climbing up the rope. He went up it quick and silent as a hummingbird.

When he got to the top, he found a handhold without hanging his fingers up in the wire, tossed the blanket over the wire as a barrier between himself and the barbs, climbed up, hesitated momentarily at the top, then dropped to the other side without use of the rope.

Jim Bob went up next with his blanket and his shotgun dangling on the shoulder strap. He went up as quickly as Booger and put his blanket on top of Booger's to make it even safer and pressed the wire down even more, then he was over the wall and out of sight. I followed with my blanket and my strapped shotgun. When I dropped over Jim Bob and Booger had already moved on. Leonard dropped down beside me, and I heard him take a deep breath in anticipation of what was to come.

The big shed was right in front of me and Leonard. Jim Bob was moving to the left, through some cars, toward some high-rising carnival equipment and, beyond that, the ring of mobile homes. Booger was going at the homes from the other side, threading his way through rusted cars on blocks and time-crusted wheel rims.

Leonard and I darted toward the shed. I went on the right side, and he went on the left. Easing along, I came to a door, tested it gently to see if it was locked, and it wasn't. I took a deep breath and cracked it open and stuck the shotgun inside, flicked on the light at the top of the gun. There were a couple of large pickups inside, and there were shelves all around. I slipped all the way in and waited until I heard Leonard come around from the other side and across the front and over toward the door. He came to the door and in a soft voice said, "Don't shoot."

"You're good," I said, and he slipped inside.

It was a pretty big shed, and there were two wide doors pulled together at the front of it for the trucks. We looked around, and what we found made my blood grow cold. On all those shelves were a lot of fruit jars, and I mean a lot. I thought at first they held canned goods, but when I put the light on them I saw that what was floating in the liquid in the jars wasn't new potatoes or jelly. In each jar there were testicles, sometimes in the sack, so to speak, and sometimes free of it. The liquid was yellowish, and in some of the jars were thick streaks of blood. In one of the jars I saw something red and floating, like a bloody jellyfish. Up close I realized it was a red toupee. Red Mop. They had not only taken his balls but also his cheap-ass hair.

If I had any doubt that we had the wrong place and the wrong people, it was gone.

"There's got to be well over a hundred of them," Leonard said.

"Easily," I said, and I could feel my skin crawling as if it were trying to tear off my bones and make for home.

We walked and looked around, me on one side, Leonard on the other, using the flashes on the tops of our weapons. There were a lot of old photos in cheap frames along the shelves. They were dust-coated and showed of a lot of people who looked alike. Family photos tucked among jars of balls. Nothing more homey and nostalgic than that. I leaned in and looked at them carefully, realized they were shots of the dead, men dressed in suits, women dressed in long white dresses, maybe the same suits and dresses for all of them. It reminded me of the old Victorian photographs of the deceased, where they dressed the recently departed up in Sunday-go-to-meeting clothes and photographed them. The Victorians didn't think it was weird, and apparently neither did the ball snatchers.

Leonard joined me. "I think these are all family photos."

"Yep. And all dead."

"What?"

Leonard took the flash off his shotgun and looked closer.

"Goddamn, fuck a lame goat in the ass. You're right. I have seen some shit, my friend, but in some ways this creeps me out more than the balls in the jars. All we need now is to come across an altar for animal sacrifice."

"I think this is the ball-snatcher dynasty," I said. "One dies, they have another to take over the work. I think it's like Doug said, incest and continuation of the line. They get old enough, they move into the family business."

"Could be more here than seven or eight," Leonard said.

"Doug was pretty certain."

"There you go. Doug, a fucking big-time criminal gave you the true dope, and why doubt his word?"

"Because us killing these folks is to his advantage. If he's right, we are looking at the last of the line."

"If he's right."

Leonard replaced his light on top of his shotgun.

"How do people end up like this?" I said.

"Choice."

"Can't all be choice. They had to have been treated like shit. They think this is normal."

"Tell you what. We get through here, you get rested, you write a paper on it, and I'll read it while I'm scratching my balls. But since there's no one in here except these balls and some cheap photos, and since that paper ain't written, let's get down to business."

We slipped out the door and trotted smoothly toward the circle of homes.

Jim Bob and Booger were by this time both out of sight.

52

Leonard and I spread apart. I went closer to the center of the homes, where there was a sizable gap between them. Leonard started in the direction Booger had taken. I hoped to hell Jim Bob and Booger didn't shoot us. I thought of Vanilla up there in the deer stand with her makeshift rifle, and that gave me some comfort.

I cruised past one of the outhouses, and the stink was strong. I thought, who in this modern age lives like this by choice? But a better question would have been, who cuts people's throats with wire and cuts off their balls with the wire and keeps them in mason jars in a goddamn shed with pickup trucks?

I hustled on until I could slip through the gap in the circle of homes. They had plenty of ways to keep you outside, but so far nothing I had seen that would alert them you were inside. To my right I saw Booger. He was pointing at the trailer where the light burned. I nodded and joined him. The trailer's front door was on the inside of the circle. There was a set of wooden stairs, sloppily built, that led up to a wooden porch with a short roof that extended out from the trailer and over it all.

I went up first. The stairs creaked, and when I stepped onto the porch it squeaked sharply. I took a deep breath and put my ear to the door. I could hear a TV going inside. I looked down at Booger.

He came up without so much as a creaking sound. A house cat would have made more noise. He leaned his weapon against the door, got a lock pick out of his pocket, and went at it. It wasn't much of a door, and it wasn't much of a lock. It came undone as easy as a whore's bra.

Booger put the lock-pick kit away, picked up his gun, and looked at me. I took hold of the door handle with my gloved hand and turned it and went inside. It was dark inside, and I had turned my flashlight off. I slipped in and stood on the left side of the door, then decided to squat down. Booger came in and took the right. There were only two ways to go in that trailer, left or right. I went left, Booger went right.

Drifting toward the sound of the television and the weak, yellow light, I came to the section of the trailer that served as a living room, slipped through an open space without a door and into the room. The back of the couch was facing me, and there was a man sitting on the couch. All I could see was the back of his head and broad shoulders. He had long, greasy, dark hair. The little light on the left side of the room near a window, and the flickering motion of the TV, made the whole scene surreal. Worse, he was watching an episode of some fucked-up reality show.

Slipping the rest of the way in, I pointed my shotgun at the back of his head. I hadn't gone more than a foot forward when I heard a shotgun cut loose in the yard. The man on the couch stood up suddenly and turned. He had a gun in his hand. That figured. Guys like this probably went around armed 24-7. But that's all he had. He was naked except for underwear, though at that point I couldn't see his feet. He might have been wearing high heels for all I knew. He saw me and let out his breath. It sounded like a snake hissing in high grass.

"Don't do it," I said. And he didn't. He tossed the gun on the couch.

Booger came in then. "Got you one, huh?"

"Who fired that shot?" I said.

"Let's hope Jim Bob."

"Who are you two?" the man behind the couch said.

"Motherfucker can at least count to two," Booger said.

"Ease around here where I can see all of you, much as I hate the idea," I said.

He did. He was skinny and white as snow, and from what I could tell in the lamplight, his hair could have been brown or black or purple. He wasn't wearing high heels. He was barefoot. On the walls were shelves, and on the shelves were jars. I knew without examining them what was in them. They had quite a collection. There were photographs as well as a faded framed invocation: GOD BLESS OUR HOME.

"How'd you get in here?" the man said. His accent was East Texas, but it seemed of some other era, not tampered with by time and association with others. The legend they might be mutes was squashed.

"Teleportation," I said. "Lean your ass into the couch. Booger, why don't you check on who fired that shot, just in case it wasn't Jim Bob?"

Booger went away, and I heard the front door open. Me and the man in the dirty underwear stared at each other until I glanced again at the rows of jars. I said, "You couldn't just buy a few knickknacks?"

The man said nothing. I stared at him, amazed at the banality of it all. This man was part of a tribe of infamous killers who traveled under a single name, and he was really nothing more than an average-looking man in stained underwear. A psychotic sitting around watching TV, scratching himself, drinking beer, and now and again taking a peek at his nut-sack collection. Nothing monsterlike in his appearance, nothing special about him in any way. He was merely a psychopath who liked reality shows, needed a shower, and a lethal injection.

I don't know how long we stood like that, but it seemed like a lot of time passed before Booger came back. He had Jim Bob with him. Jim Bob said, "Shot one coming out of the toilet. I went around to the trailers and looked and didn't see anything."

"You shot Derrick?" said the man.

"Did he look a lot like you, but had pants on?" Jim Bob said.

The man nodded.

"Don't expect him at breakfast," Jim Bob said.

"Leonard?" I asked.

"Didn't see him," he said, shaking his head. "I went and looked inside a couple of trailers, and no one was there. I came around on the side to look in the others, and here come a guy out of the outhouse carrying a roll of toilet paper in one hand and a pistol in the other. He saw me, and he didn't know if he should wipe his ass with the paper or the gun. He decided to shoot at me. With the gun, not the paper. I took him out, and not to lunch. Did you hear a twenty-two fire after my shot?"

"No," I said.

"Pretty sure Vanilla hit him in the back of the head about the same time I shot him. It was a pretty quiet shot. Damn. Look at all those jars full of nut sacks."

"I want to know where Leonard is," I said.

"Told you, don't know," Jim Bob said. "Hell, that's a lot of jars. Cut my nuts off they're going to need a lot of room, lot of jars, more likely a washtub and about ten gallons of rubbing alcohol to preserve them."

"What do we do with this one?" I said.

"You know the answer to that question," Jim Bob said.

"You ought to just go on and find someplace to hide, you know what's good for you," said the man. "You got some chance like that. Not much, but some. Better yet, you might want to get over the wall before my brothers find me."

"And when you and your brothers aren't fucking each other in the ass," Jim Bob said, "where might we find them?"

"Go fuck yourself with a dog's dick," the man said. "They'll be back soon enough, and you'll wish they wasn't."

Booger laughed and lifted his shotgun quickly and cut down on the man. It was messy.

"Goddamn, Booger," I said.

"We didn't come here to sort out their issues," Booger said. "We came to rid them of them."

"Jesus," I said. "He gave up his gun. He wasn't armed."

"Sounds like a personal problem," Booger said.

53

We went out through the door we had come in one at a time, quickly, Booger first, me, and then Jim Bob. We walked inside the circle of trailers. No one shot at us, and there was no sound of movement until Leonard came through the gap in the line of trailers I had come through.

"I heard shooting," Leonard said. "Saw one out by the shitter who will shit no more."

"Me and Vanilla nailed him," Jim Bob said.

"One inside got caught with his pants off," Booger said. "He won't be around for the holidays."

"Where are the others?" I said.

"Now, that's a good question," Leonard said. "I didn't see anyone among the junk and cars. Been in all the trailers?"

"Just one," I said.

"I was in a couple others," Booger said.

"I checked some," Jim Bob said.

We sorted out that only one trailer hadn't been checked.

We didn't bother with a lock pick this time. Jim Bob kicked the door down, and we went inside. It smelled like a buzzard's breath. There was no one there, and there were no balls in jars. It looked more like it was used as their crash pad. Mattresses were thrown about on the floor, and there were sheets and blankets twisted about on those. There were a number of automatic weapons leaning against the wall and on hooks. Their bedroom was also their armory.

In the corner there was a yellow curtain supported on metal poles and stanchions. We walked over and looked behind the curtain. There was a window that looked out over the compound. There were no curtains on it. There was a small wooden table with a couple of thick books on it. The moonlight and the compound light came through the window. There was a hospital bed. It had an electronic device, a little plastic bar with buttons on it, for raising the bed up and lowering it. There were metal stands with metal racks around the bed. There were empty glass containers hanging from the racks, tubes dangled loose from those, like snakes that had died of boredom. The ends of the tubes were fixed with rusted needles. The bed itself was yellowed by time and stank of human waste long left and long rotted. The pillow on the bed had a head on it, and the head had some dark hair on it, though most of it had come loose and lay on the pillow. Attached to the head was a body. It wasn't exactly mummified, but it wasn't completely gone, either. It was simultaneously in mid-rot and mid-mummification. I wasn't sure which was going to win out. Obviously, it was the source of the smell. The light through the window caused it to appear to be coated in a thin film of cheese. The eyes had a strip of duct tape over them. There was a thin once-white gown on her, and it had become one with the rotting flesh.

"Okay," Jim Bob said. "We killed two, and the rest of them ain't here, unless you want to count this guy. Woman. Whatever. Jesus."

"They torturing somebody?" Booger asked.

Jim Bob picked up one of the books on the table, flipped it open.

"I think they were doctoring somebody," Jim Bob said. "A relative. Doing it themselves. This is a medical book."

"I'm going to go out on a limb here and say no one on their staff actually had a medical degree," I said.

"At least someone could read," Leonard said.

"Not well enough," Jim Bob said. "The page is turned down on delivery."

"Delivery?" Booger said.

"Babies," Jim Bob said. "They were trying to deliver a baby."

"Since we haven't seen any babies," Leonard said, "I'm going to take it this is the potential mother and they failed."

"It's like Doug was saying," I said. "They ran out of sisters."

"Looks that way," Leonard said, wrinkling his nose against the stench.

They may be awful people, I thought, but they had tried to save one of their own, give birth to another. I liked it better when they were faceless killers who needed killing and there wasn't any humanity involved. I wondered if they propped her up and photographed her after she died.

The stink was making me sick. I was starting to cough. We went away from there quickly, outside into the circle at the center of the trailers. As we were starting back to the wall, we saw automobile lights coming down from the hill, between the trees. They were high enough up that the lights shone down into the compound and lay on us like laser beams. Then there was a loud clicking, and I saw red-dot lights on the inside of the gate go off, and I could see the butt ends of half a dozen machine guns positioned below those dots in the gate, just the way Booger had said. Soon as those dots went off, the big gate sprang open electronically, groaning like an old man straining at stool, and into the compound jetted a black Hummer.

As Underwear Man had said, they'd be back soon enough, and here they came.

We scattered like quail as the Hummer braked to an abrupt stop inside the compound. The Hummer's doors were thrown open on the passenger side, front and back, and two men who looked like stockier versions of the one in his underwear came out into the open with automatic weapons that sprayed the air full of lead. I barely had time to jump behind some piled-up washing machines, and still the bullets tore through them and scattered rust and one nicked my ass as I dove. Once I was on the ground, I immediately began turning my head, looking for Leonard.

I didn't see him, but I heard him off to my right, opening up with his shotgun. That old Remington of his had a certain sound when you pumped it. He was pumping fast. There was another rattle of automatic-weapons fire, all of it in Leonard's direction. I lifted my head cautiously and looked through a gap in the washing machine pile and saw that both armed men were hurrying toward me. Neither had been hit that I could see. And then one of them snapped his head forward and then back, and where his eye had been there was a leap of liquid spurting into the lights of the Hummer. The man with him yelled out something, dropped low, and then turned to race back for the Hummer. By then the spray of bullets ceased, and Jim Bob and Booger rose up from the old cars they had ducked behind and starting firing, but that bastard must have been blessed, because he didn't get hit, or if he did it was minor. It damn sure didn't stop him.

There came that faint snapping sound from the deer stand, and Vanilla nailed him. He turned his head suddenly as if to look in our direction, then banged into the Hummer and slid down it slowly until he fell with his head under it. His ass humped a little, like he was fucking the dirt, and then he was still.

"That bitch can shoot," I heard Booger yell out.

That's when the Hummer roared and burned backwards, running right over the man who had been humping the dirt, squirting what passed for brains out of his head in all directions. The Hummer roared on through the gate, swung around, and turned its nose up the hill with the tires tossing gravel. All of us were firing at it, but nothing we hit on the Hummer caused a problem.

Up in the deer stand, Vanilla snapped off two shots, and I heard the Hummer windshield crack, but it kept going, climbing the hill. We all started running after it.

When it got to the top of the hill, the Hummer turned and ran off the road and went straight for the deer stand, hit it and sent it flying, breaking it apart, launching Vanilla out of it in a flash of black clothes and blond hair. The Hummer tried to run her down then, but she limped behind a tree and the Hummer hit it, backed off, spun around, and started out of there.

We ran up the hill, and by the time we got up there, Vanilla was limping up to us, and the Hummer was gone.

"Get me to the car," she said, "and I will teach them to knock me out of a tree."

"Deer stand," Booger said.

"Whatever," she said, throwing the rifle across her back by a strap she had fastened to it.

She got between Leonard and me, threw her arms over our shoulders, and with Jim Bob and Booger in the lead, we carried on. We made it to the brush gate, or where it used to be, but the Hummer had gone right through it.

"They just thought they were badasses," Booger said, "and then they got a load of us."

"We got lucky," Jim Bob said.

We limped Vanilla along until we got to the end of the trail that led to the outer road. Booger leaned down with his light and said, "They went to the right. You can see where they dug in turning."

Our problem was that the Buick was to the left, so we limped Vanilla along that way, finally got to the car. I thought the Hummer might at this point be all the way to the North Pole.

I was still closing my door when Vanilla got the Buick started. She put her good right foot on the gas and spun us out of there backwards, braked, hit the gas, changed the gears, and away we went. Every time Vanilla shifted gears the car roared louder and flew faster. Vanilla was down the road a piece before she turned on the lights, which was a good thing, because the road was growing narrow and there was a bar ditch on either side. The headlights caught standing water in the ditches and made it shimmer.

"We'll never catch them," Leonard said.

"Yes, we will," Vanilla said, and she hit another gear. She wasn't kidding about the car being souped up beyond reason. We tore along like that for what seemed like ten or fifteen minutes, and then we caught the taillights of the Hummer. Vanilla pushed her foot down, and the Buick's engine sang like a siren; the tires clawed the road with a vengeance.

I hadn't thought to put on my seat belt, but right then I remembered and snapped it into place and tried not to shit myself. We were going so fast the car was starting to wobble and the trees to either side of us looked like a solid wall. One thing about a Hummer is it doesn't run that fast, and the Buick was a goddamn ground jet.

We were closing fast.

54

Let me tell you how I screamed. It was loud and long and it blended with Leonard's and Jim Bob's screams and it was almost loud enough to smother Booger's cackling laughter. Vanilla made not a sound.

What caused the scream was that it appeared we were going to run right up that Hummer's ass. We were so close, had the Hummer had a bumper sticker we would have collided. The Hummer had a modified door, so that the back end swung open, and as it did two men with automatic weapons, down on their knees, started firing.

Vanilla braked and drifted sideways into what I thought would surely be a bar ditch or a tree, but we were lucky. There was a wide spot there, and the next instant we were beside the Hummer. I saw that the windshield in our ride was punctured in several places and the punctures sprang fractures and then the fractures spread rapidly with a sound like thin ice cracking under a fat skater's feet.

The glass blew back on us just as I ducked, and I heard Jim Bob yell, "Goddamn it."

When I rose up the windshield was gone and there was blood running down my face. I glanced at Vanilla. She had cuts on her forehead and cheek, and there was a small piece of glass sticking out of the top of her hairline, but if she'd even blinked when the glass shattered, I didn't notice it. Then again, I had just had my head between my legs and had been trying to crawl up my own asshole, so I might have missed something.

I looked back over the seat. Leonard raised a hand in a polite wave. His mouth made a wiggle that I was supposed to think was a smile. He didn't even seem to be cut. Jim Bob was using a gloved hand to pull a bit of broken glass from his shoulder. Booger was on the right-hand passenger side. He rolled down his window and stuck his head and arms and the sawed-off out of it. Blood drops flew off the cuts on his face and blew back into the night like red drops of sweat. The back windshield was gone, too.

I turned back to the front, rolled my window down, and looked at Vanilla.

"I'm going to brake."

"I know," I said.

She downshifted and braked so fast it was like a single motion. The car's hum lowered to a purr, and as we slowed that sent the Hummer flying in front of us again. When it did, I hung my head and arms out the window with my shotgun and hoped Booger wouldn't shoot the back of my head off. Me and Booger fired close together, and the sound of those shotguns made my head feel as if a horde of crazed monkeys were beating on bongos inside my brain.

Booger yelled, "I was born for this!"

I pumped the shotgun, fired again at the open back door where the men stood, and one of them dropped down and rolled out even as the other man tried to grab him. The Buick went over his head with a bump and a loud squish.

Vanilla shifted gears, and we swung to the left side of the vehicle again, just as the other man tried to fire at us. He caught the tail end of the Buick, dancing shots across the trunk and into the woods before we pulled directly alongside the Hummer.

The Hummer driver tried to take the middle of the road and drive us

off of it. We were coming up on a narrow bridge, and there wasn't anywhere else for us to go but off of it or back behind the Hummer again.
We eased back behind it.

Me and Booger opened fire. By this time Jim Bob had rolled down
the window on his side and was sitting in the window with his shotgun
swung over the top of the Buick's roof, firing. I heard Leonard say, "I'll
just sit here quiet in the middle."

The Hummer clumped its tires over the bridge, and the man in the
back who was on his knees firing went backwards and dropped his gun,
got himself together long enough to close the back door. No sooner was
the Hummer over the bridge than Vanilla was riding the Hummer so
close we were like a hemorrhoid on its ass.

The Hummer braked, and in that moment I thought we were all going
to be sitting in the front seat with the driver, but Vanilla jerked the wheel
left and went forward and alongside the Hummer so close it took the
mirror off on my side and scraped the door handles front and back. Since
me and Booger had just pulled heads and arms inside, the timing was
perfect, even if it hadn't been on purpose.

Vanilla started rolling her window down. She said, "Hap, take the
wheel."

"What?"

"Take the wheel and sit on my feet."

I snapped off my seat belt and grabbed the wheel. Vanilla was out the
window, drawing her big automatic as she did. I slid over, and she locked
her feet under my ass. I put my foot on the gas and pulled us directly
alongside the Hummer driver. His hand came out his open window, and
it was full of pistol.

Vanilla, sitting on the window frame, twisted and fired over the roof
of the car. The driver was close enough to our car I heard him make a
sound like a gasket blowing, and then the Hummer went off the road and
into a bar ditch and out of that and through some small trees, fetched up
finally against a large sweet gum with a soul-breaking impact that scattered bark like confetti. A burst of white smoke rolled out of the back

of it, and on the far side a door opened, and I caught a glimpse of a man making a run for it through the woods, carrying a long gun.

Vanilla swung back inside the car with such force she knocked me out from behind the wheel, and the Buick wavered. She caught the wheel and whirled it and hit the emergency brake even as she downshifted. The Buick swung around, facing back in the direction we had come from.

"Yeah," Jim Bob said. "But let's see you make it dance."

Vanilla gunned us forward, came to a stop across from the place where the Hummer had left the road. We all got out of the car. Booger went about three feet and fell down. "Shit," he said. "Took one through the leg. It's broken."

Me and Jim Bob and Leonard ran to the Hummer. Jim Bob jerked open the back door. There was the wounded man with a pistol in his hand and the barrel pressed up under his chin. "I just wanted you to know I made my own way," he said and fired the pistol, launching the top of his skull with its greasy hair against the roof of the Hummer, spraying it and us with brains and blood. The skullcap hit the floor of the Hummer, spun around like a hubcap that had come loose, rattled against the flooring, then stopped moving.

There was no one else inside.

When I turned around Leonard was gone. I went the way I figured he had to go, where the trees and brush were thinnest. I had almost caught up with him when he came to a spot where the trees were sparse and the moon was bright. He went along quick-like—too quick-like, because the man he was hunting lifted up as he passed, pointing an automatic rifle. I fired quickly with the shotgun, and the blast tore through the brush, but if I hit him it wasn't a killing blow. He turned toward me, his teeth flashing in the moonlight, his rifle swinging around, and when he did Leonard turned and shot him, knocking him down behind the brush where he had been hiding.

We were both on him now. We peeled back the brush. He had dropped his rifle on the ground. He was hit bad but not dead. He was reaching for the rifle. I kicked it aside. He lay on his back and looked up at us. He looked small and pale and like someone you wouldn't notice twice. He looked like all the others that made up the Canceler, as if they had been cut from the same bolt of cloth. The moon floated in his eyes.

He turned his head toward me. His mouth opened and closed, trying to find air. I remembered when I was a kid and had a BB gun, thought I was a mighty hunter, and shot a bird. When I went to pick it up, its beak was open and it was trying to find the air it couldn't put back into its small lungs. That was the end of killing birds for the hell of it. I still have that bird's soul on my head, and a lot worse things now. Leonard raised his shotgun to shoot, but then hesitated.

The man quit gasping. The moon floated out of his eyes.

55

Me and Leonard have a veterinarian friend who sews us up in secret when we need it. He charges a lot. He has to. If he got caught he'd be sewing up shank wounds in Huntsville prison.

We went to him. He took care of us, Booger in particular. A fragment of a shell had found a place in his leg where it wanted to live. It was pretty deep, and maybe someone else would have died of shock, but Booger had him take it out without deadening the wound. I think he enjoyed showing us how much tougher than us he was. I thought it showed how much smarter we were.

The vet cut the piece of metal out of him, and Booger only grunted, but when the vet started sewing the wound up, he passed out.

"If he dies," Jim Bob said, "we can call it a win-win."

"That's not very nice," I said.

"Oh, but so true," Leonard said and kind of laughed, or maybe it was a cough.

We all had some cuts and such to patch up, and we got that done. None of us had been cut badly by the glass, though Vanilla was going to have a small scar right in the middle of her part. I looked at her while the vet doctored her up. She was cut in places, and there was blood in her hair, and damn if she still didn't look like a goddess.

When it was all done and Booger came awake and consented to some pain pills, we paid our vet friend with Jim Bob's money and went back to the safe house. Soon as we were there, Booger, who found a place on the couch, said, "I counted seven, not eight."

"I thought about that," I said. "Maybe there were only seven to begin with."

"And maybe," Booger said, "the ones in the Hummer were coming back from some paid mission, and the guys we caught at the compound were holding down the fort. That means there could still be one more out there prowling around, on a job, and when he comes home, boy, is he going to be mad."

"It's possible," Jim Bob said. "Problem is, it's hard to figure out how much was real about those guys and how much was myth. One thing is for sure, they had a lot of balls in jars."

Me and Leonard told them then about the shed and what we found there.

"Jesus," Jim Bob said. "That's a lot of killing these creeps have done."

"I always heard there were eight," Vanilla said. She had just come out of the bathroom, where she had changed into jeans and a loose T-shirt, slipped on white tennis shoes.

"But you don't know it for a fact?" Leonard asked.

"No."

Next morning I made a call to Marvin, and later in the day me and Leonard went to town to the Japanese restaurant, arriving at 12:15. Leonard waited in the car, and I went in. I promised to bring him an order of rice and hibachi beef.

I walked past the SUV parked out front, this time with two guys in it. They didn't look like they were taking their bodyguard duties seriously. One was sitting behind the steering wheel with his head thrown back on the seat and his eyes closed. The other sat on the front passenger side reading something on his cell phone.

Inside I found the Barbecue King in his usual spot. I pointed at him when the waitress came over. I slid into the seat across from him.

He looked at my banged-up face, with its bruises and Band-Aids, observed my stiff movements.

"You look like you shaved with a brush hog."

"I feel worse. Lunch is on you, and I want a takeout order."

"I assume I'm paying because you have good news."

"Your exile ends. Be here tomorrow, and a policeman named Marvin Hanson will be here to visit with you. You will go away with him. More policemen will show up at your place at the same time, and the guys outside, any others that might be around, will have their ass in a crack before they can ask, 'Are those handcuffs new?'"

"I have to take your word for it that you killed the Cancelers?"

"You do," I said. "Here's the thing, pal. It's best you have the meeting, set yourself up to have a chance at rolling over on the others. Maybe the feds will decide you're more important and will find you a nice warm spot in Albuquerque with a new name and a retirement plan. They've been protecting those you say are worse than you, so now you get your chance."

"I'm no angel, Collins, but yeah, they're worse."

"If you got some information you want to show Marvin, and it's something you can have with you when you show up here, I would. That way nothing gets lost in the arrest and no one can say they just found it and you didn't give it to them. Put you out of the deal altogether. You want Marvin first, not the feds."

"I can put it all on a memory stick and have it in my pocket, close to my heart, but since I'm having to give it to the cops, I'll put it in my front pants pocket, close to my cock."

"You can put it up your ass for all I care, just have it. Or you will go down, and in a lot less pleasant way."

He leaned back and crossed his arms. "I've conned my way out of the police before."

"I wasn't talking about the police."

He smiled at me.

"Waitress," he called out, "we're ready to order."

56

Now, let me tell you, for a few days I worried about that eighth member of the Cancelers, but after a while I didn't worry so much. I decided, as Leonard did, that there were only seven.

Booger went home, and so did Jim Bob, and Vanilla stayed at the safe house with us for a few days. She came to me one night while I was sleeping, limping a little still. She wore nothing. She crawled into bed.

"It's not going to happen, Vanilla."

She stretched out and put her arm over my chest.

"At least I hope not."

"No?"

"Well, I mean I hope not. Jesus, Vanilla. Really?"

She giggled a little. It was the only time I had ever heard her sound less than reserved. She could talk about anything and sound reserved, but that giggle, it wasn't like her. It was girlish.

"Nobody need know but us," she said.

"I would know."

"You know what I mean."

"Sorry, Vanilla."

"Let me put it like this, Hap. You called me. I came. This is the price."

"And if I don't pay?"

"Don't ever call again."

"Maybe I shouldn't have called in the first place."

"Think about how it went down out there and tell me that again."

I couldn't tell her that again.

"I just don't feel right about it, Vanilla."

"You will," she said.

"Jesus, Vanilla. You're making it hard."

"That's the idea."

"Not what I meant."

She ran her hand over my crotch, said, "There seems to be some activity."

"Damn it," I said. "Don't do that."

"You're not fighting me that much."

"I want to."

"Do you?"

"Less than before," I said. She pressed her lips to mine, and we kissed. I pushed her away and got out of bed and pulled up my pajamas that she had pushed down.

"I'm going to shower," I said. "In cold water."

She slipped out from under the covers and stood by the bed. It was dark in there, but there was enough moonlight from the window to see her standing there in all her glory. I could even tell she didn't shave down there, at least not completely. Good. I didn't like women to look like children. I thought I might tell her how much I appreciated that later, but right then, a shower.

"Good night, Vanilla."

There was a bathroom off the bedroom, and I went in there and closed the door and took off my clothes and turned on the cold water and got in and pulled the shower curtain. A moment passed. I heard the door open, and then the shower curtain was pulled back, and Vanilla reached out and turned on the warm water, and then I just couldn't fight it anymore. I kissed her and held her. But finally I had a moment of strength and pushed her back from me.

"It isn't right, Vanilla. I made a promise. I intend to keep it."

Vanilla looked at me with those beautiful eyes of hers.

"You know, Hap Collins, I think that's why I'm in love with you. You keep your word."

"I try. But I won't lie. I don't know how much longer I can keep that promise if you stay in the shower, so one of us is getting out now."

She took my chin in her hand.

"Oh, Jesus, Hap Collins, you don't know what you're missing."

"I have a pretty good idea," I said. "I have a feeling that tomorrow sometime I'll drive off by myself to someplace private and scream for a while."

She laughed and kissed me, and it was almost enough to undo me. Then she got out of the shower.

I turned the cold water back on.

57

So the others went away, and that just left me and Leonard. I was surprised that I missed them so much. Except Booger. I didn't miss him at all. We continued to stay at the safe house for a time. With Vanilla gone I didn't have to lock my door and spend the night in a steamy sweat hoping she didn't take an ax to the door, because one more time and my resolve might crumble like old cheese.

We found out from Marvin that the material the Barbecue King had given him was good. The super crime ring in Houston came apart quick, with lots of arrests in conjunction with not only the Houston police but the FBI, the latter being kind of ironic. But alliances change rapidly in the world of crime and law enforcement. I'm sure it had a lot to do with what could come out if the FBI didn't comply.

Marvin had me and Leonard meet him in town at a sandwich shop for lunch, told us all about it.

"Sandy Buckner, she calls herself something else now."

"We know," I said.

"I know you know, but I'm just saying. Her days as Lex Luthor are all over."

Leonard shook his head. "It's so unsatisfying, being out there on the search, and then when we find her, we find her secondhand. We didn't actually see her in person, just a photo in the paper."

"And it turns out she wasn't worth finding," I said.

"She is worth sending to prison, though," Marvin said.

Leonard said, "She stole that money from her grandmother to get herself in the business deeper. Screwed who she had to, backstabbed who she had to, set herself up sweet, and she cared about her grandmother the way a lion cares about a baby gazelle. She got away with her shit for a long time."

Marvin nibbled at his chicken salad sandwich, said around chews, "That's right, but thanks to you guys, and to my fine professional police work—"

"What the hell did you do?" Leonard said.

"Kept your asses out of the blender, that's what I did."

"Oh, yeah," Leonard said. "Okay."

"You killed them all?" Marvin said.

"We won't answer that on grounds that it might incriminate us and lead to a long prison sentence and possible death by lethal injection," Leonard said.

"Good reason not to answer. But let's speak hypothetically, just so I would have some idea what might have happened."

"Us and a few helpers killed all them son of a bitches," Leonard said. "I mean, that's what might have happened."

"Do I know these helpers?"

"Maybe," Leonard said. "Some."

"Went out there to the address you gave, the spot where the body was in the woods," Marvin said. "Birds had been at that old boy in the woods."

"One in the woods," I said. "You're talking about the fellow who hypothetically got killed near the hypothetical Hummer with the dead bodies in it?" I asked.

"That would be the one, and the dead guy in the road looked like a jelly roll someone had stepped on. Others in the Hummer, and the ones at that fucked-up compound, didn't look so good, either. Someone was shooting good. Looked like a twenty-two had been at work. Gun like that, had to be some good shooting. And thanks for the tip on the booby traps. That was some sneaky shit they had out there. Tell you something you don't know. We found a bunch of graves out under the Ferris wheel. Don't think they were murder victims. The graves were well tended, and there were markers on them but no names. Just numbers. I think it's their own clan, but we won't know for sure until they're dug up, checked for the ways they died, and if there's a DNA match with the seven dead fellows."

"They were just some guys," I said. "Nothing really amazing going on there. The Cancelers were people willing to kill, and there were a lot of them to do it. I pretty much heard that definition from Dougie."

"That definition could fit you boys, hypothetically."

"Don't give Hap any more of a complex than he already has," Leonard said. "You know and I know the right thing was done. There's no comparison between us and them. Hypothetically, of course."

"Of course. Fact is, the feds, they think it was some kind of turf war. You know, other hitters wanting to take them out to take their place or some such theory."

"So hypothetically," Leonard asked, "how are the chances for those guys who hypothetically killed those seven guys?"

"If, hypothetically, you did do anything, you are in the clear. Frankly, those boys being dead, and all those balls in jars, nobody gives a shit who killed them. By the way, lunch. You're buying."

"You should be buying us lunch," Leonard said.

"You're buying for me out of sympathy."

"And why are we sympathetic?" I said.

"Because everybody be hating on the po-po," Marvin said.

58

We went over to see Lilly Buckner, but found out from a neighbor that she had been taken downtown to the hospital, and we drove over there. She was in a private room—the last of her money, I guess, or maybe her Medicare. I don't know. But when I asked the plump female nurse about her condition, she asked if we were relatives.

"No," I said. "But we know her."

"You're the only ones who have come to see her."

I repeated my question. "How is she?"

"Not good."

"What's wrong?"

"Old age. So pretty much everything."

"Can we see her?" Leonard asked.

"You're not supposed to," the nurse said, "but you might as well. She's awake, but I don't think she has long."

"How long?" Leonard asked.

"No one can say for sure, but I can say this for certain. The doctors have given in. She won't make it out of this hospital alive. I'm sorry to tell you that, but I believe it's best you know."

"We're not really all that close to her," I said.

"Like I said, so far, you're all that have come to see her, and we haven't found any living relatives."

"And you won't," I said, knowing full well there was one, but considering all that had gone down, I doubted they would let Sandy come see her, and I doubted Sandy gave a damn. She had chosen a different path.

We got the room number, rode an elevator up. We went into her room, and she lay in a bed that seemed far too large for her. She was under white sheets with a big white pillow under her head. She didn't have any makeup on, and she looked even older than before. Her eyes were closed. She reminded me of a starving bird lying in the snow.

I went to one side of the bed, Leonard the other.

We stood looking down at her. I gently took her hand, and Leonard took the other.

She opened her eyes. "You two," she said, and her voice was as raw as if she had been drinking lye.

"Yeah, us two," Leonard said.

"So it's down to this. Two people I don't really know coming to see me before I take the big siesta . . . Sandy? Anything?"

"Yes," Leonard said. "We found her."

Her eyes brightened a little. "Is she okay?"

"She is," Leonard said. "She is married and living in Oregon."

"No shit?"

"No shit," Leonard said.

"You lying son of a bitch," she said. "Something is wrong, isn't it?"

Leonard pulled a chair up with one hand but never let go of her hand with the other. I did the same. We sat beside her bed.

"It's true," I said. "She's in Oregon."

"Why the fuck would she be in Oregon?"

"Maybe she likes the climate," Leonard said.

"I been to Oregon. I don't think the climate is all that good. Now, tell me the truth."

"Truth is," Leonard said, "she is in Oregon. She got in a bit of trouble with cashing bad checks, so she took your money, meant to pay it back, and then she met someone and got married. You have great-grandkids."

I thought to myself, wow. Leonard is lying his ass off.

She looked at me. I nodded.

"She was embarrassed to come back and tell you, having taken the money. She was cleaning up her check debt."

"So you saw her?"

"Absolutely," I said. "Why it took us so long."

"She was ashamed more than embarrassed," Leonard said. "She has two kids, your great-grandkids, two girls. One is named Lilly."

"She did that?" She could hardly speak now, her voice was so full of phlegm and emotion.

"Yeah."

"The other?"

"I think she said Buddy," Leonard said. "I'm sorry. Don't remember for sure."

"A girl named Buddy?" she asked.

"I probably have that wrong," he said.

"Brenda," I said. "Not Buddy. It'll be in our report, the correct names. She'd like to come see you, but the thing is, well, she's kind of wanted in the state of Texas still. The checks."

"Can't they arrest her in Oregon?" she said.

"Maybe so, but no one is pushing it," Leonard said. "I think that's just an excuse, though. Like I said, she's ashamed. That's the main thing."

"Tell her I don't care about what she did. Can you do that? I got a feeling this bed is going to be my last friend."

"Ah, hell, you're tough," I said. "You'll be all right."

She squeezed my hand and smiled. She didn't have in her false teeth, so her mouth deeply wrinkled more than smiled. "You two are the biggest fucking liars I have ever known. Thought you really had me buying into that shit, didn't you? Thought, throw the old lady a bone, like I don't know when bullshit isn't strudel."

"I thought I'd done pretty good," Leonard said.

"Buddy. What the hell, son? No. No, you didn't do good. You looked kind of cute telling the story, though. But I appreciate it. A man from the FBI came to see me. Being Sandy's grandmother and all, he thought I might know some things. He told me a little about her. She fucked up, and now you boys come lying to me because you know I'm dying."

"Yeah," Leonard said. "We aren't worth a shit."

"What I been trying to tell you."

"We shouldn't have done that," I said.

"You did it out of kindness, not something I've received in a while, mostly because I don't deserve it. Even if I hadn't spoken with that FBI turd, I still wouldn't have believed you. But as I was told when I was young, if someone gives you a shitty present, you pretend you like it, because it's the thought that counts. I'm tired now. So damn tired. Will you sit with me a while?"

"Sure," I said.

"Good. I'd like that. I still love her, you know?"

"Of course," I said.

"I thought she'd do well, but she didn't. She turned out to be a bitch on wheels. She stole my goddamn money because she wasn't anything other than a goddamn thief."

"Looks that way," Leonard said.

"She was here right now I'd punch her in the nose. Course, I'd have to ask her to raise the bed first, puff my pillow, and bend over within reach."

A small tear rolled out of her right eye.

"It's such a disappointment," she said.

"Wish it would have worked out better," I said.

"Stay with me, boys."

We did. She closed her eyes and slept, and a half hour later or so, a nurse came in and saw us. Not the same nurse as before. A male this time, but still plump. He looked at us and said, "You're not supposed to be here."

"We know," I said.

"Let me check her vitals," he said.

He did. When he finished, he stood there looking at her for a moment, and then he looked at us, and said it like he meant it. "I have bad news. I'm sorry. She's gone."

I knew that before he did, and I'm sure Leonard did as well. Her hand in mine had turned cold as ice shortly after she closed her eyes.

59

Me and Leonard ended up staying at the safe house for another two weeks. Brett and Chance and Buffy were still traveling. I called Brett one Saturday afternoon from the front porch of the safe house.

"You can come home," I said.

"Good," she said. "I was about to anyway, hell or high water. We've had fun, but I think we're both a little sick of it. And I don't like to think I need protecting. Besides, we're running out of money."

Leonard went back to his home, and damn if John didn't come around again, and damn if they weren't trying again. John wasn't talking religion anymore, and he brought his sixteen-year-old niece with him. She wanted out of her father's home, and part of that was due to her having realized that she, like her Uncle John, was gay. She came to live with Leonard and John in the loft, and at least for the time being, things were good for my brother.

The DNA test was in the mail when I got home, and that was two days before Brett and Chance and Buffy came back. I just couldn't open it. The morning before they were home, I did. The note inside said the sample had been ruined accidentally, and would we like to try again, no charge?

The air went out of me.

Brett, Chance, and Buffy arrived that same afternoon, and I was so glad to see Brett I teared up. Buffy, who seemed like a different dog, happier and more sure of herself, came bouncing up to me with great excitement. She hadn't forgotten me, or maybe she was just the kind of dog that was happy to see anyone but that asshole who had kicked her for entertainment. Chance was smiling and nervous. She took the news about the DNA test stoically. She hugged me, and I hugged her. Damn, I really hoped she was my daughter.

When I took Brett in my arms, I have to tell you, right then I was glad I had turned Vanilla away. Another heartbeat that night and we would have been at it. I was a little ashamed of how far it had gone, even if I hadn't initiated it. Jesus, that woman.

But the one who came back to me was every bit as delicious.

More so.

Because I loved her.

60

We sent off the new DNA sample, but we didn't do it until the fall. I can't tell you exactly why we waited that long, but that's how it was. I think we feared the answer might not be what we wanted.

As October blew in with a gust and the leaves turned yellow and brown and blew down from the great oak in the front yard by the curb, I was at peace. It gave me great joy to walk across the yard and crunch those drying leaves underfoot, because I damn sure wasn't going to rake them up and burn them.

We had done a number of jobs at the agency since Brett came home, and they had all been simple, and even Chance helped on a few occasions. Nothing big—little things, like watching someone who needed watching, making notes and snapping photos from concealment for divorce work, that sort of thing. She had a kind of knack for it, and with her beauty she was easily welcomed most anywhere.

So life was good, and one night in late October, on my birthday, we invited Leonard and John over, John's niece, and we had a kind of birthday celebration that turned out to be large pizzas and too many side dishes, including Leonard's favorite, vanilla cookies.

I received a few small gifts, little things I liked, mostly gift cards to food places, a box of animal crackers from Chance, and then it was over and everyone was going home or preparing to turn in for the night. Leonard decided to stay behind awhile and visit, and I agreed to take him back to his loft after an hour or so. We helped Brett and Chance store the remaining pizza away. I put the trash from the feast in a bag, and then we sat and had cups of decaffeinated coffee so we wouldn't be up all night. Leonard and I talked about the old days, how we had first met as teenagers on a dark night in the Sabine River bottoms. Brett and Chance sat and listened to us talk. We were on a roll.

When the ladies left the room, Leonard said, "Think I'm going to give John one more chance."

"You said that four chances ago," I said.

"I mean it this time."

"Did you not mean it the other times?"

"Not enough."

"Okay," I said.

"You don't fucking think I ought to, do you?"

"It's not about what I think. It's about what works—"

"Shut the hell up. Be straight with me. No psychology horseshit. Should I or shouldn't I?"

"You don't, you'll feel miserable," I said. "You do, you'll feel miserable."

"No opinion, then?"

"Frankly, Leonard, I'm fed up with the motherfucker."

"I should be."

"You were last time we talked, I think. I lose count. I think you've kicked him to the curb for good, next thing I know he's back greasing your asshole."

"I get fed up, and then I get over being fed up. Right now I'm over it. One more time into the breach, and you know what I mean, and if it don't work this time, seriously, I'm out."

"Brother, you got to make yourself happy if you can. Go for it."

"Thing is, I don't know I can. I'm starting to think the best relationship for me is a fresh box of Kleenex and a bottle of baby oil."

"Eeew."

The women came back then, and Leonard picked up his coffee and sipped it.

We all visited awhile, talked nonsense, mostly, and then the talk died down and our energy died with it. I decided to take the garbage out before I took Leonard home. I carried the bag out the back door, toward the garbage can. My mind was so engaged with the pleasantries of the evening I didn't sense the presence of someone in the yard until it was too late. He rose up from between the two garbage cans by the redwood fence, and as he did, I dropped the garbage bag and turned toward him. I was pretty quick for being distracted, but he was quicker.

There was a glint of light on an edge of steel, and I tried to use both hands to catch the man's wrist, but I was late and the blade was long, and it got me. It went into my stomach, and I groaned. I felt as if a cold wind had washed over me, and there was a numbness followed by a sensation like an electric shock, and then I stumbled backwards and fell against the garbage cans, knocking them over with a loud clatter, but somehow I managed to stay on my feet. The knife, a bayonet, actually, came loose of his hands, and I sort of melted backwards until my back came up against the fence. I clutched at the blade, cutting my hands, making them slick with blood.

He came at me again, bare-handed. I felt strange and detached, like I ought to do something but suddenly didn't know how. And then there was a great shadow looming behind my attacker, and the shadow struck out with two ridge hands to the man's temples and dropped him. The shadow was Leonard. The man on the ground turned and grabbed at Leonard's legs, and took him down. The man tried to scuttle onto Leonard's chest, but Leonard grabbed him by his jacket and jerked him down close and slapped a palm over one of the man's ears, a man I now realized had to be Number Eight, the last Canceler.

Number Eight screamed with pain, and then Leonard rolled him over and was on top of him. Leonard hit him in the throat, I think, because I heard a gasp from the man and then a gurgle, and then Leonard's hand went down two more times, the last in a clawing motion and then a ripping-back movement.

I saw all this as I eased down to the ground with my back against the fence. I so wanted to get up, but my legs weren't working and my mind seemed to have hit the Pause button. Next thing I knew Brett was bending over me, and she was screaming in a way I had never heard before, and then there was Chance bawling and Buffy was licking my face and whimpering.

Leonard reached down and picked me up and carried me out the redwood gate as if I were nothing more than a small sack of feathers.

Leonard lifted me into the back of the car with Brett, and away we went, Leonard at the wheel. Me holding my stomach with both hands, the bayonet still in me, my head in Brett's lap, Chance up front beside Leonard. Chance leaned over the seat and touched my face. Her hand was cool.

Number Eight had found out Leonard and I were involved, no mean feat if anyone from the car company had escaped arrest. Hell, Frank, from behind bars, might have given them the word to make it less likely they would pay someone in prison to stick her. It could as easily have been Leonard who had been stabbed. I was glad it wasn't him. I hoped Jim Bob was okay. Vanilla, I knew, would be long gone and damn near impossible to trace. And Booger. Well, fuck Booger.

As he drove, Leonard yelled from time to time, just some kind of wild exclamation full of fear and disappointment. I thought, happy fucking birthday, Hap.

61

By the time we got to the hospital I was weaving in and out, and as the folks came out with the stretcher and loaded me onto it, they began to do something to my stomach—apply pressure, I guess. I couldn't really feel much by then. The pain had gone away. I realized I wasn't wearing a shirt anymore because I felt the cool October wind. I wasn't wearing a bayonet, either.

As we entered the hospital hallway and Leonard raced alongside me, I saw an odd thing on his shirt. I couldn't figure what it was at first. Some kind of sea creature, maybe. It had a small, bulbous body and lots of bloody tentacles. I was studying on that when we went through some swinging doors, and one of the ladies pushing the stretcher said, "You'll have to leave, now, sir."

And I heard Leonard say, "Screw you. I'm here to stay."

"We'll call security," said the nurse.

"Tell them to bring a couple days' rations. They're going to be here awhile," Leonard said.

I realized then what was stuck on Leonard's shirt. It was Number Eight's eyeball. That clawing and ripping motion he had made, he had tore it right out of that bastard's head.

• • •

The lights came and went, and I closed my eyes and felt weaker and more tired than I had ever been. When I opened my eyes I was in a big white room, not unlike the one Lilly Buckner had been in, and by my bedside were Leonard, Brett, and Chance. The only one missing was Buffy, and I'm sure she would have liked to come.

I might have laughed at that thought. It's hard to be sure.

And then I blinked, or it seemed that way, and the only one in the room was Leonard. He was in a chair pulled up close to the bed and he had my hand in his and his head was dipped, and I knew he had fallen asleep. I tried to speak to him, but the effort of it sent me spiraling again, down into blackness, around and around, and I came out I knew not where. But sometime down in that place of no recognition, I heard a voice I didn't know, a nurse, maybe, a doctor, say, "He probably won't make it past another night."

I went away again, and there was a tunnel of light, but I went backwards, away from it, and when I came out of the unknown place with its tunnel of white light, I was glad to be back, not thinking that long, white tunnel was any goddamn path to heaven, knowing full well it was merely my brain trying to die, my focus narrowing, the kind of tunnel vision beginners get in a fight. I told myself that I was no beginner, and I would not go gently into that good night.

I fought hard, and I came back, and I was glad to be back. I rose up from the darkness like a ship on the peak of a wave, and when I did, there were Leonard and Chance and Brett, all by my side, and I think I said, "It's okay. Doesn't matter anymore," but maybe I just thought it.

I looked at them and loved them, and I thought, there stands my brother, who ripped a man's eye out of his head for me, and I love him as if he were my own blood. It was him I hated to leave the most, the way you think you'd like to keep both legs, because in that instant I knew I was leaving. The tunnel of white light was beckoning. I felt my ship on its wave starting to go down on the other side, my timbers squeaking with stress, my sail folding with pain.

I heard Leonard say, "You're just getting even cause last time it was me in the hospital. Let's just call it even."

He smiled when he said it, but he couldn't hold the smile, and I heard him say, "Goddamn it," and I continued to sail away on those dark waters, and then I felt calm, as if I had made it to the dock. I felt good. It was a strange kind of good. Free of all pain except regret. And then I felt those dark waters stir again, and my ship slipped loose of its moorings, sailed away from the pier toward what could have been the rising or the dying of the sun.

I looked up and saw Brett's face again, crying, then Chance, trembling, and finally Leonard. He was bawling like a child. My hand couldn't feel his hand anymore, but I knew he was holding it.

Then my ship sailed out farther into deep, dark water, toward that great light. I was having trouble breathing. I heard Leonard yell like he was trying to get my attention from across a great distance.

The bright sky beyond the black sea went as dark as the waters that were carrying me away, and I wasn't sure I could make it back.

ABOUT THE AUTHOR

Joe R. Lansdale is the author of more than three dozen novels, including *Paradise Sky,* the Edgar Award-winning *The Bottoms, Sunset and Sawdust,* and *Leather Maiden.* He has received eleven Bram Stoker Awards, the American Mystery Award, the British Fantasy Award, and the Grinzane Cavour Prize for Literature. He lives with his family in Nacogdoches, Texas.

. . . AND *RUSTY PUPPY*

When Hap and Leonard look into the case of a young black woman whose brother was murdered by police, the duo come head-to-head with crooked cops, cross-eyed hit men, and an illegal fighting circuit where the losers become "rusty puppies" when their broken bodies are dumped into a toxic pit.

Filled with Lansdale's trademark whip-smart dialogue, colorful characters, and relentless pacing, *Rusty Puppy* is Joe Lansdale at his page-turning best.

Following is an excerpt from the novel's opening pages.

1

I was still getting over being dead, and let me tell you, that's a comeback.

I died twice in the hospital after being stabbed, and the last thing I remember before I awoke from death was Leonard being there, shoveling vanilla cookies into his face, waiting for me to wake up. Actually, I was awake, but I couldn't fully open my eyes other than just enough to see him. I repeatedly felt as if I were drifting away on a slow boat to nowhere with a stick up my weenie. That turned out to be a catheter, but it felt like a stick. A big one.

Doctors and nurses saved me from the big, dark plunge, and I didn't thank Jesus when I came around. I thanked the medical staff, their years of schooling, their tremendous skills. I always figured if I was a doctor and I saved some person's life, and the first thing they said when they came around was "Thank Jesus," I would have wanted to stick a pair of forceps up their ass and tell them to see if Jesus could yank those out for them.

Bottom line was, I was back. It took me a few months to pull it together, but finally I was out and about regularly, and on this day I was totally on my own. I had lost a few pounds while being on the tube-down-your-throat diet (not the same tube as the one in my pecker, I hasten to add) but as of recent, my strength was back. I felt like I could bench-press two-fifty and beat an angry gorilla's ass, but maybe not in a fair fight.

That said, I also had days when I would weep uncontrollably and had the concentration of a squirrel. Doctors told me there would be days like that, days when I not only knew I was mortal, but had come smack up against the concept. Watching cartoons helped. I came around pretty quick, and the doctors were amazed that I didn't have any real posttraumatic stress. I didn't mention it to them, but I thought, *No, I only have that when I kill people,* and I'd learned to live with that stress as if it were merely a quarrelsome comrade. I had plenty of practice there, having known Leonard much of my life. But as far as quick recovery went, I've always been like that. Recuperation skills and a hard head have served me well in life.

So there I was, doing better, back to work, feeling mostly normal, only having brief visitations from the mortality fairy and a now-and-then concern about the eventual heat death of the solar system from the inevitability of the exploding sun. I'm something of a worrier.

On this day I had office duty at Brett Sawyer Investigations, where I worked for my girlfriend, Brett, worked with my best friend, Leonard. I was sitting with my feet on the desk, noticing my socks didn't match, feeling like a classic private eye, though my detective skills were right up there with my mathematical ability, which means you shouldn't ask me to do your taxes. But I'm persistent. That's another good trait you can add to quick recuperation time and a hard head. When I was sixteen my dad got me a job with a fellow who had me help him haul brush and tear down old houses he had bought to sell for scrap lumber. My dad said to him on my first day at work, "He might fuck up a lot, but he's no quitter."

That was kind of my motto.

I was at the office alone because no one else could be there that morning. Leonard was in Houston having sex with some guy he met on the Internet, which made me nervous for both of them, and Brett was nursing a cold. She shared her cold with a young woman named Chance who had turned out to be my daughter. DNA tests proved it, and I was damn happy about it. I had only known about her a short time, but she meshed with my family of Brett and Leonard and Buffy the dog as if she had been with us since birth.

Chance was staying at our house and working part-time at the local newspaper as a proofreader, looking for full-time employment. She had a journalism degree, which is kind of like a degree in Latin. The uses are small.

Like Brett, Chance was off work, home with her cold, resting on the couch. I figured I was next to get the bug, but so far I felt tip-top. After being stabbed in the stomach and dying for a while, coughs and sniffles could kiss my ass.

Buffy, the German shepherd Leonard rescued from an asshole who was kicking her, was with me at the office, lying on the sofa. She was remarkably well mannered, and much better housebroken than I was. Ask Brett. She'll tell you.

It was a pleasant morning, sitting there in the office wearing a pair of new blue jeans that my lady Brett said for once fit me in the ass, and I had on some new tan shoes that Buffy had chewed only slightly. I had on a nice green pullover shirt without food stains. My underwear was clean. My thinning hair was combed, and I had a cup of coffee with real cream in it and one package of Sweet'N Low. I had an open bag of Leonard's vanilla cookies that he had hidden behind our office refrigerator, and they were so good. Not only because of the taste, but because Leonard thought they were well concealed. I planned to eat them all and put the empty bag back behind the fridge. I might even put a note in there that said *Cookie Fairy was here. Fuck you. You didn't share at the hospital.*

As I sat there, contemplating on my return from the dead, I think I was starting to catch on to something about that whole nature-of-the-universe thing, bordering on some incredibly brilliant revelation that might be written up into some kind of philosophical paper, when the door opened and a black lady came in.

She was well groomed, overweight, wearing red stretch pants, a loose green top, and pink house shoes. All she needed was a church-lady hat with a fishing lure and a golf ball sewn onto it. She was carrying a purse about the size of an overnight bag. She could have been forty. She could have been fifty. She was certainly tired-looking.

I took my feet off the desk.

She said, "You the only one here?"

"Yes, ma'am."

"Where's that black one?"

"Leonard or Marvin?"

Marvin was no longer there. He had sold the business to Brett, but I thought she still might be referring to him.

"They black?" she asked.

"Yes, ma'am. All the time."

"They both work here?"

"Actually, only one of them does. Like me, he's a worker bee."

"Which one of them black fellows looks like he's pissed off?"

"That would be both of them. One is stocky and sometimes carries a cane, and he's maybe five or six years older than me. He's no longer here. The other one is muscular and my age and likes vanilla cookies. Just like these."

I patted the bag.

"I guess it's the muscular one I saw."

"Now that I think about it, they're both muscular. But one is older and heavier, like a bear that was trained to wear clothes."

She was studying me hard.

"As you can see," I said, "I'm not either of the black ones."

"I was just thinking I can't tell how old you are. White people, they're hard to judge. Can I have a cookie?"

"Take two. Would you like coffee?"

"You got a clean cup?"

"You bet I do."

She told me how she liked it. I got up and fixed her a cup. No artificial sweetener for her; she took four packages of sugar, stirred it with one of our plastic spoons, tasted it, asked for one more package, and I gave it to her. While she drank her coffee, she dunked one of her cookies in it and nibbled. She knew what was up.

"I guess it don't matter which one it is. I seen him come up the stairs and go down, so I figured he worked here, and him being black, I thought I'd want to talk to him."

"Some of us white folks talk and investigate pretty good."

"I guess so."

"How'd you see him?"

"What do you mean?"

"The black guy, Leonard. I assume you weren't in the tree by the parking lot with a pair of binoculars."

"Are you being a smartass?"

"Only a little."

"I live across the street, Master Detective. That's why I'm here in my house shoes. I sort of put on what was in front of me."

"I guessed that."

"No you didn't," she said.

"All right, I didn't."

"I got some money. I don't want anything for free."

"I've offered nothing for free."

"Uh-huh," she said. She removed a change purse from her very large handbag, which had enough room for an alternate universe, and probed around in it like she was digging for King Solomon's gold. She took out a wad of bills that would have choked a dinosaur and slapped those on the desk, poured some coins on top of them.

She looked at me. I reached over and pulled the money close and counted it out. It was a big wad, but most of it was in small denominations. Forty dollars in ones, a five, a dog-eared twenty with a chewed corner, chewed by an actual dog, maybe. There was twenty-eight cents in change and a nice pile of lint and a round chunk of peppermint wrapped in plastic. She took the peppermint back and dropped it into her purse. I bet that peppermint is still falling.

"What's that buy me?" she asked.

"Honestly? A cup of coffee, some of these cookies, and maybe you and me could go to the movies."

"I don't date white men."

"I know how to show a lady a good time."

"I ain't prejudice, mind you. I just don't deal with white people any more than I have to."

"That's kind of the definition of *prejudice*."

"So that won't get me nothing?"

"Tell me what's going on, and maybe I can see what this will do for you. It might be a simple business that I can take care of quickly."

"I need you to talk to a fellow."

"I guess we'll be talking about something specific?"

"What's that mean?"

"Means you have a point to all this. You would want me, or the darker gentleman, to talk to him about something that's on your mind, right?"

"I suppose you could say that," she said. "I think my son was murdered."

"Oh," I said.

Now I was truly interested. I had feared this would be a lost-cat job, and though I've nothing against reuniting folks with their lost pets, most of the time a cat will just come home.

"I want the black man to do it 'cause he's black."

"You think that would help?"

"You might not fit into the projects in Camp Rapture."

I nodded. "That could be true. Sounds to me like you need the police. I know a good cop that can help you."

"I been to the cops. They say I need proof."

"Yep. That's the way it works."

"This *is* in Camp Rapture," she said.

"Ah," I said. "The pit."

"Shit hole is more like it," she said.

"Cop I was talking about is one of the black men you saw here, Marvin Hanson, but he's a LaBorde cop, not Camp Rapture."

"Then get the other one," she said. "I want the black man here to get proof. Dealing with cops makes my ass hurt and nothing gets done."

"When I'm not toting a bale for them ole white masters or hoeing a row of cotton, I work here as well. And I gave you the vanilla cookies. Trust me, the black one, he wouldn't have given you the crumbs in the bottom of the sack."

"You ain't never hoed no row of cotton."

"And neither have you. Only cotton around here in the last fifty years is in an aspirin bottle."

That made her grin.

I said, "I have done farmwork, though. Used to work in rose fields. I worked in an aluminum chair factory, had an unfortunate period of employment at the chicken plant—"

"You worked there?"

"I didn't fit in. It was what you might call an unsuccessful period in my work history."

"I worked there."

"When?"

She told me.

"I was there then," I said.

"Say you was?"

"I was."

"You remember that woman got attacked on the other side of the fence, and a white fellow climbed over it and saved her?"

"That was me."

"No it wasn't."

"Yes it was."

"You the one . . . you was thinner then, wasn't you?"

"Thanks for noticing."

I had just been congratulating myself on how much weight I had lost, and now she was telling me I was thinner then. Certainly I had been a bit more spry.

"I was right there in the crowd," she said. "I didn't know that was you."

"Yep. I got a free vacation from the employer out of it. It wasn't as refreshing as I would have hoped. But that's neither here nor there."

I didn't mention the black man she wanted to take her case had gotten us left by a cruise ship, and then we had been attacked by thugs on a beach, and Leonard had gone around wearing an embarrassing hat and a bad wound. We got wounded a lot. We had a way of annoying people.

"Okay," she said. "Okay. That's good. You was the one, that's good. You did good by that girl. Saving her like that. You're hired."

"Keep in mind I can only do so much for this amount of money."

"You talk to this fellow seen the murder, that's all I want. Start there."

"All right. Tell me what it is me and this fellow will be talking about. Besides murder, I mean. I'm going to need details. I'll want to visit with the cops too."

She shook her head. "I don't like that. I said I talked to them. Shit. I'm pretty sure they was the ones done it."

2

Her name was Louise Elton, and she had a hell of a story. When she finished giving me all her details, I called Leonard. He didn't pick up, so I left a message. I'd hoped he might be back in town but didn't expect him to be. He and John, his longtime lover, were still broken up, something they did about as often as cows went to pasture, and Leonard had decided to play the field. That's how he met the guy on the Internet.

Louise's son's name was Jamar. There wasn't any proof the cops killed him, except there was a guy who claimed to have seen it. But there were problems with his story, or at least that's how the cops saw it. She was convinced this guy had information I could use.

I thought I could at least talk to him and get a read. His name was Timpson Weed. The projects in Camp Rapture were where Timpson hung his hat, if he wore one. It was not a nice place and white people were still considered the enemy down there. Thing was, though, I was bored, and Leonard wasn't around, and I had a number for the apartment.

After having a lunch of some very bad soup I heated in the office microwave, I gave Buffy a pat, got my coat, and drove over to Camp Rapture. It was a fairly short drive from LaBorde, and the projects looked like a place where dreams went to commit suicide and hope got screwed in the ass.

It was a cold day, and my breath came out white when I got out of the car. I pulled my coat tighter around me, started walking along the cracked sidewalk toward a row of apartments. They looked rough. The bricks were chipped, the walls were painted with graffiti, sweet nothings like I FUCKED YO MAMA AND HER PUSSY STANK.

There were similar remarks here and there, names plastered on the wall with what the police liked to call gang signs. Sometimes, if the same signs were on an underpass, they claimed they were satanic. They liked to keep it simple. Whatever they wanted them to be, they became.

Cops in Camp Rapture had really gotten a bad rap of late, though for that matter, they had always had a bad rap, and there was some evidence it was deserved. Not six months ago, they had "discovered" a car thief in a ditch near the car he had stolen, and he'd been shot in the back of the head five times. He was written down as a suicide. That didn't hold up, of course, but I think they thought it might, which gives you some idea of their level of professionalism.

I saw a group of young black men moving in my direction. Late teens and twenties. They were walking that kind of tough-guy walk where one leg seems to drag behind the other. They had their hands in their pockets and there might have been something other than hands in those pockets. Not expecting a shoot-out, I hadn't brought my gun with me. I hated how it was for them, young men without jobs or much in the way of future plans, but mostly I hated there were five of them and there was one of me.

"How are you gentlemen?" I said as they gathered around.

"We fine," said one of them. He was a tall kid with long, lean muscles and a red shower cap on his head. I've never quite understood that fashion statement, but I will say this: If it rained or he decided on a quick shower, he was ready.

"What you want?" said the one with the shower cap.

"Money and fame, of course."

"You a smartass?" said Shower Cap. This question came up frequently.

"Yep."

"You won't be so smart with your teeth on the ground and your ass kicked up around your neck."

"I would neither be smart nor happy if that were to happen," I said. "I'm looking for a fella. You might know him. I have an apartment number."

"We know him, you can bet your white ass we won't be pointing him out," Shower Cap said.

"Well, as I prefer not to bet my white ass, thank you for your time," I said.

I walked through a gap in the near circle they had made and didn't look back. When it came to young men with nothing to do and chips on their shoulder, you handled it the way you handled junkyard dogs. Show no fear, don't make eye contact, and walk away slowly and hope they don't bite you on the ass.

I walked toward where I thought the number of the apartment might be but wasn't. The numbers were wonky. I went around the other side of the apartment. There were a bunch of kids playing on that side, boys and girls, eleven years old or so, kicking a ball around.

They stopped as I came around the corner. White-man sightings were as rare as Bigfoot in those parts. One of the little girls said, "What you doing around here?"

She was rough-looking, had her hair in cornrows, and was wearing clothes that looked to have been handed down from someone larger. She had on pink tennis shoes with dirty white shoestrings in them. She wore an oversize T-shirt with writing that said MY ASS MATCHES YOUR FACE.

Charming.

"Looking for someone?" I said.

"You po-po?"

"I am not the po-po. Aren't you kids supposed to be in school, or maybe setting fire to something?"

"It's Saturday, fool," the girl said.

"You know," I said, "it is."

"Course it is, and tomorrow be Sunday, and the day after that be Monday."

"In school, I bet you make As."

"Naw I don't."

"But your marks in personality are high, aren't they?"

"What?"

"Nothing. I'm looking for a man named Timpson Weed. I got five dollars for the first person points me to where he lives, and if he actually lives there, I got another five when I come back from seeing him."

I was already out a large part of my initial down payment on the case.

The little girl gave me the hairy eyeball, like a banker considering your credit report. "Let me see you money."

I took a five out of my wallet and held it between my fingers.

"Right there," she said. She pointed at a door on a landing above us.

"I was told number nine-oh-five, not six-oh-five."

"You know so good, why you asking?"

"That is a very good point."

I had asked because the lady who hired me said she couldn't remember if it was a nine or a six. This way I had confirmation. Either that or I had just been worked out of five dollars.

I gave her the bill, went up the stairs and over to the door. I could smell cooking food from under it, chicken and dumplings and a lot of onions. I could also hear the TV going, a game show. I knocked on the door. I waited through a couple of ice ages before it was opened.

It was a short woman with a flower pattern on her housecoat. She was about thirty-five. She had her hair cut close. She was a little thick, with breasts that appeared to need somewhere else to live, there not being enough room in the housecoat. She wore fluffy pink house shoes, a fresher pair than those Mrs. Elton had worn; must have been a trend. They were open in the front and her toes stuck out and her toenails were painted silver. Her fingernails didn't match. They were red.

"What you want?"

"And good afternoon to you."

"What the fuck you want? I got things to do."

"I was told this was the address of the charm school."

"The what?"

I was being uppity and an asshole, but all I was trying to do was help Louise Elton get a fair shake for her son and I had gotten nothing but shit from an eleven-year-old on up. For all I knew, Louise's son Jamar was a bad guy and had died being bad, but the idea was to find out, and so far I was batting nothing. On the other hand, considering how it was in Camp Rapture, at least in some sections, I'd be suspicious too, especially if they thought I was a cop.

"Who's that at the door?" I heard a voice say.

I tried peeking around the woman in the doorway, but that wasn't possible. She had a way of moving so that she was in my eye line. A moment later a big black man without a shirt came to the door and eased her aside.

"What's all this racket?" he said.

"This peckerwood done here asking questions," the woman said.

"Go on back in there and watch the stove. And pull that goddamn housecoat together, woman."

She gave me a look that almost knocked me over the railing, then disappeared in the back to watch the stove and whatever was cooking.

"What you want?" the big man said. He was really big. Tall, wide, and though he had some belly, it wasn't all fat that was moving around under it. Somewhere in there were some abdominal muscles that wanted to show me they were still hard, just slightly marbled.

"Are you Timpson Weed?"

"What if I am?"

"Louise Elton sent me?"

"She did? She still on that business with Jamar?"

"Still is."

"That nigger's dead and most apt to stay that way. Ain't nothing else for it."

"I'm a private investigator, and she hired me to check into his death. See if maybe there was more to it than the police say."

"Course there is. Always is."

"Police aren't always out to screw you," I said. "I know some good ones."

"Ought to try being a nigger for a day."

"Black cop, I'm talking about."

"Yeah, he's just a white man painted over. I've had some experience."

I didn't see any point arguing.

"I'm just trying to help her out," I said.

"Taking her money, you mean."

"Not much money."

He studied me for a while. "I ain't got nothing much to say."

"Tell me the little you have to say?"

He had grown quiet, as if there were spies in the woodwork.

"I don't know," he said.

"It's to help a lady out. If it's not what she wants to believe, then that's better than not knowing what happened."

"Tell you what, you buy me a beer."

"Where?"

"The joint outside the city limits. Seven o'clock."

"Joint have a name?"

He laughed. "That's just it. It's called the Joint."

"Seven p.m. I'll find it."

"Might want to bring a razor and a billy club with you. The clientele is old-school."

"Meaning?"

"They don't like white guys. Hell, they ain't that fond of each other."

MULHOLLAND BOOKS

You won't be able to put down these Mulholland books.

• •

RED RIGHT HAND *by Chris Holm*

IQ *by Joe Ide*

RULER OF THE NIGHT *by David Morrell*

KILL THE NEXT ONE *by Federico Axat*

THE PROMETHEUS MAN *by Scott Reardon*

WALK AWAY *by Sam Hawken*

THE DIME *by Kathleen Kent*

RUSTY PUPPY *by Joe R. Lansdale*

DEAD MAN SWITCH *by Matthew Quirk*

THE BRIDGE *by Stuart Prebble*

THE HIGHWAY KIND *stories edited by Patrick Millikin*

THE NIGHT CHARTER *by Sam Hawken*

COLD BARREL ZERO *by Matthew Quirk*

HONKY TONK SAMURAI *by Joe R. Lansdale*

THE INSECT FARM *by Stuart Prebble*

CLOSE YOUR EYES *by Michael Robotham*

THE *STRAND MAGAZINE* SHORTS

Visit mulhollandbooks.com for
your daily suspense fix.